Dear Reader:

Lee Hayes is nothing short of amazing. In his prior books, he has mastered the art of storytelling through strong, suspenseful storylines and unforgettable characters. Now he has widened his prolific range and has stepped over into the supernatural arena with *The First Male*.

The main character, Simon, is changing into "something" that he does not recognize. He is plagued by dreams of things unknown and his world will never be the same. Before he was even born, his destiny was predetermined. He was to be special, to be a leader, to potentially be a destroyer of worlds. That is a heavy load to carry but an exciting one as well. Hayes once again astounds readers by showing that he is a talent to be reckoned with. I am confident that you will enjoy *The First Male* as much as I did.

As always, thanks for supporting the efforts of Strebor Books. We strive to bring you fresh, talented and ground-breaking authors that will help you escape reality when the daily stressors of life seem over-whelming. We appreciate the love and dedication of our readers. You can find all of our titles on the Internet at www.zanestore.com and you can find me on Eroticanoir.com (my personal site), Facebook.com/AuthorZane, or my online social network PlanetZane.org.

Blessings,

Zane

Publisher
Strebor Books International
www.simonandschuster.com/streborbooks

ALSO BY LEE HAYES

Passion Marks

A Deeper Blue: Passion Marks II

The Messiah

ZANE PRESENTS

THE FIRST MALE

LEE HAYES

SBI

STREBOR BOOKS

NEW YORK LONDON TORONTO SYDNEY

Strebor Books
P.O. Box 6505
Largo, MD 20792
http://www.streborbooks.com

ISBN 978-1-59309-439-3
ISBN 978-1-4516-7567-2 (ebook)
LCCN 2012943215

First Strebor Books trade paperback edition September 2012

Cover design: www.mariondesigns.com
Cover photograph: © Keith Saunders/Marion Designs

10 9 8 7 6 5 4 3 2 1

Manufactured in the United States of America

For information regarding special discounts for bulk purchases,
please contact Simon & Schuster Special Sales at 1-866-506-1949
or business@simonandschuster.com

The Simon & Schuster Speakers Bureau can bring authors to your live event.
For more information or to book an event, contact the Simon & Schuster Speakers
Bureau at 1-866-248-3049 or visit our website at www.simonspeakers.com.

*Thank you to my friends, family and fans
who have supported me on this incredible journey
for the last ten years. Onward and upward!*

AND

*Special thanks to DeTerrius Woods and Ronda Brown,
my advance readers. You rock!*

⚜ CHAPTER 1

In the immutable black of night, something ungodly stirred; something unholy devoured the light.

Deep in a swamp far from the mainland, angry winds hissed through the giant pine trees, covering the dense marsh with the unnerving sound of agitated serpents. Sharp pines needles, ripped violently from the trees, shot through the air like deadly daggers. Frequently, brilliant lightning flashes tore open the sky in a dazzling display of power; thunder shook the earth.

Sheets of blinding rain crashed against the dilapidated shack, its rotting wood punished severely by the unnatural tempest. The ramshackle structure quaked and quivered and its roof viciously shook; but, it held its ground. The shack bent and buckled, but did not break.

She would not let it succumb to the storm.

Inside the house, a woman howled in pain. Her child was coming, even in the midst of such profane turmoil. The woman did not fully appreciate all that was taking place inside or outside the shack, but she knew something otherworldly was afoot and she was a focal point; this knowledge only exacerbated her pain. She knew—she had always known—that the child in her womb was special. At the very moment of conception she felt a jarring that rattled her body, sending a wave of nausea that almost toppled her. She knew in that moment, as sure as she knew her name was

Rebecca Saint, that her child was conscious, aware. Now this very special child was coming and she felt as if she was being ripped apart. Her pain was excruciating. She screamed in agony, wishing she was in a hospital in Baton Rouge so that she wouldn't have to endure such aching; she longed for an epidural. She focused on her acute pain and the life bursting brutally from her womb. She had never experienced childbirth before, but she knew there was nothing natural about what she was feeling. The pain she felt radiated in her bone marrow; it ignited every cell in her body. She felt as if her entire body was wrapped in flames, burning from the inside out.

In her periphery, she could see the woman's gnarled fingers pulling particles of colorful light out of thin air in highly choreographed movements. She thought pain had altered her perception of reality, but she continued watching the woman conjure waves of dancing, glittery light out of nothing at all. Each strand of light flashed brilliantly for a few seconds and then dissipated shortly after its appearance, only to be followed by more iridescent hues.

"I...I...need...hospital. Who...are...you? What are you doing?" she managed to utter with breath broken by pain. She wanted to scream out, but she could not; she was lucky to speak at all.

The woman paid her little attention. She continued her hurried ritual.

The baby in her belly pounded as a voice echoed in her head.
Push.

The pregnant woman looked around the room, half-expecting to see a child huddled in a corner talking to her, but there was no child. She was going mad. The voice in her head was not hers.
Push.

The voice rang again and the woman shut her eyes tightly in

an ill-conceived effort to blot out the sound. She tried to shake the voice out of her head, hoping that her pain would mute the sound. Pain she could understand. The voice clawed at her core.

Push.

The voice sounded low, like a cry somewhere in the dark, but it frightened her enough to momentarily forget her pain. She'd gladly endure the pain if it blocked the voice.

Push.

"Stop it!" she screamed in a clear, strong voice. She didn't know her own strength.

Push.

The voice was now forceful, threatening. A force snatched her eyelids up and held them open so that she could see.

She screamed again.

"Are…y-y-ou doing this to…me?" she asked the woman in a quivering voice. The woman stopped and eyed her curiously, but she did not reply.

Push. Push. Push.

The command jangled inside her skull as tears streamed down her face.

Push…Mother.

The voice was now gentle.

"Get out of my head!"

The voice terrified her. It belonged to the child on the verge of being born. She pushed with all her might. She wanted this child out of her stomach as much as he desired freedom. She was not prepared for this. No childbirth should be like this. Who was this child? Had the whole world gone mad?

She inhaled and exhaled rapidly, as she was taught in Lamaze class, but the pain did not relent, nor did the voice of the child, or the scalding voice of the woman in the corner. Rebecca turned her head and looked directly at the woman. Sounds escaped from the woman's lips, but they were indecipherable; spoken in a language unknown to her that struck her ears as foul. It was unlike any language she had ever heard. The clamor she made filled the room; she spoke feverishly.

"Help me...please," Rebecca pleaded. Her cries fell on deaf ears. She could feel her body shutting down; the proverbial white light was sure to claim her.

"I am helping you, child. I am protecting you. I am protecting us from...*him*," the woman finally said, as she nodded in the direction of the woman's full belly.

As Rebecca pleaded with the woman, the face of a child flashed in her head. The child's face was gentle and loving, like a cherub. His marvelous beauty left a permanent imprint in her head; yet, her heart was filled with so much dread. Her heart beat furiously against the bones in her chest. She had seen the face of her child, even before he escaped from her womb and before he had taken his first breath.

Outside, the undead things bellowed in celebration; the sounds of their dark jubilation echoed as vitriolic laughter in the hissing wind. It would only be a matter of time. Although the witchy woman inside, Adelaide Thibodeaux—who had stolen Rebecca—was of great power, they knew she would not be able to last forever against their unrelenting force. Already she had expelled a great deal of power—traveling a great distance, shattering their cloak that surrounded Rebecca, and erecting her own magical barrier around the shack. Yet, they remained gleeful of her imminent demise. From the way the house rattled, they sensed her weakness as a shark smelled blood in the water. For victory, they only had to continue their assault.

He was being born, bursting from his mother's womb during

the storm of the century—a storm his birth had invoked, as told by prophecy.

Beneath a cold, blood moon, of the shortest day, He shall come forth, in flame; in storm.

The shadows could feel his presence on this winter solstice; his young power intensified the storm; such unbridled power, even in the womb. His birth had been foretold for eons, but never had been made flesh; that is, until tonight. The heaven's alignment made it possible.

To topple the shack and claim the child was their ultimate goal. The ancient scrolls outlined the stakes:

He who controls the child, shall control the world.

The undead things chanted an unbroken chain of shadow speak, hissing aberrant sounds into the depths of the night, using their power to strengthen the gale.

Amongst the shadows, he walked; part flesh, part bone; not alive, yet, not dead. He was something else. Something ancient. Something evil. His heavy feet pulverized the frozen earth; hardened stones crumbled like saltines beneath the heels of his ancient boots. Shadows at his feet moved like serpents coiling around his legs, hissing. Underneath his ragged black hood was a faceless, horrifying hollowness, except for a pair of yellow eyes. His voice was terrifying, spoken through lightning, thunder, and pounding rain. The fearsome wind flung his putrid scent across the land, polluting the night with the grimy stench of decaying flesh.

Inside, Rebecca's screams continued, shrill enough to shatter glass. Her blood-curdling yelps carried more force than the rabid wind. The shadows and undead things would one day worship her; they would exalt her and prepare a special place for her within the new kingdom, a kingdom her child would lead. In the days beyond the last days, she would sit to the left of her child and he on the right—a vulgar triumvirate. She was his mother, the Dark Mother, and she had been cloaked and protected by shadows since the moment she conceived. At the moment of the child's conception, a fiendish delight erupted in the Shadowland, a wretched place that existed in the space between worlds. The Shadowman had rejoiced for the first time in more than three hundred years.

The time had arrived. His rapture.

Inside the house, Adelaide Thibodeaux, or Addie, as she was called by her clan, wielded the ancient power of her sister-clan for what she believed would be the last time, making her final stand against the shadows. The stakes could not have been higher; the fate of the world rested in her hands.

Addie chanted. Her eyes rolled to the back of her skull. The long sleeves of her red flowing robe swayed back and forth. She commanded awesome power; force that belied her diminutive frame; power that they feared. She weaved a spell as strong as the night was black; a spell deeply rooted in the primordial blood magic of her sister-clan; a spell unlike any spell that had ever been cast before.

As her heart raced and her palms sweated, Addie's goal was clear: endure long enough for the child to draw its first breath; then, she could imbue it with all the goodness she knew and bind its powers; hopefully, forever, but she had no way of knowing if it would work. A binding spell of this magnitude had never before been attempted. To bind this child's power was tantamount to binding the night itself.

In spite of the grave uncertainty, in spite of her unsteady hands, in spite of the shadows pounding against the house, she pressed on. She had no other choice. If she failed, the child would most certainly become the abomination long prophesized. The ancient texts could not have been clearer: *the first male born of the first born Thibodeaux male would be the destroyer of worlds.* The warning sounded in her head from a place that was not a part of her. *Destroyer of worlds.* Her ancestors were speaking, warning her of the cost of failure. She had to complete the ritual or this child would one day plunge the world into abysmal darkness that would last until time ran out of time.

Fear tightened Addie's heart and squeezed her lungs. Even if she could complete the ritual in time, there was no guarantee it would take; the child's soul, ordained by fate, already belonged to the shadows, but it was believed—through no real evidence except the intuition of a powerful elder Seer-sister long since dead—that the power of the sister-clan could cleanse the shadows from his soul and bind his powers forever. It would take the collective force of the entire sister-clan, past and present and maybe even future, to complete such a feat. How long could such a spell last? Addie wondered. A day? A week? A year? Ten years? Was forever even possible? No one could be sure. Either way, Addie didn't expect to be around to bear witness to the aftermath. After tonight, after such an outpouring of power, she suspected that she'd ascend to The Higher Plain with her sisters.

A powerful lightning bolt struck the shack, setting the roof ablaze. The fire caused by his lightning could not be extinguished, even from the pounding rain. For the first time, the smell of smoke seeped into the house through Addie's defenses. Her barrier was falling. The ground beneath her very feet swelled and shook, as if a chain of perfectly timed mini-earthquakes exploded in rapid succession. She stumbled into a small table that slid across the room, but she managed to regain her balance.

The pounding against the shack was unyielding.

Addie called on her ancestors again, seeking their strength. She needed her power to combine with their strength.

"In this darkened hour, I invoke your ancient power. In this darkened hour, I invoke your ancient power," she repeated in a rapid-fire whisper that filled the room.

Then, she heard their voices. Her ancestors; the sister-clan. She heard many, many voices speaking in unison, in a tongue foreign to anyone outside her clan; an ancient language known only to them. Their voices sounded like blessings raining down. The ancients—members of her sister-clan who had long ago departed—spoke to her in hasty whispers.

Imbue the child. Bind his power. Imbue the child. Bind his power. Imbue the child. Bind his power. Imbue the child. Bind his power…

Wind blew through the house, violently scattering loose papers about the room. The papers fluttered across the room as if carried by a tornado. Within the spinning air, a dim light grew brighter and brighter until the entire room was bathed in a yellow glow. The light was warm and comforting, in spite of the dire circumstances. Addie saw the ethereal and disembodied faces of her ancestors. She saw Aunt Sarah. She saw Ambrosia. She smiled when she saw Doshia. And Whitney. And Lucretia. And Alala. And Amaka. And Irena. And Sethunya; and many others. Most of the churning faces she had only seen in the ancient texts of the clan, but they were connected through blood and magic, which stretched back farther than time. Addie would need their power if the spell had any chance of succeeding. Their faces swirled swiftly about the room as they chanted.

Imbue the child. Bind his power. Imbue the child. Bind his power. Imbue the child. Bind his power. Imbue the child. Bind his power.

Rebecca screeched. The force of thunder collided into the house, shaking it to its core. Addie's power flickered, and then she heard the rejoicing of the Shadowman; his laughter shook the sky. With the use of the strength of her ancestors, Addie had sight beyond sight so that she could see what was unseen. Her gaze focused on the Shadowman outside of the shack, and she saw him in his wretched form. She watched as he rotated his hands counterclockwise and raised them suddenly to the sky, pulling down a bevy of fierce lightning bolts that struck the roof of the house in powerful succession, leaving pulsing and bleeding cracks in the structure. Fire burned into the roof, in spite of the heavy rain.

He had succeeded in cracking her barrier in multiple places.

Addie's ancestors' faces faded.

In her mind's eye, she watched the shadows merge together and glide forward carefully, to exploit the weakness. They did not know what to expect from Addie, but they knew better than to underestimate her magic. She had more than proven her power to them. She was a Priestess Supreme.

Once the smoke reached the decrepit front porch, the shadows stopped. The undead things fanned out and created an unbroken circle around the house, preventing escape; they were ready to pounce when the order was given.

Addie focused and sealed the cracks in the roof. She kneeled over the woman and commanded her to push.

Adelaide, why do you resist? You cannot prevent that which is meant to be.

The voice—his voice—filled the room and covered Rebecca's screams. His voice was gentle, almost comforting. The smell of fresh flowers descended, as if from a field, and Addie felt a peculiar sense of peace trying to overtake her. She imagined herself in the comfort of her mother's arms as a child. She felt warm and protected; she had always longed for that sense of security, but peace was not part of her destiny. She was a born protector, and she fulfilled her duty with honor. And she knew it wasn't peace that was trying to take her; it was surrender. She would have fallen for this trick of the enemy had it not been for the burning in her heart.

We will raise him as a king of kings. How could you deny him that? He is your blood.

Addie could not engage him in conversation. She had to concentrate. Sweat poured down her face and her hands violently shook.

You cannot win.

Addie steeled her disposition and connected with her ancestors. She felt their spirit, their ancient power. She chanted and channeled them as Rebecca continued to howl. Her frantic shrieks filled the airy space. Addie felt unprecedented power surge and swell within her blood. She tried to hold it back, to control it, as a dam would hold back raging water. Her power ignited the atmosphere, swirling about the room like a contained hurricane; visible sparks ignited indiscriminately around the room, like fireworks.

"You have no power here!" she shouted with more force than she knew. The strength of her voice rumbled deep into the sky and cast the shadows away, sending them hurling and screaming into the night. The circle of undead things broke as they scattered out of fear deep into the forest.

Addie's force hit the Shadowman hard, causing him to collapse to one knee, but it wasn't enough to send him into retreat. It weakened him, but he did not flee. He could not flee. Now was his time and he would fight until the bitter end to claim what was promised to him.

Addie's expulsion of the shadows and undead things sent her power into a frenzy and her temperature rose, as if the power was too much for her body to contain. She thought she might explode and incinerate the entire room before she finished the ritual.

Addie placed her hand gently on Rebecca's forehead, as if to comfort her.

"Are…you…gonna…help me?" Rebecca asked. Her words were broken and breathy. Addie smiled at her and placed a damp towel on her forehead.

"Yes, child. I am going to save us. You must push, child."

Addie took the sharp thumbnail on her right hand and dug it deeply into the vein of her left wrist until she drew blood. She winced. She took her wrist and forced it onto the mouth of the woman, who protested, but was too weak to put up a decent fight. The woman had to ingest Addie's blood while the child was still in the womb in order for the binding spell to have any chance.

Rebecca spat out the blood. "Stop!" Then, she wailed an unearthly cry. Addie knew the scream wasn't from the woman—it was from the child.

Addie removed the towel from the woman's head and dipped her right forefinger in the blood that dripped from her wrist. She anointed the woman's forehead with a single bloody red dot. The woman twisted and howled as if she had been set on fire.

"Push, child! Push him out!"

Addie anointed each one of the woman's limbs with blood and marked the belly as she called upon the ancient power. The child was near. Addie ripped open the woman's shirt—her breasts spilled out; she drew a symbol in blood on the woman's chest, above her heart. Rebecca's body bucked and twisted as Addie held her down.

"Push!" Addie commanded of the woman. The woman pushed until the head of the child could be seen. "Push, child! Push!"

Rebecca's face was knotted with fear, but she pushed. And pushed. And pushed until the child was free. Rebecca immediately lost consciousness. Quickly, Addie cut the umbilical cord and fed the child her blood. She held the child—her grandchild—in her arms, and looked into his face. In the eyes of this child, she saw beauty personified. The sweetness of this infant could captivate the world and melt even the most hardened of hearts. The softness of his skin and the shine in his eyes entranced her. The color of his mesmerizing eyes, which were an almost unnatural blue, enchanted her. She had never seen eyes as bright. She was almost mesmerized until she realized it was nothing more than a trick. The child was deceitful.

Addie chanted as she let drops of her blood fall into his mouth. The child lapped up her blood as if it was mother's milk. He could not resist the taste of blood. She anointed his head and his heart with her blood as she chanted, attempting to bind his power and imbue his heart with light. She felt weak, as if the child was draining her life force. Her eyes rolled to the back of her head and her knees buckled, but she continued her appointed task.

She did not hear the heavy footsteps of the Shadowman punishing the rotting wooden floor until it was too late. A sudden force sent her careening into the wall, knocking a few wooden knick-knacks off the shelf. A figurine in the form of a bright-faced angel fell to the floor and rolled toward him. He raised his muddy black boot and crushed the angel without thought.

Addie had been blasted by shadow magic and it drained her already weakened frame. The dank air, contaminated by his wretched odor, offended her nostrils and sent her lungs into a spasm.

She waved her hand across her face and blocked his stench—she had no time for distraction. When she looked up, she saw the Shadowman walking slowly toward the child, who was held suspended in the air by his power. The child's cries were intermittent and uneven, not at all like the cries of a normal newborn.

Addie shook off the shadow magic, conjured a force as powerful as the one she had been hit with, and blasted the Shadowman. He crashed into the wall, his shadows howling; the part of him that was flesh took the lion's share of the blow.

Addie stood up and called for the child. He floated easily through the air into her arms as the Shadowman stood.

Why do you resist what is meant to be? The voice came from the faceless blackness under his hood. His question sounded sincere, as if he had struggled to understand her resistance. When he spoke, his voice sounded musical to Addie's ears, but she knew it was another trick.

"You cannot have this child," Addie retorted forcefully.

He belongs to me.

"He is of my blood. He belongs to me."

He is The One.

"He will never be yours."

By prophecy he is mine; the first male born of the first male. You could not prevent his birth; it has been ordained. He is mine. This time when he spoke, thunder cracked so loudly that the shack clattered.

"You do not scare me with your feeble tricks, Eetwidomayloh."

Be not afraid of what is and what will be.

Addie looked once again into the face of the child. She could not imagine this beautiful child as the destroyer of worlds; she simply would not have it. The spiraling colors in his eyes dimmed a bit, which told her that her blood and her magic were taking root; maybe his powers could be bound.

Then, Addie felt her body stiffen, as if encased in stone. The child floated out of her arms toward Eetwidomayloh. She looked on in panic, fearful that she would not be able to prevent him from taking the child. If he succeeded in stealing the child, he might be able to undo her very immature binding spell. She could not let that happen. She would not let that happen. She focused the last bit of her strength and freed herself from his stranglehold.

She was breathless and dizzied, but she continued to use the ancient power. As the child reached his arms, and as she had years ago with her son, she snatched the child away. In a harrowing split second, she opened a portal on the back wall that looked like a portrait of slick, black oil; the portal vibrated like waves in a still pool that had suddenly been disturbed by a pebble tossed into the water.

With the child in her arms and with her last bit of strength, she jumped into the portal and vanished, as did the portal.

No! The Shadowman's cries poured deep into the night; the ground beneath his feet trembled, and every living thing—every plant, every blade of grass, every tree, every bug and every swamp creature in the near vicinity—died.

The child was gone.

And so was Addie.

Simon Cassel dreamed of serpents.

They covered his body with their cold scales and slithered arrogantly across his bedroom floor. Snakes of every kind and every color, in numbers far too great to count, commandeered his home, as if they had no plans to vacate the premises; they claimed his tenement as their permanent residence.

Colorful coral snakes, with their deadly red, yellow, and black combination, wriggled in his bathroom sink and tub; black mambas, with their intimidating speed, darted across the floor of Simon's kitchen, curling themselves around the legs of his table; rattlesnakes, making good use of their bone-chilling sound, lay in wait in the half-open drawers that contained his socks and underwear. Huge Burmese pythons hung from the railings in his closet and balled themselves in the corner on the floor, covering his sneakers and the only pair of dress shoes he owned. Aggressive king cobras, flaring their trademark hoods, hissed loudly and attacked and cannibalized a few smaller members of their species. A massive ball of red-sided garter snakes spilled from the top shelf of his kitchen pantry and swirled around each other, seeking to mate with the lone female among them; green tree snakes made themselves at home, blending in with the pine branches of Simon's anemic Christmas tree that stood against the bay window that overlooked the busy sidewalk below. An indistinguishable combination of large and small snakes squiggled and squirmed around each other on his bedroom floor, almost playfully, giggling and hissing his name as if they were seasoned friends. They crawled across the massive stacks of medical, historical, and technical books that occupied space against the walls around the perimeter.

Sssss-simon. Sssss-simon. Sssss-simon.

Hundreds of serpents writhed carefully over Simon's bare body as he lay in bed, asleep. By their casual movements, they seemed comforted. They hissed his name with care, as if they wanted to wake him, but did not dare startle him.

A black snake, who had been satisfied to watch the orgy from the darkest corner in the room, slowly began to crawl across the floor. It slithered haughtily, in no particular hurry. It was completely black, except for its dull, yellow eyes, and it looked to be carved from solid black marble; it was glossy and void of scales, its body having the appearance of a long, gleaming oil slick. It moved with purpose and ego, and the other snakes parted like the Red Sea so that it could pass, unobstructed.

It slithered up one of the legs of the bed and crawled across the blood red comforter that was tangled up at the foot of the mosaic queen panel bed. It moved calmly toward Simon's face, pausing momentarily before it continued its forward motion. It crawled unhurriedly through his legs, past his ankles and calves, between his thick thighs and over his exposed genitals. When it reached Simon's chest, the serpent raised its head and looked on, as if in admiration, with its forked tongue darting rapidly in and out of its mouth.

Sssss-simon. Sssss-simon. Sssss-simon.

There was no venom or malice in its sounds; instead, the hissing was like a gentle whisper tickling the neck of an old friend. It was tender, almost nurturing; yet, Simon awakened from his dream in a panic, clutching his chest. He sat straight up in bed, and looked around the small enclave that served as his room. His chest heaved rapidly, and his body was drenched in sweat. He tried to cut the darkness with his eyes, but the black of night was too thick. The only light that shone in the room was an eerie green glow from the digital alarm clock on his nightstand that illuminated only a small section of the cramped space. Simon steadied himself and remained alert, but he was afraid to move, almost petrified.

The corner of the room nearest his closet was completely shaded in black. *Shadows.* Something about that corner unnerved him and wouldn't allow him to completely release the panic that held him. Then, his breath froze and his lungs tightened as a pair of sinister yellow eyes slowly came into view. In fright, he clumsily reached over and clicked on the lamp on the nightstand, his elbow accidentally nudging Brooke in the middle of her back. She moaned grumpily. A dim radiance spilled into the room.

When the light banished the darkness, Simon exhaled. There were no dangerous eyes lurking in the corner of his room; only a pair of sweat-soaked gym socks that he had yanked from his feet and tossed carelessly in the corner after his evening run through the park.

"What's wrong, baby?" Brooke asked in a sleepy voice, her eyes still closed tightly to block out the light.

"Ummmm, nothing. A bad dream." His reply was flat and contradicted the fear in his heart. He lied; he knew how she was. Usually, if he explained his dreams to her, she'd force him to stay up while she eagerly applied the knowledge she'd gained from three years of college psychology classes to make a rudimentary and crude diagnosis. Not tonight. Simon didn't have patience for psychology and its Freudian ramblings about the meaning of dreams. Sometimes, a dream is just a dream, although his dreams of late had taken on a much darker hue.

"Fine then. Turn the light off," she said as she buried her head underneath a big fluffy pillow and rolled onto her stomach with much more motion than Simon thought was necessary. Clearly, she was still angry from their fight earlier in the evening, but he didn't care—it had all been her fault. Why she was talking about the size of his dick and what they did in the bedroom to her silly sorority sisters—who he knew from now on would stare at his crotch each time he entered a room to see if they could sneak a peek at the snake between his legs—was simply beyond his under-standing. He didn't want to be objectified anymore. He knew all too well about women and their secret desires. All his life women had been drawn to him like he was honey; often pulled in by his mesmerizing eyes. They savored his flare, but were often startled by the power of his sting when he carelessly let them go. Never-theless, they loved him anyway; they always had. Beauty was a curse, he often thought. Sometimes he simply wanted to blend in instead of standing out from the crowd because of his physicality.

Simon looked down at Brooke. A wave of emotion swept through him as he recalled the rage he felt when he overheard her conversation about him to her sisters. He still wasn't sure how he had been able to hear the conversation—through the dense noise of the boisterous party—even before he stepped out onto the patio where they sat, but he had. He heard every word. He listened as details about his body, his techniques, and the movement of his tongue, slipped easily from her mouth, while she sat in the far corner of the patio sipping on wine and laughing with *those women*. She knew he was very private, sometimes reclusive, and never desired the spotlight, especially regarding something so innately intimate.

As he watched her sleep, he felt that dark feeling creeping up on him, threatening to send his mind to a place he didn't want to go. Simon was so disturbed by his own twisted thoughts that he retreated to the techniques he learned as a young child from a therapist, after the school counselor labeled him as "troubled" and having "anger management" and "rage" issues. He closed his eyes and slowly counted to ten, hoping to banish the rising tide of anger that sought to overtake him. *One. Two. Three*. He had to control the rage that was slowly gripping his heart, tightening like a vise grip. How dare she! And she had the nerve to be pissed at him, for being angry at her, for running her mouth. *Four. Five. Six*. A part of him want to yank her out of bed and shake the shit out of her, demanding to know what right she had to be angry. She was the one who had screwed up, discussing his body parts like he was a porn star. She should be apologizing to him! *Seven. Eight. Nine. Ten.*

What the fuck am I thinking?

Onetwothreefourfivesixseveneightnineten. Onetwothreefourfivesix seveneightnineten.

Simon realized he wasn't giving himself enough time to relax. Still, he counted.

Breathe, Simon, he thought to himself and then took several deep breaths, inhaling and exhaling slowly until he felt the grip loosening. The counting and his breathing techniques still worked. If they didn't, his next step was to walk away. Lately, the anger issues he thought he had mastered in his teens came flooding back to him. Just last week, when he was on the bus on the way to work, he became so enraged at some kid who refused to turn down the volume on his iPod that it was all he could do to keep himself from snatching the device from the teen's hand and tossing it out of the window. He literally saw himself doing it and forced himself to get off at the next stop, which was more than fifteen blocks from his destination; he didn't trust himself not to act on his anger.

As a child, when Simon found himself in the throes of anger, he often broke things, especially pretty glass items like vases or mirrors. He couldn't help himself. His therapists thought he was acting out; he was an orphan and had been bounced from foster homes, to group homes, back to foster homes, in a jagged pattern that never allowed him to plant himself and grow roots. Through the help of some talented therapists, he learned to control the rage and not let it control him. But, that was then, this is now. Something was going on with him. He felt angry all the time these days.

He took a few more breaths and counted until he felt relaxed. As the anger arose, it dissipated, much to Simon's relief.

He slid out of bed and walked pretentiously toward the bathroom, his muscles flexing with each step. His body was in perfect form. He looked back at Brooke to see if she had unburied her head to gaze at his glorious nakedness as he glided across the room—something she usually did when his full body was on display—but, this time she didn't stir; his ego would not be stroked tonight. He hovered in the middle of the room for a few seconds and stared at her, wondering how she could punish him for her folly. Women, he thought to himself. He'd never admit it—his pride would never allow for such a confession—but right now he'd give almost anything to have her wrap her arms around him and tell him that everything would be all right. The dream shook him, far more than his anger.

Carefully, he clicked on the light switch and glanced around the cramped bathroom, making sure there were no snakes curled in the sink or near the tub. The room looked innocuous enough, so he stepped fully into it and quietly closed the door behind him. A part of him wanted to slam the door shut; for no other reason than to frighten Brooke and jolt her out of her sleep; if he couldn't sleep, then why should she?

After he dried his face with the rough green towel that hung on the wobbly wooden rack on the wall beneath the clock, he examined his eyes. Already, he could see the beginning formations of the bags that would appear underneath them in the morning; his fair skin had never been able to hide the dark circles that formed under his eyes when he was tired, and he had been tired for days; barely sleeping.

"Shit," he mumbled to himself.

Ssssss-simon.

He jerked around quickly, knocking the plastic toothbrush holder to the hard floor. It clanked loudly as it bounced across the room, eventually crashing against the side of the tub.

"Be quiet!" Brooke screamed from the other room. Simon heard the loud expulsion of her breath and her shifting violently in the bed, but that was the least of his concerns. His eyes bulged in his head as he scanned the room. Everything seemed normal. The clear, plastic shower liner was still dotted with soap scum; the brown ring around the tub was still there; the roll of toilet paper still sat on top of the toilet lid, instead of on the holder designed for it; the lumpy tube of toothpaste was still missing its cap; pieces of white soap covered the caked-on soap stains that decorated the indented part of the sink that was meant to hold a full bar. Everything was fine.

Except, he had heard a hissing that called his name.

He shook his head and rubbed his face with his hands as he leaned against the cool sink. He didn't flinch when his skin touched the cold ceramic; he needed to cool his body. The night had already been too much, starting with the party, then his fight with Brooke, then his dream and his anger, and now he was hearing hissing sounds while he was awake. Maybe he was simply tired.

"Get it together, Simon," he said to himself as he rubbed his face.

Simon had always had an unusual sleep pattern, among other unusual traits. Sometimes he could go for more than a week on practically no sleep, stealing tiny naps and nods during breaks at school or on his lunch break at work; other times he'd sleep so hard someone would think he was comatose. When he was eight years old, his foster parents told the social worker that something was wrong with the boy; he never slept and was never tired. They were so spooked by him that they returned him to the system with the same ease as they would return an unwanted birthday gift to a department store. He never forgot the quizzical expressions on their pale faces as they drove away in their dark blue Mercedes station wagon. They weren't the first family to return him. It was a pattern in his life. Perfect couples, driving perfect cars, would come looking for the perfect child to complete their perfect family, and they usually fell in love with Simon's perfect beauty. Invariably, however, after some time, their perfect view of him would shatter as he displayed some unusual…talent.

When he was four, his foster mother, Danielle Robinson, who had a predilection for foreign language films, was watching a French movie as Simon played with his Tonka truck in the living room. The actress on screen burst into a room and looked at the body of a woman splayed across the sofa. With alarm, she looked at the male actor onscreen and screamed, *Qu'avez-vous fait à ma mère?* (What have you done to my mother?), to which Simon replied with ease, *Votre mère est fine. Elle a eu trop de vin* (Your mother is fine. She's had too much wine), in perfect French. This happened several times, albeit sporadically, with several different languages, until Danielle was so unnerved that she had to let Simon go.

When he was six, he *drowned* in a lake during a family camping trip. His newest foster father, Ralph Knight, sitting on the edge of a big rock a hundred yards away from the lake, saw Simon jump off the pier into the lake. He saw the splash of water leap into the air when Simon cannon-balled into the frigid water. Ralph immediately panicked; he had been told by the agency that Simon couldn't swim. He raced to the lake and jumped in head first. It was nearly ten minutes before Simon was found and was pulled out of the water, unconscious. When he was pulled to shore, Ralph frantically performed CPR to a crowd of gasping onlookers, but the boy would not breathe. Right before paramedics arrived fifteen minutes later, Simon woke up, drowsy, as if he had been simply napping. To this day, Simon recalled jumping into the lake and the horrible feeling of his lungs tightening as he inhaled water. He remembered the feeling of panic, he remembered everything going black, and then he remembered waking up.

As a child Simon could never understand what he did to offend his foster families so much that they had to return him. The things he had done were done naturally, like a child taking his first steps. Maybe Danielle would have preferred that he was dumb and barely spoke English. Maybe Ralph really wanted him to drown. His experiences taught him to temper his words and to be careful about what he did. As he grew, he learned that his talents were not appreciated and he learned to keep them to himself. Even still, Simon spent years facing rejection, after rejection, after rejection, until all he knew was rejection. So, he stopped letting people inside.

Simon stepped close to the tub, reached in and turned on the shower. He waited until he could see steam rising from the water before he stepped in. He hoped the warmth of the water would relax him and ease his anxiety. He placed his right hand on the wall of the shower and leaned into it, stretching and extending his entire body. He let the water bead down his body and cascade over his face. It felt wonderful, even though it would have been far too hot for most people. He stood motionless, with his eyes closed for several minutes, letting the water wash away his troubles.

Simon was tired. It had been at least four days since he had six consecutive hours of sleep. Maybe that explained his irritability and lack of patience with Brooke. Maybe that explained his nagging headache. Finally, he understood why people complained about having a headache. This was a new experience for him, and he didn't like it at all. Something was going on with him, but he didn't know what. All he knew was that he felt...odd.

After about five minutes, Brooke entered the room quietly. Knowing the water would scald her, she instinctively reached in and added some cold to the powerful stream. When Simon looked at her, she smiled, as if to say, "I'm sorry." He closed his eyes, not sure he was ready to forgive her.

She stepped into the tub and placed her arms around his waist from behind him. Her breasts felt like heaven against his sensitive skin; her hardened nipples tickling his back. He took a deep breath as his manhood swelled to life. She reached her hand around to his front and grabbed it. He moaned.

"I'm sorry, baby," she whispered. She planted several small kisses on his back as she moved her hand up and down his member; her hand could barely fit around his shaft. He wanted to say something, to accept her apology, but the fire in his genitals burned away his voice. Besides, she hadn't done enough work yet. He wasn't ready to forgive her. He'd withhold his absolution until she kneeled before him.

She turned him around and kissed him; her eager tongue aggressively explored his mouth. He wanted to remain firm, to punish her as she had punished him, but his body betrayed his intentions. He returned her kiss with equal zeal as his manhood rubbed the warmth between her legs. He loved her, but hated the *flesh power* she had over him. At this moment, all he could think about was being inside her, exploring her mouth, sucking her ripened nipples, licking her fruit, and digging into her treasure.

He cupped her sizable breasts and licked and sucked her nipples ravenously. They tasted sweet, as if covered in nectar. Her left one was far more sensitive than the right one, and his warm mouth covered it completely, sending her into a frenzy. He could feel her whole body shake. He couldn't seem to get enough, and he became increasingly forceful with his mouth, his teeth bearing down with a bit too much force. She winced, but he could not let her go. She moaned, louder and louder until her moans started to sound like whimpers and cries to his ears. He finally let her pull away and they stood staring at each other breathlessly, not sure what exactly to say. The tension they shared consumed the air in the room, but they had used sex many times before as a remedy to their relationship ails; sex could say *I'm sorry* in ways words never could. Slowly, she gave him what he desired most. She kneeled before him, as he knew she would.

After she finished, she stood up and kissed him again. With her hand, she guided him into the space that he loved the most. When he entered her, he was seized by such warmth and pleasure that he shuddered. At this point, he knew she had complete control of him and she worked her magic in such a way that he was ready to submit; he was ready to give in to all her desires to stay there. His weakness had always been good pussy, and she had the best.

After they finished and dried each other off, they lay back down in bed together, her head resting on his massive chest.

"Baby," she said gently, "I think you should see someone about your headache. You've had it for days now."

He kissed the top of her head. "I don't need a doctor. I'm just tired."

"No one has a headache for four days. I'm worried."

"Don't be worried. I'm fine. Really. I just need some sleep." She exhaled. He could tell that she was worried. "Besides, it's not like I have health insurance."

"I told you a friend of my dad will see you. I told him about it, and he said you should come see him."

"You've been talking about me?"

"Baby, I'm worried," she said in a soothing tone, "I want you to be okay."

"Why would your dad want to help me? He doesn't even like me. After that fucked-up dinner party we had, I'm surprised he hasn't hired someone to beat the hell out of me—a la Tony Soprano."

"Just because we're Italian doesn't mean we're in the Mafia," she said as she gave him a playful nudge in the side. "You know Daddy isn't like that. And I didn't say my dad. I said a friend of my dad."

"Oh, so you're going behind dear old Dad's back for me, huh?"

"I'll do what I have to do to make sure you're okay."

"I really am okay. Trust me. I never get sick."

"What do you mean you never get sick?"

"I mean I don't get sick. Besides this headache, I've never had a cold, a cough, the flu, or a stomach ache. I've never vomited or been dizzy or had chicken pox or any of the other shit people complain about. So, this headache will pass. It's nothing." The ease with which the words slipped from his mouth surprised Simon. Instantly, he thought of the families who had taken care of him only to return him when something about him rattled their spirit. He had violated one of his central tenets: never share too much information about himself with others. Folks would think he was odd. When he spoke about his medical history to Brooke, his words weren't boastful; they simply told the truth of his perfect health. He hoped she wouldn't freak out and leave.

Brooke sat up and looked at him curiously. As soon as her eyes met his, he regretted his confession.

"What?" he asked.

"Are you serious?"

"About what? Never being sick? Yeah, I'm serious."

"You must be the luckiest or healthiest man in the world."

"I take care of myself. I eat right, don't do drugs or smoke, and I exercise—you know how I do." He tried to make light of the situation but he felt a nervousness rising inside, twisting his stomach.

She lay back on his chest. "Well, if you've never been sick and you have a headache now, you should definitely see a doctor. It could be serious. Will you call him? For me? At least think about it?"

He paused. "Okay, I'll think about it. For you."

"Your twenty-first birthday is coming up in a few weeks and I want my baby to be healthy and happy. I have things planned for us."

"I'm sure I'll be fine by then. You don't have to worry." Simon focused his eyes upward and looked at the matted clumps of paint that made little hills on the ceiling. Sometimes when he couldn't sleep he'd stare at the clumps hoping to discern some hidden pattern. Focusing his energy on something so inane usually relaxed him and allowed sleep to overtake him. He wouldn't need such a cheap trick tonight. He was tired. Dog tired. He could feel his body succumbing to sleep. He adjusted himself slightly to allow for maximum comfort while Brooke wrapped her body around his. He closed his eyes, happy to have Brooke pressed against him. Her warmth, her scent, and the feel of her body, all felt so right. This moment felt perfect, particularly after the horrible fight they had earlier.

Sssss-simon.

He snapped open his eyes in a fright. This wasn't his imagination. It felt real. He lay perfectly still in bed, too afraid to move. Brooke didn't budge, and she clearly hadn't heard the macabre whisper in the quiet of the night; a whisper that sent chills racing up his spine. His stomach churned and tightened. Even though it was an unusually warm December night in New Orleans, the room suddenly felt as if the temperature had dropped. He swore he could see his breath leaving his mouth as he exhaled.

He remained still for several minutes more. He didn't even want to breathe.

Don't be afraid. Don't be afraid. A familiar, masculine voice, one that Simon had heard many times before, echoed inside his head. The voice was smooth and calming; Simon had heard the voice in his head at different times, over the years, though it had been many months since he had heard it last.

Now, it was back.

His body tightened.

Don't be afraid.

Something was hissing his name, and now it seemed as if someone was speaking to him inside his head. Tomorrow, he'd take Brooke's advice and see that doctor, although, at this point, he didn't think he needed a regular one.

He needed a shrink.

⇥ CHAPTER 3

S imon awoke the next morning to find an empty bed. Brooke, no doubt, had quietly slipped out in the early morning hours to make her eight o'clock class. When she stayed over the night before an early class, she was usually careful to not wake Simon on her way out. He always appreciated her thoughtfulness, but that was her nature. Caring. Considerate. Kind. In his whole life, Simon had never been doted over the way Brooke did.

Simon stretched and yawned, then rolled over and pulled Brooke's pillow to his nose, drawing her enticing scent fully into his nostrils. Upon the first inhalation, his half-engorged organ stiffened into a powerful erection, which he simply could not ignore. Memories of her firm breasts and sweet nipples replayed in his head. He thought about how good it had been only hours ago. Images of her naked flesh flashed before his eyes. Her skin. Her shapely thighs. The arch of her back. Her lips. He closed his eyes and remembered the sweet taste between her thighs. She had a power over him that weakened him in a way no other woman had, and Simon was no stranger to sex. He first lost his virginity at the tender age of twelve and had led a very active sex life since then. He wasn't yet twenty-one, but he'd had so many sexual partners that he'd lost count; but Brooke was different from the others. She was not just a notch on his bedpost. Something about her put her well above the rest. Sure, she got on his nerves and sometimes talked too much, but their sexual chemistry couldn't be denied. The more he thought about her and the more he smelled her scent, the more turned on he became. Over the last few days his lust, alongside his anger, had become insatiable, with him masturbating three or four times a day to carry him over until Brooke was within his reach. It was like puberty all over again, only worse. He could hardly focus on anything other than being with her. As he thought about her, his manhood throbbed painfully with passion. A fire swelled within him that had to be quenched. His hand was a poor substitute for her body, but it would have to suffice. He pumped some lotion into his hand from the bottle on the nightstand, closed his eyes, wrapped his hand around it, and stroked frantically, to completion.

After he finished, he lay in bed and contemplated his next move. Technically, he had a chemistry class at noon, but he had no intention of going. In fact, he hadn't attended any class in weeks. At this point he needed to drop out, but he hadn't bothered to do so yet. *Fuck the university and its rules*, he'd said to Brooke when she had suggested he officially withdraw and take his final classes next semester. All of his classes bored him to tears. Listening to Mr. Long ramble on about organic and polymer synthesis simply didn't interest him. The elementary methods employed to teach the class only annoyed Simon and he often butted heads with the professor, particularly when the instructor misspoke and Simon corrected him in front of the class. He knew far more about the subject than his instructor, who had a Ph.D.

Simon exhaled and looked around the room. Brilliant sunlight, piercing through the Venetian blinds, cut horizontal swathes across the space, dividing the room into sections. The light forced him to squint. The sun seemed brighter than usual; in fact, he was certain that he could feel the beginnings of a headache coming on—again—and he was sure it was induced by the light. By the angle of the sun in the sky, he knew that it was not yet ten in the morning. He wanted to get up and go over to the window to close the blinds, but he wasn't ready to stir yet; that would require far too much energy and the bed was far too comfortable.

Instead of getting up, he buried his face in Brooke's pillow again. After a few moments of total darkness, he reached over to the nightstand and grabbed the remote control. He aimed it at the television set and waited for voices to fill the empty space in the room. The incessant chatter of the local news team filled the room with sound. Simon could only tolerate silence for so long; silence gave him too much time to think, to ponder things better left alone. Sometimes, when it was really quiet and he was really still, he felt connected to the world in a way that he could never articulate. It was as if he knew the inner workings of the universe and was a part of it. Even as a child, it unnerved him and he never spoke of it. To anyone.

He noticed a note on the nightstand and reached over and picked it up. It was from Brooke.

Baby, you have a doctor's appointment today. Please go. Don't let me down. I want to know that you're okay.

Dr. Gregor Myles
1118 Canal Street
Appointment: at 3:30

"Fuck," he said to himself. He looked at the note in his hand and tried to suppress his growing smile with annoyance, but he couldn't. She knew how to take care of him. He thought about Brooke's sneaky ways. He knew how her mind worked; she probably had made this appointment for him days ago in the hopes that she'd break him down and get him to agree to go. She loved him and was only looking out for him, but the last thing he wanted to do was spend hours waiting at some doctor's office for some over-paid professional with a God complex who, when they finally saw him, would probably tell him to take two aspirin and get some rest. Simon knew that if he didn't go today Brooke would nag and nag and nag him until he finally caved in; or, she'd skip class one day and take him to the doctor's office herself and that was the last thing he wanted her to do. He didn't want her tagging along, and he didn't want to fight about it; he didn't have the energy. He'd go see the doctor just to appease her.

Besides, he had bigger things to worry about than some doctor's appointment. His body was going through some very odd changes that he didn't understand; changes that didn't feel medical, or natural. Everything around him seemed to be changing all of a sudden. Colors glowed with a brightness he had never seen before; his hearing sometimes was so acute that he could clearly hear conversations across a crowded room that should have been impossible for his human ear, like the conversation with Brooke and her sorority sisters. Twice already, when he was sitting alone watching television, he started sweating profusely and his heart pounded in his chest as if he had just completed several back-to-back sprints.

His body would sometime tingle, like he was being pricked with tiny needles, right before something strange occurred. The other night at work when he was wiping down tables in the dining room his skin started to feel prickly, like with electricity. He looked at his forearms and the hairs on his arms were literally standing on end. Then, the power in the building flickered and the lights in the ceiling closest to him exploded, sending glass raining to the floor. Then, the power on the whole block went out, casting the entire neighborhood in darkness. He remembered feeling a surge of energy so great that he felt like he could power the electrical grid himself.

The oddities he was experiencing in his body probably warranted a doctor's visit, but he didn't want to go. A part of him thought he should see a doctor, but he was so resistant to the idea. He had painful memories of doctors at free clinics poking and prodding him like prized cattle as a child. He had never been sick, but they wanted to inject him with all sorts of drugs that were mandated by law, so they told him. Those experiences never sat well with him.

Maybe this appointment won't be so bad, he thought, if for no other reason than to hear the doctor tell him he was okay. But, what would he tell him when he arrived? That light hurt his eyes so much that it gave him a headache? That he sweated a lot while at rest? Or, that he had really, really good hearing? Or should he tell them that he was having some really fucked-up dreams about snakes and shadows? Was that even relevant to his physical maladies?

Simon exhaled, more out of frustration than anything else. He looked at Brooke's note again. Her penmanship was exquisite, each letter given proper time and attention to develop as she wrote, especially in an age where handwriting was becoming obsolete. Her concern for him made him feel special and desired, feelings that had been foreign to him for most of his life. She was the only person in years that he believed really and truly cared about what happened to him; a small part of him believed that she always had his best interest at heart, but another part thought maybe she was pretending, in the ways that all the others had. The foster families. The fake girlfriends. He had been deceived by love, or the thought of it, so many times that his heart had closed.

When it came to that four letter word, he couldn't tell the difference between fiction and truth; even with Brooke he couldn't be entirely sure what she felt. He had been burned far too many times to trust without suspicion; but, in spite of his trepidation, he allowed himself to go emotionally farther with her than he had with anyone. Sometimes when he thought he had gone too far, he'd pull back instinctively. He'd start arguments to push her away and sometimes not call her for days, always reminding her through his actions that her position within in heart was temporary, fleeting at best. Yet, she held onto him. She held onto him tightly, in spite of offers from more suitable Southern sons whose fathers bore the riches of their fathers before them.

Her family couldn't stand him and he knew her friends didn't like him, either. He wasn't from the upper echelon of southern society. Her friends found him attractive, maybe even dangerous, and he was certain they all wanted to fuck him, especially after Brooke's conversation with them last night, but they didn't like him. They couldn't; it wouldn't be proper. Still, he saw the way they secretly cut their eyes at him when they didn't think anyone would notice; disdainful looks ripe with lust. At parties, Brooke talked him up—not in a condescending way—letting her aristocratic friends know that he was brilliant (probably an understatement) and one day, in spite of his unfortunate heritage, he'd conquer the world as the next Bill Gates, Warren Buffett or Mark Zuckerberg.

Simon never understood her world. High society was a mystery to him. Formal. Pretentious. Status determined by bloodline. He'd never fit into her well-bred world, full of cotillions and society parties, nor would he ever try. He made it clear that if they had any hope of surviving as a couple, she'd have to come down to his level. He thought that would push her away, but his plan didn't work. She met him on his level and did so without hesitation, spending many nights in his low-rent apartment when she could have been sleeping in the luxury of her canopy bed inside her sorority house, a former plantation house.

They were such an unlikely couple: the ambitious daughter of a prominent New Orleans surgeon whose life had been handed to her on a silver platter, and the mixed-up, multiracial orphan who had yet to discover the value of his worth or his path in the world. When they first met, volunteering at Habitat for Humanity and building houses for the impoverished, he had to have her. He was drawn to her in a way he couldn't explain. She was everything he was not. She was the perfect Southern belle. Beautiful. Poised. She was so unlike the fast and loose women whose beds he had stained on many a night. He wanted to possess her, if even for a short time, all the while knowing that whatever they were to share together would have an expiration date. He wasn't good enough for her and probably never would be. He was too unstable to ever offer her a lifetime of security; he could only give her this momentary pleasure. He knew that if she stayed with him for too long that he'd eventually assassinate the woman she was intended to be and she'd become something else. Bitter. Broken. Full of resentment. Angry at what she had sacrificed to be with him. Even knowing all this didn't make him want to leave her any time soon. He simply wasn't ready to let her go. They had some time left, he hoped. In the comfort of her arms she offered him something he had never experienced before—a place to be that was rightly his. He wasn't ready to let that go. He couldn't let it go; especially now.

Though their differences were great, he sincerely wanted to believe in her love for him. He *needed* to believe in her love so that there would be some justification for his unarticulated love for her. He felt love for her, insofar as he understood what love was. Sometimes, in the depths of the night when he was alone, whatever he felt for her would be so powerful that it drove him to fits. But that word, that magical little word, l-o-v-e, would never escape from his lips. That was a vow he made to himself years ago. Never. Say. The. Word.

He clicked off the television, climbed out of bed, turned on the stereo and listened to an old blues song belted out by the legendary Koko Taylor. He let her full voice fill the room as he strutted his stuff and flexed naked in front of the floor-length mirror that Brooke had given him as a gift. He considered blues music an art form mastered only by seasoned storytellers. They sang songs he could relate to, songs about pain and hurt and loss and sorrow. Those things he understood. He felt them deep in his soul.

After he took a morning shower, he checked his phone and saw a text from his boss, Cisco Gray, who ran the greasy diner in which he worked, asking him to come into work as soon as he could. Cisco's nephew, Jamal, who was notoriously unreliable, had failed to show for work—yet again. Cisco had threatened him with termination several times, but the threat lost teeth each time it was uttered without any bite.

Simon didn't mind going into work, at least it would be a distraction. He wasn't going to class and didn't really have anything to do. He figured that since his appointment with the doctor wasn't until late in the afternoon, he'd work a few hours, make a little money and then bounce, making his way over to Dr. Myles.

After he got dressed and gathered his things, he wandered down the long, creaky wooden hallway of the of the six-unit apartment house in which he rented his space. Once he reached the end of the hallway, he started descending the staircase that was covered with the most awful, dirty blue, industrial carpet that he had ever seen. Tacky silver Christmas garland was woven in between the railing of the staircase and a large, used wreath was tacked to the wall. He moved down the staircase, but stopped midway, suddenly. The front door had just closed and he heard the voice of Ms. Sanchez, his landlord. She was speaking loudly in Spanish and sounded angry.

Please don't see me, Simon thought.

Simon's rent was about a week late, which was his routine, and he wouldn't have it until the end of the week. He had hoped to avoid her until then. He listened as the floor creaked beneath her feet as she walked down the hallway to her apartment, the only one on the ground level of the building; she liked to know who was coming and going in the building. Often when Simon's keys struck the lock of the door from the outside, she'd poke her head out of her door to see who was entering. He heard her dig into her purse for her keys, as she usually did, and then listened as the key struck the lock and the door opened. He waited a few seconds after he heard the door slam before he dared move. Quickly, he descended the rest of the stairs.

He stepped boldly outside into the fullness of day. As soon as he opened the front door, his senses were assaulted by stimuli from every direction. The cool wind sliced through his skin, sending chills throughout his body and causing him to shudder. He reached into his satchel and pulled out his sunglasses, hoping they would help block the light that drilled into his head. The light seemed so bright that he thought he was staring directly into the sun. A city bus with squealing brakes trudged up to the bus stop directly in front of his house and came to a screeching halt. The high-pitched shriek felt like needles shooting into his skull. He collapsed against the door and covered his ears with his hands, partially blocking the piercing sound. Sweat poured out of his skin, in spite of the below-average winter temperature, and his knees felt weak, as if they would buckle.

When passengers de-boarded the bus and others stepped on after paying their fares, the bus pulled off and Simon slowly regained his balance. He looked around the street to see if anyone had noticed his episode. He was a bit embarrassed. From what he gathered, no one had paid him any attention. Anyone who might have seen something probably thought he was having a crack fit. In this neighborhood that was full of drug addicts and whores, he knew no one would care, even if they had witnessed it.

He took a moment to steady himself. Now, he was convinced that he really did need to see a doctor. For someone who had never been sick a day in his life, he certainly had had his share of strange episodes this week. He hadn't known sickness or pain in all of his life and found himself ill-equipped to deal with the sensory overload. He didn't know what to think or what to do, but he was becoming concerned. Maybe he had developed a tumor, he thought to himself. *Tumor.* The word rang with force in his head. As he pried himself off the door and forced himself to move down the street, the thought of a tumor stayed with him. What if he was dying? What if he got really, really sick? Who would visit him? Who would care for him? Who would care that he was sick?

The thought of a tumor pissed him off. Bad luck had always been his best friend.

As he weaved angrily down the crowded sidewalk trying his best to avoid pedestrians, he was struck by his harsh urban reality. People were squeezed into their metal boxcars on the congested roadway and others loitered on the street; some hung at the bus stop or walked easily into corner stores; vagrants, with nowhere to go and nothing to do, struck cool poses against the brick wall that was tagged with colorful graffiti. Simon was surrounded by people. Everywhere he looked, he saw them. There was no escaping them; yet, he felt, as he had always felt, alone. Even in the midst of a crowded city, he was separated from them. Brooke could only get so close. She'd never know him. Not really. He was different from everyone else, but he wasn't sure how or why. He only knew that he was something else.

By the time he reached Cisco's Soul Food Café, his anger was gone. The smell of frying bacon was so prominent that he briefly considered reneging on his vow to never again eat pork. He had given up pork six months ago after a bad experience with an under-cooked chop from some fancy restaurant to which Brooke dragged him. As he moved through the semi-crowded restaurant, he salivated at the thought of a big, juicy BLT sandwich. He thought he would have adjusted to the tempting smell of bacon by now, but the power of its aroma still had a hold on him. He could hear Cisco's teasing voice in his head saying *that swine is divine*.

Simon eased into the back of the restaurant, slipped on his apron and headed to the grill, briefly making eye contact with Cisco, who was at the front counter at the cash register. Simon was happy to see Crystal, his favorite waitress, back in the fold. She had recently suffered the loss of her father and had taken several weeks off.

When Crystal saw him, she smiled, winked and placed a cup of coffee on the table in front of a gruff-looking man, in a thick flannel shirt, who was focused more on her breasts than the menu. Simon smiled back, recalling the hot marathon sex he had shared with her one night after the restaurant closed. They must've fucked on every table in the place.

"Wassup, College Boy?" Franklin said as he moved around the corner, stopping suddenly when he saw Simon. "What 'cha doing here today?"

"That fool Jamal called out—again—and Cisco asked me to cover his shift. I don't know why he hasn't fired him yet."

"Shit, it ain't like he does anything when he's here. Cisco ain't fired him yet 'cause that's his nephew and his brother would kick his ass if he fired his son."

"You right about that," Simon said, chuckling.

Franklin looked at his watch. "Wait. Don't you have class now or something?"

"Nah, I'm good." Simon didn't want to talk about school and Franklin shot him a quizzical look as he hung a dirty white apron around his neck.

"When was the last time you been to class?"

"Huh?"

"If you can 'huh,' you can hear. I said, when was the last time you been to class?"

"You a fool, Frank. A real fool."

"How about you answer my question?"

"I don't know. Maybe a week or so ago," Simon lied easily. "Why you all up in my business?"

Franklin shook his head from side to side. "Man, you a trip. I'll never understand what goes on in that head of yours. You have a full ride at one of the most prestigious colleges in the country. You two classes away from getting yo' master's degree in what—biochemical engineering—or some shit like that. You fucking brilliant, and you slinging shit on a grill up in here when you should have yo' monkey ass in class."

"You work here, too. Ain't nothing wrong with making a little money."

"I work here 'cause I have to. This and my music is all I got and you can best believe when that shit pops off I'm getting the hell outta here and you should be working on doing the same thing. Fuck this grill. Fuck Cisco and fuck these stank-ass, rude-ass customers. I don't know why you trippin'. You know you can do anything. You can cure fucking cancer or build a new Internet or solve the world's energy problem—something."

"Dude, you have me confused with Einstein. I'm nobody. I'm a short order cook, that's all." Simon turned away from Franklin and tied his apron strings, trying to hide his annoyance with the conversation.

"That modesty shit don't work with me. I know you. I've been to your house. You got stacks of books on shit I don't even understand. Shit I can't even pronounce. Molecular this. Biological that. Just reading the titles gave me a headache. You read what, four or five books a week? The last time I picked up a book was junior high and I don't even think I finished it then."

"What's your point?" Simon asked in a heavy voice.

"My point is you can do anything you want, but you piss on yo' opportunities while a cat like me is struggling—"

"I'm struggling, too."

"Fool, you struggling by choice—there's a difference. All I'm saying is if I had what you have, my ass would be at Harvard or Oxford or inventing something in Silicon Valley; but, if you wanna keep flipping burgers up in this joint, I can't stop you." Franklin dropped a cold piece of beef onto the hot grill right in front of Simon. "Don't let it burn," he said sarcastically as he focused his attention on the meat in front of him.

Everything Franklin said to him was true. Simon knew that. He didn't want to hear it. Everyone had high hopes about his future. Brooke. Franklin. The dean at his school. His scholarship committee. Simon wanted all of them to leave him the fuck alone. It was his life to do with as he pleased. Simon felt that familiar burning in his chest and thought quickly about slamming Franklin's head on the hot grill. He could hear the sizzle in his ears.

"Yo, I got this gig on Saturday night at The Black Cat," Franklin said, breaking Simon's violent thoughts. "You should come through. Bring Brooke. I wrote this new song and my vocals are on point. I can't wait for you to hear it. I'm going to the top with this one."

"I just might do that." Franklin grabbed an order written on a small white piece of paper from the counter. He read it and immediately reached for two eggs, cracked them over the grill and added a dash of salt and pepper and a handful of shredded cheese. If Simon had ever had a friend, Franklin would have been it. In the few shorts months they had been working together they had bonded as brothers. Franklin was a struggling vocalist trying to make a name for himself in the New Orleans music scene with the hopes of making it onto the national R&B charts one day. He had an amazing voice with a range that defied expectations. He was a hot-headed, rail-thin Creole who stood right at six feet with a mixture of French, Spanish and Haitian blood who could sing anyone under the table.

"How are things with Brooke?" he asked in his typical rapid speech. "We should go on a double-date soon."

"You'd have to get a date first," Simon shot back playfully.

"That was cold. I told you, me and Nikki are back together."

"You and Nikki? Ninth Ward Nikki? The last time the four of us went out together y'all showed y'all's asses at the Fantasia concert. I thought Nikki was gonna shank you. I seem to recall security having to escort y'all outside," Simon said while laughing.

"Why you gotta bring up old shit? We were having a bad night, that's all, but we good now. Real good."

"Okay. I was just checking. I don't want no shit. I'm just saying." Simon plopped a thick piece of country ham on the other side of the grill. He watched the piece of ham sputter as the smell wafted into his nose.

As the day wore on, Simon felt a sense of fatigue overtaking him. The diner had been busier than expected with almost nonstop food orders. He hadn't taken a break in the four hours he had been laboring over the hot grill, not even stopping to go to the bathroom. He was thirsty, feeling like he was dehydrated. He reached for the bottle of water that he kept at the back of the counter and poured the cool liquid down his throat. As he returned the bottle to its proper place, he felt a tingling in his toes that started moving its way up his legs. He felt the tingle in his shins and then his knees and then his thighs and then his chest. The uncomfortable sensation enveloped entire his body.

"Oh shit," he said in a voice much louder than he had planned.

"Dude, you okay?" Franklin stepped closer to him and eyed him with concern, touching his shoulder. Franklin snapped his hand back as if he had been zapped with static electricity. Franklin looked at his fingers.

"Yeah, I think so." Simon flipped over a sizzling piece of beef meant for a burger. The prickly sensation continued through his body and grew sharper as large beads of sweat pooled on his forehead. His palms were sweaty and the collar of his shirt was making the nape of his neck itch. Simon wanted to move into the restroom, but he couldn't. His feet felt like they weighed a thousand pounds. He dropped the spatula onto the counter next to the grill and grabbed onto the counter for support. His skin felt like it was on fire.

"You don't look good. Maybe you should sit down," Franklin said with worry, but Simon didn't pay attention to his words. He felt a stabbing pain in his head and saw bright flashes. With his head held low, sweat dripped from his face. A bead of moisture fell from his face and splattered against the dirty floor. When it hit the floor, it sounded like an explosion in Simon's ears. He saw more flashes in his head:

A man with a dirty beard, in a black bubble coat that looked like a trash bag.

The man was walking down the sidewalk near the diner.

He fiddled with something in his pocket.

It was a gun.

He burst into Cisco's Soul Food Café and fired a single round into the ceiling.

He demanded money.

He pistol whipped Crystal and she hit the floor hard.

Then, he shot Cisco in the chest when Cisco pulled a pistol from underneath the countertop. Blood gushed from his chest. He was dead.

"What the fuck is wrong with you, man?" Franklin's voice grew desperate. "Hey, Cisco! Something's wrong with Simon. You better get back here!" he called out. As soon as Cisco rounded the corner to the kitchen, Simon broke free from his vision. He was sweating profusely and struggling to breathe. He felt as if someone was strangling him. He needed air. Fresh air. The smell of frying bacon fat and grease was clogging his nostrils. He raced out of the kitchen and ran quickly past Crystal, almost causing her to drop the hot plate of shrimp and grits that she was carrying.

He sprinted to the front of the restaurant and as he leapt out of the door, he collided with a man in a black bubble coat. Both men hit the sidewalk hard, with Simon falling on top. The gun in the man's pocket flew across the sidewalk and a female passerby screamed.

"He has a gun!" she yelled as she ran for safety into a storefront shop. Pedestrians scattered and screamed.

"Get the fuck off me, fool!" the angry man said as he pushed Simon off of him. His face was mangled with rage. Simon looked at the man. He wore the same bubble coat as he saw in his head. The man had the same unkempt beard. It *was* the same man as the man he had just seen moments ago in his head. The man scampered to his feet and raced immediately for the gun, which was wedged between the wheel of a SUV and the curb. When he couldn't retrieve it fast enough, he looked around at the crowd and took off running down the sidewalk, shoving people to the left and the right as he made his escape.

As Simon lay on the sidewalk, the magnitude of what had just happened hit him like a ton of bricks. He had seen the future and stopped Cisco's murder.

CHAPTER 4

What the fuck is happening? Simon thought to himself as he sat alone in a seat on the bus heading to the other side of town to make his appointment. He hadn't managed to catch his breath since *the incident* at Cisco's and he felt jittery, like he was wired on caffeine or some other drug. His head rested against the window of the semi-crowded bus and his arms were folded across his chest. The bus smelled of stale food mixed with a hint of body odor and it agitated his stomach. He watched the couple who sat a few seats in front of him kiss and hug as if they didn't have a care in the world. All their energy was directed toward each other, and Simon tried to force a smile, hoping they could serve as a distraction from the odor and the thoughts that still made it hard for him to breathe. As the bus wound its way through the city streets, his mind was focused on his transformation. He didn't feel right. Nothing about him felt right anymore. The strange occurrences that had plagued him all his life were happening with much more frequency and at a higher intensity, as if they were building to a climax. He didn't want to think about what that climax would be, but he wanted to do everything he could to prevent it. There were no reasonable or rational explanations for what he was going through. Deep inside him he had always known that he'd undergo a remarkable remaking, a rebirth, but he never understood why he felt that way. He just knew, and now it seemed as if that time was near. He was terrified.

Simon's mind struggled to process what happened. *I'll pretend none of this is happening. If I don't believe it's real, then it's not. I'll go about my business, like everything is fine and not worry about it. Yeah, that's what I'll do. Everything is fine.* He tried to convince himself, but worry still held him tightly.

He arrived at the red brick building that housed Dr. Myles' office, stepped into the elevator, and hit the button marked "10." The elevator was populated with a few people who paid him little attention, even though he felt as if all eyes were on him. Christmas music piping through the speakers of the elevator relaxed him only slightly, and he pulled himself tightly into the corner in the back and folded his arms, hoping he could reach his destination before anything else strange happened to him. He wasn't sure he could deal with another episode.

He stepped into the office and walked to the counter with unsure feet. His mind was still elsewhere, but he tried to focus on the task at hand. *Let me get through this.* This was a new experience for him. A doctor's office. He was definitely out of his element. He smiled, almost timidly, at the woman behind the counter and informed her of his appointment. She handed him a stack of forms on a clipboard and he took a seat in the waiting room.

After filling out a set of five different forms that all seemed to ask for the same information, Simon returned the papers to the woman and returned to his seat in the waiting room, hoping to relax and pull it together. He felt a slight cramp in his hand from all the writing, in addition to being annoyed at the questions that he found to be too intrusive. He had long since grown tired of filling out forms that asked him to identify his race. Truth be told, he didn't know his race. No one knew his race. His phenotype baffled everyone. He had full red lips and his skin was very fair. His hair was jet-black with a wavy texture and his eyes changed color, depending on the light, but usually were a deep-ocean blue. He surmised he was part African-American and part Caucasian, but there were so many other parts of him that remained a mystery. By any standards, whatever race he was, he was considered a thing of extraordinary beauty, a reflection of the best the world had to offer. One of his foster mothers said he was an *amalgamation of the world's races*. She praised him as representative of a bold, new world in which the boundaries erected by race would all tumble. *We shall be as one race*, she used to say to him. She was an optimist, but Simon didn't care much about her "we are the world," one race, rainbow theory. He just wanted to know who he was.

He scanned the people who sat around him in the waiting area. They were a diverse group, myriad races, sizes and shapes, and ailments. Some sat with sullen faces that hung low, while others wore blank expressions; all trying to pass the time by toying with their cell phones or flipping through outdated magazines that were scattered across the table in the center of the waiting area. Simon looked at a pale-faced, red-headed boy who sat in the corner near the window, and the child looked at him, too. The sunlight dissecting the room illuminated the child's tear-stained face. The child was no older than four, but his eyes were heavy, as if he had been to hell and back and hell again. The child, with his head resting in his mother's lap, stared at Simon as if he knew him. Something desperate and something familiar in his eyes prevented Simon from looking away, even though he wanted to, more than he could express. Simon felt uncomfortable, shifting his weight in his seat, but he couldn't turn away. The boy's gaze held him and would not let him go. When he looked at the boy, he felt something stir deep inside of him. The boy raised his tiny hand and waved at Simon, who, after an uneasy pause, waved back; it would have been rude not to.

Simon studied the face of the child. He had freckles and little red lips like thin slivers of meat. He was small, even for four. He looked like a Raggedy Andy doll.

Then, Simon's fingers and toes began to tingle. He felt his body temperature rising, heat radiating from some internal source.

"Oh no," he said to himself. "Not again." The child continued to stare at Simon, his gaze remaining unbroken. Simon couldn't deal with the pleading in the boy's eyes, especially with the prickly sensation he was feeling. Simon closed his eyes and took slow, deep breaths. The tingling became less intense, but he still felt hot.

As he sat there in darkness, he *felt* the boy. Incoherent images flashed through Simon's head. He saw toys and hospitals and a black-and-white puppy and the sad face of a man, probably the child's father. He saw a huge two-story house with the address 864 Rosecrest. He saw an older woman, probably in her early sixties, dressed in a uniform, putting a plate of pancakes in front of the boy who sat at the table with the woman, whose lap his head now rested on, and the man with the sad face. He saw tears and felt a strong stabbing sensation in his gut. *Pain*. The word flashed in his head as the unfamiliar feeling rocked his body for a few seconds. Simon had never experienced pain, and it took more force than he knew he had to prevent a wretched scream from escaping from his lips.

Then he realized this was the child's life. His family. His toys. His dog. *His pain*. But how? How could Simon know these things?

Another word flashed in his head that he didn't want to see: *Leukemia*. The child had leukemia. Simon knew it.

Simon shuddered and opened his eyes. *Blaine*. That was the child's name—it just came to him.

Blaine continued with his uninterrupted eye contact.

Will you help me?

"Excuse me?" Simon said. He wiped a pool of sweat from his glistening forehead and turned to the elderly black man who sat to his right.

"What?" the man replied with confusion.

"Oh, I'm sorry. I thought you said something to me." The man shook his head and continued working on his Sudoku puzzle.

Will you help me?

Simon looked at the child again. Then, the terrifying realization hit him. The voice he heard wasn't the old man's—it belonged to Blaine, and it was in his head! He felt a powerful tingling at the base of his spine that shot through his entire back, and rested in the back of his skull. The feeling was different; unlike the tingling he had felt previously. Now, it was concentrated, un-diluted; it circulated at the place where his neck connected with his head.

Help you? How can I help you? Simon thought this before he could fully understand what was transpiring.

I don't feel good and my mommy is very scared. Will you save me?

I don't understand.

You will. Will you take my hand? Please.

Before Simon could speak again, the little boy had raised his head from his mother's lap. He slid out of the chair and landed on his feet. He stood there, looking at Simon, waiting for Simon to make a move.

His mother smiled. "I think he likes you," she said to Simon, forcing a smile. Blaine walked over to Simon, putting one tiny foot in front of the other.

"No, it's okay," Simon said to the woman when she tried to prevent the child from moving. "He's okay. I got him." The woman paused, not sure whether to trust Simon, but she backed off. When Blaine made it to Simon, she looked relieved.

Blaine didn't speak. He looked tired, as if conquering the space that had separated the two of them moments ago had taken a lot out of him. He simply looked at Simon as if he was trying to figure him out. The laden expression on Blaine's face chilled Simon a bit. It was as if Blaine was privy to a secret that involved Simon, but wasn't at liberty to discuss. Simon didn't know what to do. Or say. Blaine stood there. Watching.

You hafta take my hand. I'm not 'pose to take yours.

Then, the door to the back opened and a nurse stepped out. "Simon Cassel." She looked around and called out again when Simon didn't respond. "Simon Cassel."

"That's me." Simon stood up. He looked down at the child whose eyes were pleading with him. Then, Simon did it. He didn't know why, but he took the child's hand. As soon as he touched Blaine, he felt heat surge in his body. Blaine seemed to feel it too. It didn't last long, but for the few seconds that they connected, Simon's body felt electrified. He felt the hairs on the back of his neck stand on end and his knees buckled.

When Simon released his grip, he felt compelled to pick up Blaine. This child was now a part of him and he didn't want Blaine struggling to walk back to his mother. Simon walked over to the lady and gently placed him down in her lap.

"All betta now," Blaine said as he smiled warmly.

"I hope he wasn't a bother," she said.

"Not at all. He's adorable." Simon smiled and then walked away toward the nurse, who appeared slightly irritable. When he approached, she pursed her lips together and exhaled.

"As you can see, we're very busy. The doctor is waiting." Simon paused at the door and looked back at Blaine. He didn't know how he knew, but he had no doubt that Blaine would now be fine. His leukemia was gone and would never return.

"Mr. Cassel, please follow me." Simon tried to take a step. Then, he felt a strong wave of nausea that threatened to send him hurling to the floor. He grabbed onto the door and held it tightly, for balance. He could feel his body temperature rising again and his skin was drenched with sweat.

"Are you okay, Mr. Cassel?" the nurse asked, finally sounding concerned.

"I—I think I'm fine." Simon looked over to Blaine who stared at him with an expressionless look. Then he smiled.

Thank you.

When the thought entered his head, Simon became dizzy. Suddenly, images from the boy's life and Simon's life merged and created a whirlwind of images that swirled swiftly around his head. Flashes of IVs and cancer drugs and yellow-eyed snakes and Brooke's perfect breasts and Simon's school and Blaine's sad-faced father and his laughing mother overwhelmed him. Then, new and unfamiliar voices rattled around in his head. Thoughts and feelings from the people in the waiting room battered him.

What am I going to cook for dinner?

I bet he's with that bitch.

I hope the doctor can get rid of this rash.

I don't want to carry this baby anymore.

I hope my HIV test is negative.

I'm scared.

What are these spots on the back of my hand?

Then, Simon smelled blood.

And cologne and perfume.

And a bit of funk.

And bad breath.

And medicine.

And old food that clung to paper containers that littered the trashcans. He felt pain radiating in the deepest recesses of his body; pain so great that it stole his voice. He felt pain in the very marrow of his bones. It was as if he had taken Blaine's leukemia into his own body and now felt what the boy had felt for months. Simon's senses were in overload and he couldn't take it anymore. The pain was too intense. The floor beneath his feet shifted; tremors threw him off balance. A pounding in his head drowned out every sound indigenous to the very busy office. Even though the nurse stood directly in front of him and Simon could see her mouth moving, he couldn't decipher what she said. He couldn't hear the nurse speaking to him or the constant ringing of the telephone or the chatter of people on their cell phones. It was as if he had suddenly gone completely deaf. Fear, in addition to crippling pain, jolted him in ways he had never known. He felt himself collapsing.

Don't be afraid. Don't be afraid, the voice in his head whispered again.

Then, everything went black.

⇥ CHAPTER 5

E li Kane stepped boldly out of the shadows at Hollytree Convalescent Center. The sun had set hours ago and darkness claimed the city. Night elicited a particular kind of chaos, filling most people with feelings of unease and insecurity, as if the night would bring about the monsters they were warned about as children. In part, they were right to fear; Eli owned the night; it was in darkness that he found strength. He was inextricably and forever bound to it, lapping in its wondrous blackness.

Eli was dressed finely in a black, expensive suit that contrasted with his bold, blue eyes. His taut frame fit his clothes perfectly, as if they had been tailor-made for his body. His wavy, jet-black hair was cut low and slicked back like an old school mobster. When he walked down the busy corridor, his thunderous steps echoed off the black and white checkered linoleum floor, his long black leather trench coat flailing behind him. He was on a mission. He had to see the old woman, again. This time, he'd be much less polite. His patience had thinned considerably since his last visit days ago.

Eli rounded the corner of the hallway that led to her room, paying little attention to workers as he passed them. As he approached the nurse's station, he was stopped by a nurse who immediately stepped from around the counter, her hand raised up with the palm side out, displaying the universal sign for "stop."

"Excuse me, sir," she said with authority. "Visiting hours are over."

Eli exhaled and rolled his eyes. He didn't have much patience for the rules of this mortal world. He could snap her neck with a mere thought, but one of the lessons he was learning was the art of subtlety. Thunder wasn't always required; sometimes, a whisper would suffice.

He took a moment to size her up. By the lines that crossed her face, he could tell that she worked too much and that she took her job very seriously—too seriously. Eli smiled pleasantly at her. She possessed a fairly attractive, rosy face that had clearly seen better days; and the frizzy brown hair that hung just below her shoulders was badly in need of a perm. Remnants of her fading beauty were evident beneath her hardened exterior. Eli let his eyes slide down her shapely figure, which stretched the white material of her nurse's uniform to the limit, though he could still imagine what her flesh would be like outside of her clothes; lust ruled him. After he finished the task appointed to him this night, he might call her back into the room and fuck her to within an inch of her life while the old lady watched, helplessly.

Eli smiled again to reveal his perfect teeth.

"Pardon me. I won't be long. I promise," he said with a coy little wink. She gave him the side-eye and looked him up and down as if she was trying to ascertain his real motive; but, when he smiled again, the cold expression on her face faded.

"Well, I guess I could let you go in for a few minutes; but, you have to promise to be very quiet," she said with a playful school-girl smile.

"You have my word," he replied flirtatiously.

"Why don't I walk with you so that no one else stops you?"

"An escort from a beautiful lady? I am unworthy." He did a

small curtsy and she giggled as if it had been years since she had been paid a compliment. They walked down the hallway together, exchanging glances as if they were secret lovers.

"I don't think I've seen you here before," she said.

"I've been here a few times. I usually come at night."

"I guess you work during the day, huh?"

"Hmmmm, something like that." When they reached his destination, Eli took the lead, stepped in front of the nurse, and walked into the room as the smell of old flesh and ointment greeted him at the door. He walked over and kissed the old woman on the forehead affectionately.

"You're a very special man. I wish more people would spend this kind of time with the elderly."

"I have to make sure my...*grandmother* is being treated well."

"Well, rest assured. She gets the best care we can offer. Even though she can't speak or move, I'm certain that if you keep coming, she would make a full recovery. I've seen people on the brink of death come back and lead a full life with the help of the love from their relatives and friends."

Eli smiled wryly. "We can only hope."

"And I'm sure that smile of yours can heal the sick," she added, her voice thick with desire. "Well, I best be on my way; more patients to see."

"Thank you so much for your special attention and for letting me break the rules."

"Don't tell anyone. They might think I'm a softie," she said with a wink. "I'll definitely keep my eye on her. You know," she continued as she shifted her weight to her left leg, "sometime when I look into her eyes I swear she's trying to tell me something. I think she's going to come out of this fine, one day." She stepped closer and touched his hand. "I don't want to get your hopes up. I know she's been like this for twenty years, but the other day, I'm sure I saw her wiggle her feet. The doctor said it was involuntary, but I think she was making a connection."

Eli forced a smile and took the nurse's hand. He could feel her heat and knew that it was radiating below, dampening her panties. Lust swelled inside of her to the point that Eli could smell its sweetness.

"Thank you for the information, love. I didn't catch your name."

"It's Andrea. Andrea Anderson, but you can call me *Love*," she said as she smiled and flitted out of the room. Eli quickly closed the door and faced the old woman who sat upright in a chair in front of the television. Her grayed hair was tossed about her head and the old shawl wrapped around her shoulders looked as if it had been made fifty years ago. She didn't move or blink.

He took a deep, menacing breath before speaking. "Hello, Adelaide," he said with the tenderness of a grandson. He removed his trench coat and slung it across another chair as he eased over to where she sat. "So, we're alone now, old woman. Eetwidomayloh sends his regards." He lowered himself in front of her and squeezed her knees hard, his nails cutting into her flesh. Her eyes widened with discomfort. "So, you can still feel. I was kind of rough with you last time. I'm glad you've recovered." He stood up and sauntered toward the window.

"You know, Addie, I'm getting really bored with all of this. I've spent too much time in *this place* smelling your shitty ass and looking at your wrinkled face. I'm tired of this Tango—we keep doing the same dance. Aren't you tired yet? I dish out a little pain and you continue to resist me. I've been patient with you—far more patient than I should have—but there are limits to my mercy and time is short, as you know. Soon, you'll have to let me into your head—you won't have the strength to stop me. I get stronger every day, but you, on the other hand, are one step closer to the grave. So why don't you make this easy on yourself and let me in? If you don't, you know I will hurt you, slowly. First, I'll blind you, sticking tiny needles into your eyes. Would you like that? Then, from the inside, I'll break each one of your bones, one at a time. I'll make it so that every crack will last hours and that you feel every ounce of pain. Then, I can make your heart explode inside your chest, and I'll fix it so that you can relive the same horror over and over again. Your suffering will be legendary, and you'll pray for the death that will never come." Eli flung open the curtain to reveal the dark night sky glistening with starlight. "Don't you miss this? Going outside? Having a life? Aren't you tired of being trapped inside that wretched old body, unable to move; pissing and shitting on yourself and having someone wipe your ass everyday? Where is your pride? Where is your dignity? You are Adelaide Thibodeaux, the most powerful High Priestess of the sister-clan and look at you now. You're a fucking invalid!" A despicable laugh escaped from his mouth and polluted the air with the stench of rotting meat. His roaring voice tumbled off the walls.

Eli moved over to the mirror hanging on the wall and took a moment to stare at his reflection. "I must admit that I am impressed with your power. Even in your weakened state, I still cannot break into your mind—that's amazing. Yeah, yeah, I know how your powers work. Each High Priestess born of the same blood is more powerful than the one before her, blah, blah, blah. And your bloodline is unbroken in more than three hundred years. I get that. Your powers are indeed strong, so tonight I thought I'd do something different. Tonight, I offer you a fair trade. I could release you from this prison that Eetwidomayloh entombed you in so long ago. Clearly, you and your pathetic sisters don't have enough power to do so; otherwise you would have been freed a long time ago. Or, I could make your stay in that body last an eternity. How would you feel about immortality? In that body? Buried…underground…writhing in pain? Would you like that?"

He calmly took a seat next to her. "Of course you wouldn't. That sounds awful, wouldn't you agree? Now, you could avoid all of that by simply letting me into your head so that I can uncloak him and unbind his powers. As you know, his twenty-first birthday is coming soon and he *will* ascend. Your little binding spell may have kept some of his powers at bay for the last twenty years, but it will fail during the Ascension. Your magic will be like using a Popsicle stick to stop the raging waters of the Nile. I suspect that your spell will break any day now. We are what, a little more than two weeks away from the Ascension? When it breaks, do you have any idea the havoc his power could cause on the world? What if he ignites the living flame and incinerates everything and everyone? Would you like to see little children running through the city screaming with their hair on fire? That's not a nice image, Addie. He could consume this world and the Shadowland with a simple thought, without even knowing it. That is why we must find him, teach him to use his power, or we all are lost. We are simply trying to clean up the mess you made before it's too late. Had you not stolen the child from Eetwidomayloh years ago we would not be in this mess now." Eli's voice began to tremble and rattle the furniture in the room. "Signs are all around us. Your spell is weakening. There are thousands of dead cattle in Wisconsin. A plague of rodents in Australia. The River Thames, overflowing with dead fish. Powerful earthquakes, all over the globe, and it's all because of you. You have made so many mistakes in your feeble effort to prevent that which cannot be prevented." He opened his mouth and inhaled with a ghastly sucking sound that removed all of the oxygen from the room, essentially asphyxiating Addie. She gasped with disgusting choking sounds as her eyes bulged and her lungs tightened, trying to inhale the remaining air. "Now," he said coolly, "won't you help me?"

He paused for dramatic effect and to extend Addie's pain. When she was near blacking out, he replenished the room with air and spoke casually, as if nothing extraordinary had happened. "We want to find him so that he can take his rightful place in the universe. He's so very near. We *will* find him; we can feel his power. Your binding spell was never complete. Can you feel it, too? Each time his powers manifest, we can sense it, and I'm sure you can, too. So, it's only a matter of time before we locate him. You've altered destiny once, but our will shall be done in spite of your interference; still, it would be so much easier if you helped us. So, in exchange for your assistance, I offer you and your sisters immunity from your crimes against us. And for you, Adelaide, I offer a special gift: full restoration of your health. Isn't that wonderful? How could you turn down such a gracious offer? So, why don't you let me in?"

Eli stared directly into her empty eyes and tried to pierce her mind. He pushed and pushed until intense pain ricocheted inside his own skull. He screeched like a wounded animal and collapsed to one knee, clinging on to the edge of a chair near the window for balance.

"So, that's the game you want to play, you old bitch," he said between heavy breaths. He staggered over to her and suddenly backhanded her so hard across the face that she flew out of the chair and slid across the floor. She crashed into the wall with a tremendous clang. Eli felt her jawbone shatter into pieces upon impact and he could sense her pain; it delighted him. She belonged to him now and no one was coming to help her. They were alone and his torture would last for hours. He spelled the room, insulating it from sound and creating a shimmer, which would reflect a manufactured image he conjured to anyone who entered. If a hapless nurse or aide entered the room, they'd simply see him reading her a story, but behind the veil, his assault of her would continue, uninterrupted.

Eli strolled over to the window and stared into the night. He placed his right palm on the cool glass.

"There's a storm gathering, Addie. Can you feel it?" He closed his eyes and concentrated on what lay beyond the window, far past the horizon. "Oh yes. A storm." His voice sounded lustful, full of strong desire. "I can feel it. It's your storm, my dear. It is the breaking of your binding spell; it is the unleashing of his power. It is gathering strength." He turned and looked into her stone face. "Surely, you feel it, too?" He moved over to her and picked her up gently from the floor. He laid her across the bed, taking time to properly fit the pillows beneath her head. He pulled the covers up and stopped when they were just beneath her breasts. He looked at a chair in the corner and it slid effortlessly over to him. He took a seat at her side and stroked her forehead. He would torture her, abuse her, and then repair her body so that no one would know.

"Well, let us get to it."

His punishment would last most of the dark night.

⊰ CHAPTER 6

Simon woke up in his bed and looked at the clock on the nightstand. It was nearly eight at night and his room was dark, save for the light from the clock. His mouth felt arid and powdery, as if he hadn't had water in days. His forehead was slightly moist, but his headache had dissipated. He sat up in bed and took a moment to fully assess his health. He felt good. Healthy. Strong. He looked around the empty room and called out for Brooke, but his voice echoed off the walls. He called out again. Still, no answer. He was alone. More troubling than being alone was the issue of how he had gotten from the doctor's office back home. The last thing he remembered was walking toward the nurse. He remembered the waiting room. He remembered getting dizzy, but the rest was hazy.

Then, he started to remember.

Blaine.

The would-be robber at Cisco's.

The tingling.

Thoughts of that red-headed child suddenly consumed him. Maybe that dough-faced boy was a figment of his imagination; maybe the man in the black bubble coat was some stranger on the street he had seen previously. Simon hoped he had imagined it all.

Then, he remembered other details.

The gun.

Reading Blaine's thoughts. He remembered things about the boy he should not have known.

He remembered the pain in his head as he stood over the grill at work. The man in the bubble coat and Blaine weren't products of his imagination. They were real and what Simon had experienced was real, regardless of how much he wanted to pretend they were fantasy; two extraordinary events on one very ordinary day.

Simon leaned over and clicked on the lamp on the nightstand, letting his eyes adjust to the sudden brightness of the room. Just as he looked around, his cell phone screamed, which jolted him into alertness. He cursed the phone in his head, looked at the caller ID and breathed a sigh of relief.

"Hey, baby," he said, relieved to hear the sound of Brooke's voice.

"How are you feeling? I'm sorry I couldn't be there, but you know finals are coming up and I had a study group."

"Not a problem, babe. I just woke up, anyway." Simon rubbed his eyes. "Hey, how did I get home from the doctor's office?"

"What do you mean?"

"I remember being at the doctor's office and then I woke up here."

"Are you serious? You don't remember anything?" Brooke's audible exhalation on the other end of the phone expressed her concern. "Simon, you fainted and when you woke up, you asked the nurse to call me. You have a low-grade fever and some kind of respiratory infection. The doctor gave you some antibiotics. You don't remember me picking you up? You don't remember us almost tumbling down the stairs when you lost your footing?"

Simon didn't want to admit it, but he had no recollection of any of those events. "Oh yeah, I think I do. I feel a bit groggy right now."

"Well, stay in bed and get some rest. As soon as this study group is over, I'm coming over to take care of you, unless you need me now?" Her voice was laced with sudden concern.

"Nah, that's okay. I actually feel pretty good."

"You sure?"

"Yeah. The antibiotics must be working. Finish studying, baby. I'll see you later tonight."

"Okay. And, Simon?"

"Yeah?"

"I love you," she said with genuine affection.

He smiled, softly. "Thanks, baby. I needed to hear that. I'll see you tonight."

He ended the call and set the cell phone on the nightstand. As much as he wanted to reciprocate, he simply could not utter the words. *No matter what.* The words had far too much power to maim and to mutilate. He had witnessed it too many times in his young life. When they were together, instead of saying them, he often sidestepped the issue by kissing her passionately, hoping the power of his lips and tongue would nullify her longing to actually hear him say the words. He wasn't equipped to be that vulnerable.

He grabbed the television remote control and clicked it. When he replaced the control, he noticed a Post-It note stuck to the nightstand. It was written in his handwriting, but he didn't remember writing anything. He pulled it from the stand and looked at it closely, as if closer proximity to his face would jog his memory. The note was simple and short.

It simply read: *A. Thibodeaux*

"What the hell is that?" he asked himself as he studied the note. "A. Thibodeaux?" He searched his mind, hoping to find some trace of recognition, some fragment that would provide him with a clue, but he couldn't. He had no idea what the note meant. He quickly grew frustrated. So much was going wrong with him. His sight. His hearing. His memory. The infection. Now, he was leaving himself strange notes that he didn't remember writing. Quickly, he balled up the note and shot it into the trashcan like a basketball.

He took a deep yawn and then pried himself out of bed. He walked into the kitchen and moved over to the refrigerator, opening the top door and pulling out a very chilled bottle of vodka from the freezer. He grabbed a cup from the shelf, poured more than a healthy shot of vodka and downed it in one gulp. The coldness of the shot contrasted with the burning in his throat. The shot did little to quench his thirst, but he took another one to the head, without pause. He winced.

He walked into the bathroom and splashed some cool water onto his face. With his eyes closed, he reached for the dry towel, grabbed it, and wiped his face dry. When he opened his eyes and looked back into the mirror, he saw the reflection of a gray-haired woman standing directly behind him. Quickly, he jerked his body around, but when he turned, the apparition had vanished into thin air. He looked around the room, his heart once again pounding in his chest. More than anything he wanted to believe that his mind was playing terrible tricks on him. Maybe it was the vodka and the antibiotics. Maybe it was the infection. He would have convinced himself that he had imagined the whole thing had it not been for the depth of his fear. His palms were sweaty and his heart beat furiously. First it was dreams of snakes. Now, it was images of old women in his mirror.

Simon had never believed in ghosts, but now he had to lend credibility to the very real thought that he was being haunted by some unknown entity. Haunted. The word chilled his bones. What other explanation could there be? He thought about all of the horror movies he had seen in which some poltergeist tormented some poor soul so that the person could help solve their own murder. He always wondered why ghosts in the movies couldn't tell the person what was going on; they seemed capable of doing everything else. They could drag persons across rooms, move objects, slam doors, break glass, but they seemed powerless to do something as simple as write a note saying what happened to them. He used to laugh at those movies. Not anymore. Not after all he had experienced. He had never been much of a praying man, but now he called on the power of the Lord to save him. *Dear God, in my time of need…*

Simon gasped at his next thought. Maybe the ghost had written him a note—the Post-It—or at least used his own hand to write it; a message from beyond the grave! Maybe he was being haunted by *A. Thibodeaux.* Maybe he had been haunted all his life; that would certainly explain the inexplicable things that had happened to him over the years. Maybe, at certain times, the ghost would take control of his body and his mind, showing him things he was meant to see as a way of solving some deep mystery. The very thought of ghosts, possessions, and hauntings sent very real shivers up and down his spine.

Simon rushed out of the bathroom and hopped into the pair of jeans that lay on the floor at the foot of his bed. He tossed on a shirt, not bothering to see if his combination matched. Now was not a time for fashion. Now was a time to flee. He was not about to spend another moment in this house, not alone, at least not until he figured out what the hell was happening. Maybe this *A. Thibodeaux* used to live in his apartment and had died some frightful death. Maybe she or he was buried beneath the wooden floors or stuffed behind the panels of the walls. He slid his feet into an old pair of sneakers, grabbed a light-green jacket, his keys, and his wallet and practically ran out of the house. He wasn't even sure if he locked the door. He didn't care. He needed to get away.

Ψ

Because he had nowhere else to go, Simon ended up at Starry Nights, a local blues club located on the outskirts of downtown. The club was housed in a converted warehouse in an industrial part of the city, separated from the rest of downtown by rusted railroad tracks. Heading farther north across the tracks was the poor side of town that many of the city's wealthy had never dare visit. The railroad tracks, as is the case in many American cities, served as a clear line of demarcation, a line that separated the *haves* from the *have-nots*. A few years back, this area, known as Ivy City, was set to undergo an urban renaissance, with developers gobbling up many of the decaying structures, hoping to replace the crumbling buildings with high-end luxury condominiums. When the economy tanked, so did plans to resurrect this neighborhood. Starry Nights, which had been a part of the city since the 1950s, was one of the few viable businesses still left in the blighted neighborhood.

Simon hurriedly exited the train and had to walk a long five blocks to reach the club. As he moved down the street with purpose, he popped the collar on his jacket to help block a wind that seemed to have developed out of nowhere. As he made a beeline for the safety of the club, he walked past a few homeless people who had taken up residence along the cracked sidewalk. Some made a perfunctory gesture of holding out a cup or a hat, hoping Simon would bless them with a few loose coins. When he could spare it, he had no issue with dropping some coins or a few dollars into their cups. He had a hard time seeing people on the street suffering and not helping when he was able. Even though he wasn't religious, as he passed the less fortunate, he often thought about that song "What If God Was One of Us" and he was careful to not look upon them with disdain, as if he was better than them simply because he had a roof over his head. *There but for the grace of God…*

Simon continued his brisk walk. Usually, when he made the trek to Starry Nights, which he did twice a week, he was fearless. He lived in a neighborhood just as tough, but for some reason tonight, he felt…small. He thought a good wind could blow out of the clouds and toss him away. He needed something tangible to anchor him to reality. Thoughts of ghosts and serpents and telepathic children occupied too much space in his head. He couldn't move fast enough across the sidewalk. The cool wind licked his neck and he felt something *unnatural* in the air. It might have been his imagination, but when he turned around he saw a group of dried leaves swirl suspiciously across the street as the strong breeze scattered them.

He shook his head and told himself there were no such things as ghosts. Even though he wanted to believe his words, they lacked conviction. Something was going on with him, or that house, or both. Maybe he had done something to attract a spirit, but, what? His routine over the last few weeks had been quite ordinary. And, if he had been haunted all his life, why?

Simon saw the neon lights of the club and felt like a sprinter crossing the tape at the end of a race when he burst across the threshold into the club. As soon as he entered, his shoulders relaxed. Instantly, the smell of booze, cigarettes and cheap perfume comforted him. He took five dollars out of his wallet—his last five dollars—and paid the cover charge. Luckily, he had a credit card with him for drinks.

He eased into the room and staggered over to the bar, climbing atop a bar stool at the end of the long, dirty counter. The place was a dive by any standard, but the music was good, and the drinks were cheap and strong. He had become such a regular among the much older crowd that they served him liquor with no hesitation, even though he wasn't yet twenty-one. He lied and told them he was twenty-three and no one questioned him, particularly Debbie, the curvaceous bartender who more than flirted with him each time he was there. And lucky for him, she was working the bar tonight.

When Debbie saw him, she slung the towel across her shoulder and sashayed over to him, wearing a too-tight T-shirt that showed more than her ample bust line. Her seductive smile grew with each step she took.

As she moved over to him, Simon focused on her breasts struggling to break free from the confines of the cotton that held them back. All thoughts of ghosts were gone. By the time she made it to him, he had already stripped her naked and had her bent over the pool table and was thrusting inside her from behind. He imagined holding onto her rather large, soft breasts as he pressed into her. The image was so vivid in his head that he could smell the fragrance between her legs. He shifted uncomfortably in his seat; he felt his nature roaring to life.

"Hey, Simon," she said with a sexy smile that illuminated her entire face. He was so enthralled with his secret fantasy about her that he hadn't realized she was speaking to him until she touched his hand. The warmth of her touch made him want to jump across the bar and make love to her right on the dirty floor. "Simon, you okay?" she asked.

"Oh, hey, Debbie," he said, matching her flirtatious smile. They had played this cat and mouse game for months, all in good fun.

Simon fantasized a lot about her, but when his desire swelled too much, he always thought of Brooke. He wasn't a cheater. It wasn't in his nature. He always tried to do the right thing, even when the wrong thing would have provided so much pleasure. It wasn't easy for him to contain his lust, but he was in a relationship now and he was happy. He often thought about the days when he was single and free to fuck anything with a heartbeat. And, he did. Those days he blazed a red-hot trail through New Orleans that left many hearts broken, but smiles permanently were draped across faceless conquests.

"You came to see me?"

"Of course I did, baby. You know how I do."

"What can I get you?"

He looked at her and lust filled his eyes. "Don't ask me that."

She leaned in so close that her breasts rested atop the counter. He looked down and licked his lips. "I meant to drink."

"Surprise me."

"You got it."

She patted his hand and turned to the bar. He watched her grab a couple of bottles from the shelf and pour more than an ample amount of brown liquor into the glass. He then turned around and faced the stage. He listened to the female singer wail about the troubles of the world. Notes floated through the club, hovering just above the clashing conversations that took place at the bar, at small tables located through the tight space, and in dark, mysterious corners. She sang in a deep and throaty voice filled with conviction and pain. When she belted out her last note, it sent chills up and down Simon's arm.

He scanned the club, looking at the familiar faces. Toothless Woody was at his usual table, which was front and center. Paulette sat at a back table with a bottle of beer permanently attached to her hand. She screamed loudly and yelled, "Sang, bitch," to the woman on stage, which was meant as a compliment. Simon couldn't help but chuckle at her and he smiled at the faces in the crowd. He loved these people; they never rejected him. He felt more than comfortable here; he felt at home. Long gone were thoughts of ghosts and hauntings. All he needed was a stiff drink and a nice pair of tits to take his mind off his issues. He had spent many a drunken night in this place listening to the blues and talking shit with the older people who often shared stories about growing up in the South during Jim Crow. Simon delighted in the stories as much as they delighted in telling them. Seems these days the audience for their stories had diminished, which Simon thought was a damn shame; people choosing to not learn their history. Simon would give anything to know his.

Debbie returned after a few moments and placed a glass in front of Simon. Simon looked down at the murky, almost intimidating liquid. "What is it?"

"It's a Debbie Surprise," she said. She leaned in closer and whispered. "I stirred it with my nipple." The mere thought of that almost sent Simon into a sexual frenzy. Quickly, he picked up the glass and took a long, long gulp, savoring the taste of every drop. He often wondered what her chocolate nipple tasted like. Were they like candy? Like Godiva chocolate, deep and rich?

"Damn, this is good."

"I know," she said proudly. "Just don't tell your girlfriend. You still with that white girl?"

He chuckled. "Yeah, we still together."

"That's too bad. You need to get yourself a sistah."

"You know that white boy is still with that white girl," a voice from the middle of the bar said. "Limp dick can't handle a sistah." Simon didn't even have to look up to recognize the voice that grated so profoundly on his nerves.

"I've told you, fool. I ain't white."

"You ain't black, either, with dem white boy blue eyes."

"Fuck you, Byron," Simon said, venom seeping into his words. "We weren't talking to you anyway."

"*We weren't talking to you anyway*," Bryon repeated in an insultingly mocking tone. "You even sound like a white boy."

"Mind your business, Byron. And don't start no trouble. I'll get Mac to throw yo' ass out," Debbie chimed in, much to Byron's chagrin.

Simon had a long and painful history with Byron, who was his senior by at least ten years. When Simon found Starry Nights by accident and started frequenting the club, Byron took an instant dislike to him. Byron had been the big man in the club, the one all the women wanted, but Simon's youth and unbridled sexuality quickly dethroned the reigning king. It didn't help that Byron had been trying to get into Debbie's pants for years, only to be rebuffed time and time again. Everyone knew all Simon had to do was say the word and he could claim the prize that had eluded Byron for years.

Byron, a brick wall of a man, with huge biceps and a thick neck, did all he could do to irritate and intimidate him, but Simon would not yield. He wasn't afraid of Byron. Byron was a former linebacker for LSU, but Simon didn't care. *The bigger they are, the harder they fall*, he thought on more than one occasion. More than once they had come close to a physical altercation, but they had never come to blows. Simon had no doubt that one day they would; maybe that day would be today.

"My bad," Byron started again. "I forgot this mutt doesn't know what the hell he is."

Instantly, fire flashed across Simon's chest and before he knew it he was on his feet stomping toward Byron. He continued his approached, anger building inside.

"What the fuck did you call me, you dumb son-of-a-bitch?"

"I called you a mutt, a mongrel. Do you want me to spell it for you?" Byron stood up and a great shadow fell over the room; yet, Byron's size wasn't enough to make Simon back down. Simon, sensitive about not knowing his racial heritage or family history, had fought bigger men than him and he was not about to let this man insult him in such a public way.

Quickly, Debbie raced from around the bar and took a defensive stand between the two.

"Don't worry about him, baby," Debbie said to Simon. "He's jealous."

"Jealous of what? This pale-faced, lil'-dick muthafucka? Bitch, please."

The word *bitch* fired across Simon's ears and, before he knew it, he had thrown the first punch. He hit Byron square in the jaw, but the behemoth barely flinched. With one sweep of his arms, Byron moved Debbie out of the way and took a swing at Simon, which hit him square in the face. Simon crashed into a few stools and hit the floor, hard. Simon's eye felt as if it exploded in its socket. Byron easily tossed the barstools out of his way in his quest to reach Simon, who had leapt to his feet. In spite of his pain, he felt rage like he didn't know was possible. His entire body now tingled; he was on fire.

Byron took another swing at Simon, which connected only with air. As he swung, Simon bent low and connected with Byron's face with an uppercut that sent the giant reeling. Byron stumbled, crashed into a table, and landed flat on his back, breaking the table.

"Get yo' ass up, bitch!" Simon screamed in a voice no one recognized as his. Most patrons in the main pit of the club snatched at their belongings, trying to flee the premises before things got too out of hand. They didn't want to be around if the cops had to come in and bust up the fight; however, others like Paulette looked on in glee, egging the fight on. "Get up!"

Dazed, Byron staggered to his feet like a blind giant. Pure hatred for Simon colored his face. He balled his fists and approached Simon like an angry bull. He swung wildly a few times, missing each time. Simon swung back, but he didn't miss. He connected with Byron's face so quickly and so often that Byron didn't know from which direction the blows were coming; they seemed to be coming from all directions at once. Then, Simon sent a mighty fist into Byron's gut, causing him to double over in pain.

A voice echoed in Simon's head.

Kill him.

Through Simon's rage, he barely noticed the command.

When he was bent, Simon kicked Byron in the face so hard that he unleashed a primal scream that could be heard down the block. The kick sent Byron flying onto the stage and he crashed into the drum set that had been abandoned by the musician. He hit the wooden stage with a loud thump and then didn't move again.

Simon stood there, heaving. His fists were still balled. He wanted to tear the place apart. He saw himself shattering glass and punching through walls. His anger was a tidal wave, almost uncontrollable. He looked around the room. People had stopped dead in their tracks to eye him, their mouths agape.

He closed his eyes. *Onetwothreefourfivesixseveneightnineten.* Again. *Onetwothreefourfivesixseveneightnineten.* Again. *Onetwothreefourfivesixseveneightnineten.*

When his anger broke, he looked around the room at the dumbfounded looks on the faces of the patrons. Their expressions were a mixture of shock and awe. And fear. The smell of fear in the air was so potent that Simon felt intoxicated by it; if he could have drunk it, he would have.

Byron, who must've weighed close to three hundred pounds, had flown up onto the stage as if Simon had kicked a rag doll.

Slowly, Debbie approached him and touched his shoulder, cautiously.

"You better get out of here," she said out of concern. Simon looked at her as if he didn't quite understand. "Go." He looked at the people again. Their fear of him was thick. Simon took one last look toward the stage and exited the room quickly with his head held low, realizing that it was done—he'd never be able to go home again.

His lowered head hid the sinister smile that began to form on his face.

Ψ

Simon furiously ran down the block outside the club and turned the corner. He stopped and rested with his back against the cold brick wall of the building. All around him darkness and shadows shaded the area. His chest was swollen with adrenaline and fire, and he still felt the tingling in his fists from the fight. He had to catch his breath and figure out what just happened. He was slightly dizzy as he looked down at his hands and wondered how he had summoned so much strength. The power he felt was rabid and intoxicating; a savage joy overtook his heart. He didn't feel bad about what happened. Byron needed to have had the shit beaten out of him a long time ago, and Simon delighted in the fact that it was he who had delivered such a thorough and complete ass-whooping. In fact, Simon was so wired that he wanted to race back into the bar and punch Bryon a few more times on general principle; but, he held on to enough sense to realize that wasn't a good idea.

When he left, the man was barely moving, probably unconscious. At his core, he didn't care whether or not Byron lived or died. He couldn't have cared less if Byron spent the rest of his life as an invalid, trapped in a wheelchair or bound to a bed in some substandard nursing home. In his predatory state, he found the thought of inflicting more harm on Byron—or anyone who got in the way—to be *lustful*. He was overcome with a strong desire for blood and violence; a desire so strong that his loins ached.

He looked up toward the intersection in front of him when he heard a car screech to a halt at the red light, slamming on its brakes. A big, blue, hulking machine of a car with dark, tinted windows sat at the light with its engine loudly idling. Obnoxious rap music thumped against the windows of the car and shook the entire block. Even though the windows were pitch black, Simon could clearly see into the car, which was populated by two young black males, and a Hispanic man of roughly same age, who had a tattoo of a cross on the right side of his neck.

In one smooth motion, all of their heads turned in Simon's direction. Through the windows, Simon could feel their eyes on him and he pondered their next move. *Maybe they'll move on when the light turns green*, he thought even though he knew things would not be that simple. His intuition told him to be cautious. He was alone in the dark with no people around him, except for the thugs in the death machine at the light. He had few options to protect himself, but he felt no fear. He was still amped up on power. In fact, a part of him wanted them to approach.

The night suddenly seemed to dim around him and the shadows expanded. Something inside of him said *flee*, but something else that was far more urgent and primal told him to stay. He wouldn't be threatened or bullied. They would be fools to mess with him, especially on this night, of all nights.

The traffic light turned green, but the car didn't move. Its engine revved. *Vroooomm. Vroooom.*

When Simon saw the driver's side window slowly roll down, his heartbeat quickened and the hairs on his neck stood on end. He was in danger; there was no doubt about that. He stood upright so that he would be ready for the coming assault. He could smell it, but it didn't cause him to panic. In fact, the smell of danger excited him in many ways; that lust for more violence ignited his body.

"Wassup?" the driver said. Even though his face was partially cloaked by the black hoodie that he wore on his head, his cold black eyes clearly showed his intention for no good. "What you doin' out here?"

"Nothing, man. Just chillin'."

"This a lonely place to be chillin'." His voice was cold and filled with a veiled threat.

"I just left the club a minute ago," Simon said, already bored with the conversation. He was ready for them to make their move. *Let's get on with it.*

"Say, homie," the Hispanic dude said when the back seat window rolled down.

"You got a smoke?"

"Nah, dude. I don't smoke. Smokin' will kill ya." They chuckled at his choice of words. Simon placed his hands in his pockets and took a few steps toward the traffic light. "A'ight, y'all take it easy tonight. I gotta get going."

"So soon?" the Hispanic dude said as he stepped out of the car and walked toward Simon, cutting him off from the main street.

All right, here we go, Simon thought. The Hispanic dude, dressed in blue jeans, a faded gray hoodie, and utility boots, swaggered his way over to Simon. He stepped up on the sidewalk and faced him. His stance wasn't threatening, but Simon knew to keep up his guard. Slowly, the man reached into his pocket and pulled out a box of cigarettes and a lighter.

"I thought you needed a cigarette."

"Nah, I'm good, homie. We just fuckin' with you."

Simon watched him remove a cigarette from the box, put it between his lips and light it. Casually, he put the box and the lighter back in his pocket after offering Simon a smoke.

"I need to be going," Simon said, but the man blocked his path.

"Say," he said coolly, "my buddies want to go have a drink somewhere, but we ain't got no money. Help us out, homie."

"My name ain't homie, *homie*," Simon said with attitude. "And I don't have any money for you and your *homies*."

"That's cold, amigo. Cold. My buddies ain't gon' be happy."

"Sounds like their problem. Now, if you'll excuse me." Simon tried to move around the man but he blocked his path again.

"I can't let you go. Not 'til you gimme yo' wallet."

"You must already be high. I told you, I don't have any money; and, even if I did, I wouldn't give it to you."

"So, it's like that, homie? You want me to take it from you?"

"Nah, I want you to *try* to take it, homie."

The tingling returned, covering Simon's whole body. Quickly, the man pulled out a switchblade and pointed it at Simon.

"Give me yo' fuckin' wallet befo' I have to cut yo' fuckin' throat."

Simon didn't blink. He remained completely still while the man teetered back and forth in an effort to prevent Simon from running.

"Stop fucking around, Juan," the driver called out in a husky voice. "Stick that fool and take his wallet so we can get the fuck out of here!"

On command, Juan lunged at Simon with the knife. Before he made his move, Simon saw the move in his head and jumped out of the way. As he moved, he shoved Juan hard into the brick wall, face first.

"You muthafucka!" Juan screamed, as blood gushed from his now broken nose. He turned around swinging his blade wildly, almost blindly. Simon was fitter and faster and was able to easily evade the blade, much to Juan's disappointment. Juan grew clumsy in his frustration and the next time he lunged, Simon ducked and punched him in the nose. Juan screamed loudly, dropped the knife, and stumbled onto an abandoned Oldsmobile that was parked curbside.

Simon went on the offensive and unleashed a torrent of body blows on Juan, who was pressed against the vehicle, covering his face, helplessly. No defense from Juan would spare him from the onslaught. With each blow, Simon's appetite for violence grew more insatiable. Juan's body was pummeled like a boxing bag.

"Look at this muthafucka getting his bitch-ass whooped," Simon heard one of the other men say. He heard the car doors open and the sound of feet rapidly pounding the pavement. Before he knew it, the other two men were upon him. They threw him against the brick wall and began to punch him while Juan struggled to regain his composure.

"You let this lil' bitch fuck you up like that?" one of the men said as he looked at Juan disgustedly. "He ain't shit!" Then, he sent a strong fist into Simon's stomach. Pain radiated throughout Simon's body and he doubled over. Quickly, each one of the two men grabbed Simon's arm and threw him against the brick wall, holding him in place. Simon didn't struggle to get free. Instead, he focused on what was to come. He saw it play out in his head before it happened.

"Get yo' knife and take care of this bitch fo' I fuck you up!" the driver commanded to Juan. His lips were snarled and his voice was poisonous. Juan staggered over to the knife that was lying on the ground near the front wheel of the old car. He reached down and grabbed the blade and moved over to Simon.

"I got you now, bitch!" Juan said between clenched teeth, blood staining his olive-colored skin.

"Bring it on, bitch," Simon said. His words infuriated Juan, who sprang into action. He lunged at Simon with the knife aimed at Simon's midsection. Right before impact, Simon pulled the driver in front of him and the knife dug deeply into his back. The driver screamed as if he had been gutted. He dropped to his knees, the knife jutting from his back between his shoulder blades.

"What the fuck did you just do?" the other man screamed as he released Simon. When he did, Simon wasted no time in punching him so hard in the face that the man lost consciousness. One blow. He hit the hard concrete with a thud.

Simon turned his attention to Juan.

"Listen, man," Juan pleaded, "I don't want no trouble." He backed away with both his hands extended in front him.

"You tried to rob and stab me, and you don't want no trouble?" Simon's voice was calm.

"Man, it was them. They made me!"

"Fuck you!" Simon yelled. In the blink of an eye, Simon was upon Juan. He had crossed a distance of ten feet without taking a single step. He grabbed Juan by the throat with one hand and lifted him off the ground. Simon looked into his eyes and saw that terror had fully taken control of him; his limbs flailed uncontrollably. In a quick motion, Simon threw Juan over the thugs' muscle car and completely across the street. He crashed into the door of another abandoned building with a colossal bang, losing consciousness upon impact.

"What...the f-f-fuck are you, man?" the terrified driver asked when he saw Simon's feat of unnatural strength. His eyes were so wide that they looked as if they would bulge out of his head. He focused more on Simon than he did his deep knife wound.

Simon looked down scornfully at the man on the sidewalk; he seemed so small, so insignificant. He was like a speck of dust against the winds of Simon's hurricane. The bloody knife was now positioned at the man's side, its silver blade stained red. Simon looked at the knife and it flew swiftly into his hand. In terror, the driver shuffled on the sidewalk, trying to flee, fighting his pain, but there was nowhere to go.

Simon admired the knife in his hand, studying its design as if it was an ancient artifact. The blade was perfectly made for killing. Sharp. Sleek. Strong. Then, he opened his mouth and stuck out his tongue. He took a broad side of the knife and slowly ran it down his tongue, wiping clean the blood from the knife and then repeated his action on the other side of the blade. As he tasted the sweetness of the man's blood, his body shuddered in ecstasy; the taste was like a powerful undiscovered new street drug; it was almost orgasmic.

Simon turned his attention back to the man and kicked him in the face. The man flew into the brick wall. "Who am I, you ask? I am your nightmare made flesh."

CHAPTER 7

Ssssss-simon. Ssssss-simon. Ssssss-simon. I felt you tonight, Simon.

Simon shifted uncomfortably in his bed. While he slept, disparate and disturbing images and voices filled his head. He tossed and turned violently in the bed, struggling to regain consciousness.

In the middle of the room stood the old woman whose reflection he had seen earlier in his bathroom mirror. She was dressed in a ragged, red dress, and her image was largely translucent. She was mouthing words that Simon could not understand. He stared at her aged face. Had she been the one hissing his name? The longer he stared at her, the more he realized the answer to that question was no. The hissing he heard was from something else. There was something about her face that set his mind at ease; a kindness about her spirit, and Simon wondered why, earlier, he had felt threatened by her. From what he could gather now, there was no ill will in her intention. It seemed to him that she was trying to tell him something.

Ssssss-simon. Ssssss-simon. Ssssss-simon.

He heard the hissing again. It no longer sounded gentle. It sounded angry. Agitated. The black snake with yellow eyes materialized in the same corner of his room, but it appeared to be twice its previous size. It coiled itself in a menacing position as it stared at the hollow image of the old woman. It raised its head and let out a hissing sound that rattled the room. Its eyes tightened and it stared venomously at the old woman. Even in his sleep, Simon could feel himself sweating. He wanted to wake, but something held him on the edge of sleep.

In a flash, the snake slithered over to the woman and struck her with his enormous fangs. Pain exploded across her face and in an instant she had vanished; her ethereal image simply faded into nothingness.

The serpent then turned its attention to Simon. With no delay, it crawled up the bed and over Simon's body. It stopped when its face was only inches from Simon's head. It opened it huge mouth and hissed.

Ssssss-simon. Ssssss-simon. Ssssss-simon.

Simon woke up screaming, sweating. He heard a commotion in the other room, as if something heavy had dropped to the floor. Before he could will himself to move, Brooke burst into the room and flipped on the light. She was dressed in a pair of gray warm-ups and one of Simon's white undershirts, and her blonde hair was pulled back in a ponytail.

"Simon!" she screamed. "Baby, what's wrong?"

Simon couldn't speak; he was breathing too hard. Instinctively, he stared at the dark corner where the snake had been in his dream. Brooke ran over to him and shook him hard.

"Simon! What is it?"

"Huh? Brooke? I'm sorry. I think I had a bad dream."

Brooke exhaled. "My God, I thought you were dying, the way you were screaming. Please don't ever scare me like that again," she said with her hand tightly clenched against her chest.

"I'm sorry, baby. I didn't mean to scare you."

"It's okay. I'm glad you're okay. I was studying in the other room and you started screaming. I didn't know what was going on." She pulled him to her body and hugged him tightly. He could feel her rapid heartbeat against his chest. She released her grip and looked at his face. "Come here," she said. He leaned in and she grabbed a tissue from the nightstand and wiped his lip.

"What are you doing?"

"You have something red on your lip. It may be blood. You probably bit your lip in your sleep." She tossed the soiled tissue into the wastebasket on the side of the nightstand.

"Oh, okay. How was your study group?"

"It was fine, for the most part. I couldn't concentrate; that's why I left early and came here."

"Were you here when I got back from Starry Nights?"

"Starry Nights? What are you talking about?"

"After I got off the phone with you earlier, I couldn't sleep," he began, conveniently leaving out the details about the old woman. "I didn't want to be here by myself, so I went to hear some music. Can you believe I got into a fight with that asshole, Byron?"

Brooke looked at Simon as if he was speaking a foreign language.

"Simon, what are you talking about?"

"I got into a fight and I kicked his ass." Pride puffed out Simon's chest.

Brooke took his hand and rubbed it in a comforting way. "Baby," she said slowly, "you haven't been anywhere. When I got off the phone with you, I left the study group and came directly here from campus. I was here in twenty minutes and when I walked in, you were asleep. I've been in the other room studying for hours. I haven't left, and neither have you."

Simon yanked his hand back from her. "What the hell are you talking about? I took the train over to Starry Nights and there was a big fight."

"No, you didn't. You couldn't have. That's a forty-five-minute train ride and you were here when I got here."

Simon studied her face to see if she was playing with him. She had a wicked sense of humor and loved practical jokes, but this time she was serious. When his eyes met hers, he knew that she really believed what she said to him.

Oh my God. He's losing his mind.

"I'm not losing my mind," Simon said defensively.

"I didn't say you were," she said slowly.

"Yes, you did. I heard you."

I wonder if Daddy knows a good psychiatrist.

When the thought entered Simon's head, he was staring directly at her, but did not see her lips move. Suddenly, he wanted to panic when he realized he was reading her thoughts; this time he felt no tingling as a forewarning. He looked at the concern carved in her face and saw the tears building in her eyes. She was really worried about him. He needed to placate the situation.

"You know what, baby. I'm trippin'. I think it's the vodka I had."

"You had vodka tonight?"

"Two shots."

She smiled and looked relieved. "Simon, you're not supposed to drink when you're taking that medicine."

"I know. I thought I'd be okay, but clearly I'm not. I'm hallucinating all kind of shit. You must think I'm crazy."

She kissed him on the forehead, letting her lips linger for a few seconds. "I feel so much better now that I understand." She stood up and straightened the comforter on the bed. "Why don't you lie back down and get some rest. You look tired."

"I think I'll do that."

Brooke exited the room and closed the door. When he heard the door shut, he exhaled loudly and rubbed his face with his hands.

Maybe she's right. Maybe I am losing my mind. His emotions were scattered all over the place. He didn't know what to think or feel or say or do. If insanity was the root cause of his troubles, he could deal with that, but in his heart he knew he wasn't crazy. What he was experiencing wasn't caused by some imbalance in his brain; what he felt was real and tangible, and its explanation defied logic.

Maybe the ghost was playing with his mind, making him see and imagine things that weren't there.

As he lay in bed, he recalled the events of the night. He looked at his hands; his fists still throbbed from punching Byron. He touched his eye and it was still tender where Byron punched him. His eye wasn't swollen or blackened, otherwise Brooke would have said something, but he knew emphatically that he had been punched. He could also smell the cheap liquor from the bar. He remembered the big-boned beauty on stage who belted out the blues against her drummer's pounding rhythm. He remembered the train ride over and the homeless people on the sidewalk. He remembered seeing the neon sign above the doorway to Starry Nights that illuminated the night sky. Then, he remembered the thugs outside. He remembered the thumping bass from the music that poured out of their aggressive-looking car. He remembered tossing a grown man across the street. He remembered everything. And, he remembered Debbie; her scent still filled his nostrils.

I remember.

I remember.

I remember.

Simon's mouth suddenly filled with the taste of blood and he could smell its pungent odor in the air. A horrifying image flashed in his head and then he remembered. He remembered slowly licking the blood off the knife that was used to stab the driver. Simon grabbed his stomach, fighting the urge to regurgitate. *Blood*. He had tasted another man's blood in a vile display of domination. *Blood*. He remembered the joyous manner in which he licked the knife, savoring the sweet taste of unadulterated power; it was unlike anything he had ever tasted. He remembered craving more of it; the taste of it was an aphrodisiac.

Simon choked back the disgust that filled his throat; the man that did that disgusting act wasn't him. It couldn't have been him, but the memory was crystal clear. Could everything else he remembered be true except that one thing? Simon readily accepted the truth of everything he remembered, but digesting blood was the one thing that he could not force himself to accept. If he accepted that, then he had to face the fact that he was becoming a fiend—a beast—something born out of nightmares. This wasn't a haunting; it was a transformation.

I'm losing my fucking mind.

How could any of this be? Brooke may have spoken her truth and denied the events the way he told them, but her explanation didn't feel right in Simon's spirit—in spite of the fact that now he wanted to believe her. It would be so much easier to believe her simple truths. He'd been home all night. Sick. With fever. Medicated. But, he couldn't swallow that story. Her truths were lies. He had gone to Starry Nights and he had tasted blood. Something was wrong with him. Very wrong. He only wished he knew what it was.

His cell phone vibrated on the table. He picked up it and saw that it was a message from Debbie. Her simple text message confirmed what he knew was true.

Byron is at Tulane Medical Center. You betta lay low for a while.

Simon gasped.

Chapter 8

Addie knew that Eli was right: a storm was coming. She didn't need her full strength or power to feel it gathering somewhere in the distance. An ever-present shadow, creeping like mist over a calm ocean, occupied a corner in her mind; she simply couldn't shake it. The hairs on her forearm sometimes stood on end and she could feel the chaos in the air; it was an ominous sign of things to come. The storm would hit when the dam she erected to hold back his power finally broke. Over the years, the wall had endured much, and there were times she felt it would crumble; but she willed it to stand, sealing the ever-increasing cracks with the sheer power of her mind. She wouldn't be able to patch the wall much longer; she knew that. She had grown weary; her powers, stretched thin. And, he grew too strong as the date of the Ascension drew near.

She feared what would happen when her spell broke. Even more, she feared that darkness lurked in his heart.

If she could contact him before his twenty-first birthday, the date of the maturation of his powers, she could possibly influence him—sway him to stay in the light; but ultimately she knew that when he saw the proverbial fork in the road, he, and he alone, would decide his course and consequently, the course of the world. She prayed that the goodness she had planted in his heart at birth had taken root and blossomed. She prayed for the world.

As the day neared, her connection to him had grown stronger, strong enough now that she was able to isolate his energy in the spirit realm. Her powers were muted, tame in comparison to what they used to be, but she had been able to transmit sounds and images to him; but, she wasn't sure how her messages were perceived by him in the real world. They could have been anything: a faint whisper in the night; a faded image while he slept; an oddly shaped cloud during a thunderstorm; or some strange electrical flicker as he watched television. Anything. And, any day now, he'd grow strong enough that they all—including the shadows—would feel his powers; enough that they'd be able to locate him—the sum of all her fears.

Addie kept trying to find him, even through her present difficulties. She had enough power to uncloak him now, so that she could find him; but if she did, the shadows would instantly feel him as soon as the veil was lifted, and they would claim him while she was immobile. So, she kept him hidden—even from herself—because the cloaking spell was blinding to all, and she searched for other ways to find him.

For over twenty years now, Addie had suffered silently, entombed in a shell of a body, unable to move on her own or speak. She had been locked away ever since the night Simon had been born; that night, so many things went wrong. Her prison without walls kept her physically immobile, but her mind never stopped moving; never stopped thinking. Because he was still wrapped in her binding spell, and because they were connected by blood, she had always been able to detect his presence, even faintly. Over the years—as it was with his father—there were times she could feel what he felt, but the sensation was never as strong as it had been with Thomas. She felt his spirit, but could never see his face through the haze. Then, weeks—sometimes months—would pass before she felt him again, leaving her with nothing more than a spiritual fragment of his existence. Recently, however, her body had begun twitching, and she knew it was due to his power and the weakening of her spells. The time was upon them—the Ascension. Once her spells crumbled, much of her power would return to her, but it still wouldn't be enough to beat back the dark; not if the dark owned his soul.

Addie sat alone in her room with the television turned on the nightly news and she concentrated. The nurse had just made her rounds and left the room. Now was the perfect time for her to try again to make contact. With all the force she could muster, she projected her thoughts to Simon. She hoped he was in an open mental state so that he could receive them. No doubt, by now, he had experienced extraordinary events, events she hoped would make him more amenable to her connection. If he was open to receiving, she'd have a better chance of making a meaningful contact.

She concentrated. She focused her mind and let it travel across mountains and valleys; she moved over rivers and lakes and jagged terrain. She was drawn to him, to his energy, but she was pulled in many directions, an effect of her cloaking spell. Today, for the first time, she saw a house. She saw a run-down house, located at a busy intersection, in some non-descript urban area, but she didn't know in which city the house was located. She struggled to see anything that might tell her more. Quickly, her eyes scanned the area—she knew she didn't have much time before her spirit moved on. Her mind's eye finally fixed upon a street sign partially hidden by the branches of a knotted old tree. Just before she was pulled into the house, she saw a sign tacked to the door of the house that read: *8707 Oakley*.

Her mind entered the room. She saw someone standing near

the door, their back to her. It was him. She could feel his presence. She needed him to feel her, too. She needed to see his face.

Turn around, she whispered with her mind. *Turn around.*

He twitched as if he felt something.

Turn around...Simon.

Slowly, his head began to turn, but as he did, Addie was snatched back to her harsh reality.

"Addie, how are you today, my love?" Eli's affectionate voice filled her room at the convalescent center. Instantly, her body stiffened and she was flooded with dread. *Not again. Not now.* He appeared out of the shadows and stepped forward coolly. Addie's body tensed into a tight knot. She wanted to cry out, to scream and to holler, but she had no voice and it would have been a colossal waste of her energy. Her only option was to get a message to Simon. Only he could save her—if she could reach him—but she didn't know if he had already been polluted by the shadows. By now, his heart could be as black as coal.

Eli sauntered easily across the room, slowly removing his black leather gloves and smiling delicately. He dropped the gloves onto the dresser and took a seat in a chair, crossing his legs.

"Addie, my dear," he began, his voice deep with impatience, "I hope we have a better meeting today than we had last time. I'm growing tired of this charade, and I'm sure you are, too. If you stop being so obstinate, we could find an amicable solution. Let's work together to restore the natural order before this gets out of hand. Do you have any idea of the chaos that awaits us all? Help us bring order to the world before it's too late." He huffed loudly and looked around the room as if he was bored. "The rules have changed, Addie. The world as we know it has changed. All of your prophecies and witchy stories don't matter now. Everything has changed!" His voice was thunderous, tumbling violently off the walls, and his eyes went completely black for a few seconds. "You will help us or you will suffer and die in ways you cannot even conceive. Now, I'll ask you again. Where is Simon?"

"Eli, let us be kind today." The sound of a woman's sweet voice filled the room. Addie could not move her head, but out of her peripheral vision she saw a woman almost glide into the room from the hallway. Her energy filled the space with a warm, golden light. She, dressed in an all-white gown with a golden belt tied around her waist, moved effortlessly over to Eli, her feet never touching the floor. Her straight, shoulder-length, fire-red hair blew gently in a wind that, apparently, she generated. Her beauty was refined and dignified, not overdone. She looked regal, like a storybook queen from some fairy tale that people often told their children; a story that ended with the words *happily ever after*. If she was in cahoots with Eli, Addie knew this story would not have a happy ending.

She stroked Eli's face lovingly, as a mother would a child. Addie watched the fury drain from his face upon her first touch. "Let me handle this, darling." Her voice was soothing, yet commanding; her smile affectionate. Without protest, Eli moved over to the corner and took a seat in the chair, rolling his eyes as a child would who had been chastised.

She moved close to Addie and stroked her hand, while looking directly into Addie's curious eyes. Her touch was warm.

"Hello, Adelaide. My name is Rebecca, Rebecca Saint." When she spoke, her words were very proper, enunciated with crystal clarity. Her words sound enchanted, almost musical, filling the room with a melodious rhythm. There was something familiar about the woman, and Addie wondered if they had met in a previous life, under different circumstances.

Despite her delicate appearance, Addie feared her more than

Eli; she was unsettling, like the calm before a calamitous storm. "How are you today?" she asked in a syrupy sweet voice, as if she really expected an answer. "We have come to you for your help," she continued, her voice suddenly laden with concern. She walked over to the window and stared into the night. "As you know, the time is near and there is nothing anyone can do to prevent it. Not I. Not you. Not Eli. What we can do is prevent a brutal apocalypse." She turned and leaned against the window, resting her back. Addie suddenly felt her chair turning in the direction of Rebecca. The chair screeched as it scratched across the floor; they were now face-to-face, but across the room. "Do you not know who I am, Adelaide Thibodeaux? I sense no recognition from you. Is my face so unfamiliar to you? Has it been that long?" She folded her arms and took a few steps toward Addie, her heels now clicking against the floor. She leaned in and whispered in Addie's ear. "How quickly you forget your crimes, Adelaide."

Addie searched her mind furiously. There were so many things that she had lost over the years trying to hold onto her strength; some things she had willingly let go.

"I suppose you wouldn't remember," Rebecca continued without missing a beat. "It was such a long time ago and so much was going on that night. Fire. Storm. Rain. I was there. Almost twenty-one years ago you stole my child." The woman's voice remained gentle, but her tone soured. She paused to let the knowledge sink into Addie's head. "You ripped my baby from my womb and left me to die." In that instant, Addie expected to feel the brunt of some force from her or Eli, but none came. "Did you even know my name, or anything about me before you kidnapped me from my family and left me to die? Did you know that I loved your son, Thomas, and when you killed him I almost died, too? It broke my heart. Still does. You and your band of banshees killed Thomas, incinerated his soul. How could a mother do such a thing to her one and only child?"

How can this be? Addie thought to herself, her insides twisting.

"It can be; you have made it so," Rebecca said quickly. "Do you see how easily I entered your head? You are becoming weak. It's only a matter of time before your spell falls and we have access to all that you know and to my son. Why not tell us where you have hidden him? I am his mother, after all. I deserve to know." Rebecca's face suddenly flashed before Addie's eyes. She remembered her. Then, her hair was blonde, but it was her, the girl whom Addie had stolen from an unsuspecting family. She was the vessel; the mother of The One—the Dark Mother. "I can feel him—my son—just as you can. We are of the same blood. So I *will* find him. Help us, Adelaide. Please. You now have an opportunity to right your wrong after all these years. Let us be done with it."

Eli jumped up and moved closer to Addie, his patience growing thin. He kneeled in front of her and looked into her eyes. "Look at my face, old woman. Do you even know who I am?" he asked as he searched her eyes for even the slightest hint of knowledge. "Really, you can't see it? You can't *feel* it?" Addie paid attention to his face, carefully considering his features. "Old woman, you're off your game—you're slipping. All this time I've been in your presence and you didn't know who I am; that's shameful." He stood up, adjusting his shirt. "I am a part of the whole."

He moved over to the dresser, floating up and sitting on a clear space on top, shaking his head in disappointment. "I can't believe we have to explain this to your simple, incompetent ass."

"Eli, be careful of your words," Rebecca chastised. "I have taught you better than that. Curse words are so…common," Rebecca admonished. "You'll have to forgive him. You know how impetuous young boys can be."

Eli continued, "The night you snatched Simon—I assume you know his name—from his mother and Eetwidomayloh you failed to realize something so fundamental." He leaned his face toward her, his eyes tightly drawn into dark slivers and he spoke in a sharp whisper. "You snatched one child…when there were actually two. *My* mother was pregnant with twins, you fool." Addie's heart pounded, her throat tightened. "Do you get it now? I am your grandson also, and because of your inept witchery there are now *two* when there should be *one*; two who must share power instead of The One who was to rule; but it's okay. We are kings of kings, my brother and me." Rebecca moved over and placed her arms around her son. "I bet your seer didn't *see* that one coming, did she?" He chuckled.

He blamed Addie for this schism in the universal order of things, but she knew the fault was not hers. She had not the power to create such a gargantuan shift in the natural order.

"Now, Adelaide, do you understand the depth of your crime? Not only have you deprived a woman of her lover, but also a mother of her son and a brother of his brother. You have destroyed a family—my family. How cruel. How so very cruel. You have a chance to make it right tonight, maybe your only chance."

Everything within Addie seized up and she screamed in her head with a force that was so strong that Eli and Rebecca felt it, stumbling backward slightly.

"Please calm down, Adelaide," Rebecca said, her teeth clenched beneath her smile. "We did not come here to fight."

"Who knew you had that much strength left? Impressive." Eli shook off her power as he would dust that had settled onto his coat. "Why don't we kill her now, mother? I'm tired of this. We can find Simon on our own. We don't need this old bag of bones." His voice was full of bravado, but the nervous glance shared between him and Rebecca wasn't missed by Addie. In contrast to his bold words, they wouldn't kill her, at least not yet.

"You're right, Addie. We won't kill you now," Rebecca said, reading Addie's mind again. "We know how your magic works. Let's see, how does it go?" she said playfully, as if she couldn't recall the words. "According to your Book of Light, when a High Priestess dies without an annointed heir, her powers combine with that of her ancestors and the strength of her remaining earthly spells are increased, threefold. Is that right? So, you are probably thinking that we will not kill you because, if your binding spell is increased by a factor of three, Simon may never be able to claim all the power that is rightfully his. Is that what you are thinking?" Rebecca paced around the room. "We know that you will not kill yourself, because all of your spells would be broken and your spirit could never *ascend* and you could never join your ancestors." She spoke of the truth as if she had experienced it before, directly from the Book of Light, but Addie knew that was not possible; no one other than a member of the sister-clan could read the text. Only a sister knew the language; it was unique, mystical.

This woman unnerved Addie fiercely.

"You are ignorant of so many things, Adelaide, but I am not. I know answers to questions your feeble mind has yet to even conceive," Rebecca continued, hubris tainting her voice, "It is no wonder you did not know about my twins. I must admit that even Eetwidomayloh did not know. Imagine his surprise when you vanished with Simon and my dear Eli burst from my womb thirteen minutes later!" She clapped her perfectly manicured hands and hugged Eli. "That was the happiest day of my life." Then, she stared into Eli's eyes and kissed him in a way no mother should ever kiss her child. "I want you to know that I forgive you,

Adelaide. I forgive you for robbing me of my other child and stealing my joy. I forgive you for snatching me from my family and for destroying the man I loved—your son—and for denying my children their father. For many, many years, I felt nothing but consuming rage when I thought of you; a rage only a mother could know, but in these final hours, I have forgiven you for what you did to me and my family. I forgive you; a new dawn is breaking. All is well, my dear. All will be well."

Addie wanted to cast them from her sight, to send them back to whatever rock they slithered from under, but she didn't have the power. All of her strength had to be used to guard her mind, to prevent Rebecca from so easily entering. She was using a subtle trick to penetrate the shallow parts of Addie's mind, but Addie had already fortified her mind to prevent such a reading. And, she recognized that the knowledge they shared with her now came at a heavy price; they wanted to weaken her, to shock her so much that they gained access to her inner thoughts. She had to concentrate, above all else, and not let their words distract her.

"So, do you get it now, *Grandmother*? Simon and I are one." Addie felt her heart pound aggressively in her chest. "If you think for one second that we won't find him, you should think again. And, when we find him, we shall rule as it was intended."

Addie felt dazed by their revelations. Never had anyone spoken of, or thought about, the possibility of the first male born of the first born male having a twin. It was madness! Addie continued to listen to Rebecca and Eli rattle on about destiny and their reign. They spoke as if it was already done, as if they sat on golden thrones atop the world's highest peak.

As they spoke, Addie tried to understand what had altered reality. How had it happened? Why had it happened? Were the seers of the sister-clan blind or deceived by the dark? How could the ancient prophecies be so wrong? What does it mean that there are two instead of one? Addie thought long and hard. Her mind traced the old texts of her clan. She tried to recall any passage or any word that would shine some light onto this condition. How could there be two when everything for eons had spoken of The One?

Addie's mind revisited the night of Simon's birth. She had sensed a seismic shift in the order of things, but she had attributed her feelings to the unnatural birth of the first male of the first male. Addie blamed herself for allowing this madness, for not finding Rebecca soon enough and eradicating the child—the children—that grew in her womb. The sins of the grandmother would now be visited upon the world. Nothing in their legends or in their stories or in their prophecies foretold this wicked turn of events.

"Eli, let me spend some time with Adelaide, alone. We have much to discuss, she and I, woman to woman," Rebecca said in a singsong voice.

"But, Mother—"

"Do as you're told," she snapped. This was the first time Addie heard Rebecca raise her voice in anger.

"My sweet son, you should take a walk outside—get some air." She walked over to Eli, linked arms with him and escorted him to the door. "You're such a wonderful son," she said as she kissed him on the lips. Begrudgingly, Eli smiled, glared at Addie one last time and exited the room, slamming the door behind him.

CHAPTER 9

Eli marched down the empty hallway furiously, his heels clunking loudly against the hard floor. The gait of his stride was long and sleek, fueled by his rising anger. His emotions were a violent whirlwind that caused trash cans and plants to topple over as he passed by; lights flickered and closed doors suddenly flung open. Each step he took sounded like the beating of a mighty war drum, alerting his enemies of his imminent approach. His scowled face showed the effort he exerted to keep the fire that was shut up in his bones from shooting forth like a bomb.

As he rounded the corridor toward the nurse's station, he increased his pace, blowing by the nurses in a quick flash; so fast that they didn't even see him, only felt his wind as papers blew off the counter at their station. He burst through the front doors and into the night, stopping in front of the building. The night felt good. He savored it. He wrapped himself in it, pulling its power into his body and enjoying the perfect fit. The sky rumbled loudly with thunder, signaling an arriving storm. The winds hissed through the trees, rustling the remaining leaves that clung to branches. He blinked and lightning bolts scattered across the dark clouds. He blinked again and several lightning bolts hit a large tree towering above everything else in the field across the two-lane road in front of the convalescent center. The tree instantly split with a loud crack and burst into flames.

Eli turned around and eyed the building. He tried hard to keep himself from making the entire building implode, collapse in on itself, killing every patient and employee on site. He wanted to do it so badly that his fingers trembled. He needed to calm himself. If he destroyed the building, his mother and Eetwidomayloh wouldn't be pleased.

In his heart, he had long since grown tired of following the dictates of his mother and Eetwidomayloh. He was the special one, the one they all should fear. He and Simon. They were kings. He couldn't wait until their birthday so that he and his brother could rule. Then, he wouldn't have to bend to their will. He could remake the world in his own image.

Eli was tired of waiting. Most of his life had been about waiting. He waited for his mother and Eetwidomayloh to show him his power. He waited for them to give him permission to torture Addie. He waited for them to find Simon. He waited for his birthday. Waiting, waiting and more waiting. He didn't want to wait anymore. He was a king and he was tired of playing this waiting game with Addie. He had always wanted to rip her to shreds, to lay her low and fill the mouth of her corpse with his feces, but he couldn't kill her. At least not now. His mother and Eetwidomayloh said wait and he choked back his disgust.

Now was his time to reign. With Simon. *With Simon*. All the years of his life, it had been so much about him, but now the time was near for it to be about him and Simon. He wasn't used to sharing attention, even though there had been much talk about Simon in the Shadowland since their birth. Eli already had an envious relationship with the brother he had never met. When they spoke of one, they spoke of the other, as if they were already joined at the hip. They were twins, but he was used to being alone; now, he had to learn to share the glory, even though he was sick and tired of hearing his dear brother's name. Simon. Simon this. Simon that. His name spilled so often from Rebecca's mouth that Eli could hardly stand it. He felt her intense longing to be reunited with her child, and it wasn't so he and Eli could rule as intended. She longed to be with him in the way she had been with Eli. He could feel her despicable desire in every syllable she uttered about Simon and jealousy cut at Eli deeply. He feared losing his mother and not being the man in her life.

He took a deep breath and refocused his thoughts on the task at hand. As much as it scratched at his soul, he wanted to be the one to find Simon, to claim the glory. He had to find a way to break Addie down. If his mother did it, she would look down on him, never letting him forget his failure. Eli could do it; he could find Simon. He knew he could. They were from the same womb and his connection to Simon should be greater than anyone's, but jealousy got in the way, blocking the connection. He angered himself sometimes for being so jealous of Simon, but he could not let it go. He didn't know how. Over the years, he labored hard to keep his jealousy hidden. No one could know.

Addie. I need to get into her head, he thought. *I need to find my brother*. Addie was strong indeed, but he believed he was stronger. Her powers were impressive, sometimes intimidating, but he'd never admit that to anyone. He had tortured her with almost the full brunt of his power, but still she resisted. He wondered how powerful she would be if she had all her strength. He needed his full power to deal with her. When the universe blessed him, he'd make sure he'd be the one to kill Addie. Slowly. Painfully.

"Eli, is that you?" He turned around and saw Andrea standing behind him, dressed in her white nurse's uniform. "What are you doing out here? It's about to storm," she said, looking at the night sky and the lightning that flashed across it. "I was on the road and saw lightning hit that tree across the street. I called 9-1-1. Is everything okay inside?" She touched his arm and smiled.

"Everything is good; better, now that you have arrived." He let go of all the anger he felt and let lust rule his body. He needed a distraction and she'd do as well as any other woman. She smiled and rubbed her hands over her hair in an attempt to straighten her tangled locks.

"I called you the other day," she said, smiling.

"Oh, really?"

"Yeah, and you didn't call me back." She playfully hit him in the chest, letting her hand linger longer than necessary.

"I must've missed your call. I haven't checked my messages in a while."

"Well, how are we supposed to talk, get to know each other, if you don't check messages?"

He smiled. "You're so very right. Can I make it up to you?" She shifted her weight coyly. "Do you have time to get a cup of coffee right now?" She looked at her watch and then back at the building. "It won't take long and my car is right over there."

"Well, I guess I could call and tell Sheila I'll be about fifteen minutes late."

"Great." He put his hand on the small of her back and led her to the parking lot. As they walked across the parking lot, a car door opened and another nurse stepped out.

"Hey, Andrea," the lady said with a puzzled look on her face. "Are you leaving? I thought we were on the night shift together?" She smiled oddly and eyed Eli. "Excuse me," she said to him, "have we met?"

"Hey, Courtney, this is Eli. He's Ms. Thibodeaux's grandson. You've probably seen him around, in her room. We were just gonna get some coffee." Courtney smiled faintly.

"Nice to meet you, Courtney," Eli said in a smooth baritone voice as he extended his hand. Cautiously, she met his grip with her hand and quickly took it back from him. Eli sensed that Courtney was nervous, her intuition probably warning her of danger. "We'll be right back. I won't keep her long."

"Are you sure, Andrea? I'm sure Sheila's waiting on you to relieve her. She's been here for twelve hours. I'm sure she's ready to go home."

"Another fifteen minutes won't hurt her. Can you tell her I'll be right back?"

"Sure, I guess."

"Thanks, Court. I'll see you in a few." They turned around and moved down the quiet parking lot as Eli put his hand around Andrea's shoulder. He could now smell her womanly scent tickling his nose and his genitals. Tonight would be one that she'd never forget, if she survived. Eli looked back at Courtney who was still watching them as they walked. He smiled at her and blinked his eyes. Suddenly, lightning flashed rapidly across the sky and thunder boomed so loudly that Courtney jumped, startled. She looked up into the sky as if she half-expected to see something falling from the heavens. By the time she looked back into the parking lot for Eli and Andrea, they were gone.

Ψ

Addie's conversation with Rebecca yielded no results for The Dark Mother. Even in her present state, Addie was strong enough to resist her efforts at trickery, deception, and force. Rebecca had grown frustrated, but tried hard to prevent the frown that made her thin lips quiver from overtaking her face.

For the last ten minutes, she and Addie sat in silence. Rebecca faced the window and stared into the night sky. Addie wasn't sure what she was doing or what they'd do to her body when Eli returned. As that thought flashed in her head, she felt a coolness seep into the room and watched Eli step into the room from the shadows of her bathroom.

"Mother," he said as he approached her. When he was near, she hugged him as if he had just returned from a long trip.

She sniffed him and then looked at his face. "You have been with a woman." Her eyes displayed her displeasure, but she didn't press the issue.

"Never mind that, Mother. Is everything okay?" He quickly shifted his eyes toward Addie. "Did this old bitch do something to you?"

"I am fine, darling. I have a headache."

"You sure?" His voice was full of doubt.

"Yes, I am sure."

"Were you able to get anything from her?" Rebecca's silence answered him. He then turned his attention to Addie.

"Let me handle this," he said as he moved around her and faced Addie. "Grandmother, I have some awful, awful news to share with you." The word *grandmother* sounded like a curse word in her ears, the ultimate disrespect. It was her own grandson who had inflicted the worst torment upon her for days and he did it without so much as blinking an eye. If he could do this to her, she imagined what he would do to the world, if he were allowed to reign.

"I didn't want to be the one who had to tell you this," he continued, "but your sister Bertice is dead." Eli spoke with feigned sympathy. A wry smiled formed in the corners of his mouth. "Now, there are only two sisters left, two of four. No doubt, we will find the other and when we do, she will burn. Your powers are fading. Your time is over."

His words felt like a punch to the face to Addie. Not her sister. Not Bertice. Next to her, Bertice was the strongest. The sister-clan had always been composed of four. Addie thought they had been protected, hidden from the evil. To ensure the propagation of the clan, Addie ordered her sisters to put aside their powers and erase their own memories of their heritage until such time that she came for them. She knew the dark would hunt them mercilessly and they would be vulnerable, especially without the protection of the High Priestess. Their powers would leave footprints in the spirit world that the dark would trace. Addie forced them to create new identities in other parts of the world, separated by vast distances. She told them she'd come for them when she broke free from her fleshly sarcophagus and when it was safe. At the time, she could not have imagined that she would be locked away for twenty years. She had underestimated the power of the dark.

Addie felt shame, along with tremendous grief. She had not even felt Bertice's death; she had been stretched too thin in trying to find Simon and hold her spells together. From each of her eyes, heavy tears fell. Rebecca moved over to the dresser, grabbed a tissue and wiped Addie's weeping eyes.

On the night of the birth of the twins, when Addie attempted to disappear after she cast Simon away, Eetwidomayloh angrily reached into the darkness and entombed her within her own body, but aged it considerably. She had been found days later, almost catatonic in a park downtown. Bertice found her days later, in a hospital, after she had been picked up by emergency personnel, unable to speak. She and the other sisters tried to free her, but they were not strong enough. That's when Addie issued her commands to them, to protect them.

"Awww, Addie. Do not cry. Your sisters are fine. They are with us, dear," Rebecca said. She tossed the tissue into the trash.

"Don't you want to know how she met her demise?" Eli asked. "Of course you do," he said, answering for her. "Well," he said, as he took a seat in the chair, "she was hiding in Bahrain, acting as a peasant woman. When I found her, she pretended to not understand, but I didn't care. I shackled her and burned her alive in the desert." He spoke easily, heartlessly. "You should have heard her skin sizzle. It was a marvelous sound, but that wasn't the end of it. I revived her and did it again. And again. And again. I lost count of how many times I roasted her. It really was…divine. You should have seen it, quite a spectacle. And you should have heard her dying words, so very unladylike."

"Let us not be boastful, Eli," Rebecca said. "Pride is one of the seven deadly sins." Addie wanted to believe that his words were hyperbole, but she knew of his boundless cruelty.

"I almost forgot, Grandmother. I brought you a gift." He extended his right hand, palm side up and then opened his mouth, expelling a black mist that swirled in the center of his hand. It morphed into a beautiful, shimmering red bottle that he placed on top of the dresser. He looked at her and smiled wickedly. "Do you want to know what it is? I think you'll love this. It's from Bertice—her screams. I captured them as a memento for you." He uncorked the bottle and a fiery red mist escaped. Suddenly, the room was filled with the tortured screams of Addie's sister. Her voice was pained and drenched in horror, unspeakable misery. Addie was bulldozed by grief. Bertice's ghastly voice tore Addie apart and contained despair so profound that the walls in Addie's room bled, leaving red streaks down the pastel-colored walls.

"All of this could have been avoided had you simply helped us. Your sister could have enjoyed immunity and a life so rich and full of luxury that kings would have been envious. Instead, you have condemned her to a life of burned flesh in the Shadowland. How does that make you feel?" he asked.

"Adelaide, we extend the offer of immunity to you and your other sister. What say you?" Rebecca tried to peer inside Addie, but met a solid, impenetrable wall. She had her answer.

In the dark corner of the room, a black mist was taking shape and a low hissing could be heard.

Addie. Addie.

"Aww, we have company," Rebecca said gleefully, clapping wildly. The mist took the shape of a huge black serpent with yellow eyes. "Say hello to your old friend, Eetwidomayloh." The serpent hissed violently at Addie, but did not approach her. "Eli, show Adelaide your new trick."

Eli smiled. "With pleasure, Mother."

He stood up and quickly disrobed until he stood in the room completely naked.

"Do it, darling. Let us teach dear old Adelaide a lesson in manners."

He smiled, stretched out his arms and suddenly exploded into hundreds of hissing serpents. They were angry and aggressive and focused their attention on Addie, who sat helplessly in her chair. Eetwidomayloh hissed something foul, the odor of his breath filling the room, and all of the snakes quickly slithered over to Addie. They crawled all over her body and underneath her robe. They nested in her hair, giving her the appearance of modern-day Medusa.

Then, he hissed something again and all of the snakes—all of them—dug their fangs into her flesh and injected her with venom. Rebecca clapped delightfully.

They bit her repeatedly until she could no longer endure the pain; she blacked out.

CHAPTER 10

When Simon walked into his apartment, the rich smell of Crawfish Etouffee, simmering on the stove, greeted him at the door. The scent swirled around the room and landed flatly against his nose. He closed the door and inhaled deeply, hoping to get a taste of his favorite dish from the air itself. His stomach, reacting to the enticing smell, rumbled. The sounds of Esmeralda, a local New Orleans blues singer, played softly in the background. Her sultry voice never failed to put Simon in a good mood.

He walked deeper into the apartment, dropping his keys and jacket on the couch. Brooke was standing over the stove, stirring the pot, wearing nothing but a short pink and white apron that stopped midway at her thighs. Her breasts spilled out from the sides of the apron, showing just enough skin to entice and titillate. It was a delectable sight and Simon fought the urge to rush over to her and gobble her up completely without saying a word; instead, he chose to play it cool.

He smiled, watching her watch him. She moved seductively and smiled coyly, leaning over deeply as she stirred the pot so that he'd get a better view of her lovely breasts. His love for her had become thick and solid during these troubling times, but still, it would remain silent. Instead of saying the word, he'd show her instead. He was good at that, good at expressing his love physically;

good at being tender and holding her in his arms. After all, what's in a word? It is actions that matter. He read somewhere that *love* is a verb; love is what it does, and he held onto that definition tightly. So the word itself couldn't possibly matter that much, could it?

This was Brooke at her best, anticipating his needs and desires. She looked genuinely pleased in making him happy, and he was thrilled to get back into their usual routine and not worry about the fantastical events that plagued him of late. He missed a sense of normalcy and routine in his life. He wanted things to go back to the way they were, before he dreamed of snakes and feared his dark side. It had been two full days since his last *episode*, and he was starting to think that the worst was behind him.

He let the music churn in his ears for a few more moments and then he bopped over to her, with a dip in his hip, and grabbed her by the waist. He pulled her into him and kissed her passionately, tasting the rich flavor of the dish on her lips and tongue.

"What's all this for?" he asked.

"For you, of course. Let's say it's the beginning of a two-week celebration of your birthday." Her smile was electric.

"Ahhh," he said, "my birthday *is* coming up. I had forgotten with all the shit that's been happening."

"We're gonna put all that behind us and get back to living and enjoying each other. This is a happy season. It's your birthday and then Christmas four days after that. So, let's enjoy it and each other."

"I don't want you making a big deal about my birthday, and you know how I feel about Christmas." She simply smiled and offered him a taste of etouffee on a spoon to pacify him.

Simon wasn't big on Christmas. Growing up in foster care, he received presents so rarely that he learned to not expect them.

His little heart couldn't stand the disappointment. He remembered feeling jealous when he looked out of the window and saw all the neighborhood kids riding their new bikes and playing with their toy guns and race cars.

"You still gonna go on the cruise with your parents?"

"Yes, and I wish you would reconsider. They really want you to come with us."

He raised one eyebrow at her. "Me and your father on a two-week Mediterranean cruise doesn't sound like a good idea. Besides, I have to work."

"I wish I could spend Christmas with you."

"You can. Tell your parents you can't go on the cruise. Tell 'em you'll be with me instead." Simon was only half-kidding. Just once he'd like to not spend Christmas alone, but he wouldn't dare impose on her.

"You know I would if I could. My mother would go through the roof if I didn't make it. She's been planning this cruise for three years and she finally got Daddy to agree. If I didn't go she'd disown me."

"I'm kidding, baby. I want you to go and have a good time with your family."

The word *family* rang in Simon's ears. It was during the holidays that his lack of familial ties hurt the most. Even now. "Are we still going to Franklin's show tonight?"

"If you're up to it after I finish with you," she said with a hint of things to come.

"I like the way that sounds." Simon moved over to the sink and grabbed a glass from the cabinet. He moved over to the refrigerator and poured a glass of wine.

"Simon, you shouldn't be drinking."

"It's cool. I looked up the medication online and it said wine, in moderation, was okay while I was on it." She looked at him incredulously.

"Are you lying to me?"

"Of course not. Here, see for yourself." He reached into his pocket and was about to pull up the popular website WebMD on his cell phone for confirmation.

"Never mind," she said, "I trust you."

When he moved near her he noticed a bright yellow piece of paper in the trash can. He immediately recognized it as a "Late Rent Notice" that Ms. Sanchez loved to tactlessly attach to tenants' doors.

"Ms. Sanchez was here?"

"Oh, yeah. She caught me when I came in, but don't worry about it. I took care of it."

"Took care of what?"

"The rent. I gave her a check."

Simon rolled his eyes hard. "Why the fuck would you do that? Brooke, I don't need you paying my rent. I have the money order in my wallet."

"She said you were late, but it's no biggie. I'll get the check from her and you can give her the money order."

"That's not the point. The point is, I'm a man and I can take care of my own bills. I don't need you taking care of me, not like that. I'm going to have to have a conversation with her about discussing my business with people."

"I'm not *people*. I'm your girlfriend. Please don't be mad. I was trying to help and we're having a good evening. Let's not argue."

"Brooke, you have to understand—" She stepped back and untied the apron, letting it fall to the floor. Her nakedness filled the room.

"I have to understand what?" Simon's unfinished criticism of her was overwhelmed by his rising desire. "Why don't you come over here and show me how much of a man you really are?"

☥

Halfway into the evening, Simon felt his two glasses of wine starting to work on his system. Franklin was on stage with a full band behind him while he sang with more heart and soul than a man three times his size. He voice was deep and rich with passion and power, and he hit every note precisely. His range and vocal affectations were remarkable and he held the entire room spellbound as he worked every inch of the stage thoroughly. Women swooned when they heard the fullness of his soulful voice and his intense and highly sexual lyrics; there would certainly be some panty-dropping tonight.

The darkened lounge was packed to the nines with people of varying shades and backgrounds. The Black Cat always attracted a diverse crop of people who came out to hear good music and to enjoy cocktails so strong that two of them were almost certain to knock you on your back. Their signature drink, Voodoo, had gained infamy in the city and had sent many folks to the drunk tank at the police station for an unexpected overnight stay.

The crowd that night was enthusiastic and lively, gyrating and grinding uninhibitedly against Franklin's charged lyrics and the hypnotic beats of the drummer. The vixen of a saxophonist, who was all lines and sensual curves, sent the crowd into a frenzy when she blew on her horn and sent notes so carnal into the air that legs immediately spread and backs arched instinctively.

Almost three-hundred throbbing people were squeezed into a place meant for no more than two hundred. Sweaty flesh pressed against equally sweaty and unfamiliar flesh, but no one seemed to mind. There was a spell in the air, some of that old magic only New Orleans could produce. The heat generated by the crowd caused the concrete walls to perspire. The crowd was on its feet and Simon felt the old floor shift underneath him. He was pressed hard against Brooke from behind, acting as part protector and part lover. Their bodies swayed naturally and easily together.

The end of Franklin's mesmerizing first set was met with thunderous applause from the audience and his cool, laconic reply when he leaned into the microphone and simply said, "See y'all in half an hour." His voice was confident and smooth; he was the reigning king of the room and the audience, his eager subjects. He dipped off the side of the stage with a proud smile on his face and disappeared.

"Wow," Simon said. The music of the club blared through the speakers. The crowd didn't stop their dancing; they simply changed their rhythm. Simon grabbed Brooke's hand and led her through the crowd toward the back bar. He wanted to use the restroom and to get a bottle of water

"Can you get me some water?" he asked Brooke, making sure that he handed her money to pay for it. "I'll be right back." Simon walked down the dimly lit hallway toward the bathroom. He had walked this walk many times in the past, during Franklin's many shows, but the distance to the restroom seemed much longer this time. Maybe he was in a hurry to pee. He moved around a couple that was grinding against the wall. Usually, he'd watch for a few minutes, but he feared any delay now would cause him to urinate on himself.

As he continued the long march, the overhead lights flickered and the hallway itself seemed to shift out of focus. Simon rubbed his eyes with his hands and pushed opened the door to the john. Surprisingly, it was empty. Immediately, he rushed over to the urinal, ignoring that sour smell of urine and alcohol that permeated the thick air in the tiny room. He unzipped his jeans and exhaled with relief as he released the liquid that had built up in his bladder.

The lights flickered again.

"*Sssss-Simon.*"

Simon spun around in a panic, spraying the wall with urine. The lights flickered rapidly and the room itself seemed to be changing shape, as if the walls were malleable. Quickly, Simon finished, buttoned his pants and turned around. The lights went out completely, covering the room in a dense black. He couldn't see anything, not even light seeping under the door from the other room.

"*Sssss-Simon.*"

"Leave me the fuck alone!"

Don't be afraid. Don't be afraid. The familiar command came in a voice that contradicted the one hissing his name. This hissing voice harshly grated on his ears while this one offered—or at least attempted to—a peculiar kind of peace; a dichotomy that his present fear couldn't reconcile.

Suddenly, a white light flickered like a strobe light in the corner. A shape of a man was being carved out from the shadows in the room. Simon held his breath and watched. He was too terrified to even move. The shadows gathered and created a hooded man that must have been eight feet tall. The man had no face; only yellow eyes inside of a dark hood. The shadows that made up the man moved like flames in a strong wind, giving the giant Shadowman the macabre appearance of black fire.

"*Come to me.*"

The room shifted in and out of focus, as if Simon was looking at an image through the broken lens of a camera. Then, the smell of rotting meat overtook the scent of hot piss and beer. The smell held a tight grip around his neck, choking the breath out of his body.

He felt unsteady, wobbly. He pushed his body against the sink for leverage just as the Shadowman raised his arm. His long, bony finger reached out across the flashing light toward Simon, who watched helplessly as the finger curved close to his face. Simon's eyes bulged and the stench of decay lodged in his throat.

"Go away!" Simon screamed. He gripped the sink tightly and closed his eyes.

"Fuck you, man. I gotta piss." Simon opened his eyes in time to see a wiry black-haired man stumble to the urinal. Simon watched him, almost expecting him to morph into a ball of shadows. He looked around the room and there was no sign or trace of the Shadowman. Gone were the shadows and the flickering lights and the bitter smell of decomposing flesh. Simon remained at the sink, looking around the room.

"Get the fuck outta here. This ain't no peepshow!" Simon didn't have to be told twice to leave that room. Hurriedly, he moved toward the door. He couldn't have gotten out of that room faster if he had been an Olympic sprinter. In that room, he had felt unfettered evil.

As he burst through the door and wobbled into the dark hallway, he clutched the black wall for support, pressing his back firmly against it as his chest heaved. His heartbeat pumped furiously against his ribcage. With his head held low, he took a few jagged steps down the long hallway, barely avoiding collisions with a few people scattered about the space. His balance was off kilter, thrown by something so wretched that he'd have difficulty articulating it.

When he entered the main area, he saw Brooke at the end of

the bar with her fingers wrapped around a bottle of water. He bulldozed his way through the crowd and made his way over to her and practically snatched the bottle from her grip. Eagerly, he poured the liquid down his bone-dry throat, hoping that the water would drown out a thought even more disturbing than the image of the Shadowman and the smell of dead flesh.

Undoubtedly, he knew that he had been in the presence of wickedness, of death. Even more troubling, there was a part of him that liked it.

CHAPTER 11

S imon stood at the water's edge absentmindedly tossing pebbles into the Mississippi River. When it was warm, families came out in full force to enjoy the water, but not today. There were people around, but fewer than he had expected. Simon tossed another pebble. He watched the waves ripple throughout the murky water, and every few seconds or so, he'd look up and gaze into the horizon, hoping divine intervention would show him the way, or, at least, provide him some answers to the questions that he could not shake.

It was an unseasonably cool day in December and the wind skimming across the water cut through his light jacket. The squawking sound from a group of birds that flew overhead temporarily stole his attention. A wounded bird, no doubt a part of their flock, struggled on the ground to take flight. Simon watched the tremendous effort of the bird, which took a few ragged steps and flapped its wings forcefully, only to fall flat. The bird meandered near Simon, who noticed a tear in its left wing. The bird struggled and struggled to take flight, but its efforts were pointless. Simon, watching the other birds soaring above, felt sorry for the damaged one. The bird reminded him so much of himself; they were kindred spirits.

Lonely.

Damaged.

Struggling.

Unsure.

As he desired for himself, he wished the bird nothing but peace.

Fly away, little birdie.

He noticed a tingling in his fingers and as the thought left his head, Simon watched the bird take a few confident steps and take flight. It soared!

Simon stared, completely mesmerized by the effortless flight of the bird. It flew proudly and Simon watched it join its group that had gathered atop a naked tree in the distance.

Did I do that?

With all that had happened, Simon wasn't surprised. He didn't take responsibility for the bird's recovery, nor did he discount his intervention, either. At this point, he thought anything was possible. He simply exhaled and moved away from the water and took a seat on the wooden stump a short distance away. He had more pressing issues than wounded birds.

He loved this spot. He had spent many days here staring at the water, people-watching and finding his inner peace. Something about the lapping sounds of the water and tranquility of the scene never failed to ease his mind, regardless of what was going on in his life at the time. It was here that he found his center. Whenever Brooke stressed him out, or when school became too burdensome, or when he didn't know where his next meal would come from, he'd come here and leave his troubles down by the riverside.

Simon tossed his last stone into the water and rubbed his face with his hands. For the first time in a long time, he truly felt afraid. He wasn't so much afraid of what was happening as he was of what he was becoming. He could feel a change coming. He thought back to the night he had the fight with Bryon at Starry Nights. He felt power surge through his veins in a way that simple adrenaline could not explain. He felt as if he had the strength of ten men. He could have easily ripped Byron apart, limb by limb. He remembered the tingling in his fingers and the fire he felt in his fists when he balled them for combat. They felt heavy, like thick stone, but he wielded them easily and crushed his adversary. He knew Byron never stood a chance. Simon was grateful that he hadn't knocked his head off his shoulders. As odd as that thought sounded to him, he knew that on that night it was well within the realm of possibility.

What disturbed him more than the brutal beating he handed out was what he felt after it was done. After Bryon lay unconscious and Debbie pressed him to leave, it took all the strength Simon had left to contain his joy.

Joy. An unusual emotion to feel when someone was near death, he thought.

How could I find pleasure in nearly beating a man to death? That was the question that Simon had asked himself over and over and over again. The question stayed with him and drove him to distraction. It was like he was becoming someone else.

Then, there were the thugs. They're lucky they escaped with their lives.

And then the tasting of blood.

Simon huffed wearily and watched a few people move rapidly down the jogging trail. Some jogged; some ran, while others simply walked. In spite of the cooler than usual breeze coming from the river, it was a lovely Sunday afternoon to be outside near the water.

Simon tried to find peace. He hadn't told Brooke about Byron actually being in the hospital lying unconscious, at this very moment, because of his temper. Since that night they talked about it, he hadn't said anything more to her about Bryon, even after he received Debbie's text message, which proved the veracity of the events of that night. He chose instead to let her dwell in the explanation that made sense to her. There was a part of him that was itching to tell her, to call the hospital and check on Byron, if for no other reason than to prove his sanity to her; but the words he needed simply would not form in his mouth.

He didn't tell her about the thugs outside of Starry Nights, either; nor did he mention the devil in the bathroom at The Black Cat. It was all too much to comprehend.

Simon stood up and moved back to the edge of the water. The breeze created a calm ripple effect that usually proved soothing. He looked down and was drawn to something shimmering in the shallow water. At first he thought it might have been a colorful fish whose scales simply reflected the sun's rays, but as he examined it closer, the golden light began to morph into something else. He looked closer and the light took shape and form. It was a face! The face of the woman who had been haunting him.

Simon was shocked and wanted to back away, but this time he didn't flee and neither was his heart flooded with dread. He was simply tired of being afraid. Instead, he felt a sense of wonderment. In order to figure out what was going on with him, he knew he'd have to confront everything that he saw, including this old woman and the yellow-eyed snake. Something deep inside him told him that she had the answers to his many questions.

He dropped to his knees and brought his face close to the water, close enough to stick his tongue out and taste it if he wanted. He watched her mouth move. She was trying to tell him something, but he wasn't able to discern her message. He concentrated on the movement of her lips, but, still, her words were lost to him.

Behind him he heard laughter. He looked up and saw a young woman and a small girl riding their bicycles on the sidewalk behind him.

When he looked back into the water, the face was gone.

"No, come back!" Simon shouted out loud, getting the attention of the woman and the small girl. They looked at him oddly and peddled faster to escape his madness.

"Who are you? What do you want from me?" Simon slapped the water with his hand out of frustration. He suddenly felt despondent. He needed answers and he knew this woman, this apparition—whoever she was—could provide them to him. He knew what he had to do: he had to find her, find out who she was and what she wanted to tell him.

"Simon, what are you doing?"

Simon looked up and standing behind him was Brooke, her facial expression peppered with worry.

Simon ignored her and refocused his attention on the ghost in the water, slapping it with his hands, hoping that his touch would bring her back.

"Simon. Simon! Do you hear me?"

"Brooke, what are you doing here? How did you find me?" he finally said, realizing the woman was lost to him.

"Baby, what are you doing down in the mud? Come on. Let me help you up." She bent down and grabbed his arm, helping him to his feet.

Simon snatched away, visibly upset. "Brooke, I'm fine. I don't need help."

She took a step back, folded her arm and looked at him. "Who were you talking to?"

"What?"

"Just then. You were talking to someone and then you splashed the water."

"I wasn't talking to anyone. I was…thinking out loud."

"Baby, come over here and sit down with me." She took his hand and led him to the wooden bench. When they sat, she placed her

hand on his thigh and rubbed gently, the way you'd comfort someone who had just been given terrible news by a doctor.

"How did you know where I was?"

"It wasn't that hard. This is one of your favorite spots. It didn't
take me long to figure out you were here, after I went to your
apartment and you weren't there." He leaned over and kissed her
on the cheek. It was his apology for being so abrupt moments ago.

She reached into her small purse and pulled out a note. "I have
something for you."

"What is it?" he asked. He wanted her to give him whatever it
was so that she could leave. He was anxious to get back to the
water. Brooke was the love of his life, but there was no way she'd
understand what was going on with him.

She angled her body in his direction and forced a smile. "It's
the name of another doctor—a psychiatrist."

He rolled his eyes. "I don't need a shrink, Brooke."

"Something is going on with you and it's scaring me. We need
to figure out what it is." She moved the hair out of her face. "Last
night, you kept mumbling something about the devil and a shadow
in your sleep. I couldn't wake you up. Baby, I'm really scared.
We need to know what's going on."

They sat in silence for some time. Simon remembered having
a restless night, tossing and turning after his unnerving experience
at The Black Cat, but he didn't know he'd been talking in his
sleep. No wonder Brooke thought he was insane. There was no
telling what he had said in the midnight hour.

He continued tossing pebbles into the river that skidded off the
water. He didn't want to look at her for fear of breaking down.
His emotions suddenly threatened to overwhelm him; he felt a
great sadness inside. He wanted so much to confide in her but he
knew she wouldn't believe him.

"Will you not even consider it?" she finally said, cutting through the silence that separated them.

"I am not crazy!" he yelled with more force than he realized. Brooke recoiled at the fury in his voice.

"Brooke, baby, I'm sorry," Simon pleaded, as he laid his now-tingling hand on her thigh. "Will you answer your phone?"

She looked at him as if he had lost his mind. "What?"

"Your phone. Please answer it." Just as Simon finished speaking, Brooke's cell phone exploded to life. She jumped back, startled.

"How...how did you do that?"

"Will you tell Jordan that you'll see her at the study group?" Brooke reached into her purse and pulled out her cell phone. She looked at the name on the caller ID. She silenced the phone, but did not answer it. "Simon, you're freakin' me out. What the fuck is going on?" she asked as she stood up and backed away from him as if she felt threatened.

"Brooke—"

"How did you do that? How did you know who was on the phone?"

Simon stood and tried to approach her, but she backed away. Simon could no longer control his emotions. Tears formed in his eyes.

"That's what I've been trying to tell you. Something is wrong with me. I'm a freak! I don't know how I knew who was on the phone. I just did. Crazy shit like that has been happening to me for days now. I don't know why."

Brooke stumbled back a few more steps.

"Don't be afraid. I would never hurt you. You know that, right?"

Brooke took a few seconds to compose herself and looked at the sincerity reflected in his eyes. "Of course, I do. I don't understand."

"I don't know what's going on with me, either." She moved over to him and hugged him tightly. He felt so safe in her arms that the tears began to flow. For the first time since he was an abandoned little boy, he allowed himself to really cry. Tears stung his eyes and he sobbed quietly with his face buried into her shoulder.

As he cried, the sky suddenly darkened and a bitter wind blew, sending brown leaves scattering. A menacing storm cloud hovered above the river and blocked out the sun; a low rumble of thunder announced the coming storm.

"We better get out of here before we get soaked," she said. Simon pulled away from her and when she looked at him she screamed. He saw blood on her jacket.

"Oh my God!"

"What's wrong?" Simon said, alarmed by her exclaim. He *felt* her fear; it was so strong it almost knocked him to the ground.

She pointed her finger at his face. "Your...your eyes."

"What's wrong with my eyes?" he asked with panic coloring the texture of his voice.

"Your eyes are...bleeding. You're crying tears of blood." Quickly, she opened her purse and pulled out a small makeup compact. Simon snatched it out of her hand and popped it open. When he saw his face, a chill raced up his spine. From both his eyes, a bloody trail ran the length of his face.

"Oh, my God!" Simon exclaimed, not knowing what else to say. He was very afraid and his emotions almost leveled him.

"Here," she said, as she took a tissue out of her purse and handed it to him. When he reached over to grab it, they both heard a thud behind her—a bird fell out of the sky.

They both looked at the dead bird and then at each other. "What the hell is going on?" she asked.

Then, they heard another thud.

And another one.

And another one.

And another one.

Dead birds were falling from the sky all around them. They were caught in a thunderstorm of dead birds.

⊰ CHAPTER 12

"I don't…understand. What's going on?" Brooke's words were broken and listless. They walked into Simon's apartment and she removed her jacket, tossing it on the couch. Simon walked past her and plopped down in the brown leather recliner, tossing the bloody tissue he had used to clean his eyes in the car into the trash can. His eyes were now clear, but not his mind. He buried his face in his hands and sighed audibly, painfully. "None of this makes any sense," she finished.

"I know it sounds crazy, but you saw what happened." He looked into her face.

"Everything I saw can be explained, I'm sure. I don't know how. Birds die all the time, and maybe you need to see an optometrist."

"I was crying—blood." His words were resolute, leaving no wiggle room for logic. "A doctor can't explain that, and even if he could, he couldn't explain me knowing that your cell phone would ring and who was on the line. How did I know that, Brooke? Can you explain that?" He pressed her with his voice, putting the burden of proof in her hands, and he waited for an answer. He needed something to make sense, for her to say something insightful, although he had no real expectation that her logic would offer him any peace.

She took a deep, calming breath. "I admit that one is a little weirder, but it's probably no different than talking about someone you haven't seen in years and then you suddenly see them at the mall or they call you or something. We've all experienced that; it doesn't make us psychic."

"I didn't say I was psychic." He got up and moved over to the mirror on the wall, finally checking his face for any residual blood. He turned and faced her. "Brooke, you've got to listen to me," he said, hitting each syllable in each word. "Something strange is going on with me and it's scaring the hell out of me. It ain't natural."

"Baby, you're sick and you're sleep deprived, plus, you're on medication and you've been drinking. I'm sure that all has something to do with what you're feeling. I don't think anything supernatural is going on."

"Brooke," he said with frustration, "I need you to suspend your disbelief for a second and listen to me. I need you to consider the possibility that what I'm saying is real. There isn't a scientific explanation for everything and this is one of those times. What I'm feeling, what I'm going through, is real. Here, look at this." He pulled out his cell phone and scrolled until he found the text from Debbie about Byron being in the hospital. "Read this." Brooke took the phone from his hand and looked down at the message and then looked back at him.

"Byron is in the hospital. I put him there."

A firm scowl carved its way into her brow. "This message is from Debbie. You told me you weren't in contact with her anymore."

"Goddamn it, Brooke. Will you focus? This isn't about Debbie. Did you read the message? Byron is in the hospital."

"Her message didn't say you had anything to do with that."

"She said I'd better lay low for awhile. Why do you think she'd send me that message if I didn't have anything to do with him being in the hospital?"

"I don't know, Simon. I have no idea why you and Debbie are

exchanging text messages behind my back," she said, with a hint of jealousy. Simon rolled his eyes.

"Baby—"

"I know, Simon. I'm sorry. Don't say it," she interrupted. "So, let's say for the sake of argument that I believe everything you told me," she said, changing the subject, "I believe you were at Starry Nights; I believe what you told me in the car about the boy at the doctor's office, and your dreams."

"I don't think they're dreams. I think they're trying to reach me, to communicate."

"Who? The old woman?"

"Definitely her, but also the black snake." Simon paused when he heard his words echo in the room. His words sounded ridiculous to his own ears.

"Okay, but what do you think they are trying to tell you?"

"I have no idea." Simon started pacing the room. "I have to figure it out, though. I know they won't leave me alone until I know."

Brooke moved over to him and wrapped her arms around his waist. She squeezed him tightly and tried to comfort him. Simon's voice was thick with worry.

"So all of this just started happening recently?"

"Yeah, a few days ago," he said in almost a whisper, "but crazy shit has always happened to me, even when I was a child."

"Things like what?" She released her embrace and Simon moved over to the couch and took a seat.

"I don't know. I mean, stuff."

"It's okay, baby. You can tell me. I'm listening. Things like what?"

He might be schizophrenic.

Simon heard her thought, but didn't respond or react to it. Instead, he shook his head from side to side, trying to decide what to share next. The burden of his secrets had weighed heavily on him for far too long. If he didn't take this time now to release his fears, he knew he'd be crushed under their weight. At this point, he had nothing to lose with his confession. He was certain she was going to leave him anyway; he suspected his issues would be too great a load for her to bear. She came from a wealthy background, and the most trouble she had ever had was deciding which expensive dress to wear to the prom.

"Are you sure you want to hear this?"

"The only way we can figure out what's going on is to deal with this head on. So, tell me. What kind of stuff?"

"Like fluently speaking languages I couldn't know as a child, or predicting things that were about to happen, kind of like I did today. Not to mention the whole never being sick thing; that is, until now. There was this one time—I think I was about eleven—when I thought I was going to die." Simon leaned back and recalled the story.

Ψ

It was a hot and sticky summer day, even for the bayous. The unfiltered sunlight beat down on the landscape with a fierceness only Louisiana knew. Simon rode with his foster family to a family reunion in Houma. The car trip excited Simon; it gave him an opportunity to see much more of the world. As a child who was bounced from one foster home to another, his travels had been severely limited; so he fell in love with the idea of traveling and meeting new people. In his head, he always fantasized that the people he met would know his real family, and, through some twist of fate, he'd be reunited with the woman who never meant to give him up.

When they arrived in the small city, Simon felt a jolt, as if he had been suddenly energized by some unknown force. As they drove through downtown, Simon soaked up every sight and sound. Something about this place felt familiar, like he had been there before. When he saw Houma's lovely Court Square, he had a startling sense of déjà vu.

The Clintons, his foster family, drove another half-hour outside of town to reach the farmhouse of Mr. Clinton's brother, Herbert. As they arrived, Simon's stomach growled when he smelled the down-home cooking and barbeque. He had never been to a barbeque before, but his foster brother, Corey, had told him all about it, and Simon had high expectations of the event.

As soon as the car stopped, Corey raced out of the vehicle and toward his cousins who he saw on the side of the house, tossing a football back and forth. Simon looked at Mr. and Mrs. Clinton and they nodded, giving him permission to join Corey. For the first time in a long time, he felt as if he belonged, even if this wasn't his real family.

When he joined the boys playing football, he quickly mesmerized and annoyed them with his amazing athletic ability. He outran, outjumped and out-touchdowned all of them. He blazed by them with such speed, one cousin starting calling him "the blur." They looked at him with admiration, awe, and envy.

Edwin, who was the oldest at thirteen, was built like a seventeen-year-old and he looked at Simon with resentful eyes; he was used to getting the praise for his athletic prowess. Edwin, serving as quarterback, purposely threw a ball so hard that it flew over the fence, well into the yard of Mr. Grimes, their cantankerous old neighbor who despised kids, laughter, and anything that resembled happiness. The ball flew to the other side of the rusted truck that sat in the middle of his yard.

"Dang, how we gon' get the ball?" Simon asked.

"Yeah, Edwin. Why'd you do that?" Corey added.

"It was an accident," Edwin said.

"Well, I ain't gonna get it. You know Mr. Grimes got them dogs."

"Dogs?" Simon asked.

"Yeah, he got three mean-ass pit bulls. Them thangs will chase ya and kill ya if you look at them," another cousin said. "Look at my leg." He pointed to a long scar on his shin. "The white one bit me two years ago—almost killed me. Luckily, Mr. Grimes was there to get the dog off me."

Edwin smiled wickedly. "Why don't you get it, *Blur*? You faster than them old junkyard dogs, ain't ya?"

"He can't outrun no pit bull."

"I bet you ten dollars that you can't climb this fence and get that ball before the dogs get you."

"Don't do it, Simon. Those dogs will kill you," Corey said.

"I knew he wouldn't do it. I knew you wasn't nothing but a scared little sissy."

"I ain't scared," Simon said, even though his heart was pounding. "Let me see the ten dollars." Edwin reached into his pocket and pulled out the money. Simon reached for it, but Edwin snatched it back quickly.

"Uh-uh. You get it when you make it back—if you make it back." The group of kids, with the exception of Corey, all laughed. Simon hated to be made to feel small, so he took the challenge. He walked up to the high metal fence and looked for the dogs.

"Where they at?"

"Don't do it, Simon. Don't," Corey pleaded.

"The dogs are usually under the shed over there," Edwin said as he pointed to a structure at least a hundred yards away. Simon looked at the shed and then at the distance to the truck. The truck seemed so much closer. All he had to do was climb the fence, run over to the truck, grab the ball and run back. He could do it. He knew he could.

He swallowed hard and set about scaling the fence.

As soon as his feet hit the ground on the other side of the fence, he took off running toward the truck. Almost instantly, he heard the terrifying barking of dogs. The barking was so loud that it sounded like there were twenty dogs instead of only three.

He put all the energy he had into running. At some point, he couldn't even hear the sound of the boys or of the barking dogs over the sound of his beating heart. He wasn't even sure if his eyes were open, but he ran like he was guided by a force unknown to him. As he ran, he realized he had made a dreadful mistake. He thought about what it would feel like to be torn apart by those rabid dogs. Fear fueled his legs and as soon as he reached the other side of the truck, he looked for the ball with his wide eyes. He didn't see it. He looked ten feet in front of him and saw it partially hidden by tall, uncut grass that was swaying non-chalantly in the sweltering summer breeze. Swiftly, he raced over to the ball and grabbed it. The barking was so much closer now; so close that Simon knew that he would not be able to make it to the fence. His chest tightened and he struggled to breathe.

Quickly, he thought about options. He tried to open the door of the truck, but it wouldn't budge. He thought about jumping into the bed of the truck, but it was so low that the dogs could easily jump in. Any second now, the dogs would round the corner and be upon him in a flash. He saw the end of his young life.

"Run, Simon, run!" he heard voices call out, even though the truck blocked his view of the boys.

But Simon didn't run. He couldn't. His legs were frozen stiff.

Then, he saw the first dog on the side of the building racing toward him with fury and hate in his eyes. Then, he saw the other two. The pack reunited and was out for blood. Simon's blood. Instinctively, Simon stumbled back a few steps. He tripped over a piece of wood and hit the ground. His arm was cut by a piece of glass from a beer bottle, but that was the least of his concerns.

Don't be afraid. Don't be afraid, a voice in his head said.

Lying on his back on the ground, he saw the dogs not more than ten feet from him. He felt a jolt in his body again; the same kind of jolt he had felt when he was in the car with the Clintons. In that instant, he thought the word *no* in his head and closed his eyes, fully preparing to be mauled to death. He imagined the first set of teeth locking on to one of his limbs while the other attacked his face or neck. He knew his death would far exceed painful. He heard their heavy and rapid steps pounding the dusty ground.

"Simon!" Corey's voice rang hollow in his ears. Corey would not be able to help him. No one could.

Then, Simon felt a tongue licking his wound. And one licking his face. And one licking the hand on his other arm. He opened his eyes.

The vicious animals, who only seconds ago, were about to tear him apart, now licked him playfully. Simon sat up, unsure of what was going on. He could hear the boys yelling frantically, but he knew they couldn't see him.

Sit.

All three dogs sat without hesitation.

Simon stood up and patted them as if he was their owner. They loved his playful touch.

"Are you okay, Simon?" Corey shouted.

Simon stepped from beyond the truck with the three dogs in tow. They playfully ran around him and around each other. When Simon stepped out from the truck, he saw the look of shock on the faces of the boys. They were utterly astounded to see the dogs playing with Simon.

Don't bark at or hurt my friends anymore. Except for Edwin. You can bark at him; don't hurt him.

Simon threw the ball to Corey casually and climbed the fence.

"Where's my ten dollars?" he said, when he was safely on the other side.

Ψ

Brooke stared at him like he was spinning a tall tale. "Are you trying to tell me that you controlled the dogs with your mind?" Simon didn't want to answer. When he recalled the story, his voice never wavered. Not once. She knew exactly what he was saying. "This is freakin' me out." She walked over to the television, reached behind it and pulled out the bottle of vodka she had hidden from Simon a few nights ago. "I think we both need a drink right about now."

After she poured two shots, which they quickly drank, Simon went into his bedroom and dumped the contents of the trash can onto the floor. He sifted through all kind of trash until he found the small note that he had balled up and discarded.

"Here, look at this," he said to Brooke as he unwrinkled the note.

She looked at the note. "What is this?"

"I don't know. It's something I must've written when I was asleep."

"What is A. Thibodeaux? Is that a person, a name?"

"At first I didn't know what it was, but now I think it's the name of the old woman I've been seeing."

"What does the 'A' stand for?"

"It could be anything. Alice? Agnes? Angela? I don't know, but I know I need to find her."

"If she is a ghost, how on earth are you going to find her?"

"See, that's the thing. I don't think she's a ghost. At first I did, but now I think she's something else. I have a strong feeling that's she's alive and that she needs something from me, maybe my help."

"This sounds so crazy," she said.

"I know it does, but it's something I have to do."

"Let's Google the name and see what we come up with." Brooke pulled the laptop out of her bag and powered it up. As they waited, Simon thought about all the extraordinary physical and mental changes he had been going through. He didn't know what he was to become or what the final change would be, but he knew the old woman knew. She held the answers to his secrets.

"Okay, here we go," Brooke said when the search engine loaded on her screen. She typed in the letters "A. Thibodeaux" and got several hits. There was a male doctor in Richmond, a speech therapist in Lafayette. They continued scrolling entries, clicking on several of them, but they all led to nowhere.

"This is pointless," Simon said after they had exhausted the possibilities.

"You know, they say if Google can't find it, then it doesn't exist," she said, trying to offer some levity to the situation. Simon wasn't amused.

"What am I gonna do?"

"Wait, I have an idea," she said with enthusiasm. "Nah, never mind."

"Brooke, don't do that. What?"

"I can't believe I'm going to suggest this, but a friend of my mother's claims to be a psychic."

"What does that have to do with me?"

"If you think what's happening to you is…supernatural, maybe she can tell you what."

"Are you serious?"

"My mother used to swear by her. Look, you want to believe that all this stuff is happening to you, that you're reading minds, making birds fall dead out of the sky, controlling wild dogs with your mind, but you doubt someone could be a psychic?"

He thought about her words. "What time do we leave?"

"Let me call and get directions."

"Is this freakin' you out?"

"What?"

"Me; all this weird stuff?"

She moved over and placed an affectionate kiss on his lips. "Baby, this is New Orleans. We were built on voodoo and weird stuff. Trust me, I can handle it."

≈ Chapter 13

Simon and Brooke stood on the front porch of the stately antebellum home on the north side of town. A strong breeze whipped through the air, forcing the couple to adjust their jackets to block the sudden wind. The sun had already started its early descent, leaving a trail of burnt orange in the sky. Darkness slowly crept across the land.

The pre-Civil War era home was set on a large, corner lot at the busy crossroads of Cypress and Rampart Streets; the house, with its imposing presence, commanded attention in the rapidly decaying urban neighborhood. Six thick, intimidating, white pillars ran the length from the porch to the roof of the two-story structure. White paint had begun to peel and chip from its walls in various places, like burned skin peeling away from decaying flesh. The house had sustained obvious hurricane damage, but still managed to maintain some dignity from its glory days. A huge tree, hunched over and knotted from age, shrouded part of the house in shadows; its gnarled limbs reached out in every direction. The wind blew again and the house moaned as if it felt a deep, lingering ache in a place hidden far from view.

"So, this is it?" Simon asked, as he looked at a row of dead rose bushes that lined the brick walkway. Without much thought, Simon reached down and plucked a brittle leaf from the plant and crumbled it in his hand, letting the wind scatter the pieces across the dried lawn.

"Yeah, this is it."

"I don't like this place," he stated plainly. His dislike of the former plantation was visceral. "I don't know about this." He sighed heavily as another strong breeze sprayed fallen leaves across the porch.

"Well, we're here now," she said as she rubbed his arm in a reassuring way. "We might as well ring the bell and go in. We need answers, right?"

"Yeah, I'm not sure they'll come from here."

"What do we have to lose?"

"My sanity." Simon studied the house again. It filled him with a sense of uneasiness, and nerves at the bottom of his stomach tightened, preparing him for what lay ahead.

"If you don't want to go in, we can get in the car and leave. Whatever you want to do is fine with me."

Simon paused. "This house has secrets; lots of secrets." He didn't pay much attention to the concerned look on her face, but he noticed it, even when she tried to mask it with a smile. She was nervous, too. He could feel it.

"Do you want to leave?"

"Yeah, let's get outta here."

Just as Simon and Brooke turned to leave, the front door of the house opened.

"Y'all not just gon' leave, are you?" They turned around and were greeted by a beautiful coffee-colored woman dressed in a bright pink dress that contrasted with the winter weather outside. Her jet-black curly hair hung just below her shoulders and her wide, inviting smile immediately put them at ease. A green scarf that matched the green sash tied around her petite waist was draped around her neck.

"Uhhh, we didn't want to be a bother," Simon said.

"It's no bother. I knew you were coming," she said with a wink and a smile. "Y'all come on in." She pulled the door open wider, motioned for them to enter and stepped to the side. Simon and Brooke looked at each other and tacitly agreed to enter. They stepped gingerly into the huge foyer of the grand house and instantly felt underdressed for the occasion. The inside of the house was constructed mainly of dark wood, which gave the space a natural feeling of formality.

"Brooke, your mother told me you'd be stopping by. It's so good to see you. You've turned into such a lady." She pulled Brooke into her body and hugged her tightly, in a way that contradicted their insubstantial relationship. "You must be Simon," she said after she released Brooke from her embrace. Simon extended his hand to her for a shake. "I'm Clara," she said, "and dah-ling, I'm a hugger." She continued without missing a beat, completely ignoring his outstretched hand. She pulled him into her body and held him tightly. Simon was slightly unnerved by such an ostentatious display of affection, but he didn't protest. He remembered times as child when he would have given his right arm for an affectionate hug.

"I'm so glad y'all came by." Her thick Louisiana accent spun, but did not rest, in Simon's ears; instead, her voice infused the dull room with life and vitality.

"Well, ma'am," he began.

"Ma'am? No need to be so formal. You can call me Ms. Clara."

"Okay…Ms. Clara. I'm not really sure why we're here."

"It's okay, Sugar. We'll get to that. In the meantime, how about some tea to warm your bones?"

"Tea would be nice," Brooke said quickly.

"Wonderful."

As if on cue, a tall, thin woman with graying blonde hair, dressed in a black-and-white uniform, emerged from a room to the side.

"Donna, would you be a dear and take their jackets? Then, please take them into the solarium and get them some tea," she said sweetly. "I'll join you in a few moments. Something upstairs requires my attention," she said, returning her attention to Simon and Brooke.

"Certainly, Mrs. Richardson." Clara smiled and moved around the group. She strutted down the long hallway, her high-heels clicking hard against the freshly polished wooden floor, and walked up the staircase on the right, disappearing as she ascended. As she walked, Simon *noticed* her and found himself drawn to her by the confident way her hips shifted from side-to-side, like a well-seasoned woman who celebrated the power of her curves. Clara was all woman—legs, hips and breasts. Her body was shapely and sturdy, full of delectable lines and sensual curves; she was the kind of woman who wouldn't crumple easily under the pressure of his weight.

Simon snapped out of his daze when Donna took their coats, hung them in a closet near the door and led them down the hallway to the back of the house, to the solarium. The intimidating room was decorated with antique nineteenth-century furniture and made Simon feel as if he had stepped back in time, about two hundred years. Slave trinkets and totems were spread throughout the room, and Simon took notice of a shelf against the wall that was stacked with historical memorabilia.

"Please, make yourself comfortable. Mrs. Richardson will be back shortly."

"Thank you," Brooke said as they walked fully into the room. Donna smiled, turned and exited the room. Simon waited a few seconds to make sure she was out of earshot before he spoke.

"This house is creepy."

"I think it's lovely—very Old World. It has a certain charm."

"Yeah, it has all the charm of a slave plantation. I'm just waiting for Miz Scarlett's prissy ass to pop in." They laughed perfunctorily as Simon continued his methodic inspection of the room. "And what about Clara?"

"What about her?"

"She doesn't give you the creeps?" Simon's emotions swirled inside him suddenly, making it hard to understand exactly what he was feeling. He felt a growing longing for Clara's body, even though she was more than twice his age. He could almost feel the touch of her skin on his skin and the feel of her pouty lips on his mouth; inexplicably, he was both repulsed and aroused by the thought. *Maybe she had already worked some voodoo on him*, he thought. Far stranger things had already happened.

Brooke chuckled. "Not at all. She's exactly how I remember, very sweet, very beautiful, very touchy-feely—very Southern. I haven't seen her in years, but she looks exactly the same."

"I think she's fake."

"You think she's had work done?" Brooke asked in astonishment. That would be a juicy piece of town gossip that she would certainly share with her mother.

"That's not what I mean. There's something strange about her, about this house. I'm not sure what, though."

Brooke moved over to the sofa and took a seat, crossing her legs at the ankles.

Simon noticed the elaborate décor of the solarium. He rotated his body slowly, in a full circle, to make sure that he took full stock of the room. Even though the room had huge floor-to-ceiling windows, the dark decorations gave it a gloomy undertone; even the vintage furniture was of dubious intent.

On a small shelf against the wall were little figurines in the shape of a large woman with very black skin, wearing an apron around her waist and a handkerchief tied tightly around her head, coupled with statues of an equally dark-skinned male with hugely exaggerated lips and big, round white eyes. The disturbing images from a time bygone added to the tension that was already balling in the pit of his stomach.

Hung on the wall by a huge rusted nail was a pair of gray shackles, most likely used to secure slaves. Simon eyed the metal clamps with disdain and empathy. Until his recent run-in with the street thugs who tried to rob him, he had never understood the darkness or cruelty that ruled man's heart. Until that night, when he dispatched three men with a callous kind of joy, he never understood evil. Now, he was beginning to understand a lesson he didn't want to know. Evil resided within him. That night, he felt something so malevolent within his own soul that he frightened himself. He felt like a wicked marionette controlled by an even more sinister puppet-master.

"Here is your tea," Donna said, as she entered the room and placed a silver serving tray with two cups and a teapot on the center table near the couch.

"What kind of tea is it?" Brooke asked. Donna smiled and folded her hands in front of her.

"It's a special blend that Mrs. Richardson makes herself. Don't worry, you'll love it. Is there anything else you need?"

"No, I think we're good," Simon interjected. Donna smiled sweetly and exited the room.

Brooke leaned over and poured a cup of the fragrant tea into her small cup. She blew on it several times, scattering the steam that rose from the liquid into the air before bringing the cup to her lips.

"Don't drink the Kool-Aid!" Simon said suddenly as he rushed over to her and grabbed her wrist.

"What's wrong?" Brooke asked with alarm.

Simon looked at her and smiled. "I'm just fucking with you," he said as he leaned in and kissed her on the lips.

Playfully, she tried to push him away, but her resistance was weak. "I can't believe you just did that to me." She nudged him in the arm with her elbow.

"I'm sorry, babe. I'll make it up tonight," he said flirtatiously. Regardless of his situation, Simon was quick for arousal; sexual desire was an innate part of his being.

"I know you will." Brooke took a sip of the tea and twisted her face in a manner that told Simon she wasn't sure whether she liked it. He watched her contemplate the taste of the tea.

"I see y'all have settled in," Clara said when she walked into the room a few moments later. Her beaming personality was much larger than her actual size. She commanded attention with her southern charm and inviting smile. She stepped into the room, sipping from a small whiskey sifter, and took a seat in the brown and beige armless accent chair across from the couch. She crossed her smooth legs like a true Southern lady. Simon looked at her shapely legs, but did not speak.

"How does this work?" Brooke blurted out nervously. "My mother said you were a psychic."

Clara chuckled. "How is your dear mother? I haven't seen her since she left for Milan. I really must call her to catch up. Maybe we'll do cocktails next week at Emeril's Delmonico."

"She had a wonderful time. You should see the pictures. By the way, your house is amazing." Brooke looked around the room in wonderment and awe as Clara's face beamed with unrepentant pride.

"Yes, it is, isn't it?" Clara settled comfortably into her chair. "I've spent the last couple of years restoring this home. It suffered serious damage after Katrina and was vacant for a spell, but she's a sturdy old girl. She's still standing. I'm not nearly done." Clara leaned in slowly as if she was ready to spill the latest piece of salacious gossip about a neighbor. "You wouldn't know this, but this house is in my blood. This here land was toiled by my father's father's father and his fathers. You see, my family was slaves on this land. It is our blood that fertilized the soil; it was our sweat that elevated the Collingtons to vast wealth. This house is deeply rooted in my family. This house *is* me. I feel so connected to it. When I had the opportunity to buy it after the Collington family declared bankruptcy a few years back, I didn't hesitate. I was meant to live here. It's only right. In an ironic twist of fate, Donna, my maid, is a distant cousin of the Collingtons. Now, she works for me. How the tables turn." She giggled.

"Wow," Brooke said. "Amazing."

"Ummmm, so you're a psychic?" Simon said, attempting to steer the conversation back on track. Ordinarily, he would have soaked up every detail about the history of her family so that he could get to know more about this intriguing woman, but he didn't have patience for history lessons today.

Clara smiled and leaned back in her chair, bringing her drink to her red lips. Her unblemished skin and perfectly symmetrical face reminded Simon of a supermodel from a time when models ruled the world. Her eyes were large and round, which lifted her entire face. She certainly didn't look like any psychic he had ever seen. Was she for real or was this a waste of his time?

"Hmmmm," she began. "A psychic? Well, sometimes I see that which is not seen by others. I'm not sure if that makes me a psychic. More often I'm a conduit—a messenger."

"What does that mean?"

"That means if someone in the spirit world is trying to deliver a message, I can be the means to that end. It's happened before;

that a spirit will talk through me or will direct my hand so that I can write what it wants you to know. I never know how it will happen, or if it will happen."

"So, you're telling me this might be a waste of time?"

"Honey, there are no rules to the spirit world that I know. I open myself up and whatever happens, happens."

"What if it's not a spirit? What if it's something else?"

"When you open yourself up to me, I can often see all that is around you, spirit or otherwise."

"If it is a spirit, can you make it go away?"

"You first have to know what it wants, but I don't perform exorcisms."

"Do you think you'll be able to help him?" Brooke asked.

"It depends. Simon has to be open to the reading." She sipped again. "I sense some reluctance on your part. You don't trust me, do you?" she said with a smile that was too sexy for the occasion.

"It's not that I don't trust you, it's—"

"There is no room for skepticism, dah-ling. Your spirit has to be completely open, or this will be a waste of time."

"I think I'm just nervous. I've never done this before."

"Here, hon. Have some tea. It'll help relax you." She leaned forward, poured a cup and handed it to Simon. She took a sip of her drink and leaned back, watching him, waiting for him to sip. He looked at the murky liquid in his cup and smiled uneasily at her. The tea's delicate fragrance began to fill his nose and enticed him to try her concoction.

"You don't like the tea?" he asked.

"I prefer a little Southern comfort, if you know what I mean," she said with a grin as she sipped again. There was an overt sensuality in the way Clara sipped her liquid. Simon could tell that it burned her throat as it went down, but there was an undeniable pleasure in her pain. Simon watched the way her well-manicured hand gripped the glass; she almost caressed it, stroking it with gentle force. Simon exhaled, hoping Brooke hadn't noticed the wanton look that crept into his eyes. Of all the things he expected to feel for this *psychic*, lust wasn't one of them. He glanced at Brooke, who had more than halfway finished her tea, and then he took a sip. And another one. And another one. The sweetness of the tea hit his palate hard, but he did not balk.

"Tell me why you're here, Simon. What do you really need?"

"I need someone to help me figure out what's going on with me."

"What do you mean?" she asked, as Simon's eyes darted nervously across the room, skillfully avoiding her gaze. He wasn't sure what it was about her that made him nervous, but he felt something stir in his spirit. It wasn't quite a warning, but it made him tread cautiously.

"I've been having bad dreams. Of snakes."

She simply sipped.

He continued, "And, I think there's a spirit that's haunting— no, that's not the right word—let's say, trying to communicate with me." He took a much bigger drink from his cup and then exhaled. Saying the words to someone other than Brooke felt good.

"Oh, I see. What do you think this spirit wants from you?"

"That's why I'm here."

"Has anything like this happened to you before, or is this all new?"

"Nah, this is definitely new."

"Sometimes a spirit will attach itself to a person their whole life, or it will attach itself to an object, like this house—this house is full of spirits; some mournful, some scornful, some vengeful, and some are my protectors."

"Your house is haunted?" Brooke spoke with alarm, her eyes cutting across the room.

"Of course it is, chile. This is an old plantation home. Slaves were burned here. Slaves were hung here. You can't inflict that much pain on a piece of land and expect it to remain unaffected."

"Why do you stay here, then?" Simon asked.

"The spirits ain't after me. They know I have slave blood running in my veins. Let me tell you something, when Donna first started working here she had more accidents than I could count; she fell down the stairs, a door slammed on her fingers and broke two of them. Once, her apron caught fire in the kitchen. At first I thought she was clumsy, but one day I actually saw a spirit hovering about her head. I actually saw it. Well, I called Savannah—one of my friends who is descended from a long line of powerful witches—and had her put a protection spell on Donna. Ever since then, we've been fine."

"Okay, this is kinda freakin' me out," Brooke said.

"No need to worry, honey. Everything's gonna be fine. Trust me."

"Now, where was I? Oh yeah, have you recently had any traumatic experience? A head injury or car accident, perhaps?" she said to Simon.

"No. I'm fine."

"Is the anniversary of the death of a parent or loved one approaching?"

"I wouldn't know. I grew up in foster homes. I don't know my real family."

She scratched her forehead. "Interesting."

"Any special occasion coming up that you can think of?"

"No, none."

"His birthday," Brooke inserted, "his twenty-first birthday is in two weeks."

"Ahhh, twenty-one, such a mystical age."

"You think that has something to do with what's going on?"

"Perhaps," she said after thinking for a few moments, "we'll know soon enough. All right. Well, let's get on with it." Clara set her drink down, got up and moved over to a credenza in the back of the room. She opened one of the drawers and pulled out what looked to Simon like a small, colorful branch from a bush that was tied together by a blue satin string. She produced a lighter, and, with the flick of her thumb, the bush was on fire. Quickly, she blew it out. She walked around the room chanting and waving the smoking branch about the room. Simon looked at Brooke, who shrugged her shoulders.

"What are you doing?" Simon asked.

"Shhhhh," Clara said. "The room needs to be open, too." The stench of the burning twig filled the room with an odor that was a mix between burning grass and incense. She placed it in a silver chalice that sat in the center of a small table in the back. "Now, we are ready. Simon, please come here." Simon moved over to her.

"Please, take a seat." Reluctantly, Simon lowered his body into the wooden chair. Clara took a seat directly in front of him. "You must not be afraid. You must open yourself up to me if I am to help you." She placed both her arms on the table and opened her hands. "Give me your hands." Simon looked over at Brooke who watched with an attentive eye. Even from his distance, he could see that her breathing was elevated by the rapid rising and deflating of her chest. Clara's ghost story must have had really gotten to her.

Simon sat directly across from Clara and stared into her beautifully dark eyes. He was convinced she was trying to read his thoughts. She stared at him and did not blink.

"Give me your hands," she said. Slowly, Simon raised his arms and put them onto the table. "Don't be afraid, Simon. No harm can come to you during this reading." Simon inhaled loudly and placed his hands inside hers. As soon as her fingers wrapped themselves around his hands, he felt her desire; such burning desire. She shifted in her seat. He could smell the sweet stickiness of her longing gathering between her firm legs. She wanted him in a carnal way, and he was suddenly afraid that he'd give in to her. He wanted to recoil, to pull away from her grip, but he could not—it was simply too pleasurable. An erotic tingling sensation traveled through his fingers, up to his elbows and shoulders, then wound its way down into his genitals. A wonderful, warming feeling twisted its way through all of his erogenous zones, and he felt an unfamiliar, yet utterly irresistible, tickling in the depths of his balls. The sensation became more and more intense and he moaned with a deep pleasure that was usually reserved for sex.

He looked at Brooke, and she looked back at him with concern, but then he returned his gaze to Clara. He had to.

After a few elongated seconds of pleasure, Clara lifted her intense gaze and the engorging of his manhood slowly subsided, much to his chagrin. Usually, when he was turned on, only the act of release could turn him off. He looked dumbfounded and his eyes were glazed; but, he exhaled slowly several times, never releasing his gaze, hoping that whatever she had done she'd do again. This was the first time he had been fucked so thoroughly, while his clothes were still on.

"Okay, let us begin," she said. She closed her eyes, tightened her grip around his hands and took in a long, ragged breath. She held it in for a few seconds and expelled it lightly from her lips. She repeated the action a few times.

Suddenly, she withdrew both her hands quickly and opened her eyes.

"What is it?" Brooke asked.

"There is darkness here," she said in a grave tone that sent chills up and down Simon's arms, "a great darkness."

"What are you talking about?" Brooke asked as she rushed over.

"Stop, chile. Go back over there." Clara's unequivocal tone left no room for argument; Brooke hesitated, but did as she was instructed.

"Are you okay?" Simon asked, more out of concern for himself than for her. "What darkness?"

"I don't know yet, but something wants to claim you—*desperately*."

"What do you mean, *something*? A ghost?"

"No, this is something else."

"What the fuck?" Brooke exclaimed.

"Quiet!" She commanded in a gruff voice that no longer sounded like hers. She leaned over and took a lingering inhale from the smoldering bush, letting it fill her nostrils. "Give me your hands." The expression on her face was solemn.

When she grabbed his hands, she shuddered, but did not relinquish her grip. Her eyes rolled into the back of her skull and Simon suddenly felt immobile and mute. He wanted to free himself from her, but he could not. An electric current surged through his body as he watched Clara's face twist and contort. She released one hand and reached over to the pad and paper on her right. She scribbled something that looked like indecipherable hieroglyphics and then her handwriting gave way to letters that looked more modern, except it was a language he didn't know. She continued writing until she scribbled something that shocked the disbelief out of Simon. He looked at the paper and even though it was written upside down from his vantage point, he could clearly see the words *Adelaide Thibodeaux* written in cursive.

Then, a terrified voiced suddenly filled his head: *Simon, no!* The voice wasn't one that he recognized, but there was real fear in it; a fear so strong that it shook him to his core.

He suddenly found the strength to rip his hands away from her grip. When he did, a force hit Clara so hard that she slid across the room in her chair and crashed into the bookshelf behind her, sending figurines and trinkets flying across the room. When she hit the shelf, she fell to the floor hard, but her hand still gripped the piece of paper with Addie's name.

"Clara!" Brooke and Simon screamed simultaneously as they rushed to her aid. Simon leaned down and lifted her head off of the floor. A small amount of blood had pooled at the corner of her mouth and her eyes were wide.

"Clara, can you hear me?" he asked. "Are you okay?" Clara coughed, spitting out a trace amount of blood onto Simon's arms.

"They…they…both want you," she said to him with tremendous effort.

"Who?"

"He…will…come…to claim you. You must choose." Clara's voice began to fade.

"Clara!" Brooke screamed.

"What have you done?" Donna asked as she raced into the room. "What did you do to her?"

"We didn't do anything. I swear!"

"Get out of here before I call the police!"

"But we didn't do anything. We need to get her to the hospital."

"You need to leave!" Donna said again. Brooke and Simon looked at each other, wanting to protest, but they did not. Brooke stood up and turned toward the door, reluctantly. As Simon began to rise, Clara grabbed him by the collar, stuffed the paper into his hand, and pulled his ear close to her mouth. She struggled to speak, but was only able to enunciate a few words.

"I won't tell you to leave again," Donna said with more authority in her voice. Simon took one last look at Clara and moved toward the door, looking back again for a few moments. He hugged

Brooke and they exited the room and walked down the long hallway toward the foyer.

"I don't know what just happened," Simon said. His voice was low and he sounded despondent, as if he had come to the end of the road and was left with far more questions than answers. "What did I do to her?"

"You didn't do anything to her." Her words were full of doubt and offered little comfort.

"I hope she's okay."

"I'm sure she'll be fine. She's used to this supernatural stuff, I'm sure. What did she say to you just then?" Simon kept walking down the hallway and didn't answer her until he reached the front door, and then he paused before speaking. "She said, 'Be wary of shadows,' and then she handed me this." He opened his hand and unballed the sheet of paper.

"Oh my God," Brooke exclaimed. Simon looked at her face and she was genuinely spooked. "A. Thibodeaux. Adelaide Thibodeaux. Who is she?"

"I don't know, but I guess I'll find out soon enough." Simon opened the door and let Brooke exit first. He closed the door behind him and hopped down the few steps that led to the walkway. He took a few more steps and stopped in the middle of the sidewalk, looking back at the eerie structure that loomed behind. "I know why this place creeps me out."

"Why?" she asked hesitantly.

"I've been here before."

ᴄ CHAPTER 14

T here was nothing sweeter to Simon's ears than the sound of cool vodka being poured over crackling ice. It was like soothing music after a long day. He watched Brooke add a splash of cranberry juice to both glasses before handing one to him and raising the other to her mouth. She joined him on the sofa and they drank greedily and silently, savoring the cool burn.

They had barely spoken to each other on the ride home, and when Brooke attempted to turn on the radio as a distraction, Simon immediately turned it off. His mood allowed no room for the latest hip-hop lyrics or thumping bass lines; he opted instead for the familiar melody of rubber tires pounding against the ragged streets.

He sat in the passenger's seat and stared out of the window simply watching the familiar landscape pass. Run-down buildings. Kids playing in the street. Fast-food restaurants. When they crossed the Chatnum Bridge, he avoided looking at the Mississippi River out of fear its waves would make him nauseous again; but that really was the least of his concerns. His mind was numb; still reeling from his experience with Clara and the resulting assault of images so disturbing that they defied words.

In the company of Brooke, he fought desperately to hold on to his stoicism; but he was shaken to his core, and rightly so. In the sanctuary of the vehicle, watching the city pass by, everything seemed fine, but everything felt wrong to him. He felt wrong, too. The world, in his view—dimmed by an ash-gray film that muted the city lights—no longer seemed to fit. He felt foreign; as out of place as a polar bear in a barren desert. Everything had changed.

He was shaken, not only because of what had happened to Clara, but also because of what he had seen and felt during his reading; things he did not dare share with Brooke out of fear of being labeled a monster. During the reading, his head was filled with terrible—almost unimaginable—images.

A dense forest where the dead bodies that hung from the trees were so numerous that they looked like low-hanging fruit.

Burning bodies being tossed into the street; he could smell the rank scent of searing flesh.

A vast field decorated with decapitated heads atop wooden spikes.

He also saw an image of a massive hole in the ground filled with screaming and crying children; he stood over them with a wicked smile as they were being buried alive.

In the vision, he felt his own rising darkness; it was a burning force that utterly consumed him.

Simon ravenously sucked the last bit of alcohol from his glass and got up hastily to make a new drink. The images that wrested in his head made it difficult for him to find even a second of peace, but the vodka was beginning to help. He wanted to believe that what he had seen was simply his imagination reacting to the very unusual circumstances or that Clara was somehow responsible for planting the seeds of the nightmare into his mind; maybe she worked her mojo—or voodoo—and made him see what she wanted him to see in order to control him. On the ride home, he had continuously blamed her for his woes, cursing her to the high heavens and trying to convince himself that he had fallen under her spell and that she had used some kind of witchcraft on him. He even blamed her for the intense lust he felt toward her and accused her of using magic to bring him so close to the edge of orgasm during his reading.

In spite of the strong case he made, he failed to convince himself of her chicanery. What he had seen was not some nightmare or random images planted subliminally into his skull by witchery. It wasn't a drug-induced hallucination caused by inhaling the fumes from some unknown burning bush. He desperately wanted to believe he had been high during the reading, but he knew that wasn't so.

What he saw at Clara's had chilled his bones; it was what was to be; it was the future.

When he reached for the bottle of liquor to make his drink, he had difficulty holding on to it because of his unsteady hands; his hands shook as if they had been stricken by disease. Brooke saw his struggle and moved to pour the vodka in his stead, rubbing his back in a soothing way, attempting to calm his frayed nerves. Simon forced a tiny smile and retook his seat on the couch, burying his face in his hands.

He wanted to weep. During the reading, he had felt the true darkness that lived within his own heart. And, he had seen the grisly figure of a hooded man with no face. The hooded man had seen him, too. This was no doubt the man that Clara warned would come to claim him; but this thing, was not a man at all. It was something else altogether, something that hovered in the shadows, lingering between life and death.

"Baby," Brooke finally said, "we have to talk about this." She took a seat next to him and put her arms around his shoulders. "We have to talk about what happened. What did you mean when you said you had been to the house before? When?"

These days there weren't many things Simon could say with certainty about his life; he knew the sun still rose in the east and set in the west, but that was about all he'd stake his life on— except the fact that he had a connection to Clara's house. He had been there before. He didn't know when or why or how, he only knew that he had been there before; and he knew it in a real place in his soul that he couldn't reach with his mind; a place that didn't allow access; but, he was absolutely certain. Absolutely.

She sighed. "I don't understand anything that's going on."

"I don't know, either. I don't know anything anymore. Last week my biggest concern was not going to class or how I was going to get enough money to pay rent, but now, I got some supernatural shit going on. None of this makes any sense." He leaned back into the folds of the couch. "Clara was right about one thing, something is after me. I don't know what it is, but I've been sensing… something, for days now. My dreams aren't dreams at all. Something has been trying to get to me. It's starting to all make sense."

"Something like what? Is it…evil?" She broached the word *evil* cautiously as if to not offend listening spirits.

Simon lifted his head and stared blankly at the wall, searching his mind for the right response. "Nah, it's something more than that. There's evil and then there's this shadow thing." His creepy words sent a cold chill throughout the room. He turned and forced a weak smile when he looked at Brooke, whose face reflected the horror that she felt. "More than that, though, I think I'm evil, too. Clara said it. I have darkness in me. And I feel it."

"Baby," she said as she took her hand, placed it on his chin, and turned his head, forcing him to look at her, "that's not true. You are the kindest, most gentle man I have ever known. That's why I fell in love with you. Your spirit fills a room. You are not darkness. You are my light."

That's why I fell in love with you, he repeated in his head. Yes, she loved him, but would her love be enough to save him?

She released his chin and continued, "How many hours a week do you spend volunteering at the homeless shelter or the children's hospital or tutoring at-risk youth? You do so much good. If the world was full of people like you, it would be a much, much better place." She was right. He did spend a lot of time giving back, even though he didn't have much to give. He always figured that because he didn't have money, he could always give of himself. "Do you remember a few weeks ago when I screamed in the bathroom because there was a big spider? I wanted you to kill it, but you caught it and took it outside and set it free. A man who won't even kill a spider is certainly not filled with darkness."

He leaned in and placed a needy kiss on her willing lips. "Thank you, baby. You always know what to say."

"Anytime you feel like you're bad, hold on to what's in there," she said as she placed her index finger on his chest, right at his heart. "Hold on to love."

He kissed her again, this time with more passion. "I'm tired. I need to rest. Can we talk about this later?"

She smiled. "Uhhh, of course."

Simon needed to get away from her for fear of breaking down. If he lost his composure in front of her, it would be a complete breakdown and he'd have no control over what he shared with her. He'd end up telling her what he saw and felt during the reading. More importantly, he'd end up confessing what he was becoming. Finding the words to tell his girlfriend that he was becoming a beast wouldn't be an easy task; he wasn't even sure he knew the words. In the car on the way home, he realized that in order to save her he'd have to send her away, ultimately banishing her from his life, maybe not forever, but at least until he figured this thing out. He needed her to go now, but he wasn't strong enough for that, yet. Not tonight. He wasn't ready to be alone in the house with his own thoughts. He needed her comfort, at least for one more night.

A tear formed in his eye and streamed down his cheek and he quickly wiped it away before she saw it. He moved from the couch and toward the bedroom.

"Simon," she said from across the room, "I'll always be here for you. Remember that."

Simon smiled, nodded his head, and continued into the bedroom. Quickly, he flipped on the light and closed the door behind him, leaving a sliver of a crack. The idea of being sealed in a room alone terrified him.

Once he stepped into the room, he carefully inspected it to make sure that nothing was lurking about in the corners. He leaned against the wall and took a few deep breaths to calm himself and to focus. He knew what had to be done. Clara had told him everything, and she had told him how to do it. He needed to contact Adelaide Thibodeaux, whoever she was. He needed to reach out to her, but in order to connect with her, he needed to be open. As crazy and far-fetched as it seemed to him, he was going to try to make contact with her. He didn't have a trick bag, out of which he could pull any of the herbs or teas or bushes that Clara had, but something told him he wouldn't need one. After all, this woman, who might be his savior, had already contacted him.

He moved over to the dresser and lit the lone candle, although he wasn't sure why; it seemed like an appropriate thing to do, given the situation. Then, he kicked off his shoes and lay across the bed on top of the covers, his hands folded across his stomach, his back resting against the headboard. His breathing was labored so he took a few quick, shallow breaths to settle himself. What he was about to do was certainly risky. He knew that. He didn't know anything about this Adelaide woman and he didn't really understand how to reach her, nor did he know whether he could really trust anything Clara had told him. He didn't know her, either. Maybe Clara wanted to get him to this Adelaide for some nefarious purpose. He couldn't be certain of anything anymore except that his world had been turned upside-down and that sitting idly around doing nothing while he waited to be transformed into something hideous, or waiting around for some undead thing to claim him, were not options.

Then, a thought paralyzed him: what if he accidentally made contact with the hooded man, bringing him closer to him? His course of action was dangerous, but he made a decision to move forward, breaking away from the fear that almost held him back. What choice did he have? He raced through myriad options in his head, and they all led back to him confronting, head-on, the issues facing him. There simply wasn't any other option.

He thought about it again and then began to focus on the grave task at hand. He didn't even really know how to begin, but, intuitively, he stared at the flame of the candle to help center his thoughts. His eyes were wide, even though he felt relaxed. Slowly, he inhaled and exhaled as he let her name echo in his head repeatedly.

Adelaide Thibodeaux. Adelaide Thibodeaux. Adelaide Thibodeaux.

He repeated this action for several minutes to no avail. His eyelids began to sink and sleep wanted to claim him, but he resisted; mainly out of fear of what his dreams would bring. He didn't want to dream of snakes or see the hooded man or see any more graphic images of death and blood. He wanted to remain in complete control of what happened next. He adjusted himself in the bed and continued focusing; fighting back the fatigue. His eyelids drooped several times, but each time he willed them open.

Simon.

When he heard his name, it sounded like someone was in his room. He looked around, but no one was there. Then, he heard it again.

Simon.

He had connected with her; he was sure of that. His name sounded like a mere whisper; a faint echo in a vast tunnel. It was distant, but he still clearly heard it. He concentrated harder. A warm, prickly sensation washed over his body. It started in his toes and moved up through his legs, his abdomen and chest. and then his head. His entire body felt sharp, like he could draw blood if anyone dared touch him. Physically, he was immobile, and he was not concerned about his sudden paralysis; his mind had never felt so free. In his head, he moved rapidly—at lightning speed.

Now, he could close his eyes, without fear of sleep.

When he opened his eyes, he found himself in a field bursting with color. The sunlight was so bright that he had to squint and use his hand as a sun shade. All around were flowers. Purple. Orange. Yellow. Red. Blue. Butterflies flew delicately about and the weak buzzing of bees could be heard in the distance. The sky was the bluest blue he had ever seen. He looked around at the shimmering world. The entire place glimmered and was ethereal, almost fragile.

"Simon, you must come," she said to him faintly.

"How? Where are you?"

"Come to me." Her voice grew weak. He looked all around the vast field and did not see anyone stir. The tall grass bent gently in the smooth, warm breeze. Beauty stretched out as far as he could see.

"Where are you?" he called out. His voice echoed in the distance.

"I am near. Come to me and all will be revealed."

"I don't know where you are." Simon's voice sounded panicked. "Wait, you're fading. Where are you?"

"You will find me."

"Wait, can I get an address?" he asked in frustration.

"Trust no one." Her warning caused alarm in his spirit.

At that moment, Simon heard a blood-curdling hissing scream that knocked him to the ground. All of the beautiful flowers wilted, and birds fell dead out of the sky. The warm breeze turned frigid and strong; the green grass turned a brittle shade of brown; the bright sunlight was sucked away, replaced by a menacing darkness and a putrid smell.

"Wait!"

Simon woke up in a choking fit caused by the rank smell from his dream. The sour taste of bile burned the back of his throat causing him to cough violently to eject the source of the rancid taste that gathered in his mouth. The smell was tangible, like a ball of regurgitated food that stuck in his throat, only it wasn't food. It was something else. The smell was familiar, and not in a good way. His stomach churned and Simon could now *feel* boiling in his belly. His insides cooked, and he felt like the acid in his stomach would burn right through his skin. That smell was beyond an odor; it was an entity—something living that latched onto him and would not let go.

He took a few easy breaths, his lungs releasing the tension that squeezed them. He looked around his room, his body tight, and although everything looked fine, he still felt wrong—out of place. He remembered the assault on his senses caused by the shadow-thing he saw in the restroom at The Black Cat. Not only had he smelled the horror of it, but now he was tasting the rottenness of it. The scream he heard still hissed in his ears, but as he settled into the comfort of his small room, he felt protected. "I did it," he said to himself. "I made contact." He felt a sense of pride.

He placed his feet on the floor and tried to stand, but when he did, the room started spinning viciously and he lost his footing, almost falling to the floor. He grabbed onto the bedpost to break his fall and to steady himself. He paused for a few seconds and then made small, timid movements, fearful that any sudden exertion of energy would cause him to expel the content of his stomach onto the bedroom floor. He placed his hand on his stomach and yanked it back when he felt something move inside him. "What the fuck?" he said to himself. *Maybe I need to vomit*, he thought. He had to get to the bathroom. He stumbled through the room, using whatever piece of furniture within reach as leverage, eventually reaching the bathroom and tumbling gracelessly into it.

He burst into the bathroom and immediately grabbed onto the sink for balance. He clung to it for dear life. As he stood there, he couldn't convince himself that the unsettled feeling in his stomach was nausea; it felt much different, stronger. It felt malevolent. Carefully, he placed his hand on his stomach again and when he did, something moved, again. He could see his stomach rolling beneath his shirt. It was as prominent as the movement in the womb of an expectant mother whose child was changing positions. He froze.

"Simon," Brooke said when she rushed into the room. The gruesome expression on his face shot terror into her body. "Simon, what's wrong?"

"There's something...something inside me." His voice was shaking so much that it was difficult for her to understand his words. He pointed. "My stomach."

With trepidation, Simon slowly lifted his shirt. He looked down, but there was no movement. He placed his hands on his sharp abdominals, but nothing happened.

"What do you mean?"

"It felt like something...alive...was inside me, moving." He reached out for her hand and placed it onto his stomach so that she could feel the peculiar movement, too. As soon as she touched him, he screamed and doubled over in pain, slamming into the tub.

"Oh shit! What the fuck is wrong with me?" He started coughing so violently that he almost lost his balance again. Brooke placed her hands around him and moved him closer to the toilet in case he needed to throw up. He flung open the lid and leaned over, dry heaving ferociously above the commode.

"Simon!"

His coughing intensified so much that he collapsed to the floor with a thud, landing on his knees and hands. Brooke stood with her back to the door, facing Simon. She kneeled beside him as he began to spit globs of blood.

"Oh my God!" she said. "I'm calling 9-1-1."

Simon let out a long, harsh cough and grabbed her by wrist, preventing her from leaving the room. Then, he felt some squirming in his throat and he coughed again. He opened his mouth and spit out a large clot of blood. It splattered onto the floor and onto Brooke's pants. She screamed. He coughed violently again and this time bile—bitter green and malodorous—spewed from his mouth.

Don't be afraid. Don't be afraid.

Simon heard the hiss in his head before he actually saw the black snake crawl out of his mouth and slither swiftly across the floor. Brooke screamed and backed away quickly—frightfully—slamming into the wall and hitting her head before falling onto her back into the bedroom. Using her feet and the palms of her hands, she scurried backward across the floor until she reached the safety of the bed. She leapt up onto it and watched the snake slither across the bathroom floor and disappear into a crack in the corner near the tub.

"B-B-B-rooke," Simon said as he lay on the floor gripping his stomach, blood oozing from the corners of his mouth. The thought of a snake in his mouth sent a wave of nausea to his stomach and he shuddered. He raised his head and looked into the bedroom toward Brooke. She was pressed hard against the headboard, her body rigid with fright. A terror greater than anything he had ever seen was carved painfully and deeply into her face. Her eyes bulged and her mouth was agape; her body, melding into the frame of the bed.

When he called out to her again, she didn't answer. She couldn't answer. She had no words. He wanted to go over to her, to caress her and tell her that everything would be all right, but his tongue could not form the lie. Things had drifted so far from all right that he could no longer separate this terrifying supernatural existence from the life he had lived only days ago; they were painfully and forever bound together. Tonight had changed everything. No longer could he deny or rationalize or run from what was right in front of his face.

Carefully, he pulled himself up from the floor using the sink as his crutch. His knees were still a bit unsteady, and when he looked at himself in the mirror he barely recognized his own image. Sure, it was his face that reflected back in the cool glass, but there was something behind his eyes that remained unfamiliar and unsettling. He stared at his face. His expression was solemn and he watched as both of his eyes turned black, like pools of sticky tar. He closed his eyes and when he opened them they had returned to their natural color; but his eyes weren't the only things that had changed in those few seconds.

He no longer felt nauseous. Or scared. He felt powerful.

⇥CHAPTER 15

Franklin looked at the clock on his nightstand when he heard the anxious pounding against his front door. It was 3:33 in the morning, and he was dog-tired after a long night at The Black Cat. He hadn't performed, but he had partied like it was the last Mardi Gras.

The pounding continued, growing in intensity. "Go away!" he screamed at the top of his lungs. Seconds earlier, he had rolled over and covered his head with a pillow when he heard the doorbell ring frantically several times in a row, presuming it to be some dope fiend in need of a fix who mistook his door for the door of the dealer two apartments down. Usually when it happened, the crackhead would stop after a few moments; probably out of fear that the door would swing open and they'd get pistol-whipped. Franklin had seen it happen once before. The resident drug dealer had a short temper and was known to pound a person to a pulp without much provocation.

Franklin sat up in bed and continued to listen to the noise. The pounding sounded like a police battering ram that was about to break his door down. He had seen that happen, too, but he could tell that this pounding was different. The thumping this time wasn't random; it was purposeful and desperate.

He finally leapt out of bed and moved quickly down the narrow corridor that led to the front door, stubbing his left big toe against the end of the dresser on his way out of the room. He let out a yelp and bounced off the wall but continued down the dark hallway, hobbling his way toward the door. He was naked except for a pair of boxers that hung loosely over his slim hips and bony legs, not having time or even caring enough to throw on a shirt. His underdeveloped chest was tattooed with a crucifix on his left pectoral and the phrase "music man" was written in cursive on his right. A black bar with a gold ball on each end ran through his nipple, directly below the phrase.

"Franklin! Franklin!" The thudding continued, destined to alert neighbors.

"Simon?" Franklin said, recognizing the voice, even though it sounded gruff. He looked through the peephole and began unlatching the locks on the door. When the door finally opened, Simon quickly pushed past him and burst into the darkened apartment.

"What the fuck?" Franklin said, as he closed and locked the door. Simon had already moved into the living room and was pacing back and forth, mumbling to himself.

The apartment was covered in darkness, except for a sliver of light escaping from underneath the bathroom door. Silver moonlight spilled into the room through the thin curtains that hung across the big window behind the television set. Simon was disheveled, as if he hadn't slept in days. The bags under his eyes were heavy and his clothes were wrinkled. He wore a path in the carpet between the coffee table and the makeshift dining room set with the mismatched chairs.

"I gotta go. I gotta get out of here. I gotta go." He spoke quickly, as if he were running out of breath.

"Simon," Franklin said, as he flicked the switch and turned on the light, "dude, what the fuck is wrong with you?"

Simon looked at Franklin, stone-faced. "I need your car. I gotta go."

"What? You need my car? Are you crazy, bustin' up in here in the middle of the night asking fo' my car. I could've had a little freak up in here. You can't be bustin' in like that." Franklin's voice was irritable.

"I. Need. Your. Car." Simon spoke deliberately, clearly enunciating his words so that there would be no confusion.

"What's wrong with you?"

"I gotta go."

"Go where?"

"Just go."

Franklin stepped closer to him and grabbed his arms, trying to get Simon to settle down.

"What are you talking about? What's wrong?"

"I gotta find Addie. Yeah, Addie. I gotta find her."

"Who the fuck is Addie?"

Simon looked at him as if he couldn't believe he didn't know who Addie was.

"She's…she's…she got answers. Answers to the snakes. She knows about the shadows."

Franklin looked into Simon's wild eyes. "Fool, are you high? You been smoking?"

Simon looked at him and spoke in a lucid tone. "You know I don't smoke, Frank. I need to go."

"You ain't makin' no sense."

"I been seeing things. Hearing things. Shadows. Snakes. Ghosts. I can do things. I can feel things. I can fly."

"Okay, if you think you can fly, you must be high as a kite. I don't know what you took, but you need to sit down for a minute. What did you take?"

"I didn't take anything. No drugs. No drugs in my body. Only snakes. Only snakes in my body. I vomited one earlier. Ask Brooke. She'll tell you."

"Did you do something to Brooke?" he asked, his voice shaded with concern.

"Brooke is fine. I can't be around her, though. Not until I figure out what I am. Addie knows. I gotta find Addie."

"Simon, take a seat. Let me get you some water. You're kinda freakin' me out."

Simon looked at Franklin oddly, but didn't protest. He plopped down hard on the sofa and continued mumbling to himself. Franklin quickly moved into the kitchen, grabbed a glass, tossed in a few ice cubes, and turned on the tap, waiting for the glass to fill.

From the kitchen he could hear and see Simon, who now was rummaging through a pile of CDs Franklin had stacked on the coffee table. He was in the process of converting much of his music to digital files and the discs on the table were organized by genre: blues, jazz, zydeco, pop, R&B, country, classical. In order to be a good musician, he believed that he needed to listen to all kinds of music and his apartment reflected that philosophy.

Franklin returned from the kitchen and handed Simon a glass of water, which he greedily drank. He sank down into the sofa and breathed heavily. Franklin didn't want to force a conversation, so he let Simon rest, hoping that whatever he took would tire him out and Simon would simply go to sleep. Then, when they woke in a few hours, they'd have a good laugh about it and be done with it.

Ψ

When Franklin woke up and quickly looked around the room, Simon wasn't on the couch. He looked at the clock on the DVD player underneath the television. It read: 7:18.

"Simon?" he called out as he got up and moved through the house. He walked down the hallway and the bathroom door opened and Simon stepped out, wearing a towel around his waist. Franklin felt the heat from the shower as soon as the door opened, and he was relieved when he saw the Simon that he had come to know and love. Gone was the wild man who burst into his house last night.

"Hey," Franklin said. "How you feelin'?"

"Better. Much better." They stood in silence for a few awkward seconds, each one waiting for the other one to say something that would make everything all right.

"So…" Franklin began.

"Listen, Frank. About last night. I didn't mean to show up and dump my issues in your lap—"

"It's cool. Don't sweat it. We're friends—that's what friends do. Although, I don't know what the hell your issue is. You weren't making any sense last night, at all. You were talking about snakes and shadows and somebody named Addie."

Simon inhaled. "I know. None of it makes sense."

"None of what?"

Simon stepped out of the doorway of the bathroom and moved down the hallway back into the living room, with Franklin right behind him. He sat on the couch and dried his hair with the small towel draped around his neck.

"There are some things I'm going through that don't make sense. Some things I have to figure out, which is why I need your car. I have to go somewhere."

"Where?"

"That's it. I don't know. I'll know it when I get there." Simon diverted his eyes away from Franklin before he met his gaze.

"See, that's the shit I'm talking about—that don't make no sense."

"I told you I can't explain it, but there are some crazy things going on with me. Things you wouldn't believe."

"You sure you ain't high? I mean, if you are, it's cool. You know I smoke weed, no judgment."

"Damn, man, would you listen to me? I ain't on drugs." Simon leaned in closer to him. "Listen, this is real talk. I'm not on drugs and I ain't crazy. I need your help, seriously. I really need to borrow your car. I promise I'll take good care of it. I have some shit to figure out. I won't be gone long."

"How long?"

"Hmmmm, I honestly don't know. A few days, maybe. Are you gonna let me borrow it?"

Franklin sat back and studied Simon's face before speaking. "Nah, man, I can't do that," he said slowly. "You're in trouble. I'm your friend, and wherever you're going, I'm going with you."

"I can't let you do that. It could be dangerous."

"Look at these muscles," he said playfully, as he flexed his puny bicep. "I laugh in the face of danger. Ha. Ha. Ha."

"You are such a fool."

"Me, a fool? Let me tell you about this fool who was banging on my door last night."

Ψ

Simon sat in the passenger seat of Franklin's gray 2002 Nissan Maxima and pulled the seatbelt across his torso. Once he heard it click in place, he fought the urge to free himself from the restraint and call the whole thing off. What was he doing? He was in a car with his best friend about to embark on a trip with no idea of where they were going. He had some strange notion that Addie would guide him to her, but he wasn't going to tell Franklin that out of fear that he'd drive him straight to the loony bin. If he was being honest with himself, he had to admit that it all seemed insane. He was searching for a woman who, for all practical purposes, existed only in his mind.

"So, are we ready?" Franklin asked in a tone that was far too cheery for Simon, given the early hour and the gravity of the situation. Clearly, Franklin didn't understand the magnitude of their journey.

"You sure you wanna do this? We could go back in the house."

"If you're going, I'm going. Stop stalling. Tell me which way." Simon didn't know which way. He had hoped for some mystical intervention, but none came.

"What about work?"

"I'm off today."

"I'm not sure we'll be back tomorrow."

"Man, fuck Cisco. I ain't worried about him. I'll call in sick and if he wants to fire me, then fine. It ain't hard getting a job as a cook, you know what I mean?" Franklin strapped himself in and adjusted his rearview mirror. "What about Brooke? She cool with you taking off for only God knows how long?"

"I hope so. I left her a note."

"You sneakin' off on that girl? I may not be an expert on relationships, but I know women don't like their men to disappear into the night. She gon' beat yo' ass when we get back," he said playfully.

"She'll be fine. I hope."

"Where is she now?"

"At my place. She tried to leave last night, but I told her to go to sleep and she laid down. She was out within seconds, and after the night we had, I can't say I blame her. She must've been exhausted—I know I was."

"A'ight. If I know Brooke, she'll be calling you in a few minutes."

"I know."

Franklin pulled his charger out of the cup holder in the center console and plugged it into the cigarette lighter before connecting it to his phone. A red dot shone indicating the phone was charging. "So, which way?"

Simon exhaled. Franklin didn't have the first damn clue about what was he was getting himself into, but if Simon tried to get him to stay back, he knew Franklin would resist; Simon simply didn't have the energy to fight. Truth be told, Simon could use his company. If ever he needed a friend, it was now, even if he was concerned about putting Franklin in harm's way. If he could vomit a snake, read people's thoughts and emotions, kick a man across the room, and lick a bloody knife—among other things— then there was no telling what he was capable of. There was a growing darkness within him, threatening to overtake him. He could feel it. He was more afraid of himself than of anything they might find on their journey. "Get on I-10 West."

"A'ight. Sounds like a plan." Franklin put the car in reverse and backed out of his parking space. He wasted no time in hitting the city streets. "You know I can't travel without some music," he said as he clicked on the radio. "Oh, check this out, it's my new song," he said as he shoved a CD into the player. Within minutes, a smooth bass line met the subtle melody of a saxophone. Franklin smiled and bobbed his head up and down, singing out loud, looking at Simon for some approval. "You like?" he asked after a few minutes of his early morning concert. Out of obligation, Simon nodded in approval. He closed his eyes and tried to get more into the song. Franklin's voice dug deeply into the music, grabbing and unifying all chords with his moving voice. Simon wanted to revel in the song, to lose himself in its majesty; it was extraordinary, but he couldn't focus.

They hit the highway and merged with the snarled morning traffic. The sound of blaring horns and screeching tires eventually took its toll on Simon. He could feel the anger and agitation from drivers who simply wanted to move forward, in spite of the fact that the roadway had largely turned into a parking lot. The feeling was overpowering, causing his head to ache. The throbbing grew into a steady pulse that matched the tempo of the beat of the music from the radio. Simon couldn't take it anymore. He closed his eyes again and inhaled deeply, telling the noise to go away. He had to learn to control what he was feeling and not be overtaken by random emotion—someone else's emotion or pain. Like with Blaine.

"You okay?" Franklin asked after a few moments.

"Yeah, I'm cool. I hate this fucking traffic."

"Imagine how I feel. You ain't the one driving." Franklin suddenly jerked the car to the left, cutting off the driver behind him. His action was met with a loud, aggressive horn that blared right behind them as the driver laid on his horn for several seconds. Franklin looked in his rearview mirror and shot his middle finger in the air. "Fuck you!" he yelled and hit the horn on his car.

"Please don't do that," Simon pleaded. "My head is already killing me."

"A'ight, man. My bad. I'll chill."

"Thanks," he said. "You know, I really appreciate what you're doing for me. I know this is crazy."

"It's nothing you wouldn't do for me."

"I gotta tell you something, though—something serious."

Franklin shot him a concerned look. "What?"

"I want you to understand how serious this is. This isn't some kind of buddy road trip where we meet a couple of girls and drink and party and fuck our way through the country. This is me fighting for my life, trying to figure out what's going on with me. There's a lot I've been going through this past week or so that I haven't shared with you or Brooke. Some things neither of you would believe," he said as his tone became more solemn. "Although, after what Brooke saw last night, I'm sure she'd believe it at this point."

"What happened last night?"

"Before I tell you, I need you to try to be open and listen to what I'm saying. I need you to suspend your disbelief."

"College boy, what the hell does that mean?"

"It means I need you to believe whatever I tell you and whatever you see, even if it doesn't make sense. You may see some crazy shit and think your mind is playing tricks on you. I need you to believe whatever you see, even when it seems unbelievable. Can you do that? Can you trust me like that?"

"Uhhhh, okay. I can do that, but I want you to know you're giving me the heebie jeebies."

"I know. I'm freaked out, too."

"So, we're both freaked. Fine. Now, what happened with Brooke?"

Simon looked at Franklin, whose eyes were full of curiosity. He quickly thought of a hundred different ways to say what he needed to tell him; whether to broach the subject gently or to jump right into the conversation, but nothing would change the facts. *It* happened, and the words he used to tell the story wouldn't change that or soften the blow. There was no easy way to say it, so Simon spat it out. "I vomited a snake."

"Excuse me?"

"You heard me."

"I heard you, but I don't know what that means."

Simon looked out of the passenger's side window. A small boy strapped down in a car seat in a sedan made faces at him through the window. "It means what it means. I threw up a snake. Crazy, right? Last night, I felt a severe pain in my stomach, like something moving around inside me. I went into the bathroom and vomited. What came out was a live snake that slithered away." Simon spoke in a cool, easy tone. Franklin's eyes grew wide and he was seconds away from hitting the car in front of him. "Watch out!" Simon yelled. Franklin snapped his head forward and applied the brakes with a heavy foot. The car swerved and jerked to a stop, just in the nick of time.

"Damn," Franklin said between rapid breaths. "That was close."

"Too close. I'm not trying to die on this trip."

"Me either. I got a big music career ahead of me. I'm sorry. I'll pay more attention, but you can't say some shit like that and not expect me to react; that's a helluva story. You know how I feel about snakes."

"It's not a story. It's for real." Franklin eyes were filled with wonder. He searched Simon's face for the punchline to his joke, but none came.

"You're serious, aren't you?"

"Remember what I just told you? I need you to believe me. If you can't believe me, then there's no point in you going with me."

"A'ight. I got ya," he said as he focused his attention on the roadway ahead. "So, you tellin' me that a real, live snake crawled out of yo' mouth and slithered away? How the fuck does that happen?" By the sound of Franklin's voice, Simon could tell that he was struggling through his incredulity to reach a place where he could accept Simon's word at face value. Simon couldn't blame his doubt. Hell, if the shoe was on the other foot and Franklin told him the same wild story, he'd struggle to believe him, too.

"I don't know. But this trip will explain a lot."

"This is gonna be wild if what you're telling me is true."

"There's a lot more I need to tell you, too." Simon looked at Franklin and, for the first time, saw on his face the seriousness warranted by their situation. Franklin turned up the radio and let the chatter of the morning talk show hosts fill the car, easing the tension that was building between the two friends. The radio hosts spoke of Christmas toy drives for children and offered listeners the opportunity to donate money for families in need of a traditional Christmas dinner. "Before we hit the road, I need to make a pit stop. Take the Basille exit and head past downtown."

"No problem," Franklin said as he flicked on his signal light, looked into the mirror, and forced his way from the center lane to the far left one. "At least this gets us out of traffic."

"I don't know why I didn't think of this before now."

"Think of what?"

"I'll tell you in a minute."

"If you want me to start believing you, then you gotta start telling me everything. No secrets." He looked at Simon. "I'm serious. I wanna know everything you know."

"Deal."

Franklin took the exit and ended up on the highway feeder road. Once he reached Basille Street, he took a left, underneath the freeway, and headed toward downtown.

"For real, though," he began, "you'll tell me if you got another snake in you, right? I just had my car cleaned. I don't need no nasty shit all over my seats." They looked at each other and started laughing. The laughter broke through the tension, carving a path to an easier conversation. They laughed like they were at a comedy show, with deep, hearty chuckles.

But, even though they smiled politely and made uneasy jokes, both men knew this was no laughing matter.

≈ CHAPTER 16

S imon stood on the front porch of Clara's house and took a few seconds to collect himself before he rang the bell. Much had transpired in the hours that had passed since his last visit. After last night, he wasn't thrilled about returning here or even sure that Clara would see him. Yet, he felt calm, almost settled, even as unsettling thoughts jolted his head. What if she had been seriously injured? Maybe she had been hospitalized. Whatever had happened was his fault. Guilt tried to creep into his consciousness, but he forced himself to put it aside; there was no room for it inside him, he carried enough weight.

He had returned. He knew she had answers, answers to questions that, even since last night, had become more troubling. She was more than a simple, part-time psychic or mediocre medium. She had real power, even if she didn't know it. He felt it last night, and it was more intense than he had expected from her. Maybe, just maybe, she would help.

Slowly, the door creaked open and a head of uncombed hair appeared from inside. Then, the door opened fully.

"Simon," Clara said, her voice deep and serious. "It's very early, dah-ling. I haven't even had time to put on my face." She was playful in her words, but her tone was something else. Her face was smooth; her beauty, natural.

"I am so sorry to disturb you—"

"It's fine. I knew you'd be back."

"I really need your help. I'm…afraid. Something happened."

She inhaled. "I know, chile. I know." Her eyes cut across Franklin, who stood quietly at Simon's side.

"This is my friend—"

"Franklin," she said, before he could properly introduce them. Franklin cut his eyes back to her and Simon.

"How do you know my name?" he asked, his voice quivering, ever so slightly.

She smiled and rubbed her hands over her red silk robe, straightening out the fabric. She stepped aside and swung open the door.

"Dah-ling, I know a lot of things. Don't stand there. Come on in." She opened the door and allowed them to pass into her home. Franklin followed Simon and when he stepped into the foyer, he looked around the grand hallway, his face full of the same wonder Simon experienced the day before. "Go on in there," she said as she pointed to a room on the right, but neither man moved. "I'd take you to the solarium, but we had a little trouble there last night, didn't we, Simon?" She made no attempt to mask her displeasure, which showed across her face. Simon smiled, uneasily. "Shall we?" she said as she moved into the formal living room, her voice trailing behind her. Her walk carried the same saunter Simon saw last night, but the movement of her hips was subdued, lethargic. She entered the room and took a seat in a high-backed chair that more than resembled a throne. The wooden chair was painted black with gold trim and its cushioned bottom looked woven from expensive fabric.

Simon entered the room, his heart filled with trepidation; Franklin trailed behind him. They lingered toward the back, half-waiting for permission to sit on the fine furniture, and half-afraid to move.

"I wouldn't normally let gentlemen into my house without being properly covered, but these are extraordinary times." She crossed her legs and moved the robe over her legs to cover her exposed thighs.

"Extraordinary times? What do you mean?" Franklin asked.

"Come. Have a seat," she said and waved her arm toward the sofa, offering them rest. When they sat, she immediately focused her attention on Simon. Meeting her gaze, the attraction to her he remembered from last night entered his mind, but he had to focus.

"What happened last night?" Franklin asked as if he had been left out of a grand secret. His question may have been simple, but its underlying meaning was not lost to Clara.

Her face suddenly went sour. "Many things happened. So many."

"I don't understand what's happening to me. Can you help me figure it out? Can you read me again?" He reached both his arms out toward her, trying to take her hands, but she rebuffed his efforts.

"Not hardly. Last night was more than I could handle. My back still hurts."

"Your back?" Franklin asked with a goofy grin on his face; the same grin that took over his face each time Simon told him about a past sexual conquest.

They both ignored him. "What did you see, then? I need to know. Tell me." Before the question fully left his lips, Simon caught a whiff of her rising fear. It was dour, like old musk, but he immediately recognized the scent. It was the same scent he smelled from the thugs who tried to rob him. The same scent he'd smelled from Brooke last night.

"You already know. You saw what I saw. It was the future. It was the past. It was the present."

"Stop talking in riddles!" Simon's outburst rattled the room, causing some of the glass figurines to rattle on the shelf. His own fear punched right through the calm he had worn all morning.

"What the hell was that?" Franklin asked as he jumped to his feet. "Earthquake?"

"Sit down, Franklin," Clara said calmly. His eyes cut back and forth between Simon and Clara. "It was nothing…by comparison." Her eyes fixed on Simon, and his on her.

"Comparison, to what?" Once again, Franklin was ignored.

"I'm sorry. I didn't mean to yell." Simon closed his eyes and shook his head from side to side. "Please help me. What's going on with me?"

"Honestly, I don't know much. Not much more than you do. When I told you last night that there was darkness in you, I meant it. Something is eating you from the inside out. Something evil." Simon gasped; although he had already accepted that fact, hearing it from her validated his feelings. "Lately, I'm sure you've been having cravings, almost a bloodlust for…power—that's the darkness inside you. You've always been ruled by your baser emotions, such as lust," she said as she pointed at his groin, "but I knew that much about you as soon as you stepped onto my veranda. It was so thick I could almost smell it. That's how we connected so easily. From time to time, I've been ruled by lust, too."

"What does that mean?"

"It means that you've got to control your emotions, and not succumb to your base desires. Control them, or they will control you; like what just happened."

"But, *what* am I?"

"I can't answer that question. I don't know what you are. I know that you are…powerful."

"In what sense?"

"I don't know the answer to that one, either. You're special, Simon. And you have special gifts, but, you already know that. All I know is that your gifts will either be a blessing or a curse to all of us, but it is up to you to decide. They will come for you, and you will be forced to choose. Darkness has a rightful claim to you, but so does light. Always choose the light. In the darkest of times, remember love."

"Are y'all both high?" Franklin said. "What is this shit y'all are talkin'?" His face contorted with confusion.

"I'll explain later, Franklin. Be quiet." Simon's agitated voice cut Franklin off before his next sentence.

"That's really all I know." She stood up, putting a period at the end of the conversation. "I really must get myself together. I have a gentleman caller coming by to take me to breakfast in the French Quarter. You'll have to excuse me."

As much as Simon wanted to press the issue, he knew that she had closed herself to him. She was afraid; the scent had grown stronger. She was afraid of many things. Of him. For the world. Her prescience of the future overwhelmed him with sadness.

When they reached the door, she opened it and politely smiled. "Simon, death and life are in the power of the tongue. Always remember that, dah-ling." She reached her arms around the back of her neck and unlatched a necklace with a crescent moon and some odd geometric shapes. "Here, put this on."

"What is it?"

"It's for protection. My grandmother gave it to me when I was a girl. Never take it off. I think you're gonna need it." Simon didn't question her and let her latch the necklace around his neck.

"Thank you," he said as they walked out of the house. Simon heard the door slam shut, and, even through the closed door, he could hear her rapid breathing and pounding heartbeat.

eath and life are in the power of the tongue. The phrase stayed with Simon all day, even as the miles that separated them from New Orleans grew. They had driven for hours, with no real sense of direction, save for Simon's intuition. Occasionally, mixed in with the sound of the rubber hitting the road and the beat of the music emanating from the radio station that Franklin refused to turn down, Simon heard whispers—whispers that he hoped would guide him to Addie, even though he couldn't altogether be sure of the messages. A few times, he thought he heard directions like "left" or "right" or "forward," and he followed those commands, but other times, the whispers were much more vague. For most of the trip, Simon relied on his feelings, his gut reaction to guide them. He was trying to learn to *sense* things, willing himself to connect to a world that existed all around them, but remained unseen. If he concentrated hard enough, he knew he could see it and feel it, too. At least that's what he hoped. There were times when he felt in tune with things around him, but the feelings were fleeting. He was too distracted by the loud music, by cars passing by, and by Clara's cryptic words.

They had driven through Baton Rouge, Opelousas, Alexandria, Monroe, and Natchitoches and now were cruising down I-20 in Marshall, Texas. Much to Simon's surprise, for most of the trip,

Franklin was quiet, which was not his usual demeanor. At work, Franklin's mouth would rattle so often that Simon seriously thought about buying a muzzle for him. But not this time. His silence was eerie. He didn't speak much and certainly didn't complain about anything. He didn't complain about the lack of direction. He didn't complain when they drove down a back road in Shreveport that ended up taking them in a circle. He didn't complain when Simon stopped for coffee a couple of times along the highway. In fact, he had been unusually silent since they left Clara's. He had only spent a few moments singing to the latest pop song on the radio or perfecting the vocals on his newest song, which left a gaping hole of silence in the car where conversation should have been. When he did speak, his sentences were curt; usually about directions or necessities, such as food or gas. The few times Simon tried to engage Franklin in real conversation about his passion—his music—he only offered a few words, an incontrovertible sign that he wasn't ready to chat. Simon had to respect that. After all he had heard and been exposed to, Franklin clearly needed time to process. After they left Clara's, Simon told Franklin everything that had happened to him. Everything— even about ingesting blood. Now, Franklin's whole reality seemed to be shifting. Simon only hoped Franklin would come back to him and not be so freaked out that he could never look at him again. Simon longed for one of Franklin's sarcastic comments or tongue lashings over what Franklin often referred to as his "questionable" taste in music. More than that, he needed to tell his friend that he wasn't a freak. He needed Franklin to tell him that everything was going to be all right.

As they rode down the highway, Simon grabbed his cell phone and checked it to see if Brooke had called or sent a text. She had done neither. Almost more than anything, even more than wanting

Franklin to talk, he wanted to call her or send her a message, but she needed her space. He'd be lucky if she ever spoke to him again. Like Franklin, she needed space to absorb everything. It wasn't every day that a live snake crawled out of your boyfriend's mouth.

Simon drove down the Frankston Highway, fifteen miles south of the East Texas town of Tyler, and followed the signs toward Lake Palestine. He had been driving for almost twelve hours, taking a few breaks here and there, and he was tired and needed to rest. Franklin was passed out in the back seat, snoring occasionally. Simon figured he'd park by the lake and get some rest, hoping the lapping sounds of the water would relax him enough to get some sleep so that they could take up the journey in the morning. It seemed odd to him to be so tired when it was not even eight o'clock, but with the night he had just had, it didn't surprise him.

He pulled into the resort compound as darkness fell and he followed the signs with arrows pointing toward "lodging." Using his phone, he had already made a reservation for a room with two twin-sized beds. The seventy dollars he spent on the room would be well worth the cost. At first, he contemplated finding a quiet spot and sleeping in the car all night, but ruled against that when he Googled the cost of the room, and it was well within his limited budget.

When he made the reservations, he conveniently ignored the two pleading texts from Brooke asking him to call her. She had also left a voicemail message that Simon replayed repeatedly, only to hear the sound of her voice. The worry that filled her voice touched him deeply, reminding him of the love he held for her. A part of him desperately wanted to return the call, but he couldn't—he wouldn't—at least not until he had answers and could assure her that she was in no danger from him. He would never forgive himself if she came to harm at his hands.

Franklin grabbed his bag and a few other items from the trunk of the car, and, once they checked into the room, he quickly sprawled out across the bed.

"All that shit y'all were talking…I don't believe," he finally said. Simon was sitting on the edge of the bed unlacing his shoes. He looked up at Franklin, happy to hear the sound of his voice. "And, I'm sorry for being such a drag on the drive. I got a lot of shit going on in my head. Plus, I was tired as fuck. I barely slept last night. But, I still don't believe y'all."

"It's cool, man. I know this is unbelievable."

Franklin sat up on the edge of the bed and faced Simon. "Really though, what you think is going on with you? I still think you got hold to some bad crack, or something, and now you trippin'. I ain't seen you do nothin' crazy."

Simon chuckled. "Wait around. I'm sure that'll change."

"Whatever, dude. You tryna freak me out."

"Why the hell would I do that? You felt what happened at Clara's."

"That could've been a big-ass truck going by or a minor earthquake. Stranger things have happened. Why don't you do something now? Make the room shake."

Simon was growing frustrated with Franklin's badgering. He wanted his friend to believe him and thought that he did. Simon was tired and didn't feel like going through a big show to prove something that should've already been proven.

"It doesn't work like that. I can't control it. It just…happens."

"Bullshit. I ought to take my ass back to New Orleans 'cause all of this is bullshit. You know it and I know it."

"Fine. Believe what you want. I'm tired and I need to get some sleep. Your ass slept in the car. I didn't."

"Look, man," Franklin said with a heavy tone, "I'm your friend. Why don't you tell me what's really going on? Who you runnin' from? What you do?"

"I ain't running from nobody. I'm running *to* someone—Addie."

"Right. This mysterious woman who's been communicating with you in dreams." Franklin rolled his eyes. "Bullshit."

"You know what? You don't have to believe me. Like I said, I'm tired and I need to get some sleep."

"It ain't time to sleep. It's time for some answers. I mean, you practically break down my door last night and drag me all around the states of Louisiana and Texas, and now you want to sleep. Fuck that." Franklin jumped to his feet. His deep voice thumped across the room, fueled by his agitation.

"What the fuck do you want from me, Franklin? I've told you everything I know—everything."

"You've told me shit."

"Why can't you accept what I told you, huh? Why do you always have to be so damned argumentative?"

"'Cause this shit you tellin' me don't make sense. You been watchin' too much damn Harry Potter."

Simon shook his head from side-to-side. "This is pointless."

"If you can do all that you said you can do, why don't you fuckin' try, instead of sittin' there tryin' to convince me that you're some dark lord."

"I never said that."

"What you said was some bullshit. B-U-L-L-S-H-I-T. Now, I want the real story. I've gone along with all this shit for as long as I can. What's going on?"

"You heard Clara. You were there."

"I don't give a fuck about Clara or what she said. I don't know that bitch."

"Would you watch your mouth?"

"Or what? You gonna spit a snake out yo' mouth or make the earth move? Or, maybe you gon' pick me up by my collar and throw me across the parking lot. Come on then, Superman. I'm waiting." Franklin stood near the door with his arms outstretched, wiggling his fingers as if to say *bring it*.

Simon was taken aback by Franklin's level of anger. His voice quivered when he spoke, and his eyes had tightened into little slits. He puffed out his little chest like he was ready to do battle, but to what end, Simon didn't know. He wasn't going to fight Franklin nor was he going to argue with him anymore. It had already taken too much out of him, and he could feel his head beginning to hurt again, which was never a good sign for him.

"We can talk about this in the morning. I'm going to bed." Simon kicked his shoes under the bed and climbed under the covers. "Would you mind turning off the light," he said as he rolled over.

"Yeah, whatever."

♆

When Franklin woke up at 2:38 in the morning, the room was quiet and dark, except for a slice of light cutting in from the room's door, which was cracked slightly open. Cold air seeping in from outside chilled the room, and Franklin could see his breath in the air when he exhaled. He sat up and looked at Simon's bed, which was empty. The covers were tossed about, and one of the pillows was on the floor. The necklace Clara had given him was on the nightstand and an eerie silence blanketed the room. Even though it was early morning and he knew that most people were sleeping, the night still felt unsettled, like there was more to come. He called out Simon's name, but no answer came. He looked around the room and saw Simon's shoes in the exact place he had left them, but Simon was nowhere to be seen. He got up and moved to the door, closing it. The bathroom door was pulled shut and the light in the room was out. Slowly and cautiously, he moved over to it, carefully tiptoeing across the faded carpet as if he expected tiny pieces of broken glass to be embedded in the fibers.

"Simon?" he called out again, a question in his voice. He lightly knocked on the bathroom door, but there was no response. He placed his hand on the knob and slowly turned. It was unlocked. Finally, he pushed open the door and turned on the light. The room was empty and quiet. He breathed a sigh of relief. He half-expected to see Simon unconscious on the floor.

He reached over the table and turned on a light switch. Everything about the room was in place, except there was a half-empty bottle of vodka on the table a few inches from the lamp. He looked around the room for a note, for something to indicate where Simon was. He turned his attention to the nightstand and saw Simon's cell phone. Simon wouldn't travel far without that. Then, he noticed his jacket lying across the back of the chair in the corner. His shoes. His jacket. His cell phone. Yet, no Simon.

Franklin walked over to the window and pulled back the curtain. Across the parking lot and near the water he could see a figure sitting on a bench at the water's edge. He looked deeper into the night to ascertain who it might be and was reasonably confident that it was Simon. The shape of the head and the posture seemed to match Simon. Franklin threw on his jeans, a shirt, and his shoes and grabbed his jacket.

The cold air slapped him hard across the face when he stepped outside of the room. He looked around and didn't see or hear anyone else, nor did he see light coming from the other row of rooms that faced the lake. As he hurried across the parking lot, loose gravel crunching beneath his feet, he wondered what the hell Simon was doing outside in the cold. It must've been thirty degrees.

"Simon," Franklin said with care, as he rounded the bench where Simon sat. "You okay?" Simon didn't respond; instead, he lifted a plastic cup to his lips, a cup that no doubt contained vodka. He was alone on the bench, wearing a thin white T-shirt and a pair of jeans, with no socks or shoes. Moonlight glistened off the cool water, partially illuminating Simon's stone-cold face. "Where are your shoes?" Franklin asked, putting his hand on Simon's shoulder. "Dude, you're wet. Wassup?"

"Hey, Franklin," he said in a light voice. "I was out here thinking, resting. You know."

"All I know is that you gon' catch yo' death of cold, if you don't get yo' ass back in the room and put on some dry clothes. It's cold as fuck out here."

"I'm fine. Really. Except my body is tingling." Simon looked up and Franklin noticed the distant look in his eyes. His eyes were red and his gaze detached. Franklin took a seat next to him.

"That tingling is probably hypothermia setting in."

"Nah, that's not it. I'm not cold. In fact, I'm burning up." Simon took Franklin's hand and placed it on his forehead. "I'm wet because I'm sweating."

"You must be gettin' the flu. We need to get you to a doctor before you pass out."

"A doctor can't help me; I'm not sick—at least not like that." Simon took another sip and passed the cup to Franklin, who quickly took a swig. The breeze skimming across the cold water chilled Franklin's bones, and he hoped the liquor would provide some internal warmth.

"Man, I'm sorry for earlier. I was an ass. I didn't mean to go off like that. You know how I get when I'm tired."

"It's fine. I understand your feelings." Simon's voice settled into a creepy coolness. He spoke lightly, in a sharp whisper that seemed to cause the atmosphere to vibrate slightly. But, for Franklin, there was something else in his voice, too. Something that chilled him even more than winter's night air. Underneath the coolness of his voice was a texture that didn't even sound like Simon. The whisper covered the growing rasp.

"Do you hear that? Feel that?" he said as he looked around and up in the night sky. Simon didn't reply. He continued looking off in the distance, beyond the lake. "Man, something doesn't feel right out here. Let's go back inside." Franklin stood up and nudged Simon in the arm. "You hear me? Let's go in."

"Okay." Franklin moved to the back side of the bench as Simon slowly stood up. Franklin took a few steps toward the hotel and then turned around to look for Simon, who was now moving toward the lake.

"What are you doing?" Franklin asked in a panic.

Simon turned to face him. A discomforting smile spread across his face and his eyes went black for a second. Franklin gasped and blinked hard. In the silvery glow of the moonlight, he couldn't be certain what he saw.

"Get...get away from the water. Let's go inside."

"You wanted to see something?" Simon asked as he continued walking toward the water, leaving smoldering rocks beneath his bare feet. Franklin's eyes grew wide as the smoke rose from Simon's prints in the dirt. This time, he was certain that his eyes weren't playing tricks on him. A hard lump formed in his throat, making it difficult to breathe. He felt his knees shake, and he wasn't sure his legs would support his weight. He wanted to sit down on the bench, but he was frozen in place. He watched with nervous anticipation as Simon approached the water's edge. Franklin thought maybe he was approaching the water to cool his feet, but when Simon reached the edge of the water he stopped and faced Franklin.

"I want to show you something," Simon said in a rasping voice as he turned and faced the lake. He put his left foot forward as if to test the temperature of the lake, but Franklin quickly realized that wasn't his intention; he was simply toying with him. Then, Simon took a bold step *onto* the lake. And then another step. And another one. And another one.

Franklin had to steady himself to keep from collapsing when he realized…Simon was walking on water!

ᴴCHAPTER 18

Eli and Rebecca stood in the foyer of Clara's house and looked around the room.

"He was here, Mother. I can feel him." Eli closed his eyes and let his head fall back so that his face pointed toward the high ceiling. "I can really feel him." Rebecca smiled and proudly cupped Eli's face with her hand, but she did not speak. She listened to Eli's words cautiously. She loved her son, but she had learned to never blindly trust his notoriously unreliable *feelings*. He often misinterpreted his emotions, which led to false proclamations that hid the truth. He was still young and would learn to hone his talent one day, she often told herself. He was undoubtedly powerful but often unfocused. Power was his birthright, but he remained the child of a lesser god.

Rebecca released her grip and took a few steps, meticulously surveying the room and everything around her. She wouldn't be caught unguarded in a house that she knew had secrets. Deep secrets. All remained quiet in the house, except for the clicking sound of her heels on the hardwood floor as she sauntered about, trying to discover its treasures.

"The question, my dear son, then becomes, where is he now?"

"Don't worry, Mother. We'll find him. After all, he is my brother and our connection to each other grows every second."

Rebecca offered a tiny, worried smile and moved into the formal living room. She stood in the center of the area, looking around inquisitively. Her attention was drawn to the weathered bookshelf built into the wall on the left; she was attracted to its sheer enormity. The case was stacked from top to bottom with books and odd trinkets. When she was near it, she ran her fingertip across its ancient wood, which was splintered in several places on several shelves. Scratches, undoubtedly made by an unruly child with a sharp object, gave the shelf a thrift-store feel, despite the splendor of its construction. She tilted her head to better view the titles that were etched on the spines of some of the books. She didn't notice anything unusual. *The Bible. The Koran. War and Peace. Gone With the Wind. To Kill a Mockingbird. Beloved. The Color Purple.* There were a few books on the history of New Orleans, on voodoo, and on the slave trade, and there were dozens of fictitious works written by contemporary authors that remained unknown to Rebecca.

Rebecca moved over to the fireplace and looked at the trinkets and figurines that adorned the mantelpiece. Their faces seemed to focus on her and Rebecca half-expected them to move. They didn't feel like ordinary store-bought knick-knacks to her, and they gave her reason to pause; however, when nothing happened, she quickly grew bored with the toys and moved on.

She touched the back of the black throne-like chair and quickly withdrew her hand. "There is power in this house. I can feel it vibrating. It is subtle, so very subtle."

"I can feel it, too," Eli added anxiously, in that voice he used when he sought her approval; that tone grated on her nerves, but she always allowed him to speak, never chastising him over it.

As they strolled throughout the room, a voice called out to them from the doorway. "Can I help you? How did you get in here?" Rebecca turned her head toward the voice that belonged to Donna, who stood in the doorway with a scowl deeply carved into her brow. She set down her bags of groceries. "Who are you?"

"Who are you?" Eli asked impetuously, snarling. He took a quick step toward Donna, but Rebecca extended her arm to block his forward momentum.

"I am Rebecca Saint and this is my son, Eli. We knocked on the door and it came open," Rebecca stated in her honey-sweet voice.

"That's not possible. I locked that door myself."

"Well, here we are anyway," Rebecca said, smiling.

"What do you want?"

"What can you tell me about this lovely house?"

"What?"

"You heard her," Eli interjected. His boorish comment didn't sit well with Donna and in response she folded her arms across her chest and shifted her weight.

"Please forgive my son. It has been a long day. We are looking for the owner of this house. Is he home?"

"*She's* not here right now. Who shall I tell her stopped by?"

"When do you expect her to return?"

"I can't say."

"You can't, or you won't?" Eli asked, impatience digging into his voice. Donna looked at him, suddenly concerned. In an instant, her indignation turned to fear. "I think you need to leave before I call the police."

"No need for that, *Donna*," Rebecca said.

"How do you know my name?" Rebecca quickly glided over to the doorway and Donna took a few clumsy steps backward, bumping into and then bouncing off the wall. Eli was suddenly upon her, circling and sniffing her like a wolf.

"Let me play with her, Mother. She has a lot of years on her, but I could still teach her a few things. I have a special game, a new game I want to try. Do you want to play with me, Donna?" he asked, as he pushed her hard against the wall and then cupped one of her breasts. Donna's body recoiled at his touch.

"Most women do not survive your games, Eli." Rebecca's comments were not meant to strike fear into Donna or to be boastful; her statement was a simple matter of fact.

"I'll be gentle this time. I promise." Eli stuck out his forked tongue and licked her neck, slowly. He ran his finger gently up her forearm, leaving a trail of seared skin. Her body shuddered and the rank smell of smoldering skin wafted into the air. Donna tried to scream, but Eli's other hand around her neck stifled her sounds. The rattling of her bones could be heard over her gasps for breath and over her burning skin.

"That is enough, Eli. We do not have time for this," Rebecca said, interrupting. "Tell me, Donna, when will *Clara* return?" she asked as Eli relinquished his death grip on her neck. Rebecca tried to probe Donna's thoughts, but was only able to go deep enough to pull out a name, Clara's name. "Interesting. What are you, some kind of witch?"

Donna looked at her in confusion and shook her head wildly from side to side. "Wha-what do you mean? I'm not a witch."

Rebecca paused and rolled her eyes from Donna's feet to the top of her head. "You speak the truth. I sense no power from you, yet, oddly, you are protected by some kind of spell. You have consorted with witches, have you not?" Again, Donna shook her head *no*. "It is of little consequence, though. This power that protects you is rudimentary, at best. Amateurish."

"I don't know what you're talking about."

"Let me be clear. I do not care about you, Donna, but if you value your life you will tell me when Clara will return to this house."

"I...I don't know. I swear."

Rebecca paused and stared at Donna with her cold eyes. "Well then," she said as she took a few steps away from her, "we shall wait." She moved deeper into the room and took a seat in the black throne. "I love this chair," she said as she ensconced herself in it. She took a few seconds to find the perfect sitting position, adjusting herself until she found a regal position. "Donna, be a dear and fetch us some tea."

"Yes...yes, ma'am." Donna covered her burn marks with her hand. "Right away." Donna stumbled a few steps, moving cautiously around Eli.

"And, Donna," Rebecca said.

"Yes?"

"I advise against doing anything improper like trying to run away or calling for help. I assure you it would end disastrously for you and your whole family." The sweetness of Rebecca's voice belied the threat of her words, but it was clear by the expression on Donna's face that she would do exactly as she was told.

After a few moments, Donna returned with a fresh batch of tea served on Clara's finest china. The tray shook in her trembling hands, but she was able to serve it without spilling a drop. When she turned to walk away, Rebecca stopped her.

"Where are you going, Donna?"

"Back...to my work."

"You work for us now, and I want you to stand right there in that spot and keep us company."

Donna stood for hours.

♆

As soon as Clara crossed the threshold of her home, she knew something wasn't right. Instantly, her breathing quickened. She set her shopping bag on the floor near her feet, slowly closed the door, and removed her big red hat with the wide brim. She carefully removed her coat and laid it across her bag on the floor.

"Donna?" she called out. Her voice echoed throughout the house but returned empty, unanswered. The house was quiet, too quiet, and devoid of almost any usual signs of life. No music playing. No voices from the television. Not even Donna's customary hum as she moved about the house. Even the air was still, eerily undisturbed.

Clara's eyes carefully scrutinized her surroundings, darting around the room, trying to take in as much as she could. She didn't see anything unusual; yet, the warning in her heart remained. The hairs on her forearms stood on end, validating her suspicion that something was dreadfully wrong. Even the illumination in the house was unusually dim, except for an odd glow reaching out from the back. Clara knew Donna well enough to know that she didn't like a dark house, and if she had to leave, Clara knew that Donna knew her well enough to leave enough lights on so that the house wasn't shrouded in shadows.

Shadows. That's when Clara really noticed the shadows. In every corner they seemed menacing, almost threatening in ways she couldn't define. There seemed to be shadows everywhere, even in places there shouldn't have been.

"Donna? Where are you?" she called out again and took a few guarded steps toward the living room, which was empty. Even though the room was empty, she still felt a presence; something that didn't belong there had disturbed the energy of the room. Cleverly tucked underneath the silence of the room was an almost undetectable hissing sound. It was faint and familiar; she had heard the sound before—when she read Simon. Then, it was so light that it simply blended into the background. But hearing it again, she instantly remembered it. It was there, in her vision, and now it was in the house, everywhere. The sound was distinct.

Her attention turned toward the back of the house as she took a few more steps, moving stealthily so that her heels did not click against the floor. The deeper she moved into the house the more she felt the same energy and the hissing sound grew. The air became less settled the farther she went. It was a different vibe than the energy she usually felt from her ancestors, who had left pieces of themselves in the wood, the walls, the furniture and other fixtures. This energy was far more kinetic than the spiritual energy sustained in the slave ornaments that adorned her house. The energy usually emitted by the house and its possessions was a comfort, often in her time of need; but *this* energy was disturbing, malevolent. Clara raised her hand to her throat and clasped the gold protection necklace she had made for herself and moved toward the solarium. Whatever awaited her was there. She could sense it.

When she reached the room, the stench of whatever it was suddenly slapped her hard across the face; the smell was so strong that it forced her to cough, announcing her presence to the *thing* that occupied her house, even though she knew no announcement was needed. From the moment she entered, she had been aware of it, as she was certain it had been aware of her.

When she peered into the room, shock gripped her tightly around the neck and she swallowed a hard lump of fear that almost stuck in her throat. As a spiritual medium and from living in New Orleans, Clara had felt evil before, in many different ways and forms, but what she felt now churned her guts. Her innards felt as if they were on fire. Instantly, she recognized that the evil in this room was pure, undiluted. Her eyes widened as she saw Donna's naked body hanging in mid-air in the corner, her arms extended as if held in place by an invisible crucifix; her head bowed. She hung several feet in the air, her head inches away from the ceiling. Trails of dried blood snaked from the corners of her mouth and her puffy flesh was stained with burn marks. Clara wasn't sure if she was conscious.

In front of Donna was a fiery shadow thing that must've stood eight feet tall. It was hooded, with yellow snake-like eyes. Most of its body did not appear to be corporeal, save for a few bones; she could see through the shadows that comprised its torso; still, it had power. The only thing about it that seemed tangible was its dreaded hood. Yet, the stench that she knew could only come from him covered the room, stained the carpet, embedded itself into the walls, and latched onto objects; claiming the room's possessions for itself, as if it was sentient. Clara's throat constricted, in part to prevent the smell from entering her body, and in part, out of pure fear.

Her heart grew heavy, like it would sink out of her body, when she realized that she had seen this shadowthing before; she had seen it when she read Simon. It was there, in her mind and all around Simon. In her reading, it wasn't in the form it was in now; instead, it was everywhere, ubiquitous, like air.

Clara scanned the room. A woman sat in her chair, her silhouette visible. Across from her was a man she recognized. Simon. Clara backed away, slowly.

"Come in, Clara." The woman didn't even turn in Clara's direction, but her voice floated across Clara's ears, compelling her to move, in spite of Clara's strong desire to stand firmly planted where she stood. "Do not be afraid of us." The woman swiveled around slowly and faced Clara with a frightful delight painted on her face. Panic seized Clara when she lost complete control of her own limbs and her body moved forward on its own, one hard step at a time. "Do not fight. Come. Join us." Clara's body moved mechanically and her joints popped like an unoiled machine as she struggled for control; a wasted effort. Her body continued moving forward, despite her resistance. Her forward motion was labored, her movements rough.

"So, you're the one," Eli said as he eyed her up and down lustfully. As soon as he spoke, Clara recognized that he was not Simon. He was someone else; yet, they were identical. She quickly wondered if Simon knew he had a twin brother. Eli was sitting in front of the woman and then, suddenly, stood in front of Clara, sniffing at her. "I can smell him on you, *in* you. Mother," he said, turning to face Rebecca, "this one has touched Simon; she has been inside him. She's stained with his power. I can use her to find him." Clara stared into his hateful eyes and trembled as Rebecca's face exploded into wicked delight.

"How wonderful, my dear son," she said as she stood and clapped wildly. Then, she turned her attention to Eetwidomayloh. "I told you my darling Eli would not fail you. He could never fail us."

"I had no doubt." Eetwidomayloh's voice filled the space of the room, his low voice rumbling like thunder.

"We will deliver Simon to you, and all shall be as planned," Rebecca continued. "We will have dominion over this world and will open The Great Gate so that you may enter, permanently, and not just in shadows."

A booming sound that Clara could only assume was a laugh slipped from underneath the hood, shaking the entire house. "Make it so," he said. The windows in the solarium rattled mightily when he spoke, and the horrible hissing sound fluttered beneath his rumble. Then, the bones that gave him form cracked, collapsed in on themselves, and turned to powder, and the shadows that bonded his bones together in this world retreated into the dark recesses of the room, and he vanished; the powder blowing across the room.

"Clara, do you understand the power before you? Are you the one that spelled this poor creature?" Rebecca said, referring to Donna. "You tried to protect her from harm, from us with this little trinket?" Rebecca held in her hands a necklace identical to the one she had given Simon. Clara did not answer. "As you can see, your power is feeble and we are strong."

"What—what do you want from me?" Clara's voice was strong and curt. Her courage, in some small measure, had returned to her when the shadows vanished, taking the hissing with them.

Rebecca calmly walked over to Clara and eyed the shining necklace that was hanging around her neck; digging into her cleavage. She let a rambunctious laugh escape from her mouth that created sparks in the atmosphere.

"Do you think this silly thing will protect you?" Swiftly, she snatched it from Clara's neck and tossed it onto the floor, grinding it beneath her heel. "It will not. Only we can protect you. Or destroy you."

"Where is my brother?" Eli screamed, as if he could no longer remain silent.

Clara's body tensed, but she remained silent.

"I did not hear an answer, Clara. I must warn you that my son has a temper, and I can only keep him *leashed* so long. It is in your best interest to tell us where Simon is. I could pull it out of your mind, but I would much rather you told us voluntarily."

"I-I-I don't know where Simon is. I don't even really know him." Even in the clutch of an increasing fear, Clara spoke clearly, defiantly.

"What was he doing here, then?" Eli asked. "You at least know that."

"He came for a...reading. He thought he was being haunted."

"Silly boy," Rebecca said, more to herself than to Clara. "Silly, silly boy. What did you tell him, witch? What did you show him?"

Again, Clara did not speak.

"Let me rip it out of her mind, Mother. We don't have time for this. Simon is out there alone. He needs us."

Rebecca sighed audibly, rolling her eyes. *This witch may have more power than we know. We cannot risk entering her head unless we bind her powers and we certainly do not have time for that.*

But Mother, I can do it. I know I can. I am strong.

We cannot risk you this close to your ascension. I forbid it.

Clara tried to maintain her calm when she realized she was privy to a conversation Rebecca and Eli were having with each other in their heads. Never before had she been a mind-reader; she had always been more empathic, but the presence of their power in the room had obviously strengthened hers. The information she gathered she could use to her advantage. They wouldn't probe her mind out of fear. They feared her. Clara didn't quite know why, but they did.

"Clara, look at this unsightly woman before you. Look at how she hangs there, almost lifeless. She is being disciplined for forcing me to repeat myself. I never liked that. If you value your life you will learn to answer all of my questions, the first time, or Eli will rape you in ways you cannot even conceive. Am I clear?"

The word *rape* burned fear so deeply into Clara that she felt it in her bones. It felt like fire burning her from the inside out. She hoped it was only a threat, but Rebecca's words carried weight, real power. Her threat was a promise; yet, Clara wasn't ready to capitulate. If she told them what she knew, she had no doubt they'd kill her, perhaps torture her—without a second thought. She had to use her cunning. Her survival depended on it. Her mind raced.

"Now, Clara, what did you show or tell Simon?"

"Nothing. I mean, I couldn't—he wouldn't let me. He was closed." Rebecca and Eli circled her, displaying their usual predatory posture.

"She's lying, Mother. She's a lying bitch!"

"Eli—"

"I know, I know, but now isn't the time for delicacy, Mother. This woman—this mortal—is all that stands between me and my brother, between me and our crown. She knows where he is. I know she does. We need to know what she told him."

"You are right, my son. You are right."

The smile on Eli's face deeply disturbed Clara. Whatever he had planned for her, he planned on enjoying it.

"You will tell me all that you know, or I will shred you." He spoke through tightly clenched teeth.

"I told you all I know. I don't know where Simon went." Eli took his fist and knocked her across the room. She crashed into a chair and fell to the floor as pain ricocheted across her face. Blood poured from her lips, staining her chin red. She lost partial consciousness. Teetering on the edge of blackness, she forced her eyes to open, and, when she did, she saw Rebecca looming above her, smiling. But, she also saw something else. Spirits. Spirits of her ancestors, circling her; protecting her.

"I'm all out of patience, witch!" When Eli screamed, all of the glass in the solarium exploded. Every figurine, light fixture, and window shattered, and jagged pieces of deadly glass ripped through the room like razor blades. The glass cut deeply into Donna's flesh and sliced into Clara's face, ending her reign as a great beauty. She cried out in agonizing pain. She wondered where her protection from her ancestors was.

"You poor dear," Rebecca said, gloating.

Eli's eyes had turned completely black. He snapped his head in Donna's direction, and her body was immediately gobbled up by flame. Her eyes popped open, and her skin fried as her screams clawed across the room; her body convulsed, writhing in unbearable pain.

"Donna!" Clara screamed. "Make it stop, make it stop. Please," she sobbed.

"Certainly," he said.

Instantly, the flames extinguished, for a second. Then, the fire returned, but it was far more ferocious than before. It quickly devoured all of the flesh on Donna's body, leaving nothing but skeletal remains. The horrifying smell of cooked flesh stuck in Clara's throat; she *tasted* Donna.

"Now, tell us what we want to know," Rebecca said, "or your fate will be much, much worse—lasting an eternity."

Clara tried to speak, but her words were lost somewhere inside her inconsolable sobs.

"Fuck this," Eli said abrasively. He quickly moved over to Clara and looked down on her bloodied face. He yanked her up and brought her close to his face, squeezing her chin. He leaned in and whispered in her ear, his hot breath singeing her skin. "I'm going to take your power, witch. And then I'll know every-thing." She instantly felt a pounding in her head that convinced her it would explode. Eli was inside her mind, probing clumsily. Suddenly, he kissed her hard on the mouth, inserting his tongue into her mouth and tasting her blood.

"Eli—no!" Rebecca screamed, but it was too late. Suddenly, he screamed and stumbled backward and fell onto the floor, twisting and hollering in pain.

"Eli!" Rebecca screamed and moved over to him.

"My head, my head!" he screamed and continued to roll violently around the floor. A thick, black, tar-like substance formed in the corners of his mouth and ran down each side of his face.

"Eli, baby, what's wrong? What did you do to him, witch?" she bellowed at Clara. "It is going to be all right; everything will be fine. Mother is here. Do not worry," she said as she kneeled to be closer to him. She pulled him into her arms, tears falling from her eyes. "You did this to him! You did this!" she yelled, pointing an accusatory finger at Clara, who did not comprehend.

From the corners of the room, an offensive tearing sound suddenly spread across the room as shadows pulled themselves from the corners and sprung to life, crawling across the floor toward Eli. The shadows moaned deeply, painfully, as if near death. They left black oily smudges across the beige carpet, and they struggled to reach Eli, using clots of carpet to propel themselves forward like giant slugs. They moved purposefully, slowly, but did not stop.

"You will pay for this in ways that will cause angels to cry—I promise you that." Her voice was so shrill that Clara felt claws scratching her arm, breaking the skin. Rebecca stroked Eli's forehead all the while maintaining unbroken eye contact with Clara as the shadows began to cover her and Eli. "You cannot leave this house. You are bound here from this day, forevermore. The glass buried in your skin is permanent—it can never be removed. And, you cannot die, not until I kill you. This is your curse, from this day forward, until the end of time." As the shadows completely engulfed the duo and they began to fade, all that could be heard was Rebecca's wailing moans as she held Eli in her arms, rocking back and forth.

That night, a great storm ripped through New Orleans.

CHAPTER 19

T homas Thibodeaux was in a panic. His shallow, rapid breaths dug deeply into his chest as he slid deep down into the folds of the cold, leather seats in the borrowed, sky blue, '67 Ford LTD with the white rag top. It was a tank of a car with a dull, foretelling grin that looked as if it knew it was, someday soon, destined for the junk yard. Thomas's body was on fire with adrenaline, but panic choked off the giggle that tried to escape from his mouth. He knew he had been wrong. He never should have grabbed that girl by her waist and shoved his tongue down her throat, but the danger in the air, mixed with the promise of the taste of her cherry red lips, created an almost irresistible temptation. He had to kiss her, it was destiny. And when he kissed her, she only protested because her hairy beast of a boyfriend was across the room, at that very moment, leaping across the pool table, ready to separate Thomas's head from his shoulders.

Thomas let the kiss linger a beat longer than it should have, but the reward far outweighed the risk. He was spry and knew there was no way the beast with the thick neck, skin tight blue jeans, and heavy cowboy boots would be able to catch him once he got moving.

Thomas hadn't counted on the beast having friends.

As he zigzagged through the crowded bar, dodging swinging fists and beer bottles hurling through the air, he didn't notice a burning tingling in his hands, but in his head he realized he was seeing events happen a few seconds before they took place, giving him the edge. He knew who *would leap out to try to tackle him. He saw a skinny boy with frazzled brown hair swing a pool stick before he actually did it. He heard the sound of the black eight-ball whizzing through the air before it was actually thrown by the dark-skinned dude, who had been playing pool with the girl's boyfriend. Thomas ran through the crowd as if his life depended on it; he was quite sure it did. If they caught him, they'd beat him to a bloody pulp, or worse. Luckily, he made it outside and disappeared into the parking lot before they laid hands on him.*

With care, Thomas dug the keys out of his jacket pocket, making sure that they didn't jangle against each other as he searched for the ignition key. He had to get out of there. He had no problem fighting one dude, but he wasn't thrilled with the thought of taking on up to five.

Outside the car, Thomas heard frantic voices; voices desperately out for blood, searching for him in the dimly lit parking lot. Heavy footsteps pounded in succession against the hard black asphalt outside of the Lux Lounge. The thumping sounds fanned out in different directions as the gang sought to corner its prey. Thomas felt as if he was surrounded, trapped like a mouse in a maze. The parking lot was full of cars, their drivers, inside, heavily drinking and furiously dancing away the blues of their troubled lives; that is, until Thomas flirted with the wrong girl, a bad habit he had perfected. For him, there was nothing more satisfying than the forbidden pleasure of another man's woman. The moment he slid into a prohibited sweet place that belonged to another was the moment his ego swelled. He could have any woman. Any time.

During the evening, he had purposely made eye contact with the girl's boyfriend on several occasions, smiling wryly from the corner of his mouth when she pointed him out to Thomas. He was across the room at the pool table with his brow furrowed deeply into a sharp crease, a sharp wooden toothpick clutched tightly between his thin lips. Despite his formidable presence, Thomas made very little attempt to disguise his intent. The two men's eyes slashed across each other with shallow cuts, finally settling into a permanent sour glaze. Periodically, between shots of tequila that ignited the back of his throat and bottles of Corona that cooled it, Thomas looked at him as if to say "tonight, I'm getting between her thighs" and "fuck you."

The boyfriend returned Thomas's stares, walking menacingly around the pool table while gripping the pool stick, fire in his belly, daring Thomas to push too far.

The waitress—Carmen Delgado—pushed Thomas away several times, but he recognized the faux protest that glinted in her eyes. Her mouth may have said, "Stay away, I got a man," but her eyes said, "Come closer and fuck me now." Thomas would have, had it not been for the gang now circling the lot, looking for him.

He only had one shot at getting away. If he tried to start the car and the engine didn't turn over, the vultures would descend upon him and peck him apart, piece by piece. And they would enjoy it; Thomas had antagonized them so. If it came down to it, he'd fight and take a couple down with him, but he'd lose. The odds weren't in his favor..

He had a clear shot out of the parking lot if the car would start; a clear, direct path into the street. The car belonged to his elderly landlord and neighbor, Ms. Irene Bell, and it wasn't in the best condition. By the time the goons hopped into their cars, he'd be gone, cloaked in the safety of the dark streets.

Slowly, he inserted the key, said a little prayer, and turned it. *Vroooooooommmmm.*

"Thank you, God," he said to himself. He sat up in the car so that he could see over the dashboard, threw the car into drive, and pressed hard on the gas pedal. His tires screeched as he burned through the parking lot, shooting the middle finger at the guys as he blew by them, narrowly avoiding a full on collision with the girl's boyfriend when he jumped in the path of Thomas' escape route.

"Yeah, and fuck you!" he yelled as he watched their agitated bodies

grow smaller in his rearview mirror. Once again, he had avoided
catastrophe.

When Simon opened his eyes, he was sitting straight up in bed
in the hotel room. He was naked, except for a thin white sheet
that was draped across the lower half of his body. Brilliant sunlight spilled into the room from the partially open blinds, and he
could smell the fragrant aroma of freshly brewed coffee. Images
of his dream—or vision—still claimed a part of his mind. He looked
around the room, which seemed much smaller than before, as if
the walls had been pushed closer together. He expected Thomas
to burst from the bathroom, having escaped the clutches of
Carmen's boyfriend. He had never dreamed of Thomas before,
yet he felt a spooky closeness to him, an inexplicable bond. Now
that he was awake, he felt robbed, as if the waking hour had
stolen a part of Thomas's life that was yet to be discovered in the
dream.

He shook his head in disappointment and noticed a lid-less,
half-empty Styrofoam cup of coffee sitting on top of the dresser.
From the outside, voices of a passing family seeped into the room
and stole his attention. A father, Stephen. A mother, Lana. Two
daughters: Christina, seven; and Carrie, five. The girls sang an
off-key rendition of "Santa Claus is Coming to Town," but they
sang so joyfully that it made their parents giggle. Simon listened
to the pitter-patter of eight feet on the sidewalk until they
rounded the corner. At this point, he didn't even question how
he knew so much about the family he had never even seen, except
in his mind's eye.

Simon shifted his body to get out of bed, planting his feet on
the floor. He stood up and stretched, feeling as if he had just
awakened from a much-needed slumber. As he placed his arms at

his sides and took a step forward, the doorknob jiggled and Franklin stepped inside.

"Oh shit," Franklin said as he closed the door quickly behind him; surprise stained his face. His eyes grew wide as he stared at Simon as if he hadn't seen him in months. "You—you up," he managed to say after a few seconds.

"Of course I am. Why wouldn't I be?"

Simon, unashamed in his nakedness, stood and waited for an answer from Franklin, who seemed at a loss for words. Franklin diverted his eyes downward, moved over to the dresser and dropped the car keys on the wooden top, next to the coffee cup.

"Dude, could you put on some clothes?" Simon looked down at himself, as if he didn't realize that he was nude. He grabbed the bed sheet and wrapped it around his waist. He watched Franklin move nervously through the room, carefully avoiding eye contact. He could even hear Franklin's shallow, quick breaths. Clearly, he was ill at ease. In contradiction to the disharmony that surrounded Franklin, Simon felt perfectly calm, at peace. Gone was the tight ball that had resided in the pit of his stomach and served as a constant reminder of his overwhelming sense of fear. He felt rested, at peace. He was at peace with whatever had happened to him over the last few weeks and, as much as he could, made peace with whatever was to come. He no longer dreaded the future.

"Are you gonna tell me what's wrong?" Simon finally asked as he sat back down on the bed.

Franklin stopped dead in his tracks and looked at Simon. "Everything. Everything is wrong."

"What do you mean?"

"First, Brooke called a bunch of times, but I didn't answer 'cause I didn't know what to tell her. And, the credit card you used to pay for this room was declined and the manager is gonna bang on the door at any minute to kick us out. Shit, I had to hide in the parking a lot a for a few seconds 'cause I saw him coming our way."

"That doesn't make any sense. The room was like seventy dollars, and I had a couple hundred dollars on that card, at least," Simon said, ignoring the information about Brooke.

"Simon," Franklin said as he took a seat on the twin bed across from Simon, "we've been here four days."

"What? We just got here last night."

"No, we didn't. You been asleep for three straight days, every since…" His voice faded.

"Since what? Franklin, since what?"

"Since you…since you, walked on water." Franklin's voice trailed off at the end of his sentence and he diverted his eyes away from Simon, who watched as Franklin's body shifted uneasily as he sat on the bed. Simon wished he had words of comfort to offer, but he didn't. He couldn't explain his extraordinary feats and, at this point, didn't have the inclination to even try. Walking on water? Sleeping for three straight days? It all sounded so normal to Simon now. It never ceased to amaze him, the things that people can grow accustomed to.

"Franklin," Simon began, but he was cut off, mid-sentence.

"It's cool, man. Really. Walking on water ain't the only shit that's been going on around here the last few days."

"What else?"

"I mean you. You've been freaking me out, sitting up in bed at night while you still sleepin'; talkin'—I guess it was talkin'—in a language that didn't sound…human. I don't know what the fuck it was. You were like, talkin' to someone, and the crazy part about that shit is that I swore I heard whispers in the room, but wasn't nobody here but me and you." Franklin spoke rapidly, leaving little room between his sentences for Simon to process what he was saying. "I woke up one night and you were standing in the middle of the room, sweating like it was a hundred and twenty degrees. I couldn't wake you and I couldn't move yo' ass, either. I tried to pick you up, to lay you down, but it felt like you weighed a ton. Shit, I couldn't even push you down. Then, you started moaning like you were in pain and black shit starting running out of the corners of your mouth. It was slimy, like oil and it stank to the high heavens. I had to open the window to let the smell out, even though it was cold as hell outside. I almost froze my balls off. I didn't know what to do. I thought about callin' 9-1-1, but then I didn't know what the hell I'd tell 'em, so I didn't, but it's safe to say that you done officially freaked me the fuck out." When he finished speaking, Franklin exhaled loudly and looked at Simon with droopy eyes that begged for better days. "Is this shit real, or am I losin' my mind? Am I crazy?"

Simon spoke frankly. "It's real. I think you know that."

"Well, I guess that's a relief. I can deal with anything 'cept losing my mind. My granddaddy had Alzheimer's, and I seen how it can mess up yo' mind. I don't wanna be like that."

"Trust me, you're not losing your mind." Simon's voice was flat, offering little encouragement. Franklin commanded part of his attention, but a greater part of Simon's mind was still with Thomas. He wanted to know more; he didn't need to be told that what he saw wasn't a simple dream. He'd stopped having random dreams some time ago. Everything he saw now, in his sleeping hours, turned out to be warnings or messages, but this time was even different than that. This time, he felt as if he had lived a part of this man's life in his dream; Thomas's life was his life, too. He experienced everything Thomas felt that night. He felt Thomas's lustful exhilaration, the frantic pace of his heartbeat, the enormous adrenaline rush prompted by the fight, and Thomas' celebratory moment when the car started and he realized that he'd live to fight another day. "We better get out of here before the manager comes. I don't have any more money," he said, focusing on the immediate issue.

"Neither do I. I got just enough gas money to get us home, maybe a little breakfast, too." Franklin hopped off the bed and started tossing his clothes in his open gym bag. "What the hell are you waitin' fo'?" he asked when he noticed Simon wasn't moving.

Simon needed a few seconds. Without warning, it dawned on him, like truth. "Oh, shit," he said.

Franklin stopped. "Oh shit, what?"

"I met my father last night." The truth could not have been any plainer to Simon.

Franklin's face cringed. Instantly, Simon regretted his words. The part of him that had grown accustomed to not sharing his life with others suddenly became more prominent, and he wished he could recall his words, like an e-mailed message that was sent in error. Franklin had seen too much. Simon felt guilty for dragging Franklin with him and laying his troubles at his feet.

"What do you mean?"

"Nothing. Never mind"

"Look, answer the damn question. I saw you walk on water. At this point, nothin' would shock me."

"I guess you're right."

"So, what you mean about yo' daddy? You met him?"

"Kinda. In my dream last night, but I didn't just meet him, I *was* him. He's dead, though. I was living a dead man's life. His name was Thomas," Simon said slowly, "Thomas Thibodeaux."

"Thomas," Franklin said, letting the name wash across his tongue, "you said that name a few times last night in your sleep. Thibodeaux. Isn't that ole girl's last name, the one we're looking for, Addie?"

"Yeah. She's my grandmother, I think. No, I know. She *is* my grandmother." Franklin plopped down on his bed and exhaled. Simon expected him to run screaming from the room, finally having reached his limit.

"So, let me break this down. This woman we been driving around lookin' fo' is really yo' grandmamma that you ain't never met, and now, you say that you lived a part of your dead father's life in your dream? Is that what you're telling me?"

"Yeah, that about sums it up."

"Well," Franklin said. "I guess it's another day in Simon's bizarro world. I always knew you was a freak," he said teasingly.

"Speaking of freaks, I'm not going to ask you how I got naked," Simon said with a chuckle.

"Hold up. No homo. I ain't into that freaky-deaky shit. I'm a pussy connoisseur," he said proudly, tugging at his shirt. They looked at each other and laughed until their stomachs hurt. Simon hadn't laughed in so long that he had forgotten the feeling; now, it swept over him like the memory of a long, lost love. It was familiar, comforting, and it lifted his spirit to the clouds.

Franklin continued. "Yo' ass was soakin' wet after you pulled yo' little *walking-on-the-water* trick. You came in here and collapsed. I had to pry yo' clothes off to keep you from catching pneumonia. Trust me, it wasn't one of my finer moments. Be happy I took care of yo' ass, a'ight?"

"A'ight, man. Calm down. I was wondering. I've seen the way you been looking at me. I'm just saying," Simon said playfully.

"Look at these nuts." Franklin grabbed his testicles through his sweat pants. "Stop playing, and get yo' ass up befo' these crazy Texas muthafuckas call the cops and lock our asses up."

⚔

After slipping away from the resort and driving for an hour, Simon nodded off in the car while Franklin sped down the highway. He awoke, after some time, when he felt the car bounce and bob as it moved across a rough patch on a country dirt road. Simon looked around and all that he saw was thick trees and dense shrubbery. Franklin followed deep tire tracks left in the red dirt that eventually ended when a fallen tree blocked their path forward.

"Where are we?" Simon asked, wiping sleep from his eyes. "What are we doing?"

Franklin threw the car into PARK and turned off the ignition. "Get out," he said as he unhinged his seatbelt. Before Simon could respond, Franklin was already out of the car and walking briskly toward the dense trees. Simon hopped out of the car and quickly followed, leaping over the fallen tree to catch Franklin. Dead leaves padded the forest floor, and broken branches that were scattered about made walking more treacherous than Simon expected; he had never been a big fan of the great outdoors. He hoped the rural obstacle course would slow the stride of Franklin's gait, but Franklin continued to move easily, his long legs covering great distances in a single leap.

"Hey," he called out to Franklin, who moved with purpose and surprising agility. He seemed focused, like he knew exactly where they were going, even though Simon knew there was no way Franklin was familiar with these woods off some lonely Texas country road.

Finally, they reached a clearing and Franklin stopped, looking around as if to inspect the place. Simon caught up to him, breathing heavily.

"What the fuck is going on?" Simon asked between quick breaths.

"We're here."

Simon eyed Franklin oddly and then took a moment to assess his surroundings. They were standing in the center of a circle of enormous pine trees. Near them was an old, rusted barbeque grill that looked as if it hadn't been used in decades. Cigarette butts, old food wrappers, and broken glass from beer and soft drink bottles decorated the landscape. Knee-high, brown weeds, bent over and bowed, created a foreboding wall at the edge of the forest.

"Okay, where's here? What are we doing?"

"We're doing a little experiment," he said, sounding like a professor. "I've listened to all this stuff you been talkin', and I seen some crazy shit with you over the last few days, but one thing stuck in my mind about it all."

"What?"

"You ain't never tried to control it."

"Huh?"

"This…*power* that you have. You ain't never tried to control it. You said shit keeps happening to you, but I say its time you stop lettin' it happen and you control it. That's why we here. I wanna see what you can really do. Ain't nobody around. Just you and me." He took a breath and folded his arms across his chest. "Now, do something."

"What? Franklin, it doesn't work like that."

"How do you know how it works? You ever tried to do something on your own?"

The simple truth of his words shined like a beacon on a darkened night. Simon realized that he had been so freaked out by things that he never even took a second to understand that maybe, just maybe, he could control this thing, whatever it was. Maybe he didn't have to succumb to random events—maybe he could control them!

Simon shook his head from side to side, acknowledging the

wisdom of Franklin's simple words. "Damn, you're right. You're fucking brilliant!" Simon ran over to him and hugged him tightly, even though Franklin playfully protested.

"Get off me, fool! I don't want yo' hoodoo rubbing off on me!"

"A'ight, a'ight," Simon said as he took a few steps backward. "What should I do?" Simon was suddenly anxious, ready to prove that he was still the captain of his fate.

"I don't know. Make something move, like this bottle." Franklin kicked an old bottle with a faded red-and-white label toward Simon.

"Okay, okay. I can try." Simon shrugged his shoulders and rolled his neck as if he was loosening himself up right before a title fight. "Wait, I don't know what I'm doing."

"Try something. Focus on it. Tell it to move."

"Okay, I can do that," he looked at Franklin, then down at the bottle. "Bottle," he said as he deepened his voice, "move." Nothing happened. "Bottle, I said, come to me." Still, nothing happened. Simon repeated the phrase several times, but to no avail.

"Stop. That don't even sound right. It sounds fake. Look, be natural with it, and stop trying to sound like Merlin the Magician."

Simon didn't know why, but he felt nervous, like he was playing to an audience. He had never been one for attention, often preferring to blend into the background; however, this was his show—The Simon Show—and he really wanted to perform, if only for himself. He wanted to make something happen, make some magic. The possibility of taking control over his life filled him with excitement. If he could make the bottle move, then he wouldn't be a slave to his powers. He could control them.

He took a few, deliberate breaths to calm himself down. Then, he steeled his resolve and tried again, speaking in his most natural voice, but nothing happened. The bottle didn't budge, not even a centimeter. As he repeated his commands something about that relaxed tone in his voice seemed far too casual for the task at hand. After all, he wasn't playing some silly game; he was trying to defy the laws of physics and in deference to those laws, he needed to be more somber, more focused.

"This ain't workin'." The frustration in Franklin's voice wasn't disguised. "Are you even tryin'?"

"Yeah, I'm trying. It's not like there's a *How-To* book for this." They both exhaled in disappointment.

"Okay, maybe we takin' the wrong approach. How do you feel when something happens?"

"Scared."

"That ain't what I mean. I mean, when it's happening, what's going on with your body? Didn't you say something about some tingling you felt? And, right before you walked on water, you were sweatin' like a hooka in church. Maybe you need to get hot and sweat before something happens."

"What are you suggesting?"

"Do a few sprints, get your heartbeat up. Sweat." Simon pondered the idea and it seemed as plausible as anything else.

"Fine, but if I slip on some leaves and bust my ass, I'm going to punch you in the face," he said.

"I'd like to see you try, *College Boy*."

"Stop calling me that." The moment Franklin called him that name, Simon felt irritation building in his chest. It felt like a spark.

Simon moved over to the edge of the circle of trees where the weeds stood tall. With a sudden burst of speed, he ran through the clearing where the circle began to the group of trees on the outside. He repeated the action for several minutes until his heartbeat was raised and moisture dampened his forehead.

"A'ight, now try it again," Franklin commanded, which also irritated Simon. Simon closed his eyes and took a deep breath. "Hurry up!" Franklin screamed. "We ain't got all day."

"Would you shut the fuck up! Damn."

"Whatever, College Boy."

Inside, Simon felt the spark become a flame, like the moment a match is struck, before it burst into flames. He felt a small prickly feeling in the bottom of his feet. His eyes were still closed, yet he could see the bottle clearly. In fact, he could see everything around him clearly, even the sour look on Franklin's face. The tingling sensation moved up his leg and soon he felt it all over his body, but it wasn't painful. It felt as if every cell in his body suddenly ignited. He imagined the bottle moving, flying swiftly through the air, and as he did, he heard a loud crash and the sound of glass breaking, which startled him. He opened his eyes and saw Franklin lying against the dirty grill, his eyes wide.

"What happened?"

"The...the...the bottle. You did it," he said as he pointed toward a tree. "It flew into that tree and broke. It was like a fuckin' missile. I thought it was going to hit me in the head!"

"Oh shit, man. You all right?"

"Yeah, yeah. I'm fine," he said as he dusted pieces of rust and black soot from his jacket. "I wanted you to move it, not kill me in the process."

"Man, I wasn't trying to kill you. I was moving the bottle, like you told me to." Simon's voice didn't reflect the level of concern he knew that it should have, considering the speed in which the bottle whizzed by Franklin's head. Simon had seen in it his mind; he had even heard the bottle slice through the air as it soared by. There was a vacant place in Simon's soul that would have smiled if he had opened his eyes and saw Franklin's skull split open, blood gushing from his head; that was the part of him that scared him to death.

"All right, let's see what else I can do." Before Franklin could respond, the old metal grill shook and then shot through the air as if it was a football that had been kicked through a goalpost. It flew beyond the top of the trees and disappeared. They heard it clank loudly against the forest floor as it thudded to the earth.

Quickly, Franklin moved to Simon's side. "Just gettin' out of the line of fire," he said, swallowing hard. Now, Franklin emitted a scent that emboldened Simon; the sweet smell of his growing fear swept across the area, fueling Simon's lust for power. Simon looked at him hungrily, his nose greedily inhaling his scent. Franklin's fear made him strong. Power swelled in his veins. He felt dizzy, intoxicated. He took a few steps forward so that he was standing in the center of the circle of trees. From his vantage point, he could see all around him with a simple turn of his head. He saw deep into the forest, far beyond where they stood. He saw a couple of deer standing near a creek and an abandoned vehicle that had been taken over by forest vines. "Fire, there's an idea," he said, repeating Franklin's words. Simon inhaled several times and looked upward, toward the sky. Suddenly, the tops of all of the trees in the circle burst into roaring flames and all that could be seen was an enormous ring of beautiful fire. The sweet harmony, made by the crackling of the dried branches as the flames consumed them, filled Simon's heart with tremendous pride, as did the ostentatious display of his awesome power. He had never seen anything so spectacular; and, it was all his doing.

"Oh shit!" Franklin exclaimed. "Put it out befo' somebody gets hurt!"

Simon smiled dryly when he looked at Franklin, his eyes completely black. Franklin took a few steps backward. Suddenly, the fire was on the ground, running the circle at the base of the trees, enclosing them. "Don't worry. It won't harm you. I won't let it." Simon walked closer to the flame. Franklin did not follow. The fire began to move forward, fed by the abundance of dried leaves and twigs, and began to encroach upon the center of the circle where they stood. The heat of the blaze pushed hard against the duo, with Franklin struggling against the waves, but Simon reveled in its intensity.

"Dude, this ain't funny," Franklin said, trying to hide the panic in his voice.

Simon cut his eyes at him, as if his words had somehow offended him. He then focused on the flame and spoke, with his arms extended and the palms of his hands pointed toward the wall of fire. "Stand back and behave," Simon said to the flame. The entire circle of flame moved back in one motion, upon command. The fire burned, but did not consume.

Whispers and hissing sounds could suddenly be heard, as if a thousand snakes suddenly awakened underneath the leaves, which now rustled with life. Simon looked back and saw Franklin with a terrified expression gripped his face.

"Simon, make it stop!"

Instead of diminishing, the flames grew higher and higher, showing no signs of relenting. Simon reached into the fire with his bare hand and rotated his arm. He felt as if he had become a part of the fire and the fire was a part of him; he knew no harm would come to him.

He looked back at Franklin, whose eyes were wide with fear, as his gaze darted between the circle of fire and the rustling of the hissing leaves. Simon turned away and walked through the flames, leaving Franklin trapped.

CHAPTER 20

"You sure this the right place?" Franklin asked in a dry voice, looking straight ahead at the black-and-white sign, attached to the red brick building, that read *Hollytree Convalescent Center*. They arrived in Houma as darkness robbed the sky of all light, draping the world in an eerie gloom that was void of even a sliver of moonlight. The darkness seemed to spread out endlessly in all directions, cutting the center off from life itself. Franklin noticed that the center's lawn was in a state of disarray, much like a battlefield after a midnight melee. A fallen tree lay horizontally across the lawn, and a few benches and trashcans were tossed carelessly on their sides. Clearly, a storm had ripped through the area, but they had business more pressing than a passing storm.

The drive back to Louisiana from Texas had been even quieter than the drive to the Lone Star State. The return trip was filled with so much that simply couldn't be summed up in words. Simon didn't know how to fully articulate his fear that the evil growing within him had metastasized; he harbored tremendous dread that he'd soon lose the man that he was and that the Simon everyone knew would be cannibalized by the Simon he was sure to become. So, for most of the trip, he sat in the passenger's side of the car and barely moved. Not only were his thoughts heavy, but the unleashing of his power in the forest had drained him, leaving him weak and wobbly; too tired to speak, even if he wanted to. It had been too much for him to endure. Even now, he wasn't fully recovered.

Simon let out a hot puff of air. "Yeah, I'm sure." Simon didn't move, not even an inch; he didn't even blink.

"You know you hafta to go in," Franklin said, thinly veiling the urgency that colored his voice.

"I know." The weight of what lay inside felt like heavy stones on his shoulders, forcing them into a downward slump. Inside were answers to questions he no longer wanted to ask and the weight of his worry could be measured in pounds. "She's in there—Adelaide." She might be his grandmother, but Simon knew nothing else of her, except this extraordinary connection they shared. Maybe she was locked away in this place for a good reason, hidden from the world by a higher power. Maybe she was the ultimate evil, lying in wait for him for some wicked purpose. Or, maybe she was his savior, his light. He simply couldn't be sure.

"What you waitin' fo'?"

"I don't know."

"You scared?"

"Terrified." When Simon awoke in Franklin's car after their visit to the forest, he felt more than weak; he felt cut-off from everything, including the world and his feelings. He was like a container whose contents had been emptied; he didn't feel fear or curiosity or remorse or any emotion. He simply felt empty. Now, he felt terror. Tangible fear.

Franklin shifted in his seat. Out of his periphery, Simon could see his friend's head turn in his direction. "You scared me, man. I thought I was gonna die. I thought you was gonna let me burn." Franklin's voice was thick, heavy with unspoken emotion. "You like my brother and I thought you were gonna kill me. If there's a chance this woman can help you figure this shit out, you hafta go for it." Simon turned his head toward Franklin and met his gaze; Franklin then looked down at his nervous hands. "I'm terrified, too."

"I told you no harm would come to you. I don't care what happens." Simon grabbed one of Franklin's hands. "Look at me. I will protect you with my life, if necessary. You gotta know that. You're about the only family I have." Even before the words fully passed his lips, Simon had begun to doubt them. Until he learned to control the darkness in his heart, he knew that he wasn't in any position to make promises, regardless of how sweet the lie sounded. When the fire had raged in the forest, more than a few minutes passed before he even thought of saving Franklin. In fact, had it not been for the memories of their friendship that suddenly entered Simon's head, Franklin would have been burned beyond recognition by now; his body, nothing more than a pile of ashes carried away by the wind. In order to hold on to himself, Simon had to hold onto Clara's words when she told him to "remember love." In those moments, when his powers raged in the firestorm, he barely remembered love; it was a fading feeling, a flicker, no more than a small candle deep inside a vast cavern.

"Will you go in with me? I'm still a little weak."

"I got you, man." Simon opened his car door and struggled to pull himself out of the vehicle. His feet were heavy, like stone, and his stomach remained unsettled. The cold night air bit into his skin, and snowflakes fell from the sky, suddenly. Snow in Louisiana was an anomaly, and this storm appeared out of nowhere. Simon knew its cause; it was him, and moreover he knew this was the beginning of more odd occurrences. A deep sense of melancholy drifted down on him, like the snowflakes that fell in soft clumps. He moved slowly in front of the car, which was parked directly in front of the building, and leaned his hip against the grill. From his vantage point, the building seemed enormous; its brick walls expanding half a city block. It was a formidable structure, full of sharp angles and intimidating lines.

Simon heard the door close and Franklin shuffle his feet across the asphalt parking lot toward him. Franklin moved to his side and they leaned together against the car in silence, watching the snow fall.

"What if she can't help me?" Simon inquired after a few elongated seconds. His voice carried his concern deep into the empty night.

Franklin paused. "Then God help us all."

Simon pried himself from the hood of the car, stood tall against the sharp wind, and then moved laboriously forward to his future, with a prayer in his heart.

Ψ

Addie wiggled her fingers and toes as she sat in a stiff, upright position in the recliner in her room, a tell-tale sign that her binding spell was weakening and that she was becoming stronger in these final hours; strong enough to possibly break the spell that kept her crippled. At this point, she could even move her neck from side-to-side, if only slightly. If her spell broke completely, the power she had used over the years to keep it in place would return to her in full measure, albeit slowly. Even though her strength was returning, she was still afraid to use her power on herself; instead, she chose to strengthen her binding spell. Her efforts may ultimately prove futile, but it was all she knew to do.

Over the last couple of days, her connection to Simon had been severed and she had tried desperately to reconnect; her efforts were in vain. When she had tried to reach him all she saw was a vast, all-encompassing darkness and a deafening silence. She feared the worst. Maybe he had given in completely to the darkness. Maybe she was already too late.

Inside her room, everything was quiet—too quiet—even the television was silent. Outside her door she heard occasional voices from the staff going on about last night's storm and talking about the minutia that filled their days, living in ignorant bliss of things yet to come. They were concerned about silly things such as car payments, taking their children to soccer practice, the latest celebrity gossip, or the newest high-tech gadget they wanted to buy when they got paid, when all around them there were signs of the coming apocalypse; raging wildfires, seismic shifts in the earth, violent storms—such as the one that sprang up suddenly last night. By comparison, their concerns were silly, but they had the luxury of not knowing what Addie knew. Indeed, ignorance is bliss.

The unexpected storm that tore through the state the night before was widespread and fierce. Its violent winds toppled trees, ripped roofs from buildings, and tore houses from their foundations. The rain, which came down in sheets as thick as blankets, flooded the streets and forced residents to recall memories of recent storms. Weather forecasters, caught off guard by the sudden storm, were left dumbfounded by its raw force, blaming it on an unusual weather pattern in the atmosphere.

Addie knew better. Whatever had caused the storm certainly wasn't natural. Deep in the clutches of night she heard a wretched scream that shook the sky so ferociously that she thought it would tumble and fall. Seconds later, the heavens split open and rain fell with torrential force, hammering the earth with heavy drops. No, this storm wasn't natural at all; it was birthed by an unholy force. She felt it.

And now it was snowing; hardly a natural effect.

Addie had felt something else last night—pain. Somewhere, in a place hidden far from view, the shadows cried. Addie wondered what could have happened to cause such agony, especially when they were perilously close to the Ascension. If they were in pain, then maybe, just maybe, she could still undo her mistakes from so long ago, but time was running out. For everyone.

As the snow continued to fall in hard, fast flakes from the black sky, Addie felt a sudden chill, like a stabbing pain at the base of her spine that caused her body to jolt. She tried to cry out, but had no voice. Her pain was sharp, like a warning. Her intuition suddenly overwhelmed her senses in ways she hadn't felt in years. Something wasn't right. The atmosphere was charged with power unlike she had ever felt. Immediately, her mind raced toward Eli and Rebecca. Could her feelings be related to them? She focused her energies and quickly dismissed that thought. What she felt now was different. This power was feral—unchained—much different than the contained evil she always felt from them.

She focused again to try to find the source of this awesome power and shuddered when the stabbing pain returned, threefold; the pain was acute. Then, she knew. Something wasn't coming for her; something had arrived. Her day of reckoning, at long last.

She had waited so very long for this moment and now that it was upon her, she wasn't sure how to react. She bore the mark of shame for this abomination, wearing it like a scarlet letter. Her shame had burned in her soul for twenty years. She had relived her mistakes over and over again every day for two decades, cursing her naivete and her arrogance. All of this was her fault. All of it. From her own womb, the first Thibodeaux male in seven generations had been born, much to her horror and the horror of her sister-clan. Many generations ago, the women of the clan had cast a powerful spell to prevent the male chromosome from taking root in their bloodline, effectively preventing the birth of a male from any woman whose veins pulsed with even the most infinitesimal drop of Thibodeaux blood. As powerful as the sister-clan was, and had always been, it was not infallible. Their magic was not foolproof; nature had its own power and the shadows had many tricks.

Prior to that ill-fated night twenty years ago, it had been 372 years since the last first male born of a first male had been conceived. The destroyer of worlds could only be born on a winter solstice—the shortest day of the year—underneath a full crimson moon caused by a lunar eclipse. The last time a lunar eclipse occurred on a winter solstice was in 1638. Back then, the Thibodeaux sister-clan pooled their power and burned the vessel carrying the child long before he had a chance to take his first breath, beating back the rising darkness, expelling it from the world and entombing it in the Shadowland...until now.

From the beginning, it was ordained that any male born unto any Thibodeaux woman would be anointed with blood and put to immediate death by fire, his ashes scattered across hallowed ground.

When Addie discovered life growing in her womb, she called her sister-clan and they blessed the belly to supplement the ancient spell cast by their ancestors.

But, something went wrong.

For a split second—just a split second—Addie lost concentration when the spell had demanded complete focus. In that millisecond, a shadow swept across her mind. She denied to herself that she had seen it, fooling herself into believing it was her imagination, a product of her nerves. Deep down in a place in her soul, she knew what she had seen and the possibility of what it meant. Yet, she remained silent, foolishly believing their power was enough to beat back the shadows, hoping the ancient spell and the blessing ritual her sister-clan had performed would bless her child and prevent the unthinkable.

She had been wrong.

During the pregnancy, the shadows were able to cloak the gender of the child, even from Addie, tricking her into believing she would welcome the next generation of Thibodeaux witches into the world.

When her child, Thomas Thibodeaux, was born at 3:33 in the morning on December 21, 1956, the horrifying screeching of the sister-clan echoed throughout the hospital, short-circuiting machines and plunging the entire hospital into complete darkness. His birth into the world immediately weakened the clan, albeit temporarily.

In the darkness, the sister-clan felt the shadows skulking. The shadows tore through the umbilical cord still attached to Addie in a brazen attempt to claim the child who would father their master—The One.

The sister-clan grabbed hands and united their power, hoping to expel the shadows. Their weakened force stunned, but did not stop, the darkness from seizing the child and vanishing into the black.

But Addie would not surrender her child to them. She simply could not. If they escaped with the child, it would set the stage for the entire world to burn. While clasping the hands of her sister-clan, in a frenzied exhibition of raw power, she reached into the dark and snatched the child away. She had not had enough strength to kill the child or to bring it back to the hospital; she could not risk that. She had just enough strength, on that darkened night, to create a portal and to rip the child from their arms. She flung it without direction into the vast and empty blackness; the child spun aimlessly into the wild night. Where it would land, she did not know; but, neither would the shadows.

The sister-clan and the shadows spent years trying to find her child, *The Father*. Their powers tore through the earth, wreaking havoc as hurricanes, earthquakes and tornados. The light and the dark clashed fiercely and left a trail of destruction all over the globe; from Asian tsunamis to Haitian earthquakes; from Californian wildfires to European blizzards; their powers met on a great battlefield, all in search of *The Father*. He had to be found.

To the shadows, he was a blessing that would help free them from an eternal underworld; his seed would bring forth The One and when he reigned, they would be free to walk the earth in their various and hideous forms. They would bring endless torment and destruction to mankind and plunge the world into a darkness yet unknown.

To the sister-clan, *The Father* had to be destroyed before he could impregnate a woman—a vessel—who would give birth to The One. The birth of The One would be a nightmare that defied imagination. His reign of terror would be marked by rivers of blood and plagues of epic proportion. He would have unmatched power.

Somewhere on the earth, in the flesh, *The Father* walked. He could be a fisherman in Tanzania or a student in Belarus or a diplomat's son in New York; he could be a Mexican farmer or a Moroccan soccer player; he could be anything and anywhere.

Addie had one advantage over the shadows: this child was flesh of her flesh and blood of her blood; his blood pulsed with the magic of the sister-clan, although he had no real power of his own; his power was singular—he was used to bring forth The One. But, they were united. Occasionally, especially in the depths of night, she would feel him; his presence seemed to hover over her like a gray mist over a cool lake. At inconvenient times, she would feel what he felt. She had awakened many a night over-wrought with emotion, emotion she knew did not belong to her. She felt him. She felt his desires and his longings. She felt his happiness, his joy. Many nights she felt his burning lust; a lust so strong that it made her moist, saturating her empty bed with her sweet nectar. She felt his pleasure and his pain and his anger and his sadness, too. His rage, his burning rage, sometimes consumed her.

When she felt him, it never lasted long enough for her to pinpoint his location, but the feelings lingered long enough to give her direction. There were a few times over the years in which she thought she had found him, but each time she was mistaken. She could not give up the search. She was resolute. She had to find him before his seed could take root. She had to prevent the coming apocalypse.

Then, on his twenty-first birthday, Addie felt her child in a way she had never before. The feeling was so strong that it knocked her down as she stood in the kitchen. She collapsed to the hard floor, dropping the plate of berries and herbs which constituted her diet (her body needed to remain pure.) The plate exploded on the floor, spraying colorful food across the span of the room. She knew where he was. She could see his face clearly for the very first time; the bond between mother and child was not easily broken. Immediately, she and her sister-clan set out to dispatch her one and only son; if the father dies, the son can never be born. She had to right her wrong from so long ago. It would be her sacrifice to the world.

Through the conjuring of the sister-clan, on a Los Angeles freeway on a very ordinary day, a car crash ended the life of Thomas Thibodeaux. Addie ensured that his death was quick; not painless, just quick. The sisters made certain that his body was consumed by fire. Addie gathered his ashes and scattered them across sanctified ground, saving a few ashes in a crystal bottle for herself that she would hide from the world.

The Father had been destroyed; but, they could not be sure if he had begat a child, so the sister-clan continued to search and to cast locating spells. The Seer of the clan could not see anything beyond the death of Thomas and the clan rejoiced.

Addie remained uncertain.

In the flicker of time before the semi-tractor trailer ended the life of her child, she thought she felt something. It was enough to give her pause, in spite of the assurances from the Seer. She wouldn't be fooled twice.

Over the years, Addie continued to seek, using her power to break through veiled walls that divided light and dark. She looked in mirrors between life and death. She peered into places forbidden to her; she had no other choice.

Addie's feelings were validated when she felt the impending birth. The pain she felt was as real as the pain she felt when Thomas had been born. She did not have time to summon the sister-clan. Instead, she cast a locating spell and propelled herself hurriedly through space to the woman whose womb contained the destroyer of worlds.

Addie stole the woman from her house in the dead of night. The woman was waiting for her family to take her to the hospital. When Addie appeared out of nothing, the woman screamed, trying to alert her family, but by the time they made their way upstairs to the bedroom, the room was empty; Addie and the woman were gone. Addie took her to the shack her grandmother had lived in before her death. Her grandmother had had consecrated this place deep in the swamp. Addie hoped to gain power from this ground, which was hallowed by the bones of her mother, her mother's mother and her mother's mother's mother. This place was the ceremonial burial ground of her ancestors, made fertile by generations of their blood.

When Addie had a chance to examine the woman, her worst fear had come to pass—the child was near. The first male born of the Thibodeaux clan could be burned to ash; the first male born of the first male—and his mother—could be destroyed by fire only if they were consumed by flame before the breaking of the woman's water. If Addie burned the woman and the child this close to his birth, her power and his power might combine and be set loose into the world in a living flame that would incinerate everything in its path. No method made from man would be able to extinguish it and any effort she put forth to quench the flame would be futile. She could not risk it. Once the child took his first breath, he'd become immortal, and her power would not be able to destroy him. Her only option was to bind his powers and to pray.

CHAPTER 21

W hen Simon walked through the doors of Hollytree Convalescent Center, with Franklin following closely behind, he instantly felt a charge in the air that almost caused him to double over. The air was alive, aflame with an energy that penetrated his flesh and bore deeply into his bones. It was sticky sweet and felt like molasses filling his lungs. The more he inhaled, the more he struggled to breath. A violent cough dug deeply into his chest, forcing him to grab onto Franklin's shoulder to steady himself as the world spun around his head. Even though his feet were planted firmly onto the floor, he felt airy, as if he was floating above everyone and when he looked down, everything seemed fluid and malleable, as if he could bend the entire world to his will.

The bustling area—full of nurses, other staff, and visitors—was bathed in an effervescent yellow haze that gave the room an ethereal appearance. As Simon gazed slowly around the room, he inhaled, pulling life into his flaring nostrils; realizing with sudden acuteness that he knew and could feel the emotions of every single person that he saw. He felt their happiness and their sadness; their pain and their pleasure; their worry and relief. He knew their failures and their triumphs and he could feel every sickness that ailed every patient in the facility. He even knew those patients who would not survive the long night. What he felt now was the same feeling that overwhelmed him when he went to visit the doctor, only amplified several times. This time, however, he wasn't sickened by feelings. Now, he felt strong, almost omnipotent.

Then, he felt the familiar dark rising within his soul, evidenced by a fiery bubbling in his belly. His mouth filled with the taste of something foul, rancid. Forcefully, he swallowed back the taste, but not before a small stream of black spittle oozed from the corner of his mouth. Quickly, Simon wiped it away before anyone could notice.

Onetwothreefourfivesixseveneightnineten.

Onetwothreefourfivesixseveneightnineten.

"You okay?" Franklin's concerned voice pulled Simon down from his perch and pushed the dark back down inside of him. Simon didn't know how long he would be free of the dark, but he knew he needed to be in control so that he could speak with Addie with a clear head. "You need to sit down?" Before Simon could respond, Franklin had started to lead them in direction of the group of bland beige sofa and chair sets that filled the waiting area.

"No, no. I'm fine." Simon released his grip from Franklin's shoulder and forced himself to stand on his own. He stood on suddenly strong legs. His cough dissipated and his breathing stabilized, leaving him feeling invigorated. "I'm good. Really." He looked at Franklin's face, which was colored with incredulity, and moved briskly toward the nurse's station.

He approached the nurse's station cautiously. A group of three nurses was huddled in the back, speaking in whispers. By the smell of the emotion that wafted from the trio to Simon's nose, he could tell they were in despair. Simon inhaled deeply and let their grief enter his body. Their faces were torn with sorrow; their eyes were red, puffy sagging bags. A great sadness shrouded them, and they fought back a river of tears as they spoke about a missing nurse named Andrea, who was last seen a few nights ago, leaving with a man in the parking lot.

One of the nurses looked up and saw Simon standing at the counter. She wiped the tear from her cheek, tugged at her uniform in an effort to straighten it out and approached the counter, forcing a smile when she was near him.

"May I help you?" she asked.

"Yes, I'm looking for a patient—a resident—I think. Ms. Thibodeaux?" Simon asked meekly as he looked at the nameplate attached to her uniform. It read "Courtney."

"You mean Adelaide?"

"Yes. Adelaide Thibodeaux. " For the first time, Courtney looked directly into his face, a flash of familiarity sweeping across her eyes. "Do I know you?"

"No, I don't think so. I've never been here before."

"Really? Your eyes, they're so familiar." As she stared into his face, Simon started feeling uncomfortable. He could feel her mind working hard to match his face with a name or place him into some context in which she would recognize him. Simon didn't like being looked at that way.

"Could you tell me her room number?"

"Oh, uh…it's room 173. Down that hall." She pointed, and Simon turned his head.

"Thank you." He waved for Franklin to follow him and they began their walk down the long hallway. Simon turned his head around toward the nurse's station and Courtney was still staring at him; still searching. If he had been more in control of his powers, he would have tried to read her mind, but he hadn't yet learned to call on them upon command, and he had more important things to deal with.

They walked down the hallway quietly, as if they were too afraid their voices would alert Addie of their impending arrival. The corridor was narrow and as they passed by room after room, they tried hard not to peer into open doors out of respect for the privacy of the residents. The numbers on the door increased the farther they walked, and after a few moments they reached the one seventies. With each step he took, his connection to the swell of power started to fade, leaving him feeling breathless. He slowed his pace and took deeper breaths, feeling as if his energy was being siphoned off the closer he got to her. As quickly as the wave of sudden power had manifested, it was passing, and his shoulders slumped, slightly. The manic swing in his energy level concerned him, but he knew it was symptomatic of much larger issues.

"Simon, wait," Franklin said. He grabbed Simon's arm as they neared her room not noticing the change in Simon's posture. "What's the plan here? You gon' walk in and say, 'Hey, Grandma, it's me'?"

Simon paused. Franklin's question threw him for a loop. After all he had been through, the last few days, he had never thought about how to start the conversation with this woman. What would he say? What could he say?

"I don't really know," Simon said, trying to hide the fact that he was somewhat winded. "Hadn't thought about it."

"We need to have a plan. What if she's…you know, like Medusa or something."

"I doubt seriously Medusa is living in an old folks' home."

"I guess you have a point," he said, appearing to really consider Simon's words, "but you do seem to have an attraction to snakes— that's gotta come from somewhere. Maybe she's some kinda snake lady. I'm just saying. Or, what if she starts trippin', like actin' all angry or crazy or violent?"

"You don't have to worry. I told you, no harm will come to you."

"You say that shit with such confidence, but I ain't convinced." Franklin rolled his eyes.

"Follow me and be quiet," Simon said after he could no longer endure the alarm in Franklin's voice. It had been Franklin who, only moments earlier in the car, had urged him to go inside and meet this woman, and now he was having cold feet. If this was a different circumstance, Simon would have told him he was acting like a bitch. Instead, he shook his head. "You aren't going to let an old woman scare you, are you?"

After a few more small steps, they stood outside of room 173. The door was almost closed; only a sliver kept it from being tightly shut. Simon leaned his ear closer to the door, hoping to hear some sound. The room was quiet. With trepidation in his heart, he slowly pushed on the door, which opened with an eerie creaking sound that seemed to reverberate off the dull white walls of the hallway. As the door swung open, an old woman with tousled salt-and-pepper hair came into view. She sat in a chair that faced the television, which was not on. Her eyes were glazed and at her feet was a pair of knotted blue slippers that were stained with dirty brown specs. The room was pleasant enough, with a painting of sunflowers hanging on the wall opposite her twin-sized hospital bed that was fitted with metal rails on the sides. The curtains on the window were wide open, revealing the fast-falling snowflakes.

Simon took a few more steps. He had expected to feel something profound the first time he laid eyes on his grandmother, but the keenness of his senses had dulled considerably. The room felt like an emotional vacuum in which nothing could exist, or escape; in stark contrast to the surge of energy and emotion he felt when he first entered the facility. She sat there in silence, her eyes absently fixed on the wall in front of her. Surely, this feeble shell of a woman could not have been the one that had haunted him in his dreams.

"Excuse me. Are you Adelaide Thibodeaux?" he asked, his eyes fixed upon her aged face; his voice was shaky. The woman in his dreams was older, but certainly not as old as the woman he saw now. His eyes drew into tight slits, focusing on her face, searching for some recognition, waiting for her response, which did not readily come.

Simon didn't really need a response. He knew. He knew this *was* Adelaide Thibodeaux, in the flesh, or what was left of her flesh. She looked to be nothing more than loose skin struggling to maintain its grip on her aged skeleton. Her face was so sunken in, he could see the outline of her bones. To say she looked fragile would be an understatement.

"What's wrong wit' her?" Franklin asked meekly. "Is she even breathin'?" They stepped deeper into the interior of the room and jumped slightly when the door behind them closed on its own, suddenly. "What da fuck?"

Simon inched a few feet in her direction; Franklin stayed close. Simon froze in place when her head slowly, almost painfully, turned toward him.

"You...are...the one," she said in a creaky voice that sent chills up his spine. Both men froze in place, horrified by her wretched voice, which sounded like it came from the grave.

"You...you've been trying to contact me...in my dreams?" The question in his voice carried very little weight. "I'm...Simon."

"You...have...come...for me?" She struggled to speak and coughed as if choking on her own words. Her shoulders lurched forward in a hard jerk and instinctively Simon quickly moved to her, thinking she might fall out of her chair and hit the floor.

He moved a few paces backward when her coughing stopped and she didn't flop onto the floor. He looked down at his feet and nervously shifted his weight. He didn't know what to say or what to expect from her, but even in her decayed state, she still exuded power that Simon felt in his bones. His feeling of omnipotence had been replaced with a feeling of impotence; he felt limp, almost voiceless. "Something is happening to me and I think you know what. I need...answers. Can you help me?"

"Are you his grandmother?" Franklin's hurried question shot from the back of the room like a spear, but it landed flat; his question went unanswered.

"Sit," she struggled to say. Simon looked around the room and pulled up a chair next to her. She seemed to be wrapped in the stench of death, which oozed from her pores.

We have much to discuss, you and me. Her voice, which was much clearer and stronger, echoed inside his skull. *I have felt you. Should we fear you, Simon?*

"Fear me? I think I should be scared of you."

"Who are you talking to?" Franklin asked, looking around the room making sure no one else was around.

"Franklin, please be quiet." Simon's tone was suddenly author-itative.

Have you become death?

"Huh? I haven't killed anyone," he said impatiently to her, but then his mind was drawn immediately to the thugs in the street. He didn't know whether the one he threw across the street or the one who had been stabbed were alive.

They are alive. Simon shuddered when he heard her words; then, he breathed a sigh of relief. He wasn't ready to become a killer.

Many may die.

"No. No. I don't want that. How do we stop it?"

Release me.

"What?"

Release me.

"I don't understand. Release you? From what?" He looked around the room, searching for some clue or sign. Maybe he was looking for a key or a secret code. He looked at Franklin, who simply shrugged his shoulders out of complete confusion.

Simon looked at her again and suddenly understood. "Oh my God," he said in astonishment. "You're trapped—in that body." He jumped up suddenly.

Release me.

"What's wrong?" Franklin asked as he moved closer to Simon.

"She wants me to release her—from that body."

Franklin looked at Simon, then at her and back at Simon. "You can do that?"

"She seems to think I can."

Time is short.

"What do you mean 'time is short'?"

They will come for you.

"Who will come for me?"

Release me.

"I don't know how." Fear and frustration strained his voice. "She keeps telling me to release her, but I don't know how." Franklin grabbed Simon and pulled him to the back near the door.

"I don't think you should release her."

"I don't even know *how* to release her."

"If she says you can, then I believe her. I've seen yo' ass walk on water and walk through fire, so I'm sure you can do this. I just don't think you should."

"Why?"

"We don't know anything about her. Whoever put her here,

I'm sure they put her here for a reason. I don't think we should be messin' around with this shit."

"Franklin, she's my grandmother."

"You don't even know her."

"We share the same blood. That's all I need to know." Simon moved toward Adelaide and took his seat, staring into her hollow, blue eyes. For the first time he realized that her eyes were his eyes; they shared the same sapphire sparkle, although her eyes were clouded with haze.

He concentrated and tried to project his thoughts to her as she had been doing to him.

Before I release you, I need answers. Projecting his thoughts came easier to him than expected when he focused. The slight tingling returned to his body, but by now, he had grown accustomed to it. *Who am I?*

You are The One.

The One? What does that mean?

You are life and you are death.

I am none of that. I am Simon. Simply Simon. I just want my life back—my normal life.

You are The One.

Stop saying that. Simon said with exasperation. *That tells me nothing. What the hell is going on with me?*

Release me and all will be revealed.

He looked around the room and found Franklin's face. He needed reassurance that releasing her, if he could, was the right thing to do, but reticence carved deep lines into Franklin's brow. Simon could feel his deep apprehension from across the room. Yet, at his core, he knew he had to release her; he was as sure of this as he was sure that it was snowing. He had come too far and had endured far too much to leave here without answers.

What do I do? he asked her, caution imbuing his voice.

You must focus.

Not knowing what else to do, Simon cracked his knuckles and inhaled deeply. He felt as if he should close his eyes, but her hollow gaze told him otherwise; instead of closing his eyes, he focused on her eyes. Her eyes, even though glazed, gripped him tightly. His body constricted as if he were restrained by a strait-jacket. Instantly, he felt his temperature rise; his breathing quickened.

Focus.

His body twitched, suddenly, when he felt a sharp pain puncture the base of his skull, as if it had been pricked by a thick needle that was pushed deep into his head. The taste of salt and blood and bile filled his mouth and he thought he would retch, but he swallowed hard. He felt her power in his body, in his bloodstream, connecting with him, but it wasn't a smooth union; it was tantamount to mixing oil and water.

The air in the room became thin, making Simon and Franklin feel lightheaded. The lights flickered on and off as her connection to Simon's powers tightened. Simon could feel her in his head, in his blood, on his skin—he felt as if she were becoming a part of him.

Focus.

She kept telling him to focus, but he wasn't sure what he was focusing on: the fire in his belly or the taste of vomit in his mouth or the tightening of his lungs? Or, the fact that he felt like he was being choked by a giant boa constrictor? There were so many things happening at once that he couldn't focus on any one thing.

Then, he physically felt her tap into a place in his soul that he wished would vanish; the dark in him. It was housed in a physical place in his body, although he couldn't identify exactly where. It felt distant, yet so close that he could smell it, touch it. When he felt her probing that area, the pain in his head amplified. He thought he was going to pass out and hit the floor with a thud. The room spun swiftly around his head, or so he thought. Quickly, he realized the room wasn't spinning, but items in the room floated around the perimeter in a circular motion. The lamp, the remote control to the television, a few magazines, an empty cup, a few pillows from the bed and some miscellaneous papers spiraled around the room even though there was no discernible wind. He didn't even have to turn his head—he actually couldn't—to know that Franklin had taken cover in a corner, squatting and covering his head like a child.

As Simon was becoming used to the sensation of being violated at his core, he realized that he was not breathing—at all. He tried to force himself to inhale, but nothing happened. Given the circumstances, he felt fine, but the knowledge that he wasn't breathing, or didn't require air at this moment, disturbed him more than the actual lack of oxygen itself. He looked down at his chest, hoping to see the faint rising and falling of his breastbone, but when he didn't, his eyes returned to Addie's in a panic.

What disturbed him more than the fact that he wasn't breathing was the subtle hissing he now heard in the room. He diverted his eyes again—momentarily—from her solid gaze and saw the shadows in the corner of the room begin to coalesce, slowly.

Do not lose focus, she cautioned. *Do not lose focus.*

"But—" he said out loud.

Fear not. Only focus. The sound of her voice released Simon from the throes of panic. Her laconic words were soothing, peaceful. Simon had no doubt that she heard the hissing, too, but if she wasn't worried he decided he wouldn't worry, either. Instead, he took her advice, and with all the strength he could muster, he focused on freeing her.

Then, something extraordinary began to happen; the connection he felt to her faded and the floating objects in the room hit the floor. The lamp shattered and pieces of glass sprayed across the hard floor. Right before his eyes, he witnessed years fade from her face. Her prune-like skin tightened and smoothed out, leaving her cheeks full and unblemished. Her thin, graying hair thickened, its black color deepening. The age spots on her olive-colored skin vanished and flesh seemed to wrap itself around her brittle bones, filling out her sagging skin. In a few minutes the decrepit old woman was replaced with a much younger, fresher-looking woman. The woman who sat in the chair now looked to be in her early forties.

Simon watched her stretch her body deeply, and he listened to the cracking of her bones when she rolled her neck. She suddenly looked lively—alive! Even the haze that glossed over her eyes was gone, leaving shimmering cerulean pools. Now, he could see himself in the richness of her face. She was indeed his blood.

With great effort, she extended her legs and let her feet hit the floor with a plop. They sounded heavy, like stone. He watched her struggle to stand, using her arms to push herself out of the chair. Her arms, weak from atrophy, could barely sustain her weight, in spite of their strong appearance; but, she managed to stand and take a few steps. Her movements were reminiscent of a newly born fawn; shaky, unsteady, but determined.

"Do you need some help?" Simon asked, finally.

She offered a tiny smile. "We must leave. They are coming." Simon had stopped paying attention to the hissing sound, but when he listened closely, it was still there, albeit subtly.

"Who's coming?" Franklin asked, looking around the room nervously.

"Come," she said to Simon, who moved quickly over to her. She threw her arm around his shoulder. "You come, too," she said to Franklin. He stood in place for a few seconds and only moved when he noticed the irritated expression on Simon's face. Then, he rushed over and supported her from the other side. They struggled to take a few steps.

"Wait," Franklin said. "Where we goin'?"

"I don't know. Out of here," Simon shot back.

"What we supposed to tell the nurses outside? How we gon' explain draggin' her out of this room?"

"We must go," Addie urged.

"I don't know. I'll think of something. Let's go," Simon said. They took a few more steps before the hissing sound filled the room. Instinctively, they all froze. The hissing sound seemed to come at them from everywhere in the room simultaneously.

"What the fuck is that?" Franklin asked as the shadows pulled themselves up from the floor in front of the door, slowly taking the shape of a man.

"Simon," the shadow hissed in a voice that sounded so much like Simon's own voice that it unnerved him.

"Simon, do something!" Franklin urged.

"I can't—I don't know how."

"Make some fire, or blow some shit up. Don't just stand there!" Suddenly, Addie removed her arms from their shoulders and slapped the palms of her hands on each of their chests. A blinding bright light filled the room, almost as if the sun itself had fallen into the room. Using their life force to magnify her power, they all vanished in an instant.

In seconds before their disappearing act, Simon got a good look at the shadow-thing that was forming in the room. Even though the flashing light was bright enough to blind, his eyes cut through the brilliance and landed squarely on a face that was exactly like his. Was this some kind of dark trick, some attempt to play with his mind? In that flash of a second, he felt a connection that was so strong that he knew it would, one day, be almost unbreakable. He knew, beyond the shadow of a doubt, that he had a brother. An identical twin brother. And a grandmother.

He was no longer alone in the world.

CHAPTER 22

"Noooooo!" Eli screamed when he saw Adelaide vanish in a flash with Simon. The agonizing sting of anger caused him to shake his head from side to side, trying to understand. If only he had arrived sooner, maybe he would have been able to stop her from absconding with his brother. He was still ailing from ingesting the poisoned magic through Clara's blood and wasn't exactly prepared for a battle with the old woman; but, he wasn't coming to fight. He was coming to simply talk to Addie. He hadn't known that she had been freed from her prison. Only Simon could have released her. Eli was confident that once he stood face-to-face with his twin brother that Simon would have come with him willingly; instead, he lost him. To Adelaide. That bitch. Another failure he'd have to explain to Rebecca and Eetwidomayloh.

As if the shadows needed anything else to worry about.

The Shadowland harbored deep concern—albeit secret concern—that Adelaide's binding spell would hold long after the Ascension and that Simon's powers would never fully develop, thus preventing the foretold reign of The One. She was the most powerful witch that had ever existed and this was uncharted territory; no one knew what was to come. No one *could* know what was to come. The prophecies were bogus and the future remained largely unwritten. But Eli was confident that once his brother learned of his existence, that they'd write their own stories, together. There had to be a part of Simon that felt him all these years, even if only faintly. Eli had to believe that. Through the years, he had felt Simon, too, and there were times he was certain he could have located him, but he chose not to. He wasn't yet ready to give the shadows what they desired most, the other half of the whole. Nor was he was ready to see his mother smile after so many years of enduring her disappointing gazes. He wanted her to suffer and to worry just a bit more; he had never been much of a pleaser.

When he materialized from the shadows into Adelaide's room, he fought the wave of nausea that grew inside his stomach. Being sick and traveling on the wings of shadows wasn't a great combination. Immediately, he latched onto the wall for balance, only to be temporarily blinded by the flash of light that filled the room. In the fleeting seconds before they were gone, he *saw* Simon and was confident that Simon *saw* him, too. They connected, if only for a millisecond. This was the closest he had ever come to his brother and Simon's power was awesome—Eli felt its flare in that infinitesimal flicker of time before they vanished. Even now, traces of his strength lingered in the room. Eli smiled. With the traces of Simon's energy, he'd be able to find him again and when he did, together, they would be unstoppable.

Eli stumbled over to a chair and plopped down, hoping to catch his breath. He looked around the room, wanting to set fire to everything with his thoughts, but any manifestation of his power now was usually followed by a great sickness in his stomach. His strength waned and wavered as his body reacted to Clara's poisoned magic like it was fighting a deadly infection; that bitch Clara would suffer. If she thought what she was going through now was painful, she had no idea what was to come once he fully recovered.

What angered Eli even more than being sickened so close to the Ascension, was the sound of Rebecca's berating voice admonishing him for being brash and impulsive. Her *I-told-you-so* tone in warning him to be wary of Clara struck him at his core; he was tired of being treated like a petulant child, like someone who needed guardianship. He cringed when he thought of the grating sound of her voice chastising him, this time for letting Simon escape.

There was only so much shit he would take from her. By prophecy, everything belonged to him, it was his birthright. He was sovereign over everything and didn't need permission or approval to do anything. He was highborn, a prince—soon to be a king—but she made him feel like a servant. Once he ascended, his powers would multiply, as would Simon's, and they would rule without the nagging voice of his mother or the overbearing oversight of Eetwidomayloh. They were nothing without him and Simon. *Nothing.*

Shadow prophecies had long predicted how their reign was to unfold, with Eetwidomayloh positioned on their right and Rebecca on their left. Eetwidomayloh would be free to walk the earth, his chains loosened and she would be treated as royalty, praised in the streets as The Dark Mother.

Fuck the prophecies.

Eli had other plans; plans that didn't involve either of them.

He and Simon would rule, alone. Once they ascended and claimed what was promised to them, he would crucify her on a cross of bone on the highest hill. He would slit her from navel to nose and let the brave new world bear witness as her innards spilled from her body. Her demise would be epic, as would Eetwidomayloh's. Eli wasn't sure whether or not Eetwidomayloh, the source of all shadows, could actually be killed, but it didn't matter too much to him. Eetwidomayloh's head would be separated from his body—along with his limbs—and cast into a bottomless, sunlit pit for all of eternity. If dismembering him didn't kill him, the blazing light would cut through his bones forever. He would pray for death.

I bet the authors of the prophecies never saw that coming, he thought to himself.

But, in order to rule, he needed Simon. He needed Simon first to heal the sickness that grew in his body; only their combined power could thwart the poison that raced through his veins. That witch, Clara, wasn't simply some two-bit psychic—only a Thibodeaux witch's blood would have such an effect on him. If the infection wasn't eliminated soon, he knew he'd die.

He leaned over and spat a wad of blood onto the floor, violent coughing punching him in the chest. He wiped the blood from the corner of his mouth and steeled his disposition. He wasn't going out like this. He was stronger than this sickness. He was stronger than any poisoned magic. He was The One—or at least half of *The One*.

Eli sat in the chair and he felt his strength returning to him as he ignored the calls from the Shadowland to return. Hissing sounds filled the room, beckoning him, but he wasn't yet ready to return. He tried to block out the sounds, but they penetrated his mind.

Eli felt rage boiling to the surface. When he could no longer bear the hissing sounds that scratched at him, he opened his mouth and let out a shriek that could be heard in every room and every crack and crevice in the center. His voice punched through walls, shattered glass, overturned heavy furniture and machinery, and knocked patients out of their beds; it was like a hurricane ripping through the place. Immediately, Eli felt stabbing pains in his stomach, but his rage was stronger than his sickness.

In the seconds right after Eli disappeared in the shadows, the entire building imploded.

⚔

Heavy snow fell continuously from the sullen sky, blanketing Louisiana and much of the southern states. The effects of the snow were fierce: snarling traffic and plunging many cities into darkness; its weight snapping power lines across much of the region. There was no warning for the blizzard-like conditions. Meteorologists across the south decried what they termed as the *freak Christmas snowstorm of the century*.

From the window of a house perched high somewhere, Simon could see and hear the winds of the storm below; yet, when he looked directly out of the window, it was all sunshine and iridescent colors. The green of the grass and the yellows, purples, and reds of the flowers in the yard almost glistened. From the subtle movements of the plants in the yard, he guessed that a warm breeze caused them to gently bend and lean. The scene was utterly picturesque, like something out of a painting. Here, he was completely shielded from the turmoil in the real world; here, in this false world, he felt, at peace.

But, it wasn't real. Simon knew that. It was something Adelaide had conjured.

Several times, Simon tried to leave the house, to open a door or break a window, but to no avail; the door simply did not budge and even when he hurled a chair against the window it didn't break or even scratch. He was trapped.

Addie was locked in a room in the back, presumably sleeping. When they arrived in this manufactured place, she told him she must rest and then stumbled her way into the room in the back.

Simon heard the heavy locks snap into place when she closed the door. It was evident that she didn't trust him.

That was twelve hours ago.

And, while she slept, Simon had waking dreams of a man with a face exactly like his; only, it wasn't a dream. It was his brother, who existed in another place, a place Simon couldn't reach. Even across the vast distance that separated them, Simon felt him and longed to connect with him. His longing was a constant itch, an almost aching need.

He continued to stare out of the window, thinking about the profound ways in which his life had changed, almost in an instant. Only days ago, life had been so serene; now, peace was a distant memory, a far-off place. Images flashed across his mind of a life that no longer existed; a life that could no longer exist. He thought of Franklin and of Brooke and of Cisco and of The Black Cat and of Starry Nights and longed for simpler days; days without magic and mystical forces; days without shadows and snakes and haunting dreams of Addie and his father and the Shadowman.

"You want to know who you are?" a voice called out from behind him. When he turned, he saw Addie standing before him. She was dressed in a free-flowing blue dress with yellow flowers. Her coal-black hair hung low, far below her shoulders. She looked youthful; the wrinkles that had carved deep rivers into her face only hours ago had simply faded away, leaving her skin luminescent and her blue eyes sparkling—eyes like his.

"I want to know *what* I am. But I also want to know what you did with Franklin. Where is he?"

"Your friend is out of harm's way. I thought that would be best. He won't remember any of this." She moved closer to him and placed her hand on his shoulder, cautiously.

"Why are you scared of me?" he asked as he returned his gaze to the outside world.

"I'm not afraid of you, Simon."

"What's that smell, then? I have smelled more fear in the last two weeks than I have in my whole life. I know what fear smells like. It leaves a bad taste in my mouth," he said, without looking her direction. "Where are we?"

"We are in a protected space between worlds. We can't stay here much longer."

"Good. 'Cause I wanna go home."

"Come. Sit," she said as she moved over to the couch. She pointed at the chair in front of her. "You have many questions." She waved her hands across the coffee table and an old leather-bound book materialized on the table. "This book will provide you with answers."

Answers. The one thing Simon had craved all his life was now the thing he feared. The answers he longed for were written in the pages of some book on a table a few feet from where he stood.

Slowly, he moved over to the chair and sat. Instantly, the book appeared in his lap.

"Read," Addie instructed. He looked at her and then down at the book in his lap. When he touched it, he felt vibrations, as if the book were alive. He opened the thick black cover and gazed at the first page, which he couldn't understand. The book was written in symbols and thick, curvy lines.

"I can't read this."

"I'm certain that you can." Simon looked down again, but all he saw were symbols. He looked up, frustrated. "That book is the ancient text of the sister-clan. It can only be read by members of the clan; yet, I am confident you can read it. It tells who you are—or will be."

Simon looked down at the book again. He closed the book and placed his hand on top of the weathered leather cover. He closed his eyes, inhaling slowly. He felt the book's vibrations grow stronger, faster. As the vibrations grew in intensity, Simon *felt* the words of the book tell its story. He learned of the sister-clan, the protectors of the light. He learned of the shadows and the shadow-creature that he saw in the restroom at The Black Cat. His name was Eetwidomayloh, which means *he who greets with fire*. He learned of the ageless battle between the light and the shadows. And, he learned of The One who would end the battle and drown the world in blood. He learned of so many things. The years of stories buzzed by, filling his head with ancient knowledge. His head snapped from side to side, sometimes violently.

He suddenly jerked his hand from the book and tossed it onto the table like it was a hot piece of metal. He leapt to his feet and moved quickly to the other side of the room, putting distance between himself and the book.

"Bullshit! This isn't me—all of this a lie, some kind of trick!"

"It is true, Simon. In your heart you know it is." Her voice was serene, calm.

"I'm not a killer or a king or this *one* everybody is so scared of. I don't want this. I don't want any of this. I want to get back to my life and back to my girlfriend and my job; forget that any of this ever happened." Angry tears burned his eyes.

"You have darkness in you. You have felt it; you have seen it manifest and you cannot ignore it," she said as she stood and moved closer to him. "But, you also have goodness in you. When you were born, I blessed your blood with goodness, with light, with love. You are more than what's written." She grabbed his hand and held it between hers, tenderly; as he always imagined his grandmother would.

"I don't care what that book says. I'm not anything like that. I wanna go home."

"I have so much to show you; so much to teach you. Let us sit." She took Simon's hand and guided him back to the chair. "I know the question in your heart. And you are right. He is your brother. His name is Eli."

"How could I have an identical twin that I know nothing about? How could you keep me from him? Do you have any idea how lonely a child I was? I needed someone—someone related to me. I've spent twenty years feeling like a freak, an outsider, and now, all of a sudden, I have family. This is some bullshit."

Addie stood up and moved over to the kitchen as she spoke. "I hid you from the shadows for your safety—for the safety of us all. Eli is lost to the light. We couldn't lose you, too." She reached into the cabinet, pulled out two cups and poured water into each one. Instantly, the water boiled and she dropped a tea bag into each cup.

"I can't get my head around any of this. All these years, the only thing I ever really wanted was a family. Where are my parents, my mother and my father?"

"Your mother is with Eli. She, too, is lost. They seek to corrupt you, to bring you to the shadows."

"What about my father? Where is he?"

Simon sensed Addie's emotions constrict. "He is dead." Her tone didn't leave much room for conversation, but Simon pushed.

"I've dreamed of him. I've felt him. Thomas. That's his name, isn't it? My father. Your son. I think he's been speaking to me over the years."

Addie quickly set down the tea. "What has he said to you?"

"Sometimes when I'm in trouble, or scared, I hear a voice in my head saying, 'Don't be afraid.' I just realized that it was him speaking to me."

"How can this be?" Addie said, more to herself. "You must tell me everything he has said to you—everything."

"That's it—'don't be afraid'—that's all he said. What happened to him?"

"He died. In a car accident."

Carrying two mugs of hot tea, she moved back into the living room, placing a cup before him. She sat down onto the couch and brought the cup to her mouth. She blew into the cup, scattering the rising steam. "Drink," she said. Simon picked up the cup of tea and let the sweet aroma fill his nostrils.

"What of my brother?"

"He is evil incarnate."

"That can't be true."

"It is. He would see this world lie in ruins. And, he would free Eetwidomayloh, giving him dominion to walk the earth." From the knowledge he gained from her book, Simon understood that only the power of The One could unlock the gates and free him from the Shadowland. When Eetwidomayloh was free to walk the earth he would bring with him every dark creature over which he had power. They would unleash an unknown reign of terror on the earth, a reign of terror led by The One.

"But, he's my brother—my identical twin brother—aren't we the same?"

"You share the same darkness."

"Stop saying that." Simon grew agitated. "Tell me how to stop this. What do I need to do?"

She sipped on her tea and Simon sipped his. The moment the tea hit his throat he felt a fire burn in him.

"What is this?" he asked.

"It is an ancient tea of my sister-clan. It provides peace of mind. Drink again. It won't hurt as much. You will need the clarity it provides." Cautiously, Simon picked up the cup and sipped again, fighting the urge to choke. The more he sipped, the more he wanted to sip. The bitterness of the beverage turned to honey sweetness, and he found himself craving more of it.

"You keep talking about the darkness in me. How do I get it *out* of me? I mean, can't you do an exorcism or something? Can't I give my powers away or bury them or something?"

"You are the first male born of the first born Thibodeaux male. The prophecies have made you what you are. I cannot undo it; no one can."

"What the hell can you do, then? I don't want to become this… this *thing*. You have to help me!" Simon's voice suddenly went from calm to frantic. He slammed the cup of tea down, spilling some of it on the table, and leapt to his feet. He felt a strong burning sensation inside his chest and a tingling in his fingers and toes.

"Simon," Addie said as she rose to her feet, "you must control it. Do not let the dark control you. Anger, lust, rage, jealousy, fear—all bring you closer to the shadows." She stepped toward him. "Control it."

"No, don't come any closer," he cautioned. "Stay away from me."

"Control it, Simon." When she tried to take a few more steps toward him, he raised his hand, and, instantly, she was thrown against the wall.

"I'm sorry. I didn't mean to—"

"Control it!" she yelled.

"I don't want to be here. I want to go home!"

Simon felt a sudden tingling in his chest as a bright, yellow light consumed the room. "You can't have me—none of you can!" he screamed out.

In a flash, he was gone.

⇥ CHAPTER 23

B efore he could complete a blink, Simon was standing in the middle of his living room when only seconds ago he was in an unknown place with Adelaide. Somehow, he had been transported here, to his home, with a single thought. He remembered talking to her about who he was predicted to become and the carnage he would inflict upon the world. He was overwhelmed by the weight of her words and remembered really wanting to be in the safety and comfort of his home, and then he was standing here.

In his living room.

Alone.

There's no place like home.

He turned his head slowly and looked around at the place, taking time to fully process his surroundings. Everything was exactly the way he left it. The remote control was on the table; a half-empty glass of apple juice sat near it. The pillows on the couch were misaligned, and the stain on the carpet where he spilled cranberry juice a few weeks ago was still there. *Damn, it felt good to be home*. He needed respite from the supernatural lunacy that had surrounded him. He felt safe here, in spite of the paranormal occurrences that continued to plague him.

He sighed.

His apartment was dark and frigid. Cold breezes seeped in

from underneath the door and from the window sill. He had complained about the lack of sufficient insulation but never raised a stink about it with the landlord; never wanting to be a bother to anyone. The entire apartment was deathly quiet, as if it hadn't known life in years. Wintry air embraced him, wrapping itself around him like the chilly arms of a long, lost lover; he shuddered while wrapping his arms around himself.

He moved over to the lamp on the table and clicked it on, expelling some of the darkness; but, shadows still lingered all around. Everywhere there seemed to be shadows; even the shadows had shadows. He then moved over to the thermostat on the wall and flipped the switch. He waited for the heating unit to start its familiar hum, but it remained quiet. He tried again. Still, it was quiet. *Shit*, he said to himself when he remembered the unpaid and unopened gas bill that littered his kitchen counter. He had meant to pay it, but there had been too much going on for him to remember something as simple as a utility bill.

Simon decided to try something. He focused on the heating unit; with a slight tingle in his index finger, he touched the thermostat and heard the unit click on. *This power has to be good for something*, he thought.

His body cut through the stillness of the apartment as he moved about, not sure exactly what to do next. He stepped into the living room and stopped when he neared the window. The heavy snowfall continued, and the land was covered in white as far as the eye could see. Cars parked along the curb were nearly buried by the snow and the street itself was hidden, blending seamlessly with the curb and the sidewalk. Streetlights cast a dim illumination on the abandoned urban block. Outside, all was quiet; the snow had forced people to retreat into their homes.

Destroyer of worlds. The words kept ringing in his head. *Destroyer of worlds.* The words taunted him. *Destroyer of worlds.* The words haunted him. All he wanted was his simple life back. He didn't want this power and he had no intention of destroying anything. Then, he remembered the feeling that consumed him in the forest with Franklin and realized that he might be capable of tearing down the world if he had the power; and apparently he did, or at least he soon would, when he *ascended*—whatever that meant—on his twenty-first birthday, which was in two days. He trembled when he thought of what could be. He was more afraid of himself than he was of snakes and shadows and the Shadowman that wanted to claim him.

Simon shook his head and then walked through the lonely house, assessing his imminent fate. Only days ago he had been happy, happy here, in his apartment. He remembered the recent card party Franklin threw with some of his buddies from The Black Cat and the laughter that filled the house that night. Simon won almost two hundred dollars that night. He and Franklin had spent countless nights drinking into the wee hours of the morning, lamenting life and blasting whatever trouble rocked their relationship of the moment; that was before Brooke. Simon's mind was pulled to thoughts of her. Her voice always filled his apartment with such life and love, especially on days when he had been content to keep the curtains pulled to block out the sun. She was often his light. He remembered holding her, and all the memories of their passion confronted him, regardless of which direction he looked in the small space; they had made love all over the place. He could smell her everywhere and, for the first time in days, it hit him hard how much he missed her; it was like one of his limbs had been removed. The pain of her absence had been there all along, simmering just beneath the surface of his extraordinary circumstances. As he stood in the silent room, the pain made itself known, screaming throughout his body, like a chill deep in his bones. He felt tears welling in his eyes, but he beat them back, unsure of what damage his emotional breakdown would cause.

He moved through his bedroom and into the bathroom. When he flicked up the light switch, he saw the ugly black marks, caused by his blood and vomit, that stained the floor. He was repulsed by the sight of it, but stopped cold when he saw a curvy black trail left by the serpent when it slithered hurriedly across the floor and disappeared into a crack. He closed his eyes and shuddered when he remembered the awesome pain he felt when the snake squirmed out of his mouth. *Where was the snake now?* he thought to himself.

As he stood in the bathroom, a familiar scent wafted into his nostrils. He opened his eyes and looked around the room, searching for its source. The scent was like fresh flowers, like lavender—like a perfume Brooke wore. The pace of his heart quickened. He stepped out of the bathroom and moved across the bedroom. As he neared the living room, the scent grew stronger. When he reached the threshold, he peered around the corner, nervously. He gasped. Brooke stood in the doorway that divided the living room from the dining area, at the edge of the room. She had never looked more beautiful to him. Her blonde hair cascaded down her shoulders like ocean waves, and the depth of the smoldering blue in her eyes had never been more mesmerizing. She wore a pink flowing gown, like something a princess would wear. She was resplendent. She smiled at him, delicately. He had never missed her more than he did in this moment. His aching for her was palpable, almost tangible. He wanted to move closer, if only to be closer to her scent, but something held him in place. Something was wrong. Her body was hazy, out-of-sync with the rest of the room. Still, her beauty filled the space, and the longing he felt for her vibrated in his pants. It had been days since he had felt an orgasmic release, and the sight of her burned deeply within his loins.

"Simon," she whispered. Her voice fluttered across the room, warming the frigid air as it traveled. When her voice landed against his chest, it took all the force he could muster to keep from running over to her, tackling her and mounting her. His love for her was deep and even though he vowed to never say the word, he felt so weak in this moment that it had already formed on his lips.

But, before he could speak, the image dissipated, like smoke scattered by the wind.

"Simon, Simon, Simon. How I have waited for this day." Simon flipped around and standing behind him was the man with a face like his—his twin. Simon jerked his body quickly, his feet tangling around each other as he tried to step away. He fell hard against the wall, but recovered instantly and stumbled into the living room. "Don't be alarmed," his twin said in a calm voice. "I didn't mean to scare you. My name is Eli, but I'm sure you know that by now." Eli's voice echoed throughout the room. "I've been looking for you, for years," he said with relief. "My brother, at long last."

Simon steadied himself and watched Eli, dressed all in black, walk toward him. His long gait was exactly like Simon's, but he stepped boldly, with far more confidence; whereas Simon liked to fade into the background, it was clear by his walk that Eli loved center stage. His stride bordered on being sinister. Eli's presence was formidable and spellbinding. Simon longed for an ounce of the self-assuredness Eli possessed in spades. Simon was simply awe-struck and studied Eli's face; it was his face. Eli's eyes burned with the same intensity as his, but his wavy hair was slicked back and Simon's was in a Caesar cut. They were the same, but very much different; and, Simon longed to know him. The familial ties that he had longed for all of his life suddenly tightened around his neck. He hadn't felt this sensation with Addie, even though she was his grandmother. He didn't want any of this *stuff* that he had been subjected to over the past days, but he wanted a family. The magnetic pull to Eli was strong, like two halves itching to become a whole. Simon wanted to know him, wanted to be him.

"Oh my God," Simon said, his heart pounding in his throat.

"No, not *God*. Just me." The corners of his mouth curled up into a twisted smile.

"But how?"

They took a few awkward seconds and sized each other up, checking to see exactly how identical they were. There was no denying it; they were exactly the same. Same height. Same weight. Same body composition. Same piercing blue eyes and olive skin. "We have a lot to talk about, dear brother," Eli said, finally breaking the tension. "Do you have anything to drink?"

"Uhhh, yeah. I have some water or juice in the 'fridge."

Eli looked at him playfully. "I was hoping for something with a little more…kick."

"Shit. I'm sorry. I have some vodka in the freezer." Truth be told, Simon craved something far stronger than juice, too. He needed something with some fire to calm his nerves.

"Now you're talking." Simon moved around Eli and entered the kitchen, but when he looked toward the refrigerator Eli was already in there staring out of the window at the snowfall. Clearly, he had the same ability to travel as Simon did. Simon didn't show his alarm. Instead, he reached into the cabinet and pulled out two glasses.

"Look at this beautiful storm," he said reverently. "I wonder if it will bury the world."

"Let's hope not." Simon opened the freezer door, pulled out the very cold bottle of vodka and poured more than a healthy amount into each glass. "Do you want some juice or something to mix it with?" As soon as he asked the question, he realized how silly it must have sounded.

Eli grabbed the glass off the table, but a rough cough rose from his chest and threw him off balance. He grabbed onto the kitchen counter for support.

"Are you okay?"

Eli didn't respond. Instead, he reached over and grabbed the roll of paper towels that sat on the counter. In the midst of a cough, he ripped one from the roll and brought it to his mouth. When he was done, he wiped a trace of black mucus from the corner of his mouth; it looked to be the same substance that came from Simon when he vomited the snake. Eli tossed the towel into the trashcan.

"You need to sit down."

"I'm fine."

"You don't look fine."

"I said I'm fine," he snapped. He grabbed his glass from the counter and raised it. "Here's to us, brothers. Reunited at last. Let our reign begin." *Reign.* Simon didn't like the way the word burned across his ear, but he raised his glass anyway, clinking it against Eli's. They each took a long pull from their cups and the cold burn from the vodka instantly warmed Simon's chest. Eli finished his drink in a hurried gulp and poured himself another.

"Let's talk." Simon watched Eli stroll into the living room. "You can't know how much effort and time we've put into finding you. You were well-hidden by the witch's cloaking spell."

"The witch?" Simon asked as he rounded the corner and entered the living room.

"Adelaide. Our dear grandmother. The one you *freed*." Eli's tone soured when he spoke of Addie, and a flash of something malevolent swept across his eyes. "I assume she used some trick of the mind to get you to free her, but I won't dwell on that. What's done is done. I would, however, like to know what she told you about us, about me."

"Nothing. I mean, not much. I left before we finished talking. I had to get out of there; I wanted to come home."

"Good. You shouldn't trust her. She's a bitch. And a liar." Eli lowered himself onto the couch, taking his time to make sure that he was comfortable. He crossed his legs at the thigh, fully ensconced in the comfort of the chair. "You know she's the one who kept you from us, right? She's the one who ripped you from the loving bosom of our dear mother. This hard life you've had," he said as he looked around the room with disdain, "is all her fault. You could have been basking in luxury, in paradise, had it not been for her."

Simon felt heat building in his chest. "Is that true?" Simon wanted to trust him, but he tread lightly. He was wise enough to know that truth changed, depending on the storyteller. Was he to put his faith in Addie or his brother? He didn't know. He didn't know either of them; both gave him reason to pause. As he listened to the slick words that oozed out of Eli's mouth a warning sounded in his heart, much as it had when he listened to Addie. He wanted to trust Eli. After all, weren't they the same?

"I wouldn't lie to you, brother." Eli sipped from his glass. "Oh, she also killed our father. Burned him alive."

"She said he died in a car crash."

"That much is true, but she probably left out the fact that *she* caused the accident. When he didn't die upon impact, she set loose a fire that utterly consumed his body—turned him to ash right there in the street. Oh, the stories I could tell you about dear old grandma." Eli spoke so casually about the death of their father that it was eerie. The heat continued to build in Simon's chest. He didn't know what to say or do. His thoughts were convoluted and erratic; there was simply too much to process.

"Oh, I'm sorry about the image of Brooke. I was reading your emotions and that's what you were projecting. I didn't mean to send her to you like that."

"It's okay."

"You love her, don't you?"

Simon paused. "Yeah. I guess," he said, slowly, as he took a sip. "Yeah, I love her," he said more confidently. "I do." He had never said the words out loud before, but they felt good on his lips.

"These human emotions will be the death of us all," Eli said, shaking his head in disappointment. "I guess I can't blame you, though. After all, you've been around *them* all your life. I can smell them on you." Eli coughed again, but Simon ignored it.

"We're not...human?"

"We're so much more than that."

"This is too much for me. In the last few days, after spending a lifetime alone, I find out that I have a grandmother and a twin brother. Now, you're telling me I ain't human? What am I? A demon? Some kind of vampire?"

Eli chuckled. "Vampire? Really? Don't be silly."

"I tasted another man's blood. And, I liked it. How do you explain that?"

"How did it make you feel?"

Simon spoke with no hesitation. "Powerful. It made me feel powerful."

Eli smiled and raised his glass. "We are indeed brothers." He leaned deep into the chair. "We are many things. We are everything. Vampires and demons—even angels—will worship at our feet. Everything that walks on the earth, crawls beneath it, or flies above it will serve our will. Everything will bow down to us. We are The One."

Simon took a long sip from his glass and shifted in his seat before speaking again. He wasn't sure if Eli's boastful words were hyperbole or if he should take them at face value; regardless, his words were enticing. "One of Adelaide's books said that I am the destroyer of worlds."

"*We* are the destroyer of worlds. *We*," Eli corrected. "And what do you mean you *read it in one of her books*?"

"She had some old book with a bunch of symbols that I couldn't read at first, but she insisted that I could. I tried, but I opened it and saw gibberish."

"Her books are written in a language only known by her sister-clan. I want to know how *you* read it."

"I didn't exactly read it. I put my hand on it and I knew everything that was in it—I knew." Eli's eyes flashed.

"Marvelous. Simply marvelous. We have been trying to read their language for eons. You are indeed powerful, and, together, we will be unstoppable. We will grind kingdoms to dust and build a whole new world; a world in which we are worshipped as deities. We will be gods." A ravenous lust flickered across Eli's eyes as his prophetic words drifted across the room, mesmerizing Simon and igniting within him ambition he never knew he possessed. Naked ambition. It warmed Simon's loins. Simon had never been strong on ambition, but Eli's words suddenly gave him a raging emotional erection; the throbbing he felt went far beyond simple lust. He was jonesing for something he had never really had before—power. He let out a slow hiss, like air escaping from a tire. The dark was rising in his soul.

He tried to hold on to memories of love and friendships.

"What if I don't wanna be this...this *destroyer of worlds*. I don't wanna destroy anything; that sounds so morbid. I kinda like this world."

Eli leaned a little closer to Simon. "We can make one that is *so* much better. This world is full of pain and death and misery. There are starving children everywhere you look. Horrific acts of war are committed on a daily basis. What is there to like about *this* world? This world is dying more and more each day." Simon didn't say it out loud, but Eli made a good point. There were so many things wrong with this world, but there were so many things that he thought were right, too. Like Brooke. Like Franklin. Like music. Like smiling and laughing children. Many things.

"Do we have the same powers?" Simon asked, changing the subject.

"I don't know. No one is sure what powers you have."

"How do I control them? You seemed to have mastered yours."

"Ahhhh, that's a bit more tricky with you, brother. That bitch Adelaide bound your powers at birth." His tone sharpened.

"She did what?"

Eli exhaled as if he couldn't believe Simon didn't know the answer. "I have so much to teach you. She *bound* them. It's a little trick witches use to block the powers of their enemies. She cast a powerful binding spell on you to prevent the maturation of your powers. That's why your powers come out in spurts—probably tied to your emotions—but who the hell really knows? The witch is clever. She's trying to deny you your birthright. You see how evil she is?"

"I'm not her enemy."

"Yes, you are and she will *try* to kill you the first chance she gets. Addie is neither weak nor foolish. She is cunning as a fox and strong as a lion. Do not take her kindness for love. Behind every smile is a plot to rid the world of you—of me."

"I was with her. She could've killed me if she wanted."

"Killing us isn't a simple task. We are unlike anything that has ever existed." Simon exhaled. The more Eli spoke, the more Simon realized that nothing would ever be the same again. Not for him. Not for the world.

"Why didn't she bind your powers, too?" Simon asked after a few moments.

"Because," he responded coolly, "she didn't know about me. I surprised everyone, including Eetwidomayloh." Eli relayed the full story of their birth and as he spoke, Simon was suddenly flooded by vivid memories of being in the womb. He remembered. He even remembered sharing the womb with someone else. *Eli.* Old memories swept over him like a tsunami. He remembered speaking to his mother, telling her to *push.*

"Oh my God," Simon said in astonishment. "I remember. I remember it all. I remember the cabin. I remember my mother. I remember Addie. There was a storm that night—a really bad one."

"Do you remember being torn from our mother? Do you remember the pain our mother felt? I remember it. I felt it in the womb and I'm sure you did, too."

That old pain came back to Simon. Pain he didn't even know he carried. It came to him in hard, jagged bursts that jabbed against his insides; it was an animal longing to be free. He lurched forward. "I remember."

"It's all coming back to you, isn't it?" Eli smiled.

Simon's eyes went black. Completely.

"That's it, brother. Remember. Remember who you were meant to be."

This time Simon didn't fight the darkness. He didn't want to. He let it wash over him. He let the pain of his birth flush through his body. He let every hurt he had ever felt in his heart sweep over him. Every part of his body tingled as if a low-level electrical current ran through his frame. His body shuddered and the feeling was pleasurable, almost erotic. He felt close to orgasm. His skin was alive, crawling with power.

"That's it, brother. Embrace the power. Embrace it."

The surge of energy that flowed through Simon completely took over him. He saw flashes of light followed by piercing sounds. His senses were on fire. He felt omnipotent, god-like. Slowly, he rose to his feet, feeling fully in control of the world. He gazed at his brother who seemed astonished by the energy Simon emitted.

"You are sick, my brother," Simon said in a voice so deep it seemed to drop to the floor. "I will make you whole."

"No, Simon. You can't. When we ascend, my powers will heal me."

"That's *if* you make it to the Ascension. You are sicker than you know. I can smell your death." Eli's eyes widened, in shock. "I will heal you now."

"No," Eli protested, "to heal me you have to take my sickness into your body. I can't let you do that."

Simon smiled confidently and then let out a chuckle. "You worry too much, my brother." Before Eli could utter another word Simon was upon him, the palm of his hand firmly planted against Eli's forehead. Simon closed his black eyes and felt a rush of heat throughout his body. He looked down on Eli whose body convulsed violently as pools of the black substance gathered in the corners of his mouth before flowing slowly down his face. Simon felt the poisoned magic leave Eli's body and enter his. He felt sharp pains in his stomach, but he withstood them, fearlessly, all for his brother. Tonight, he would save Eli. He had no doubt.

When Simon removed his hand from Eli's head, he was blasted across the room, landing hard on the floor on his back. He felt the foreign magic inside of him, struggling to take hold, to control him, but Simon held it back—he wouldn't let it take root.

Simon let out a scream so primal that it sounded as if it originated from the depths of hell itself. It was a raw, scratching, unhuman yell that could not be contained. The yell lasted for several seconds, and then it was over.

Eli stood over him, his chest rising and falling with rapid breaths. "Simon, are you okay?"

A smile formed in the corner of Simon's mouth. "*We* are fine," he said, knowing they both had survived.

"You…you…saved my life. This is incredible. I didn't think it could be done until we had our full power." Eli eyed Simon curiously, his voice full of awe and wonder.

"I knew I could," Simon said as he reached for Eli's extended arm to pull himself from the floor. Simon stood, feeling slightly queasy, but he steadied himself.

"Now, let's go have some fun."

W hen Addie materialized inside the foyer of Clara's house she felt the presence of evil. The pungent odor of it was unmistakable. The foul odor permeated every inch of the house, as if it had been born there and had continued to multiply unchecked over the years. With her first inhalation, Addie felt pains of dread stab her in her stomach; the smell was sharp, stabbing. It took her a few moments to steady herself and adjust to the smell.

When she adjusted to the odor, she looked around the room carefully. The darkness in the house was thick, almost impermeable. Addie felt it grip her tightly, trying to consume her, to swallow her whole. She calmed her temperament and focused so that she could cut through the void with her eyes. Her senses were acute. Shadows covered the room and at any moment she realized they could spring to life and assault her. Much of her power was still being used to hold together the binding spell, but she was far from defenseless.

She took a few meek footsteps, moving with feline-like finesse so that the wooden floor beneath her feet wouldn't betray her position with sound. She surveyed the room, using her magic to feel it out. She couldn't detect any evil in the immediate area, save for the smell of the room. In fact, the evil that she sensed seemingly poured into the room from upstairs. She knew she had to venture to the second floor, but she couldn't leave the downstairs area unguarded. For her protection, she weaved together golden light that transformed into a net. She gently pushed the net into the air and watched golden webs of light spin. Within seconds the golden light faded, but the entire downstairs area was draped in a spider web-like net that would trap any and all shadows and prevent them from moving. The web was invisible, as well as impenetrable, to any creatures that lurked in the dark.

Once she was confident that the area was secure, she moved to the staircase and looked up toward the second level of the house. She could hear voices, faint voices, but couldn't decipher the words. Were the words threats or simple conversation? She wanted to materialize into the room from which the voices came, but it would be too dangerous. If whatever evil that was in the room detected her appearance before she fully came into form, it would have the advantage and would be able to strike first, possibly a fatal blow. She couldn't risk it. She placed her hand on the banister and slowly lifted her weight onto the step. It creaked. She froze, her heart pushing into her throat. She waited a few seconds to make sure she had not been detected. She listened closely and the voices continued to speak, uninterrupted.

Then, one by one, she carefully glided up the stairs.

Once she reached the second level, she surreptitiously moved toward the room at the end of the hallway—Clara's room. The stench was striking; much more bitter on this floor than on the lower level. It lodged deep in Addie's throat and she fought the urge to cough violently.

Addie glided closer to the room. A faint light spilled from the cracked door into the dark hallway, enough light for Addie to see Rebecca's fiery hair. Rebecca stood to the left of Clara, pacing back and forth. It took all the strength Addie could muster not to gasp out loud when she saw Clara's face; pieces of jagged glass were buried deep into her once-beautiful face, and fresh blood ran down her cheeks. Clara's pleading eyes were only half-open, as was her twisted mouth. Rebecca leaned in and screwed a shard of glass deeper into Clara's face. Clara's body jerked and she let out a moan that told Addie that she was close to death. Addie could see Rebecca's hands, which were stained red with blood, Clara's blood.

"Is this what you had in mind for yourself when you poisoned my son, *witch*?" Rebecca asked, her voice a scathing whisper. "Because of you, my son is wandering this world, not answering my calls. He is lost to his mother and to the shadows. Do you know the pain I feel as a mother, unable to protect my child from harm?" She brought her hands to her chest. Her voice carried pain, a mother's agony. "He could be anywhere, lying dead or dying because of you!" she yelled. She stepped back and took a few seconds to calm herself. "Until I find him, you will not have a moment's peace. I will keep you teetering on the edge of death forever, so I can have the pleasure of torturing you and tasting your blood," she said as she licked her fingers clean. She slapped Clara across the face. Clara made a gurgling sound, as if blood were caught in her throat.

Addie fought back angry tears that burned in her eyes. This madness was about to end. Abruptly. She balled her fists and clenched her lips tightly together as a tremendous force suddenly pushed through the room, blowing the door off its hinges. The door hurled swiftly through the air and flew directly into Rebecca, one of its edges hitting her directly in her chest. She crashed into the wall with a bang and let out a painful scream.

Addie flew into the room, her feet hovering inches above the ground, her black hair blowing in the wind. She watched Rebecca struggle to dig herself from underneath a pile of rubble and lurch clumsily to her feet. When Rebecca looked up and saw Addie's face, shock caused her body to shudder.

"You!" she screamed. Rebecca flicked her wrist and attempted to throw Addie across the room with her power, but Addie absorbed it and sent it back to Rebecca, who once again crashed into the wall, banging her head hard.

"You may be The Dark Mother, Rebecca, but I am the Priestess Supreme of the Thibodeaux Sister-Clan. You have no power here, *demon*." Rebecca stood on wobbly legs, her beautiful white dress now stained red with blood. "You will not touch her again." Addie's words were absolute. "You will not even look her direction."

Rebecca stood up and her eyes rolled to the back of her head, as if she was dizzy. She steadied herself and then faced Addie, letting out a maniacal laugh. "Is this your payback, my dear? Payback for all of the things we did to you while you were locked in that decaying body for decades? Is that why you are here? Vengeance does not suit you, Adelaide Thibodeaux. If vengeance is what you seek, you shall not have it!" Rebecca waved her arms and attempted to disintegrate into shadows, but Addie clenched her fist and held her together, firmly in place. Rebecca's neck craned as she looked around the room, shocked that she had not been able to easily fade away.

"Your powers are great," she said to Addie, "great, indeed. Enjoy them while you can, *Priestess*. The Ascension—your day of reckoning—is upon us. We will rid the world of your kind, once and for all. We—my sons and I—shall usher in a glorious new era. And when my sons reign as kings I will make them give you to me. You will be kept as my slave, chained and gagged. I will have you walk across hot glass on all fours, like the animal you are. I will feed you the feces of goats on a silver platter; after all, you are a *high priestess*." Rebecca spoke in a pleasant tone as a smile formed in the corners of her mouth.

Addie didn't speak.

"Have my words frightened you? Are you afraid of the truth I speak? You cannot win. The time of the great protectors—the sister-clan—is over."

Addie would never show weakness or concern, but Rebecca's words about the Ascension had, indeed, unsettled her. The thought of the world plunging into darkness chilled her to her bones. She would do anything and everything to prevent that from happening. Her options were few, but until her last breath, she would remain resolute in her opposition.

Addie chuckled. "Idle threats from The Dark Mother. Is that all you offer? The world of which you speak shall never come to pass. It was your son who freed me from the dark magic. He is good and decent and will never succumb to your will."

Rebecca's head recoiled as if she had been struck by Addie's words. "I am certain that you used one of your witchy tricks to convince him to free you."

"The only trick I used was love. Simon is full of love."

"Love; an unstable emotion. Love will not save you. I am his mother. I can feel his longing for me in the whispers of the night. His spirit calls out to me. You can never compete with that, old woman."

"And yet, you still cannot find him. Pity."

"That is because of your magic, witch! You have kept me from my son and for that you will suffer!"

Addie flicked her wrist again and Rebecca screamed out.

"You will not threaten me again."

"Listen, Adelaide. Listen carefully," Rebecca said, taking a deep breath. "Our offer of immunity still stands. Forget what I said earlier. If you let me go, you will be allowed to live in luxury after they ascend. We do not have to be enemies. You are the grand-mother and I am the mother—we are forever connected; neither of us can change that."

Addie released a snide chuckle. "Is that all you have to offer? Moments ago you were going to feed me goat shit—on a silver platter."

"I spoke in haste, out of anger. Forgive me, my dear. Let me go and I can assure you that you will have a seat at the table when we discuss the new world order."

"There will be no new world order."

"Do not be naïve. Look around you. It is over for you; don't be a fool, you do not have to perish. Death does not have to claim you. You do not have to dwell in this frozen wasteland. Let me go, and come with me. Let us bask on sunny shores." Rebecca's smile lit up the room. Her voice had taken on an enchanting musical quality as she spoke. Addie found herself becoming lightheaded, feeling as if she were floating. Rebecca continued speaking, her spell spinning into Addie's ears. Addie's eyes closed and she felt as if she were no longer tethered to the floor. The pleasant sound of Rebecca's voice filled the hollow spaces in Addie's heart; the space that longed for her sisters, the space occupied by fear of the future, and even that silent space that still mourned the death of her son, Thomas. When Rebecca's voice tickled that space in her heart that was Thomas, Addie snapped out of her trance, quickly. She remembered that it was Thomas's seed that brought forth The One.

"Your mind tricks won't work tonight." Addie spoke in a scathing voice. "Dark Mother, I bind your powers—"

"No. Stop," Rebecca protested.

"I bind your powers now and forever more. I bind you. I bind you. I bind you."

"Fuck you!" Rebecca screamed, the obscenity projecting from her mouth like a missile. She suddenly became infuriated, her body squirming violently with anger, trying to loosen Addie's grip on her. Her face contorted into an obscene caricature, her jaw unhinging and her mouth twisting into an enormous black hole. Strands of her flaming red hair became agitated serpents, snapping angrily in the air at Addie. "I will drag you to hell myself, Adelaide!" she hissed. Addie suddenly remembered the snakes that Eli routinely set loose on her; she remembered their fangs plunging deep into her flesh, injecting her with their venom. The pain she felt had been unimaginable, and her body often swelled beyond recognition.

Addie blinked and tossed Rebecca into the wall, again. She landed with much more force. Then, Addie moved across the room and stood over Rebecca, who was laid out on the floor. Rebecca's gruesome transformation would not save her now. The hissing snakes continued snapping at Addie, who didn't step close enough to be in any real danger. "I bind you, I bind you," she repeated and watched Rebecca transform back into her natural state.

As she stood above, Rebecca's words rang in her ears. *I am his mother. I can feel his longing for me in the whispers of the night. He calls out to me.* Addie knew beyond any doubt that simply binding her powers wouldn't be enough to remove the threat. The bond between mother and child was not easily broken. As long as she lived she was a threat. If her connection to Simon was as strong as she claimed, then it was only a matter of time before *he* sought her out. If he found her, she would complete his transformation into the beast Addie feared; that was not a risk she could take. Rebecca had to die.

Rebecca wouldn't be the first casualty in this war, and she certainly wouldn't be the last.

Clara made a choking sound that stole Addie's attention for a quick second, and when she turned her head back to Rebecca, she had already disintegrated into shadows, attempting to flee. Seconds before she vanished, Addie clawed at the shadows with her fingernails and slit Rebecca's alabaster throat. The floor of the room shook violently. In the back of the room, in the places where darkness dwelled, the shadows bled. Bright red blood oozed from the cracks between the wooden boards of the floor and began to consume the objects it touched, like acid. A pair of high-heeled shoes, a purple blouse and a pair of silk panties melted right before Addie's eyes. She watched, almost mesmerized, as steam rose from the blood, which moved like molten lava. Addie had never witnessed such a spectacle. The blood began to eat away at the floor, dripping onto the first level of the house. The crying and hissing of the shadows could be heard throughout the house, even above the deep rumbling that shook the cold sky. Addie waved her arms and froze the blood, stopping it from consuming the house.

Then, everything was still.

When her eyes landed upon Clara, tears burst from them. The wretched sight of her was almost too much for Addie to bear. She sank to the floor on her knees at Clara's feet.

"My dear sister. I'm so sorry. I should've been here, to protect you." Addie waved her hand in front of Clara's face and instantly her face was restored to its former beauty, the glass shards that jutted from her face only seconds ago had completely vanished. Clara shifted her body, but didn't fully open her eyes; they hung low as if life had been suctioned from her soul. Addie knew it would take time to assess how much harm the dark powers had done to her sister.

When Addie waved her hand over Clara's face, she also removed the veil that covered her mind and prevented her from knowing her true identity—a Thibodeaux witch. Years ago, as a measure of protection, Addie had cast a spell to hide Clara's identity from the world, even from Clara herself. Addie knew that if something happened to her the night Simon was born that the dark would hunt down every sister in an effort to wipe out the entire clan. Without Addie's protection, her sisters would be vulnerable to the shadows. Two of her sisters had already been lost, severely weakening the clan. But, two remained, assuming Clara survived The Dark Mother's torture. Addie would not lose Clara. She simply could not lose her. She would will her back to health, even if it took all her strength.

Addie laid her head in Clara's lap and sobbed. Her tears were hot and flowed heavily, dampening the raggedy robe Clara wore.

"Clara, please come back to me. I can't do this alone. I need you. The world needs you."

"Addie?" Clara said in a voice that struggled to be heard. Addie slowly raised her head and met Clara's vacant gaze. Her eyes were wide now, straining to focus. "Is that you?" Addie jumped to her feet.

"Yes, yes, it's me." Addie grabbed Clara's hand and clutched it tightly. Clara forced a smile.

"Where...where have you been?"

"It doesn't matter now. All that matters is I'm back." Clara slowly turned her head and looked around the war-torn room.

"What's happened here? What's happened to me?" Addie wanted to explain the events of the night, but she didn't want to worry Clara. She knew that Clara, being the seer of her clan, could soon see the past and know what had transpired; if she had the strength. "I remember. I remember who I am. I remember every-thing now. What did you do to me, sister?" The accusatory tone in Clara's voice filled Addie with sadness.

"I tried to protect you. I tried to save you."

"How? By...by...wiping my mind? Binding my power?" Clara coughed and spat up blood. Addie wiped it on the rag that was draped over the arm of the chair.

"I didn't take your memories, only buried them deep inside you, as I did with your powers so that the darkness would never know you were a Thibodeaux witch. I did what I had to do. I couldn't be around to protect you."

Clara forced a weak smile. "You are the Priestess Supreme. I do not question your wisdom, sister." Clara tried to pull herself from the chair, but quickly fell back down. "I feel so weak, so... sick. Dying..."

"You are *not* dying," Addie quickly corrected. "You need rest, sister."

"Maybe you're right. I need to rest." Clara leaned her head back and closed her eyes. Addie kept a close eye on her chest, making sure it continued to rise and fall with breath.

Addie stood above her sister, tears burning her eyes. She tried to shake the thought from her mind, but thoughts of death invaded it.

"Don't blame yourself for my fate," Clara said, her eyes still shut. "I can feel your pain—your guilt. We both know I am dying. I can hear the music of The Higher Plain."

"No, I can't let you go."

"My sweet sister, you can't stop me, even with all your power," she said with a warm, playful smile. "Some things are meant to be. My time here has passed."

"All of this death is my fault. *All of it*. I gave birth to the father, and the father begat the sons. I have lost all my sisters. Now, the whole world will perish because of my incompetence. We shall die. The binding spell will break. I cannot stop the Ascension, especially without you. I'm afraid, Clara. Terrified."

"Save Simon, and you will save the world," she whispered. "I have felt the goodness in his heart. I have seen so much in these days. The closer I come to death the clearer things become. Come here, Addie," Clara said, her voice sounding formal. Addie moved closer, and Clara placed her hands on Addie's head. "Love will save us all. Find the one who owns his heart."

"What if love isn't enough?"

"Love is always enough."

"No, sister, sometimes love fails; look at my failures."

Clara coughed loudly and then spit out a wad of blood into her hands. Her eyes rolled to the back of her head and then closed.

"Clara!" Addie screamed. "Clara." Addie shook her.

Clara's eyes opened. "I...I...have seen it. Blood of the father."

"What?"

Clara looked at her one last time with eyes that were crystal clear. "B-b-blood of the father." Suddenly, the room was filled with a warm, yellow glow. A sweet smell filled the room and wiped the entire house free from the stench of death and the shadows. Addie held onto Clara's hand.

"It is my time, sister, but I bequeath to you my gift, the gift of sight. May it serve you well in these trying times." Addie kissed her forehead and stepped back, letting nature take its course. Addie could hear choir bells as the life force from Clara drained away, leaving her body an empty shell.

"Dear sister. I'll see you on the other side."

Addie wept for hours.

CHAPTER 25

"Where are we, Eli?" Simon and Eli sat atop a hill higher than any mound Simon had ever seen. The hill was surrounded by the most vibrant colors, and the sun shone down with a brilliance that hurt Simon's eyes, which had returned to their natural blue color. As far as his eyes could see, vivid colors sparkled in the hillside, creating the most spectacular vision he had ever seen. Even from their great distance Simon could see two great streams of the purest blue water that ran on either side of the peak. The calming sounds of the running waters rang out in a perfect, peaceful melody. The valley beneath them was fertile, full of life. In the center of the valley stood a huge edifice, a glittering castle made of what appeared to be solid gold. The word *paradise* echoed inside Simon's head.

"We are at the top of the world—*our world*. From there we shall rule," Eli said, pointing to the castle. "All of this is ours. The entire world. Our castle. Our land. Our rivers. Our people."

"How did we get here?" Simon asked while looking around, seemingly unimpressed by what he saw. The darkness had settled in his spirit and he scratched his forearm to rid himself of the sudden itch that he felt over his body. He tingled.

Eli opened his arms wide and spun in a small circle. "I bring you to the top of the world and all you can ask is how we got here? Brother, don't you know by now that we can move with our thoughts? We can do anything, and soon we'll be able to do everything. Our powers have no bounds. The sooner you realize that, the better off we'll be." Simon pulled thin, cool wisps of air into his lungs and exhaled loudly, as if bored. He folded his arms and looked around casually. There was beauty everywhere and wonders abounded on every side of the mountain, but the majesty of their vantage point didn't impress him much.

"Eli, what will happen during Ascension?" Simon asked, suddenly.

"We shall take our rightful place atop the world."

"No, I mean what will *actually* happen? Will it rain and storm? Will we be bathed in blood? Will fire shoot from our eyes? Will the ground tremble beneath our feet? What?" As the words left his lips, Simon felt empowered by them. He thought of what it would all mean. Power. Blood. Pain. Terror.

Eli chuckled. "You're funny, brother. Funny, indeed. Truth be told, no one really knows what'll happen, except that our powers will…*mature*." Eli said with a sparkle in his eyes, "An Ascension has never happened before. By the way, did you learn anything useful while you were in Grandmother's captivity? The witches are powerful seers and they may have more information about the Ascension than we do."

"I wasn't in captivity," Simon corrected and then searched his mind for any answers the book may have provided him, but none came.

"Think hard, brother."

"I don't think they know anything. They are as ignorant as we are. Simon rolled his eyes. "I am amazed that with all the power gathered on both sides no one knows more about the Ascension."

"Well, it's only a matter of days now. We shall all soon find out, together."

Simon plucked a purple flower from the ground and brought

it to his nose. "And, what about my power? You said it was bound by Addie. Will the Ascension break her spell? Do you even know the answer to that question?"

Eli paused. A speck of worry flashed across his face. "The universe has ordained our strength. There is no power on this earth that can prevent that which was meant to be."

"You speak with such confidence, Eli, but I can feel something inside me. It's like a noose tightening around my neck. What if her spell cannot be broken?"

"It shall break," Eli said with impatience. "It *must* break."

"If it doesn't, what will happen?" Simon scratched his arm, again. Eli looked at him, but did not mention it.

"Simple. We'll be denied enough power to rule, and I'm sure the witches will attempt to seal all of us in shadows forever—that cannot happen. The spell *will* break and so will her neck. Eetwidomayloh said so."

Simon smiled. "Eetwidomayloh. Tell me about him."

"Didn't you learn of him in Addie's book?"

Simon looked at Eli with impudence; a hint of anger seethed just beneath his skin. "I want you to tell me about him, Eli."

"He is the source of all shadows. He is the bringer of the fire. He *is* death and he is father to the shadows. He has always been. He is endless."

"Endless and apparently impotent."

By the expression on Eli's face Simon surmised that his words shocked his brother. "What do you mean?"

"He is the source of all shadows but remains entombed. He is powerless to free himself from the Shadowland."

"Only The One—only we—can unlock the door to his cage and allow him to walk the earth; that is our power—the power of The One."

"Oh, I see. Do you love him?"

"Love? What is love? I respect him."

"Does he respect you?" Simon's voice was peppered with sarcasm.

Eli contemplated the question, pausing momentarily and then speaking introspectively. "He will. They all will."

Behind him, Simon hid his smile and paced around the hillside, his mind suddenly on fire with thoughts of things to be. He could still feel the darkness crawling inside him, *becoming* him. His skin itched. It felt like thousands of hairy spiders crawling slowly over his body, inch by inch, weaving together a web of new skin that would finally fit his face, his true face. It was a joyous feeling. He stepped closer to the edge of the mountain and inhaled deeply, filling his lungs with power.

"And what of Mother? I want to see her."

Eli frowned. "In due time, brother. In due time."

Simon felt a surge of hatred rush through him; it was thick, like molasses. "Why do you hate her so much?"

"Who?"

"Our mother."

Eli raised his left eyebrow and looked at Simon. "Who said I hate her?"

"Don't be coy, brother. I can smell the hate on you. What did she do to you?"

Eli smiled. "Let's just say we have a complicated relationship."

Simon shook his head from side to side, disappointed in Eli's words. "One of my recurring childhood dreams was that my mother would one day find me and whisk me away from the orphanage, or whatever foster home they stuck me in. I dreamed of her being a famous movie star or a singer and that when she found me we'd live this wonderful life. Suddenly, I feel disappointed."

"Don't let my words or feelings disappoint you; you'll have more than your fair chances of being disappointed by her."

Simon wanted to find out more details about Eli's complicated relationship with their mother, but he didn't want to bear Eli's burden. He turned his back and took a few aimless steps away and he focused on expelling Eli's hate for their mother from his system. Eli's cross was too heavy for Simon to carry.

"Eli," Simon said, his voice solemn as he changed the subject, "with all the power you have and the shadows have, I don't understand how *you*, of all people, couldn't find me. We are one, aren't we? Are you telling me that one witch's spell is more powerful than all of you? Is the dark really that weak?"

"She's not just any witch. Grandmother is a witch of the highest order. Her powers are…great."

Simon shrugged off his words. "Still, she will have to die. She stole me from my family. Deprived me of my heritage. Killed my father. She is the enemy." Simon spun around quickly and faced Eli. Then, he spoke in a booming voice that spread out evenly in every direction. "I want you and every shadow everywhere to know that *I* will have no patience for weakness. In the new world, failure will be dealt with harshly. Instantly." His voice bounced off the side of the mountain, causing large stones to shake and roll down the hill.

Eli's face froze in a half-smile, one part admiration, another part uncertainty. Maybe fear. Then, his smile cracked. "Spoken like my true brother."

"And what should I know of you, Eli?"

"You already know me. I am you. We are the same, you and I."

Simon walked over to him and stood side by side, draping his arm around Eli's shoulder. "Yes, we are, aren't we?" Eli pulled away and took a few steps closer to the edge of the mountain and looked down on the glimmering castle. His eager face was filled with wonder, excitement and awe. Simon could feel Eli's strong desire and his dark aspirations.

Simon looked at his brother and the world through newly formed eyes. "I thought you said we were going to have some fun?"

ᛣ

In a flash, the brothers stood outside the huge golden doors of the glittering castle. Slowly, the doors swung open and they stepped inside a great hall with large alabaster columns lining the long aisle. The other hues in the room were dark, dull shades of metallic gray and basic black. There were no windows in the hall, and even though not a sliver of sunlight could be seen, Simon could still see everything with crystal clarity, even the shadows lurking in every corner. The darkened room was in stark contrast to the heavenly scene outside.

Eli marched down the hallway with his usual harsh footsteps and Simon followed behind him. When they reached the end of the hallway they took a left and ascended a long staircase that led to another long hallway. Eli stopped and looked back at Simon, when they reached the end and were greeted by a double-set of black doors. Eli placed his hand on the knob and slowly turned. The doors opened and they stepped inside a cavernous room decorated in earthly brown tones.

"Welcome, Simon," Eli said as he ushered him into the room. "These are my quarters. Make yourself at home." Simon stepped inside and the doors closed behind them.

Simon looked around the room. An expensive-looking, brown leather sofa was pushed against the wall. On the opposite wall was a bar that was complete with exotic liquors and drinking glasses of every kind. Behind the bar were a few small stairs that led to a vast bookshelf built into the wall. Simon eyed the shelf and tilted his head upward, realizing that the bookshelf rose endlessly into the ceiling and probably beyond.

"This is the dark library. Every spell that has ever been written by a shadow is archived here. There is much power here."

"Oh, I see," Simon said.

"Impressive, isn't it?" Simon nodded. "Would you like a drink?"

"Certainly. Surprise me." Eli moved over to the bar and began mixing various liquids together. He clanked ice cubes in a glass and poured a clear concoction over the cubes, which made cracking sounds the moment they came in contact with the beverage.

"Here, try this." Simon moved over to him and brought the drink to his nose, smelling it before he sipped.

"What is it?"

"You said surprise you. Try it."

Reluctantly, Simon took a sip and immediately felt his knees buckle. He felt as if he was drinking hellfire. A burning sensation moved down his entire body, igniting every cell.

"Don't worry, brother. You'll get used to it." Simon watched Eli take a gulp. Not to be outdone, Simon took another sip and winced.

Simon moved to a globe of the earth that sat on a stand in the corner. The globe was the size of a huge beach ball. Simon put his hand on it and made it spin.

"This will be our world," Eli said. Simon faked a smile and half-listened to Eli ramble on about being kings and their reign.

"I wanna have some fun," Simon said, putting an end to Eli's incessant rant about power and glory.

Eli smiled sinisterly. "You sure about that?" Simon nodded as Eli set down his drink. "Let's try something. Here, take my hand."

Happily, Simon set down his drink next to Eli's and took his hand. He instantly felt a wave of emotions from Eli. He felt his ambition and his lust and his hatred and even his jealousy—jealously directed at Simon. Simon smiled as Eli spun the globe again.

"All right, Brother. Concentrate," Eli said as the globe slowed. Simon felt his body tingle. With his index finger, Eli slowly touched the globe when it stopped circling. Immediately, Simon heard a great noise and saw ripples in the waters off the island of Japan. Rising from the globe were the screams of thousands of people.

"What did we just do?" Simon asked in confusion.

"I wanted to test our strength."

"I don't understand."

"We just caused an earthquake, which will trigger a tsunami. Many will die," Eli said, nonchalantly.

Simon was in awe. "I can hear them scream. I can feel them."

"Wonderful, isn't it? If we can do that, imagine what we'll be able to do after we ascend."

Simon spun the globe again. "Let's see what else we can do." He grabbed Eli's hand and when the globe stopped he touched an area near Joplin, Missouri. Again, they heard screams, but not the sound of the earth moving. Terrified screams echoed across the room like faint whispers, but there was power in their terror. Simon breathed deeply, trying to inhale all of their fear.

"What did you do?" Eli asked delightfully.

Simon looked at him slowly and smiled. "Tornadoes. Lots of tornadoes."

Eli stepped away from the globe and strolled around the room. "There's nothing we can't do together. We will be invincible."

"I'm bored now. Let's do something else."

"What did you have in mind?"

"Something…fun."

"Follow me," Eli said with a wink. He moved quickly out of the room and down the hallway, taking a different set of stairs to reach the bottom level. They walked to the back and took another set of golden stairs that winded down into the basement.

"Are you ready for this?" Eli asked, with a wink.

"That depends on what it is."

"Put your hand on the door."

"What?"

"Just do it. Trust me." Simon watched Eli place his palm against the door and shudder, as if in extreme pleasure. Curiously, Simon placed his hand against the door and immediately felt a surge of heat race through his body. The feeling ignited a ravenous sexual desire that overwhelmed him and buckled his knees. Quickly, Eli grabbed Simon around the waist to keep him from falling.

The doors to the room flung open and the sweet funky smell of sex hit him like a tidal wave. Simon looked into the room, which was pitch-black, like he was staring into vast nothingness; yet, he knew that it was far from empty. He could hear a faint hissing emanating from the void, an enchanting hissing sound that beckoned him forward. He looked at Eli who had already started unbuttoning his shirt.

"Let the games begin," Eli said as he removed the rest of his clothing. He winked at Simon and stepped into the room, disappearing into the blackness. Slowly, Simon removed all of his clothes and stepped into the dark, completely naked.

When he entered the dark, a mass of naked bodies slowly came into view; bodies writhing around each other, hot flesh melding into hot flesh. Simon felt hands and fingers touching him as he moved through the room. The sound of the orgy of bodies slapping against each other was almost more than Simon could stand. Finally, he stopped in what he thought was the center of the room and looked around for Eli. Within seconds, he was surrounded by indistinguishable nakedness that finally brought him to his knees.

Hours later, after they had spent their sexual energy and finished ravaging the bodies of their willing consorts, Simon and Eli lay in the center of a pile of naked bodies, exhausted. The room was dark and the leftover smell of sex was thick. Simon smiled to himself as he thought of the ways in which he had unleashed upon them. His sexual storm tore through crowd, blurring the lines between pleasure and pain. His experience had been awesome and they had begged for him. Never—not even with Brooke— had he experienced such vast and endless pleasure. Here— wherever he was—all of his senses were magnified in ways that defied his imagination. In this room, the slightest touch from anyone ignited a flame in him that demanded immediate attention. He blasted through the room, all flesh and brawn, touching and licking and kissing and grabbing and pounding.

Simon stood up and began to walk through the dark room. He was spent, fully used up from his experiences, but he wanted to soak in a tub. He hoped he could recall how to get to Eli's room; this castle was gigantic.

As he moved through the room, trying not to disturb anyone, he suddenly felt queasy and he struggled for breath. Instantly, he dropped to his knees and instinctively drew his hands to his throat. He heard a faint sound and at first he thought it was a hiss, but it wasn't. This time, he could hear words; like someone chanting.

He struggled to speak, to repeat the words out loud, but his voice was a whisper. "Ties...bind...tight...night."

"Simon," Eli called out. Suddenly, Eli was upon him, his hands pressing on Simon's shoulder. "What is it, brother? What's wrong?"

"I…I…don't know. Can't breathe. Help me." Eli tried to remove Simon's hands from his throat, but when he did, Simon let out a screech that tore through the room, causing the shadows to cry out in horrific pain. The force of his yell even caused Eli to stumble back a few steps.

"Simon!" Eli screamed in a panic.

"Ties…bind….ties…bind," Simon managed to say before he lost consciousness and vanished.

Chapter 26

Brooke slid the curtain to the side, grabbed a towel and stepped cautiously out of the shower. The plush mauve bath mat felt good underneath her feet, soft; like cotton candy. She wrapped the teal-colored towel around her body and stepped in front of the mirror, wiping the condensation away with her hand. Her cheeks were still rosy and her blue eyes, pale. The soothing water that rained down on her from the hot shower couldn't mitigate the sting from the tears that burned her eyes.

She couldn't deny what was painfully obvious; she was lonely. And, the loneliness that she felt was fierce, unlike anything she had ever experienced. It felt alive, like a determined energy that attached itself to her like a Siamese twin. As soon as she parted ways with Simon, she noticed it; the emptiness had been immediate, a hollow feeling that stayed with her, no matter where she went or what she did. It had only been a few days without Simon, but with each passing hour, her loneliness became more acute. She *felt* it; it was heavy like bricks, weighing her down. Sometimes, when the hour was late and the air was still, she even thought she *saw* it, as if loneliness was an entity that could be seen. Sometimes, she saw something hazy huddling in a corner of her bedroom; or, at other times, she noticed something almost imperceptible perched high on a tree branch outside her window, peering at her; almost torturing her, never letting her forget that the loneliest place in the world is often near someone you cannot have. There were at least a hundred times when she thought about calling Simon, but she didn't; she couldn't, in spite of the pull he had on her.

She reached down and grabbed her pink brush off the sink and ran it through her wet hair. She stroked absentmindedly, hoping it would relax her and take her mind off Simon. Even in his absence, he took up so much space in her world. She closed her eyes briefly and took a long, deliberate breath. When she opened them, she screamed and dropped the hairbrush when she saw something in the mirror scurry and disappear into the depths of the bedroom behind her.

Quickly, she turned around and faced the bedroom, her chest heaving as she rested her back against the sink. She stood absolutely still for several extended seconds before deciding to move.

"Get it together, Brooke," she said to herself. "Get it together." This wasn't the first time she had seen or heard something unusual since her split with Simon; being alone took some getting used to.

She moved away from her mirror and stepped into her silent room, slowly. She looked around, but didn't see anything or anyone; yet, the hairs on the back of her neck stood on end. She felt something; a presence. And, she smelled something sweet, like cologne; Simon's cologne.

She was not alone.

"Simon?" she called out nervously. Her wispy voice fluttered through the room. She toddled over to the closet and pulled open the door, half-hoping that Simon would be there, playing some silly game; however, instead of Simon, she was greeted only by her designer wardrobe. She closed the door, suddenly feeling silly at her paranoia.

When she turned around and faced her queen-sized bed, the mattress was indented, as if someone was sitting there.

She screamed and rushed toward the door to her room, trying to escape, but felt massive hands grab her waist and push her against the wall. She was held there, her hands pinned above her head. Her body squirmed as she struggled to break free, but she didn't know what she was fighting; she couldn't see anything. She tried to scream again but when she opened her mouth, nothing came out; her voice, stolen by the entity. The only sound that could be heard was the rapid beat of her heart pounding ferociously in her chest.

The towel unwrapped itself from her body and fell to her feet. She continued to fight, trying to free herself, but then she felt warm hands caress her thighs and fingers flick against her damp nipples. Invisible lips kissed and sucked on her neck in a way that only Simon knew; her breathing quickened, burrowing deeply into a space that hadn't been touched in days. Her legs parted, not of her own doing, but by whatever force held her. She didn't want to submit to its will; her instinct told her to keep fighting, but her body betrayed her.

Fingers that she could not see inched themselves up her inner thigh; they moved torturously slow, allowing the anticipation to build. Her body quaked, shuddering with eagerness. A warm mouth covered her left nipple—the most sensitive one—at the same time fingers parted her. Her knees buckled and she winced with pleasure as she was rigorously explored.

She felt the fingers pull out of her and a lustful part of her wanted to beg for more, but she had no voice. Then, her legs parted wider and she was entered by a force that immediately brought her close to orgasm. She was pleasured just the way she liked it, the way her body craved, with deep, even strokes that filled her; her eyes rolled to the back of her head. She felt a wave of pleasure so great that she forgot she was being fucked by an unknown force. She didn't feel afraid; this wasn't the touch of a stranger, but the familiar touch of a lover deeply in tune with the nuances of her body.

She felt the tension rising in her body; the pleasure was so great that she would have collapsed had it not been for the force that held her in place. Her entire body jolted violently as wave, after wave, after wave of pleasure covered her.

Then, she was released and she slid down the wall and sat on the floor, trying to catch her breath.

Moments later, Brooke opened her eyes and was startled by the fact that she was laying on the floor near the door of her room, naked. She panicked, feeling as if she had lost her wits and she quickly looked around the room, grabbing the towel at her feet, using it to cover her flesh. She didn't know whether or not she was asleep or awake, but she was moist and tender in places that concerned her. Had she been sexed? She couldn't be sure. The sensation she had earlier, that a presence was in the room with her, was gone; now, she felt completely alone. She tightly clutched the towel that covered her body.

The room was still; eerily so. Slowly, she pulled herself from the floor and stood on shaky legs. She took meek steps forward and then stopped, suddenly. She gasped. The scent of Simon's cologne lingered in the air.

Ψ

Brooke stood at the bay window in the den of her sorority house and watched, with singular focus, the snow fall at a sharp angle, carried by the moaning winds. It had been snowing almost nonstop for days and the grounds of the house were blanketed in white. She wanted to move away from the window, but something about the storm held her in place, captivated by the majesty of it all. She wondered when the snow would cease, but secretly hoped for a white Christmas, even if she spent it alone, not that her parents cancelled the cruise. She wrapped her arms around herself; her heart was heavy and she couldn't enjoy the snowfall as much as she wanted, regardless of its simple beauty.

She tried to focus only on the snowfall, but her mind drifted back to last night, when she was in her room. When she thought about her extraordinary experience, she became unnerved, fighting back the tears that formed in her eyes, even though she wasn't sure whether the tears formed because she thought she was losing her mind, or because she missed Simon tremendously. She thought about her invisible lover and his familiar strokes; she thought about the rough and gentle ways in which she was handled, ways that were identical to Simon's techniques. She thought about the smell of his cologne hanging in the air. Had she imagined it all, including his kisses? Even if she had, it only reinforced her need to be near Simon.

She wanted to burst from the room, plow through the snow to run to him, but she resisted the urge; he wasn't safe for her; lately, strange things seemed to surround him. How does someone vomit a live snake? How had she been brought to multiple orgasms by a force that she was certain was him? Still, through the madness of what was happening, she could not stop craving him.

"Hey, Brooke," a voice called out from behind. Brooke turned and saw her sorority sister, Serenity, bouncing into the room, her long black hair cascading down her shoulders. "What are you doing?" Serenity was dressed warmly, in a thick coat, hat, and gloves in hand.

"Watching the snow. What are you doing?"

Broooooooooke.

Quickly, Brooke turned around and looked out of the window, hoping to see Simon. She heard his voice; she was certain of that, but when she faced the window she was met only by the bitter gray sky and the falling snow.

"Brooke," Serenity asked as she stepped closer. "Did you hear me? I said we are going to go play in the snow. Wanna come?"

"Huh? Oh, no."

"Are you okay?"

Brooooooooooke. She heard the voice again.

"Did you hear that?"

"Hear what?"

Brooke glanced outside the window, half-expecting to see Simon take shape out of the darkness. The whisper she heard was clear and sounded really close to her, yet Serenity was looking at her as if she had lost her mind. "Nothing."

"That settles it. We are getting you out of this big empty house. Go upstairs and put on something warm. You're coming with me and Jackson. We're going to go out and build a snowman and make snow angels and have a good time. I won't have you moping around by yourself any longer." Serenity gently took Brooke by the hand and looked into her eyes. "I don't know exactly what's going on between you and Simon, but I can tell that it's not good. You don't have to tell me what happened, but I'm your best friend and I hope you know that I'm here for you."

For a few seconds, Brooke honestly thought about confessing everything to Serenity. Her voice was full of concern and sounded so sincere; so comforting. Brooke needed to release all the tension that had built up in her bones, but when she thought about what she had to confess, she balked.

"Everything is fine. We had a…misunderstanding."

"About what?"

"It's not important."

Serenity expelled a puff of air with exaggerated effort. "Fine. But you're coming with us. And I won't take no for an answer."

Brooooooooooke.

Brooooooooooke.

Brooooooooooke.

Brooke fought hard to not react to the voice. It was like she could hear his voice on the wind, calling for her, each time it blew. Since the moment they separated, she had felt a strong urge to be near him again. She had dreamed of him; last night, she felt him. She couldn't escape him; part of her didn't want to escape him. Now, she heard his voice calling her name, and she wanted to run to him.

And, she did.

Ψ

When Brooke walked into Simon's house, she was immediately hit with a blast of heat. It felt like it was a hundred degrees in the room. The place was dark and it reeked of funk, like the rank smell of an unclean locker room. She took a deep breath and tried to stop her knees from knocking. This place that used to provide her with solace now filled her with fear. She remembered what happened the last time she was here. She remembered the snake and the vacant look in Simon's eyes. When she burst from the apartment that day, she swore to herself that she'd never come back; yet, she found herself standing with her back pressed against the inside of his living room door. She had tried to stay away, to not think about him, but he was a part of her that she couldn't shake loose. In the deep of the night she felt his fingertips on the small of her back as if he was lying right next to her, touching her in the ways she had come to love. When she walked down the street she could hear his voice, whispering on the wind. Her body craved him, ached for him, but she resisted. She resisted returning his many phone calls and text messages, even though her nipples stiffened when she saw his name on the display of her phone.

She had resisted the strong yearning as long as she could. She had even prayed that whatever bond he had on her be broken. She knew she loved him; that fact was incontrovertible, but this unnamed craving she felt for him, which seemed to grow stronger each day, wasn't love. It felt unnatural, but it wouldn't be denied.

In spite of the fear she now felt for him, she had braved the storm and trudged through the city streets, hoping for the chance to be near him, if only to smell him. She imagined his manly scent filling her nostrils; the thought of it sent chills throughout her body. Before she entered his building, she had stood outside of it for a few moments and stared at it. Her head had been telling her to flee and warning her *do not enter*, but the longing in her soul, that burned hotter than fear, overruled her thoughts and she found herself inside the building, slowly ascending the stairs that led to his apartment. She felt like an automaton, mindlessly following a set of instructions planted within her brain; the reticence in her heart told her she was more like a moth being drawn to a flame.

After she stopped her body from rattling, she pried herself off the wall, took a few steps, and dropped her keys on the table near the door, flipping on the light switch when she passed it. The clanging of the keys on the table echoed through the house, as if the sound were magnified, three-fold. She jumped, but felt silly. She wiped the sweat from her brow and moved over to the thermostat, intending to turn off the heat, but it was already off.

She flipped the switch to "on" and listened to the machine roar to life, confirming the facts that the thermostat had already told her: that the heat was off and it was almost ninety-five degrees in the room. Quickly, she turned it off, again. She had no explanation for how the apartment could be so hot when the heat was off, especially when it was so bitterly cold outside.

Oh God, she thought, fearing what lay ahead in the apartment. First it was snakes. Now, it was an interior heat wave in the middle of a blizzard. "Simon? Are you here?" Her question went unanswered. "Hello?"

She moved through the living room and looked around nervously. Nothing was suspicious. She moved into the kitchen, but saw nothing unusual. She noticed the magnetic calendar on the refrigerator in which she had circled his birthday—December 21st—which was only two days away. The special plans she had to celebrate had died when the snake came to life.

She took in a deep breath and propelled herself forward. Slowly, she crept toward the bedroom. An image of the black snake slithering out of Simon's mouth flashed across her mind. Her body stiffened, but she kept walking. When she stepped into the bedroom she immediately noticed that the room was hot and sticky, like a sauna. The linen on the bed was in disarray and one of the pillows lay on the floor near the nightstand. She walked deeper into the room, intending to peer into the bathroom, but when she turned she saw a foot sticking out from the other side of the bed.

She gasped.

Without much thought, she raced over to the body, not knowing who was lying there.

"Simon!" she screamed when he came into view. He lay on the floor completely naked, in the fetal position, covered in a gooey clear substance. His eyes were closed and his body shook, slightly.

Instantly, she knew that the smell that permeated the air emanated from the slimy material that covered his body. Quickly, she reached down to touch him and jerked her hand back instantly, shocked at how hot his skin was. It wasn't hot enough to burn her, but far hotter than she had ever known a human body to get.

She dropped to her knees at his side as panic seized her. "Simon! Simon!" She shook him hard, hoping to awaken him. His eyelids fluttered rapidly before finally opening to reveal his blood-shot eyes.

"Brrr—Brooke?" he said between staggered breaths. "Y—y—you—you came back." A tiny smile formed on his lips.

"I need to get you to the hospital," she said. "I need to call 9-1-1." She leapt to her feet, but Simon grabbed her by the arm, halting her movement.

"No," he said pleadingly. "That won't help. Help me up," he said in a much steadier voice. "Please," he said as he tried to stand, pulling on her arms for support. Quickly, she wrapped her arm around his waist and helped him to the bed. "Water." She needed no further instructions. She darted into the kitchen and poured a glass of water and then raced back into the room. With unsteady hands, Simon took the glass and emptied it ravenously. "More," he said. Brooke didn't hesitate.

After seven full glasses of ice cold water, Simon had finally had enough. He set the empty glass on the nightstand and tried to push himself off the bed, but his legs were wobbly. Brooke moved around him and placed his arm around her shoulder. Her hands slipped off of his waist due to the slimy substance that covered his body. "Help me into the shower," he said.

They walked across the room unevenly, Simon's weight bearing heavily on Brooke's petite frame. She struggled, but did not relent.

When they reached the bathroom, he moved over to the toilet, dropped the lid and plopped down on the seat, exhaustedly. Brooke turned to the shower and turned on the water. She knew that he usually liked his showers hot, but with his body already close to nuclear, she thought it best to moderate the temperature of the water.

"I wasn't sure you'd come," Simon said. "I wasn't sure you'd feel me. And, even if you did, I wasn't sure you'd come."

Brooke turned slowly to him, his words spinning deeply into her mind. "What are you talking about?"

"Nothing—just that I love you." He smiled. She forced a smile in return and moved over and helped him.

"The water's cool," she said in a meek voice. He stepped into the shower and winced immediately, but continued. Brooke watched the slimy substance begin to fall from his body and get sucked down the drain. She looked at the slimy material that Simon left on the seat of the commode. She reached into the cabinet, grabbed a towel and wiped the seat down. The unusual odor of the substance filled her nostrils and, as far as she was concerned, Simon could not clean himself fast enough; she wanted to be rid of that odor and that slime.

Simon spoke to her through the running water and the shower curtain, but her thoughts were on the words he spoke earlier: that he wasn't sure that she would *feel* him; that unnerved her. She had indeed felt him—like she had never felt anything before. What she had felt, what had led her here, was stronger than love and more potent than fear. He had called out to her, she realized. And, she had answered. Was he controlling her? Was her life no longer her own?

Even if that was the case, at this point, she'd willingly sign her life over to him.

After Simon showered, he returned to the bed. He walked with much more vigor than he had only moments ago. He climbed into the bed and lay on his back. Brooke felt his forehead, which was still hotter than it should have been. She went into the bathroom, took a small washcloth and ran it underneath the cold water. She returned to the room and placed it on Simon's forehead.

She waited a few moments before speaking. "Simon, what's going on? Please, talk to me."

"I'm...becoming..." His words drifted off.

"Becoming? What?" She swallowed hard.

He didn't respond. Instead, he inhaled deeply and closed his eyes. Brooke didn't know what to think or do; but, in spite of the grave warning in her heart, she remained certain that she wanted to be at his side.

Simon leaned forward, with some effort, and placed one hand on her cheek. "Just know that you are safe. I don't care what you see or what you hear, you are safe with me. Can you trust that?"

She shook her head, unconvincingly.

"Baby, I need you to believe in me—in us."

"I do, it's just that—"

"Trust me, okay? And love me. I will keep you safe from all harm." When she looked at his face this time, it warmed her. She believed him and she let go of the fear.

"I trust you, baby. I do."

"Promise me one thing—above all else."

"Anything."

"Promise me that whatever happens, whatever I become, that you'll never stop *seeing* me."

She leaned in and planted a kiss on his lips; not one full of passion or desire, but one that sealed their covenant. "I promise."

"I don't want you to leave. I want you to be here when I wake up."

"I'm not going anywhere."

He smiled.

Ψ

Brooke moved into the living room to let Simon sleep. She poured herself a glass of wine and dropped to the couch. The temperature in the house had leveled off, returning to normal.

Beneath her feet, something moved; more like, slithered.

Instinct told her to yank up her feet from the floor, but panic seized her heart and froze her limbs. She prayed there wasn't a snake near her feet. If she looked down and saw a serpent, she knew she'd faint.

With her heart pounding, she slowly tilted her head downward so that she could see her feet on the floor. She exhaled when she didn't see a snake.

Out of her periphery, she saw something move in the corner near the kitchen. Then, she heard a hiss.

Brooooooooooke.

She screamed. "Who's there?" she asked in a panic as she faced the corner. She didn't want to wait for an answer. She grabbed her jacket and headed toward the front door, picking up her keys from the table. When she tried to open the door, it wouldn't budge. Not an inch. She pulled with more strength than she knew she had, but to no avail.

She turned and ran back into the room, looking for an escape route. She focused her attention on the window. She looked down at the snow-covered ground from the second floor window and contemplated how she could get down.

Brooooooooooke.

In a hurry, she tried to lift the window, but like the door, it wouldn't open. Tremendous fear gripped her. She sprinted into the kitchen and grabbed a large skillet and raced back to the window. Without hesitation, she threw the pan into the glass, but it didn't break. Or crack. The skillet simply bounced on the window and hit the floor, without so much as making a sound.

She felt defeated. Trapped.

Resigned to her fate, she wiped the tears from her eyes, calmly removed her coat and went back into the living room, picking up her glass of wine and downing the contents in one gulp.

She wasn't going anywhere, just as Simon wanted.

As she sat on the couch she told herself that it was all in her head. All of this was some bizarre waking nightmare and all she had to do was to take control of her reality. There were no snakes; the doors and windows were probably frozen shut; no one was hissing her name. It was all in her head. She took slow, deliberate breaths to calm herself and soon the depressing effects of the wine took hold of her and her eyelids drooped, heavy with fatigue. Before she knew it, her eyes were closed.

"Wake, my child," a gentle voice called out to Brooke. She opened her eyes and jumped when she saw a woman standing in the living room.

"Who are you? How did you get in here?"

"Don't be scared. I'm not here to hurt you. I'm here to save you; to save us all."

"Look, lady, I don't know what's going on—" she said as she looked around the room.

"My name is Adelaide. Adelaide Thibodeaux." Brooke's heart froze when she heard the name. It was the woman that Simon had been looking for; the one he said he had dreamed about.

"You're Adelaide? *The* Adelaide?"

"Listen to me. I don't have much time. Simon is not to be trusted. The dark in him is strong. You know of the dark of which

I speak, don't you? This wretched storm is because of him; because he lives." Brooke remained silent, wishing she could disagree. "He frightens you, doesn't he? He frightens us all."

"He loves me."

"Still, he will destroy you. It is he that prevents you from leaving this place. His powers have sealed you here. No one can enter or leave this place; it is his will."

Brooke gasped.

"What has he told you? About who he is? About *what* he is?" Addie asked.

"N-n-nothing."

Addie stepped closer. "He is the destroyer of worlds. He will kill everyone you know and love. Your mother. Your father. Your brothers and sisters. Everything will burn."

"No, that's not true. You're lying."

Addie moved closer to Brooke and took her by the hand. She placed Brooke's hand over her heart. "Here, look into my heart. Know what I know."

Heat surged through Brooke's body as a rapid-fire succession of horrible images flashed through Brooke's mind.

The world on fire.

Screaming children.

Earthquakes swallowing whole cities.

Bloodied angels falling from a flaming hole in the sky.

Simon, on a throne in a golden castle, smiling.

Brooke yanked her hand back. "Make it stop, make it stop!" Tears poured from her eyes. "This isn't true! You're doing this!"

Addie smiled delicately. "What you have seen shall come to pass unless we stop him. You know this. You have *felt* it."

With trembling lips, Brooke spoke. "H-h-ow. How do we stop him?"

"Not *we*," Addie said as she pointed her finger at Brooke, "you."

Ψ

Brooke awoke with panic in her heart. She quickly looked around the room, searching for the woman she had seen in her dream, but the room was empty. Her heartbeat was rapid; pounding with force in her chest. Even as she pulled herself together, she knew that, though she had been asleep, what happened to her had been real. She was certain of that. Like Simon, she had been visited by Adelaide Thibodeaux in her sleep.

"Brooke," Simon said as he stood in the doorway of the living room, eyeing her strangely. "Who were you talking to?" he asked, an accusation coloring his voice.

"Huh?" She heard his question but was distracted by a faint, red pulsing light that seemed to be radiating from his skin, like a hidden heat source. She closed her eyes and shook her head, but when she opened them the light was gone.

"I heard you talking to someone." His voice was now stern.

Brooke shook her head and rubbed her face in her hands. "Oh, I must've been asleep—talking in my sleep. It's been a long few days."

"Tell me about it." The tension left his voice. "Would you come and lay next to me? I miss you."

Her stomach tightened into a ball. "Of course, baby." She moved over to him, watching his face brighten as he stared at her, but as she moved nearer, all she could think was: *destroyer of worlds.*

CHAPTER 27

On December 21st, at the stroke of midnight, Adelaide Thibodeaux's binding spell on Simon's powers finally collapsed.

It broke, not with a bang.

But a whimper.

As Simon lay in a tepid pool of bathwater, his body expelled the last of the slimy residue that had continued to ooze out of his pores throughout the nights; it was a sign of his transition.

And then he ascended.

Quietly.

And the snowstorm ended.

CHAPTER 28

"The ties that bind make them tight, stronger than the blackest night. The ties that bind make them tight, stronger than the blackest night." Her words had echoed throughout the room since the previous night. She had spent the evening fortifying the shack with her magic, hoping to erect a barrier strong enough to keep them out. They were coming; she had no doubt about that. Their birth date was today and presumably, they had their power, but Addie couldn't be sure. There were no signs, no omens as she had expected. The only thing she could be certain of is that they wouldn't be satisfied until they stole the power of the sister-clan and the power from this sacred ground; they'd have to come here to do that, which would be the final nail in the coffin for her. Yes, they would come. They would come to claim her; to kill her.

Let it be done, she thought.

She felt strong; stronger than she had in years. This cabin, these grounds, this swamp, was hallowed by the bloodmagic of her ancestors and it was here that she would be the strongest. It was here that she'd make her final stand. She prayed, chanted and called upon the ancient powers with a fervor she had never known. She hoped their spirit would strengthen her spell and protect the world, although she wasn't quite sure how.

In the morning light she felt calm, almost serene; this just might be her last morning and her last sunrise.

She stepped out onto the porch and inhaled the fresh scent of morning. The snow had finally stopped falling and the sun shone bright in the sky. Even at this early morning hour the temperature was far above the freezing point and the snow that covered the land began to melt. She listened as droplets of water slid from the roof of the house and splattered against the fractured wood of the porch. If this was to be her last morning on earth, she wanted to enjoy the simply beauty of nature.

She didn't fear death, at least not hers. She feared the death of the world. She feared that this day might end with the swamp water that surrounded her shack turned to blood, with hundreds of discarded corpses floating in the muck; she feared the day when the stench of death choked out any hope of life. She would willingly die if she could be certain that the world would be spared the brutality of the shadows.

But for now, she wanted to enjoy the view and remember things the way they were; the tranquility of the bright morning didn't last long.

Her serenity was splintered by the foul scent of burning sulfur. Instantly, her body tensed and she took an offensive position as she looked around quickly, hoping to find the source of the odor. Shadows. It could only be the shadows. They were here.

She heard a low rumble from the sky and watched as flakes fell from the heavens. *Was it snowing again?* she asked herself but it was far too hot for snow. One of the flakes drifted down and landed in the palm of her hand. It didn't melt. She raised it to her nose and took a whiff. It wasn't snow. It was ash. Gray ash was falling from the sky as if heaven itself were burning. The ash rained down in heavier, thicker flakes.

Addie wiggled her fingers to activate her protection spell that she had placed around the house. She heard a low rumble in the sky and rushed inside the house, closing the door behind her.

"Hello, Grandmother." Addie froze. They were already inside. She spun around and saw Eli standing in center of the room, his head cocked to the side and his mouth curled into a devious grin. He was dressed in tight, white slacks and a white vest, with his hands in the pockets of his pants. "I must say that I didn't expect to see you here, of all places," he said as he looked around the room. "I expected you to be hiding, cowering under some rock far from here. But here you are, in this place—the last bastion of your power. I will burn it to the ground myself with you in it and take its power," he said boastfully, "but, first, have you noticed the beautiful *snow* falling? It's marvelous, isn't it?" He strolled around the room speaking casually. "I've missed you, Grandmother. Have you missed me?" Addie knew that he couldn't be alone; her eyes scanned the room. "Do you like my outfit? I thought I'd dress for my big moment." Eli did a quick three hundred and sixty degree spin on his toes. "You didn't know that I'm a dancer, did you?"

Addie didn't have patience for his little games. "Where's Simon?"

"Oh, don't worry about my brother. He may not come when you call, but he's always on time," Eli said with a deep laugh. "Oh, I'm sorry—that was funny. That's what you people used to say about you know who," he said as he looked up. "I wonder what *he's* doing now as ash falls from heaven?"

"Eli, it isn't too late. You can still change—come to the light. Stop all this before it starts."

Eli paused as if he were seriously contemplating her offer. Then, his expression changed. "Why would I ever want to do that, old lady? You don't get it, do you? It's so much better in the dark. And soon the dark will lay waste to this land. Your time is up. Finally, *my* time has arrived!" He extended his arms to what seemed like the length of the room. Quickly, he put his hand in his pocket, pulled out a closed fist and extended his arm toward Addie. "You wanna see a trick?" Before she could respond, he opened the palm of his hand to reveal a fistful of dull, gray ash and then blew hard on the substance. The ash flew from his hand, but remained suspended in air inches from where he stood. Then, he smiled and blew again and the ash sprayed across the room like machine gun fire, stinging Addie's flesh so hard that it brought her to her knees.

"Eli," she said as she tried to cover her body with her hands. "Stop it! You can stop all of this!"

"Oh, Grannie. You're so funny."

"If you wanna laugh, my dear grandson, how about this?" Addie clenched her fist hard, and Eli let out a scream that bounced around the room. He fell to the floor, holding his stomach, writhing in agonizing pain. Addie stood up slowly. "I'm better at this than you are, little boy—never forget that."

"I'll fuckin' kill you!" he screamed as he curled up in the fetal position. Addie clenched her fist tighter, intensifying the sensation that his insides were about to explode. He spat up a wad of blood.

"Not if you're already dead."

Addie pointed her finger at him and made his body rise from the floor. He hung in the air, suspended by her power. She looked him in the eyes—eyes that were like hers—and then flung him hard against the wall. He screamed out again.

"You—you—can't kill me. I can't die," he stammered out, unconvincingly.

"Are you sure about that?" Addie raised an eyebrow. "You're weak. You haven't ascended," she stated. When Eli's eyes widened, Addie knew that she had gotten into his head. He was genuinely afraid that she would kill him. She could see his fear. "Surely, you weren't foolish enough to come here, to face me, without your full power. Your arrogance is your undoing."

"Please, Grandmother. Please. I'm so sorry for what I did to you when you were in the hospital. Please, don't kill me."

"My dear Eli," she began, "such a beautiful child; so full of evil. It's hard to believe that you are of my blood. This world has been protected by the blood of my sisters—your family—for eons; it is that same blood that pulses in your veins. We have nurtured every thing of beauty for so long that we are inextricably bound to the fate of this world. I love this world and will not let you destroy it. You crave nothing but blood and death. You are lost." She tightened both fists and doubled his pain. His cries amplified across the room.

Then, Addie flew across the room and crashed into the wall.

From a room in the back of the shack, Rebecca emerged. She was dressed splendidly, as if she was ready for a runway show. Her short black gown showed her long, smooth legs; her makeup was perfect, except it couldn't completely cover the deep scar on her neck where Addie had slit her throat. The sound of her heels clanked across the wooden floor.

"Adelaide, what have you done to my son?" she asked with little emotion. She extended her hand to Eli and pulled him up. "Mommy will always take care of you, darling."

Eli stumbled to his feet and straightened his vest. "Do you see what that bitch did to me? She got blood on my outfit. She tried to kill me!" Eli's fury filled the room in the form of flames that raced across the space, igniting loose pieces of wood and furniture. The fire formed a circle around Addie, pinning her in the corner, but she twisted her fingers in a circle and all the fire that raged around her coalesced in the palm of her hand; she snapped it out when she closed her fist.

"So, here we are," Rebecca said with joy, "at the final battle. This is the moment when dark overtakes light, permanently." Rebecca and Eli stood in line, almost shoulder to shoulder, and faced Addie, who stood on the other side of the room, her hands balled into tight fists, ready for battle. "Do you really think you can take us both, even in this place?" The smile vanished from Rebecca's face.

"I have no doubt about that, Dark Mother. Your power is a shadow against the sun—a mere fragment of my true power. Do you really want to do battle with a Priestess Supreme? Do you really believe your artificial power can withstand an assault by me? Gone is the feeble woman you helped keep locked in a shell for years. She's gone," Addie said with emphasis on her last two words. "I am a warrior witch; born and bred to beat back the shadows. I am not afraid of either of you." Tension, thick as fog, gathered in the room and separated the enemies; one wrong move would set off a powder keg, but neither side budged. They stood eyeball to eyeball, deciding whether to engage or whether to retreat.

"Adelaide, why do you still resist, even in this final hour? You can still join us and be spared from the death that most assuredly awaits you. Why not join us and live?"

"I will not live on my knees, worshipping false gods," she said as she motioned toward Eli.

"Fuck you!" Eli lashed out. "You will bow down to me!" He sent a blast of shadowmagic toward Addie that she deflected and sent back to him. When his own power hit him, he screamed and shook violently, as if overcome by a seizure.

Rebecca clawed the air and instantly Addie felt the flesh on her arm rip. She screamed out in pain and blood poured from her forearm. Addie blasted Rebecca so hard with her power that she flew across the room and Addie kept her pinned to the wall, as if she had been nailed there. Addie then looked down at her arm, waved her hand across it and sealed the wound.

"Release her!" Eli screamed and he flicked his wrist as if he were backhanding someone across the face. Addie felt his blow from across the room but absorbed it, painfully.

In retribution, she clenched her fists and he collapsed to the floor and screamed.

Then, the room started to vibrate, shift out of phase. The feeling sent a wave of nausea to Addie's stomach and she lost focus, momentarily. Her hold on Rebecca broke and she slid down the wall to the floor.

Everything in the room continued to vibrate, only much faster. The smell of sulfur filled the room and the ground beneath their feet rocked back and forth violently. The furniture, spaced sparsely throughout the room, slid from side to side as if tossed by an earthquake.

Rebecca stood up and ran her fingers through her red hair. "Yes, come to us. The time is now!" she screamed. "Give me your hand, Eli—quickly." Eli paused, but Rebecca took her hand into his. "We must help Eetwidomayloh."

"How? We can't open the gate."

"We can on this day and with his power, we can rid ourselves of that bitch once and for all," she said, a snarl curing her lips at the corner.

They joined hands and foul sounds escaped from Rebecca's mouth; her head snapped back as if she were possessed. The sky suddenly darkened as day instantly turned to night, and the dizzying smell of sulfur intensified in the room; the wounded sky bled thick, gray ash, which fell like snowflakes in a heavy blizzard. Tremendous claps of thunder, exploding in rapid succession, shook the antiquated walls of the cabin, causing pieces of rotting wood to fall from the ceiling onto the floor and crash with a thud. In the middle of the room a black, oval-shaped vortex appeared—a rip in the veil that separated the Shadowland from this world. From the black space of the vortex, shadows emerged, slithering out quickly and coiling around each other. The shadowserpents coiled around each other and soon began to give shape to a man. The shadow grew until finally the outline of a giant man, at least eight feet tall, stood in the center of the room. The vortex closed.

"No!" Addie screamed, but her protest was met with a severe blast of shadowmagic. The blow hit her so hard that the room spun and she felt as if she would lose consciousness.

The shadows continued to circle and coil around the man and flesh appeared on thick bones. Rebecca clapped wildly.

Addie gasped.

"Eetwidomayloh," Eli whispered.

Soon, the Shadowman stood in the center of the room, only now more flesh than shadow. His tremendous legs were as thick as tree trunks and his forearms looked as powerful as jackhammers. He stretched his body, as if to adjust to this world and to acquaint himself to his newly formed flesh.

He slowly removed the black hood that covered his face and revealed his enormous head, the size of a lumpy, overgrown pumpkin. His head was completely hairless, as was the rest of the pale skin on his body. His enormous body was void of even a single strand of hair. The angry orbs that were his eyes were the size of fists and took up half his face. His piercing gaze ripped through the silence of the room. He looked around the room as if to orientate himself to the space. His thin lips were tightly drawn, but then he opened his mouth widely and a hideous stench poured out, drowning the room in a nauseous gas.

"Where is Simon?" Eetwidomayloh bellowed. "Where is he?"

"Do not worry. He will be here soon," Rebecca offered quickly. "Very soon."

Eetwidomayloh growled with displeasure and then released a scream that sounded as if it originated from a deep, cavernous space. "He should be here now!" He took two giant steps toward Eli that shook the cabin. "Where is your brother, Eli?"

"As Mother said, he'll be here shortly. Don't worry."

"I have waited a millennium for this moment. All that we desire is at hand. I ask you again, where is Simon?"

"He won't come," Addie said, projecting confidence. "He will not serve you. You will fail as you have always failed."

Quickly, Eetwidomayloh turned and faced Addie. "Even now, you continue to resist?" he asked incredulously.

"I will always resist." Addie's fists glowed yellow; she blasted the giant with her magic and made him stumble. "Until they ascend and tear down the veil, your tether on this world is tenuous." She hit him again. Again, he stumbled. "Your new flesh is weak, Eetwidomayloh," she said as she sliced her fingers through the air, tearing his flesh. Eetwidomayloh screamed and fell to one knee, his head dangling on his unsteady neck.

"Stop it!" Rebecca screamed, but Addie simply flicked her wrist and sent the woman hurling through the air.

Eetwidomayloh screamed and raised his hand, blasting Addie. His power stung her in her left shoulder. She stumbled.

"I am many things, you foolish witch. Weak is not one of them!"

Eli stepped forward and blasted Addie. She deflected his blow. "Let's kill her now!"

The Shadowman rose to his feet just as Rebecca regained her footing. The trio—Eetwidomayloh, Rebecca and Eli—formed an offensive line, staring Addie down.

"I think we can take you now," Rebecca said gleefully.

"Three on one? Now, you might have a fighting chance." Addie's words were fused with confidence, even though her heart trembled, slightly. "I will send us all straight to hell before I let you burn this world." Addie started chanting to herself; it was a chant she hoped she'd never have to use. It was a spell to detonate her power. She was confident that it would decimate everything for miles in all directions. It might be enough to stop Eli from ascending and to blast Eetwidomayloh back to the Shadowland.

Addie's voice rattled throughout the room. As the words left her mouth they thickened the atmosphere so much that the trio could barely move. Addie continued to chant and watched as they struggled to free themselves; they moved as if held in thick molasses.

Addie felt the power in her body surge. Quick flashes of light flickered throughout the room. The temperature of her body swelled and she felt the impending explosion.

Right before the tremendous explosion, screams echoed through the swamp, including Eetwidomayloh's.

Then, everything went silent.

⇥ CHAPTER 29

"What, what happened?" Addie asked.

"There was this…this heat—this fire. I felt my skin burning," Rebecca said, speaking slowly. She looked around the room as if it were unfamiliar. "You tried to kill us," she said to Addie as if the knowledge suddenly dawned on her. She turned her head. "Eli. Are you okay?"

"I'm fine. I think," he said and looked at his arms as if he couldn't believe they were still attached to his body. "My arms were ripped from my body. What the fuck?"

"My Lord, you contained the witch's power. You are indeed powerful." Rebecca bowed.

Eetwidomayloh grumbled. "I did nothing."

"If not you, then who?" she asked.

The door to the cabin suddenly blasted open with a spectacular flash of light that ripped the flimsy wooden door right off its hinges. Eetwidomayloh cowered, grumbling loudly as he covered his face with his arms to shield himself from the flash.

"Me," Simon said, confidently, as he walked into the room with the regal swagger of an emperor. The door flew back on its hinges, closing hard behind him. Simon stepped into the center of the room and took time to make eye contact with everyone. He slowly sized them up as his eyes sparkled; his gaze was haughty and self-assured. Even though Eetwidomayloh towered over him,

Simon's gaze cut him down. Everything about Simon had changed, including the power of his gait, the strength of his shoulders and the boldness of his chest. He held his head high and wore the arrogance of a hundred kings as if it were a gilded coat; it was a perfect fit.

"My son!" Rebecca exclaimed loudly as she rushed over to him and threw her arms around her long, lost son. "I can't believe it's you; after all this time. You've come home. You don't know how long we've looked for you." She pulled back slightly, and rubbed her hands on his face, touching him to make sure that he was real.

"Simon! I knew you'd come," Eli said. "I knew you'd come."

Simon pulled away from Rebecca and looked her up and down. He smiled politely.

"Do you have no love for your mother?" she asked.

Simon wanted to feel love; he wanted to feel something—anything—for her, but there was nothing there. He emoted no love or excitement at meeting his mother for the very first time, contrary to what he had always hoped. As a child he had imagined racing into his mother's arms and feeling the warmth of her embrace. She'd tell him how much she loved and missed him and would promise to always take care of him. As he stood before her now, he felt none of that; he was empty.

Rebecca stood in front of him waiting for an embrace that never came.

"Mother," he simply said and offered a perfunctory peck on her cheek. He moved her to the side, out of his way. "And Brother. And Grandmother." Simon strolled around the room with carefully measured footsteps. "And Eetwidomayloh—the one who has haunted my dreams and terrified me for weeks. The whole gang is here. My family. I guess the question then becomes, what do we do next?" He looked around the room as if he awaited an answer.

"How did you do that?" Eli asked, confusion furling his brow.

"Do what?"

"The explosion. You contained Grandmother's power, didn't you? Not even he could," Eli said, gesturing toward the Shadowman.

Eetwidomayloh snarled.

"That was nothing, Eli. I can do things you cannot imagine." Simon's tone was boastful, gloating. He stepped closer and whispered in Eli's ear. "You see, Brother, I have *ascended.*"

"What?" Eli exclaimed.

"You heard me, Eli," he said and then turned to address the room. "What I told my brother, you all should know. I have ascended. I see the world through newly formed eyes. I know the answers to the mysteries of the world and the secrets of the universe. I am connected to everything and everyone and it is all connected to me. My body tingles with absolute power." He inhaled deeply and stretched out his arms. His eyes quickly flashed to black but returned immediately to blue. "I am a force; a hurricane."

There were audible gasps in the room.

"You ascended? When? How? Does that mean that we have our full power now?" Excitement danced in Eli's eyes and echoed in his voice. "I don't feel any different."

Simon smiled and shook his head. "No, *we* don't have our full power. I have *my* full power."

Eli paused. "Huh? I don't understand."

Simon exhaled loudly. "Would someone please explain this to my simple brother? He doesn't seem to get it. Surely one of the learned witches in the room understands."

For a few seconds the room was silent.

"He's not the first," Addie began. "I get it. You may be twins, but one of you was born first—Simon."

"Right you are!" Simon said and the boisterous sound of clapping was heard throughout the room. Then, Simon made it stop.

Eli gasped. "I won't get any new powers? I won't ascend? This is it?" The shock of his new reality carved deep lines into Eli's face. His jaw tightened and his breathing quickened. "This doesn't make sense. They said we'd ascend together; we're supposed to rule together! We are from the same womb—the same egg. I thought we were one!"

Simon waved his hand at Eli, flippantly. "Eli, calm down. The power you have now is great, just not nearly as great as mine."

"I'm not going to ascend?" Eli said to himself, shaking his head in disbelief. "I've waited all my life for this and now I get nothing? You stole my power!" Eli suddenly lunged at Simon. Simon simply looked at Eli and immobilized him; Eli immediately froze in position.

"Behave, Eli. We're brothers. Now, sit down." Immediately, Eli dropped to the floor. He struggled to get up, but could not.

"Mother! Help me!"

Rebecca looked at Eli with disdain and moved to Simon. "My son, I can feel the power in you," she said lustfully. She waved her hands inches from his body. "You are indeed The One." She took in his scent and released an orgasmic breath.

"Ha, ha, ha, ha." A gritty laugh rumbled from Eetwidomayloh's throat. He stepped to Simon and circled him, sniffing and snorting like a pig. "Ahhhh, The One. Let us end this. Kill the witch and set me free—permanently," he said. "Let our reign begin."

"There will be no killing around here until I say so." Simon spoke with authority; he had no intention of taking orders.

"Kill the witch!" Eetwidomayloh commanded in a rough voice that hammered through the room. "Kill the witch!"

"You, too, Eetwidomayloh will behave." Simon's voice was less patient.

"Who are you to speak to me like that? It is because of me that there is you. I am older than time itself; I am larger than the breadth and scope of night. I have always been. Your arrogance offends me, young one."

"Who am I, you ask? I AM THAT I AM." Simon's eyes turned black and his voice deepened, rumbling loudly and digging into the ground, shaking the earth like a quake and tossing everyone around. Strong winds hissed throughout the room.

"You are not God, Simon," Addie interjected as she struggled to regain balance.

"Aren't I though, Grandmother? Aren't I now to be feared and worshipped? Can I not part the sea or drown the world in flood? I tell you again, I AM THAT I AM. Do not question me again—none of you. And don't waste your powers on fighting each other. I have an entire world to rebuild in *my* image." Simon exhaled. "Now, who's with me?"

At that moment, the door to the cabin opened and Brooke walked in; the winds stopped howling and Simon's eyes and voice returned to their natural states. Brooke's expression was dull and her body language stiff. She looked around the room as if she was unsure whether she should be there.

"Simon," she said timidly, her voice trembling.

"Brooke, my love," Simon said as he moved over to her and pulled her into his embrace. "Ladies and gentlemen, it is my duty and my honor to present to you—your new queen. She and I are to be married and *we* shall rule as sovereigns." He hugged her tightly. "Our wedding will be seen all across the world in the skies," he said as he released his grip on her. "And, nothing would make me prouder than for my whole family to be there to witness the event. All my life all I've wanted was a family, a real family. Now, here we are, but we are not complete." Everyone looked around the room. "I knew you'd all be here—in this shack—waiting for

The Ascension like it was some grand event. Sorry you missed it; but since you came all this way, not only did I want to announce my queen, but I also wanted to complete my family."

"Simon," Addie said gently.

"Be silent, Grandmother." Simon moved to the door and placed his hand on the knob. "For the benefit of you who do not believe in me, I want you to bear witness to my power. I'm going to scream three times and *it* shall be done." His voice was full of bravado, unwavering self-assuredness.

"What are you talking about, my son?" Rebecca asked. Simon shot her a look that silenced her.

"Be silent and know that I am God," he said with impatience. Then, as he said he would do, he screamed loudly three times before speaking again. His screams were loud, piercing, and felt alive as his voice fanned out in all directions like a sudden heat wave.

"Please, come on in," he said to someone as he opened the door. Audible gasps flew rapidly around the room when he stepped into the room, looking as youthful and spry as he had twenty years ago. "Come in, *Father*," Simon said, speaking with tremendous hubris; a wide smiled decorated his face.

Rebecca screamed as Thomas Thibodeaux walked into the room with the zeal of a twenty-year-old.

"This cannot be!" Addie screamed.

"Grandmother, meet your long, lost son and my father," Simon said. Before Addie could speak, Rebecca raced over to Thomas and kissed and hugged him tightly.

"Rebecca, is it really you?" Thomas asked with astonishment as he pushed her back so that he could look at her. His eyes grew wide with excitement. "I didn't think I'd ever see you again. I was so lost."

"What manner of dark magic is this?" Addie asked. Her eyes bulged as she clutched the neckline of her dress. "What have you done?"

"Magic is neither light nor dark—magic simply *is*. Moments ago, you told me I am not God," Simon said as his eyes quickly flashed to black, "but look at what I have done. I have raised the dead! Behold my father, a modern-day Lazarus. You may have to reconsider your statement, *Addie*."

Eetwidomayloh hissed, joyously.

"Our father?" Eli said, more to himself than to Simon. "What's going on here?"

"Do you see what I have done?" Simon said boastfully. "Addie, Aunt Clara told me, 'death and life are in the power of the tongue.' She was right. I spoke it; I spoke that my father should live and it came to be. He is of flesh and blood," Simon said as he grabbed Thomas's arm to emphasize his point. "Since I was a child, I've heard this voice inside my head, telling me not to be afraid; that it would be all right. I thought I was crazy, or that I imagined it, but it wasn't a figment of my imagination. I finally realized who it was—it was my father, reaching out from some other place to protect me; to guide me. He offered me comfort when all of you failed me. So, it was only right that I brought him back from that unknown place so that he could live—he lives!" Simon exclaimed. "Yes, there will be a new world order; an order that is probably very different from what any of you imagined."

"Brother, may I stand now?" Eli asked humbly.

"Will you behave?"

"Certainly. And I want you to know I am with you and our father." Simon smiled and Eli stood up, released from Simon's power. "Thank you," he said as he moved closer to Simon.

"What will you do, Simon?" Addie asked, the shock of Thomas's presence cracking her voice. "Now that you have ascended?"

"I will create a paradise."

"What is your idea of *paradise*?" Addie asked with concern.

"You're my mother?" Thomas asked as he approached her. His face was balled with confusion. He stood close to Addie and looked at her as if he could see through her. "Mother?" He hugged her awkwardly. Tears welled in his eyes. "I have always wanted to see your face."

"Yes, I am your mother," she said as she pulled away gently. "And you are my son, my beautiful son, but you are not to be here. Your presence here is…unnatural—an abomination. Your flesh turned to ash decades ago." Addie stroked his face tenderly. "You must go back to where you came from."

"What? I don't understand." Thomas's voice sounded innocent, as if he truly didn't understand all that had happened. "I don't wanna go back—I don't even know where I was. I wanna stay here, with you and my sons. I wanna live."

"You don't remember the last twenty years, do you?"

"Twenty years?" Thomas asked.

"Yes, twenty years. You don't remember because your life ended. This life you have now is not yours," Addie continued.

"What the hell is going on? This day was supposed to be about me!" Eli snapped.

"Shut up, Eli," Rebecca said.

"And that's enough storytelling, Grandmother," Simon said, curling his top lip. "He is here because it is my will. I gave him new life."

Addie ignored Simon's warning and continued speaking. "Look at them, Thomas. Your sons are your age. How can that be? You cannot exist here; it is against nature," she said and before anyone could react Addie blasted him with her power and sent him reeling across the room. He slammed into a window and a long piece of glass sliced deeply into his shoulder.

"No!" Simon screamed. "Behave, Grandmother," he said and immobilized her. She stood in place, perfectly stiff, unable to move.

"Are you okay, Father?" Simon asked with concern. "Eli, get something to wipe the blood from our father."

"Uh—okay," Eli said and moved to a corner and picked up a rag from the floor.

"I'm okay, I think. What did you do that for?" Thomas screamed. Eli moved over to Thomas and helped him pull the long piece of glass from his shoulder; Thomas grimaced. Eli dropped the shard of bloodied glass onto the floor and helped Thomas to a chair in the corner.

"Your dear mother and her band of witches are the ones who killed you so long ago, Thomas. The shadows tried to protect you, but their powers were too great," Eetwidomayloh said.

"All better now," Eli said.

"You see what you did, Grandmother? Do you now understand why I have to remake the world? You are so used to violence and war with the shadows. I will end all of that. Don't you see? No more fighting. No more war. No more violence. Doesn't that sound wonderful? Wouldn't you like to put all of that aside and live in the glory of my kingdom?" Simon took a deep breath and continued. "I know you still fear me. I know how I am described in your *books* and your silly prophecies—which have all been proven wrong—but tell me, how you could possibly know of me when I am the universe? I am air. I am earth. I am fire. I am water. I am life itself," he said as he turned his head toward the window in the front. "I can turn night to day," he said, and the still-darkened outside instantly became light. "I am everything and nothing at all. You, too, Eetwidomayloh, got it all wrong. Your dark prophecies are false. I am servant to neither shadows nor light. The universe, which has bestowed upon me these awesome powers, had other plans. What shall become of this world is entirely my decision and I want us to be a family."

"Yeah, my brother will decide," Eli said, "so fuck all of y'all." Eli pumped his fist in the air.

Simon turned to Eli. "Brother, do not attempt to win me over with your false motives. I am you, remember? I know what darkness lies in your heart."

"Wh—what are you talking about?"

"Oh, Brother. I have felt your jealousy of me since we met; I know the contempt you secretly harbor for her," Simon said as he pointed at Rebecca, who recoiled. "Did you think you could keep your emotions secret from me?"

"Eli," Rebecca said, trying to sound shocked.

"And, I know of the hatred you have for him." Simon pointed at the Shadowman. "I know of your secret plans."

"Secret plans?" Rebecca asked.

"Not true! Not true!" Eli exclaimed. "Simon, stop it!"

Simon moved over to Eli and grabbed both his hands. "It's okay, Brother. What you felt was then; this is now. Growing up the way you did, under the auspices of shadows, it's no wonder you felt like that. No one blames you." Simon released Eli's hands and strolled around the room, hoping to sway the crowd with his words. "I want you all to know that things will change. I will change them. All you have to do is let go of whatever ideas you had about the world and join me for my eternal reign. It shall be glorious and all shall bear witness to my majesty." Simon smiled wildly and extended his arms as if to invite everyone into his embrace.

"I grow weary of words—too much talk. Open the veil," Eetwidomayloh growled in exasperation. "Open it now and let us be done with this...*talk*."

"Temper your tone in the presence of your king," Simon said. "You must learn your place," Simon stated.

Eli and Rebecca gasped.

"Enough!" Eetwidomayloh bellowed, his deep voice rumbling like thunder. In a flash his massive hand was wrapped tightly around Simon's neck. He lifted him off the ground effortlessly, pulling Simon's face close to his. "I have had enough of this insolence," he growled and loudly inhaled Simon's scent, his nostrils flaring. "You are corrupt. I smell it now; I can smell the light in you. You are not The One I have waited for; but, you will still do what you were created to do. You *will* tear down the veil so that shadows can bleed into this world. My patience has grown short, boy!" Eetwidomayloh tossed Simon across the room into the wall. Simon hit it hard, knocking several wooden beams to the floor.

"Simon!" Rebecca screamed as she raced toward him. Eetwidomayloh grabbed Rebecca by her neck and snapped it like a twig, tossing her limp body against the wall next to Simon.

"Rebecca!" Thomas raced over to Rebecca's body and pulled her into his arms. "No, she can't be dead. What have you done? She can't be dead!" he wailed as his eyes burned a deep red, and bloody tears raced down his cheek. Brooke moved to him and placed her arms around him to comfort him.

"Is she dead?" Eli asked, with a hint of a smile on his face. "Is she?"

"You will all die, and this little *boy* will not be able to bring you back with his parlor tricks!" Eetwidomayloh pounded his chest angrily and screamed at the top of his lungs. He turned his attention to Eli and he blasted him with shadowmagic. Eli hit the ground, blood spewing from his mouth. "You will all die!"

Addie, free from Simon's immobilization spell, hit the Shadowman with a ball of light that did little damage; Eetwidomayloh's uncontained anger and wrath gave him tremendous strength.

"You are next, witch!" He pointed his finger and Eli levitated from the ground. Eetwidomayloh held him, suspended, in air. "But first, I have waited twenty-one years to teach you the discipline your mother never could. You have been the shit beneath my boot from the moment you were born. I knew you were not The One; The One could never be so incompetent." Eetwidomayloh held out his hand and a long black whip with sharp barbs of bone embedded at the tip materialized in his hand. Eli's shirt ripped from his body. Eetwidomayloh cracked the whip once and, without hesitating, he brought the heavy strap across Eli's chest. When the whip struck his body, it tore into his flesh and blood gushed from the open wounds. Eli's scream was a death rattle. Eetwidomayloh whipped him again. And again.

"Puh-please, stop," Brooke said in a weak voice. "Please stop all of this. I don't know what's going on—why I'm here. I wanna go," she said, tears staining her face.

"Do not address me, human!" he bellowed out. He turned his hand toward her and the whip cut through the air fiercely. Brooke covered her face with her hands and screamed.

Then, everything stopped, including the whip.

Suddenly Simon was standing between Eetwidomayloh and Brooke.

"I told you to behave, Eetwidomayloh. Were you about to hit a woman? My queen?" The whip ripped from Eetwidomayloh's hand and flew into Simon's. "That was a mistake; a serious one. I may not be the one you wanted, but I am The One!" Simon raised his hand and brought the whip down across Eetwidomayloh's head. The whip tore into his skull and ripped a hole in it, sending pieces of bone fragment flying across the room. Eetwidomayloh's grip on Eli broke and he fell to the floor with a thud, his body battered and bloodied.

Eetwidomayloh screamed a blood-curdling cry that was equal parts shock and pain. He dropped hard to both knees and Simon continued to whip him mercilessly. Hot blood splattered across

Simon's face and the walls of the cabin, but he continued to whip the Shadowman viciously, not missing a beat. Eetwidomayloh moaned several deep, guttural sounds, and covered his head with his hands.

"Simon," Addie said as she moved closer to him, cautiously. Simon's blue eyes had gone completely black. "That's enough. Simon, stop."

He looked at her and then let the whip drop from his hand. "Back to the Shadowland you go, Eetwidomayloh; back to the depths of hell. I curse you and the Shadowland from this day forth. I curse you!" He clawed at the air and suddenly the vortex reappeared; now it was the size of a wall in the cabin. The putrid scent of sulfur and death poured from the hole. Simon peered into the Shadowland, which looked like a vast wasteland; a country-side eviscerated by a nuclear blast. Then, Simon let out a yell and kicked Eetwidomayloh with so much force that the giant flew across the room into the vortex. He was kicked with such force that the sound of him hitting the ground resonated from the Shadowland into the cabin. "I curse you forever more." A ball of yellow light formed in Simon's hand and he threw it into the vortex. Then, he whispered, "Let there be light." The horrendous sounds of thousands of creatures screaming poured out of the vortex.

Then, Simon sealed the tear in the veil, presumably forever.

"You should have let me kill him, Brother," Eli said as he spat out blood, emboldened by Simon's victory.

"Shadows cannot die. As long as there is light, there will be dark, but the sunlight I sent to them will burn and keep them weak forever. The ball of light will spin and grow and cover much of the Shadowland with light. Eetwidowmayloh and his minions will have little refuge."

"That's fuckin' awesome," Eli said. "Fuckin' awesome."

A blood-covered Simon with blackened eyes stood in the center of the room, shell-shocked. He looked at the blood that covered his hand and started licking it ravenously.

Addie stood in raw awe and fear of Simon's power. She studied his bloodied face and his blackened eyes and knew, without any doubt, that he was lost, too. Each time he bludgeoned the Shadowman, he also bludgeoned the flicker of light that remained inside of him. Tears formed in her eyes.

She looked at the war-torn room. The Dark Mother was dead, and her back-from-the-grave son, Thomas, held her tightly, weeping. Everything was wrong. Everything. Addie moved to the front of the room near the broken window.

Brooke left Thomas's side and moved cautiously over to Simon. She grabbed his hand and stopped him from licking the blood that stained his hands.

"Simon, look at me," she said gently. "Look at me." He turned his head toward her slightly. "Baby, I see you. I still see you. You made me promise to always *see* you, no matter what happened. I see you, baby." She stood on the tip of her toes and kissed his lips.

"Brooke," he said.

"Yes, it's me, baby. It's me."

"What happened?" He looked around the room and his black eyes changed back to their natural color. "Did I hurt you?" he asked suddenly, and with tremendous concern.

"No, no, I'm fine. You saved me."

"Thank God," he said as he hugged her tightly.

From behind and with a decisive blow, Addie stabbed Simon in the back with the bloodied shard of glass that Eli had pulled from Thomas's shoulder. The glass went through his body and pierced his heart. Brooke screamed.

Simon stumbled, not sure what happened.

"Brooke?" he said as he lost his balance and slammed into a table.

"It had to be this way," Addie said. "Your power cannot be allowed to exist. I have to save the world."

"What—what—have you done?" Eli asked, as he, too, lost his balance and stumbled. He looked down at his white vest and saw blood soaking through it, as if *he* had been stabbed by the glass. "You can't kill us. We can't die."

"You can. You will," she said in a voice that was confident, but not boastful; it carried a small sadness that couldn't be masked by victory. "The seed of the first born Thibodeaux male gave you life; only his blood could give you a proper death; blood of the father, as Clara said."

"Y-y-you said I had light inside of me. You said I could be saved, Grandmother," Simon said, his voice heavy.

Tears fell from Addie's eyes. "I was wrong about that." Simon flung his body wildly around the room trying to remove the glass that was deeply embedded in his back. He threw his arm over his shoulder and tried to reach the glass, but it was out of reach. He flopped desperately, like a fish out of water, gasping for life and breath.

Then, he stopped struggling.

He stood in the center of the room, looking longingly at Brooke with his sad eyes. Her tear-stained face was streaked black with makeup. She brought her hand up to her lips and blew him a kiss and he smiled.

"I remember me. I remember. Thank you," said Simon, resigned to his fate.

"I don't wanna die. Grandmother, save me. I renounce the dark! I renounce it!" Eli screamed, just before he collapsed at her feet. He hit the floor hard, his eyes frozen open with shock.

He was dead.

Then, Simon dropped to the floor.

Dead.

Thomas felt his head spin violently as the force that gave him life was ripped suddenly from his body. He put his hand to his mouth and coughed dryly, expelling flaky gray material from his lungs. Then, he looked at his forearm and watched helplessly, in horror, as his flesh quickly wrinkled and crumbled from his arm. He peered into his mother's face, smiling innocently even as his body began to disintegrate into gray ash. A gentle breeze arose inside the cabin, scattering his remains across the wooden floor.

From ash he was conjured; to ash he returned.

⊰ CHAPTER 30

B rooke sat in the solarium of the house that used to belong to Clara and sipped a cup of Addie's special tea slowly; she savored each flavorful drop. There was something about the sweetness of the drink that made her think of sweet times she spent with Simon. The rich aroma of the beverage filled her nostrils and relaxed her body. She peered out of the window into the warm light of day, which illuminated the room as if it were glowing.

Over the last few months she had learned to love the sun, the light.

She blew the steam that rose from the cup and watched it fade into nothingness. She was alone in the house, but she never really felt alone. She felt protected by the ancestors that inhabited the house; sometimes, they spoke to her. Sometimes, she spoke back. She wasn't afraid; after all she had seen, fear was no longer a part of her.

She had come a long way over the last six months; a long way, indeed. After the ordeal in the cabin and the death of Simon, she withdrew into herself for days. She shut out the world, but she couldn't shut out the voice that whispered in her head, the voice that called her *Mommy*.

She looked down at her swollen belly and missed Simon; at least the Simon that she knew. Before things became so bizarre, she had imagined being his wife and carrying his child; only part of her dream came true.

"Hello, my dear," Addie said as she entered the room. "May I join you?" Addie's face was luminescent, youthful.

"Of course you can." Addie moved over to where Brooke sat and poured herself a cup of tea. She sat upright in the chair, as a proper lady would.

"How are you feeling today?"

"I'm good," Brooke said. "Really good; the baby's been kicking a lot."

"What has she said?"

"She told me her name—Genesis. She likes to be called Jenny for short."

"Genesis; as in—the beginning?" Addie said with a question in her voice. "I guess it *is* time for a new beginning. I like it."

"I'm glad."

Addie sipped her tea, slowly. "I may have Clara's seer powers, but I can see nothing of Genesis—the offspring of The One; nor is there anything written."

"We know how well the prophecies worked with Simon," Brooke said sarcastically.

"She could be the most powerful witch in the history of the world."

"Or, she could be the most gentle soul that has ever walked the earth. I can feel the love she has. I can feel it. She *is* love. I want Jenny to live a normal life."

Addie sipped. "Is that possible? We don't even know what she is."

"She is her father's daughter; she's my daughter—your great-granddaughter."

"What does she want?" Addie's voice was void of emotion as an uneasy peace settled into the room.

Brooke exhaled. "She simply wants to be born."

Addie continued sipping her tea, slowly.

Brooke took a long sip and smiled at Addie. She turned her attention to the bright summer day that existed on the other side of the window. She felt Jenny kick a few times and Brooke placed her hand on her belly, as if to soothe her unborn daughter, who spoke to her. Brooke wasn't quite sure what it meant, but her entire body stiffened when Jenny's thoughts entered her mind. Jenny projected five stolen words: I AM THAT I AM.

⚜ ABOUT THE AUTHOR

Lee Hayes is the author of the novels *Passion Marks*, *A Deeper Blue: Passion Marks II*, *The Messiah* and the editor of *Flesh to Flesh: An Erotic Anthology*. He currently resides in the Washington, D.C. metropolitan area. He can be reached at leehayes@hotmail.com or via Facebook at www.facebook.com/leehayeswriter. Please visit his website at: www.leehayes.info

IF YOU ENJOYED "THE FIRST MALE,"
CONTINUE YOUR WALK ON THE DARK SIDE WITH

The MESSIAH

BY LEE HAYES
AVAILABLE FROM STREBOR BOOKS

PROLOGUE
IN THE BEGINNING...

Jazz McKinney

The buzzing sound of flies will resonate in his ears *forever*. That annoying, dissonant sound caused by the rapid vibrations of tiny wings that had stolen the peace from countless languid summer evenings was the only thing he could focus on, as he lay battered and bloodied in a field of orange, yellow, and blue. Stunning summer hues dotted the landscape on the grassy knoll as his world morphed from living colors to a gray and mangled mesh of madness. Jazz McKinney struggled to keep his eyes open, but he knew the uncontrolled swelling would soon blot out his vision and his view of the world would darken. *Maybe forever*.

Yet, given that grim reality, that buzzing sound kept him holding on to life.

That ceaseless buzzing—a sound that rang louder than his own listless voice—numbed the pain of the million ant bites, which stung his limp body. Each time he opened his mouth to scream for help, the sound rang hollow; not even a decibel and barely a whisper. So, he sent his silent prayers to the heavens and hoped that God was listening.

He remembered trying to scream, but there was no sound. He remembered trying to move, but the only movement was the involuntary shooting pains that kept him immobile.

Though he often thought it cliché, his life did indeed flash before his eyes. Sadly, all he could see was the nameless faces from a thousand midnight encounters. He had taken residence in a world created by fantasies and actions without consequence; a reckless world where instant gratification was like sweet nectar and remorse simply didn't exist.

He mentally erased their faces at the conclusion of a lustful rendezvous, often never knowing their names. Now, those same strangers who had been his one constant in life, were poised to be his one constant in his death. Oddly, a death he invited in part to a late-night "craving."

He didn't imagine his body would survive very long in its present condition—broken and battered. *And isolated.* In his moment of ultimate desperation, when all seemed lost, something more meaningful should have filled his head. He should have been focused on life after death and his final resting place in eternity, yet he could not free his mind of their faces. And that buzzing. That damned buzzing tormented him.

As he lay there, blood oozing from his busted body, the hollow faces spiraled around his head in a choreographed ritual of torture. *Go away*, he thought, but the reflections of his misdeeds were permanent fixtures in his mind. The images were so real to him in those fevered moments that he wanted to reach out and touch their ethereal silhouettes, but he didn't have the strength.

The nasty flies were drawn to his rotting flesh, which would soon sizzle in the intense summer heat when the sun took its rightful place in the sky. Jazz feared they would devour him and leave no remains to be claimed; all that would endure after he faded would be naked bones. The moonlit brutality he experienced at the hands of a stranger now gave way to a dazzling daylight despair. His fears of dying in an abandoned field and the intensity of his pain did not fade when the sun majestically rose.

As he lay prostrate in the field, the events that led to his predicament replayed in his head but he didn't want to remember. He didn't want to relive the attack. He wanted to pretend it never happened, but each time he attempted to move, the pain forced him to remember. Each time he looked around at the weeds and flowers and dirt and broken glass that surrounded him, he could not deny the attack.

Jazz vividly remembered what *he* did to him. He could still feel every thrust, every fist, and every kick as his body continued to throb with waves of pain.

He remembered *his* deranged laughter, which ricocheted in the night.

He remembered crying out, only to be answered by a kick to the face.

He could still see and feel the boot that caused blood to gush from his nose. It was a Timberland.

Jazz remembered the incoherent prayers that escaped from his attacker's twisted mouth while he lay in the field.

Jazz remembered begging *him* to stop and apologizing profusely for his actions, but that only caused laughter to swell and spill from *his* vile mouth.

Naked, dizzied, and pleading for his life, he remembered staring up into the dark sky as his vision blurred, while his attacker's voice shifted between manic states of rage and calm. Even as he lay bound in the field, he remembered. He could not forget. Jazz bore the shame of his lust and tried to imagine being somewhere else. He tried to imagine this was someone else's nightmare instead of his own. But the details of the night's betrayal raced through his fleeting consciousness like strong river currents.

The evening started with such promise but ended in such despair. Pain, visions, voices, and memories splashed on the canvas of his mind. He fought to push them away, but they stood their ground, refusing to leave, scrambling and heightening his anxiety. Scenes of torture traded places with apparitions of bliss; visions of violence exchanged posture with images of pleasure. After all, Jazz was facing his senior year in college—a year of promise and partying; not his death.

His roommate Montre had gone home to California for the summer and left him in Washington, D.C. to fend for himself. He felt partially betrayed since the duo had discussed subletting an apartment for the summer and working at Fashion Centre at Pentagon City to pay the bills. Jazz had envisioned a fun-filled, carefree summer. He wanted to run wild in Chocolate City and let D.C. know it had been graced by his presence.

He wanted his last summer in the city to be seared in a blaze of glory. He wanted to leave the men saddened, wobbly, and shaken, but happy that they had experienced his magic, if only for a small moment in time. So when Montre told him he had to return home to help take care of his ailing mother, Jazz was disappointed, but he understood.

He was thrilled at the thought of graduating and moving to New York City thereafter to jumpstart his stagnant modeling career. After years of local modeling, he told himself he'd give the Big Apple a two-year try and if it didn't work out, he'd get a job using the degree he was earning in mechanical engineering. *Quite an accomplishment for a disavowed stepson of a preacher*, he thought.

Just as relaxing thoughts of his past began to numb the sting of his current existence, a pain in his chest jolted him back to reality. He began to tremble as he took rapid, ragged breaths; they felt like his last breaths. He gasped for air; fought the feeling of despair that began to swallow him. He could feel his heart racing, beating in his ears, his throat, and his loins. Then everything went black.

✝✝✝

As the sun rose and illuminated the morning skies, Jazz squinted against its burning rays. His blood-caked body was now noticeably bruised and swollen. A single tear crawled down his left cheek and found a home in the corner of his mouth. He stuck out his tongue to taste its salty residue. It was enough to remind him that he was indeed still alive—but for how much longer, he didn't know. How could a night destined for pleasure culminate into an evening of so much despair? Dark memories crept in as Jazz recounted those events that would now change his life forever...

It was a quarter to midnight when he had stepped out of his car, locked the door, and kept his keys splayed between his fingers in case he needed to defend himself from some brute lurking in the shadows. An unusual vibe, which permeated the night air, unnerved him, but he dismissed his intuition as simple paranoia and pressed on.

A quick lightning flash moved across the sky, followed by a low rumble of thunder. He took a moment to scan the area and when he was satisfied that no one was around, he walked with speed toward the structure. Trepidation was his traveling partner as he moved briskly forward. During these midnight meetings, a sense of fear stimulated his desire. He walked with due speed, continuing to look around for other people, including the police, who often cruised the area on the fringes of the city. He couldn't imagine having to explain to the police why he was lurking near the abandoned church at such a late hour.

As he neared his destination, a decrepit, gnarled wooden sign pointed toward the church like old crooked fingers guiding him to the path of salvation. When Jazz was close enough, he paused for an instant and looked up at the structure. From his distance, he could read the letters above the doors: "Olive Branch Baptist Church. All are Welcome."

As he moved closer to the chained fence, which protected the deserted edifice, the warning in his heart grew, but he would not yield to that feeling. An ominous presence rode the stiff night air, as if some unseen force skulked around from all sides. Partially excited *and* terrified, Jazz pressed deeper into the night. The fear of being caught while meeting a stranger to do whatever deeds men who meet in the dark of night did is what Jazz was counting on to multiply the force of his orgasm threefold.

As he scurried across the vacant parking lot, he heard a slight rumbling behind him, which sent a cold shiver up his spine, in spite of the evening's balmy temperature. He stopped, spun on his heels, and exhaled in relief as he saw an old soda can rolling across the lot in the gentle breeze. He resumed his march toward ecstasy.

When he reached the fence surrounding the church, he prayed it would be unlocked so he could walk through it instead of going around it, but when he yanked on the chain, it barely moved. *Damn.* He looked up at the barbed wire that sat like a crown of thorns atop the fence and decided that he was not skillful enough to climb the fence without seriously injuring his body. He had to find another way in. With his hands in his pockets, he turned and quickly walked around the behemoth structure, wondering why he had agreed to meet *him* at such a place.

When he got around the corner, he found that the side gate was locked and chained, but he remained undeterred. Quickly, he looked around the perimeter and found a place in the fence in which he could pass without injury and, with surprising prowess, he scaled the fence. Nothing was going to stand between him and what *he* had to offer. He landed flatly on his feet and paused a moment to scan the area before moving toward the back of the church.

The closer he got to the rear of the small white structure, the quicker his heart raced. These mysterious encounters that he had grown accustomed to made sex wildly exciting. He had grown out of missionary sex when he was seventeen and moved quickly into things there were more titillating and dangerous.

For Jazz, sex was freedom; sex was power. Thoughts of his next encounter and taking his escapades to the next level occupied much of his daily thoughts. Pushing the envelope and stretching sexual boundaries was his drug—his driving force. He wasn't a sex addict, but he loved sex. He loved doing the unspeakable and scandalous. He loved gobbling and rubbing and pulling and yanking and plowing and breathing and using fingers and tongues and holes and toys and ropes and candles and wax and anything else he could incorporate into his romps to intensify the experience. He loved meeting people who, like him, weren't afraid to explore the universe and be used as willing vessels to help him reach that ultimate orgasm. That's all that mattered to him.

He leaned against the back of the church for only a few minutes, blowing nicotine smoke circles into the air to calm his nerves. Standing in the darkness, with no signs of life, those minutes felt like hours. He listened for any sound of movement, for the slightest disturbance, for anything that would announce *his* arrival. Jazz took a long drag from the Benson & Hedges he pursed tightly between his lips and rolled an empty beer bottle underneath his foot to take the edge off the night.

Then, he heard a faint sound coming from the other end of the structure. He didn't move. Instead, he waited for confirmation. It sounded like dry grass being crushed underneath heavy feet. Then, he heard it again. The crunching sound that dried leaves and grass made underneath a foot was unmistakable in the dead of night.

He peered around the corner toward the other end of the building. He did not see anything, but all his senses were acute. Curiosity got the best of him and he stepped out and walked toward the noise. He took a few steps forward and then stopped. Something didn't feel right. The moonlight cast a shadow on the ground—the shadow of a man.

"Hello?" Jazz called out. The hairs on the back of his neck stood on end, but he pressed on, hoping his feeling would give way to sexual pleasure.

"Hello?" he called out again, sounding a bit desperate. "What's going on?" he mumbled to himself as he let the cigarette dangling from his lips hit the ground. He stomped it out with his foot. "Wassup, man? Don't be shy. Come to Daddy," he said, trying to sound playful. As the words left his mouth, *he* jumped out from around the corner and struck Jazz across the face with what felt like the strength of a hundred men. Jazz hit the ground with an incredible thud.

"What the fuck?" he screamed. The only response he received was fists that rained down on him in torrents. Jazz threw wild blows into the twisted face of his attacker, but to no avail. The punishing barrage of heavy fists continued to pound into Jazz's body like mortar. Jazz's terrified screams echoed in the night, but ultimately went unanswered. He knew he was alone and that if he were to survive, it would be all up to him.

He covered his face with one hand while the other desperately searched for something on the ground he could use to defend himself. He grabbed at anything and everything he could, but cupped fistfuls of dried grass instead. Spit dropped onto his face from the salivating mouth of his attacker. Then, Jazz grabbed a small rock from the ground and swung wildly, the blow landing right above his attacker's left eye. *He* fell backward, covering *his* face with *his* hands.

Jazz, trying to seize the opportunity to flee, forced himself to stand. He tried to run, but he was unsteady and shaky. When he got his balance, he heard the breaking of the bottle before he actually felt the impact on the back of his skull. In the flicker of the second that it took for him to realize what had happened, he felt the presence of evil looming on the edge of night, dancing a wicked jig in the dark and laughing at his misery. Jazz fell to the ground on his back and looked up to see the menacing figure above him again.

Jazz felt his vision blur and the coming darkness ready to devour him whole, but the boot that smashed into his ribcage brought him back to consciousness with piercing pain. Jazz lay on the ground, an agonizing throbbing covering his body. He tried to scream but his voice wouldn't carry.

The stranger moved away and fell to his knees.

Even through the blistering pain, Jazz heard a voice emanating from *him* that sounded as if the night itself was speaking words which were not meant to be deciphered. *His* raspy voice rose to slightly above a whisper as *he* spoke with rapid speed. It almost sounded as if *he* was speaking in tongues.

"The Lord is my shepherd; I shall not want. He maketh me to lie down in green pastures: He leadeth me beside still waters. He restoreth my soul: He leadeth me in paths of righteousness for His name's sake."

Jazz cried out.

"Yea, though I walk through the valley of the shadow of death, I will fear no evil; for Thou art with me; Thy rod and Thy staff they comfort me. Thou preparest a table before me in the presence of mine enemies: Thou anointest my head with oil; my cup runneth over. Surely goodness and mercy shall follow me all the days of my life: and I will dwell in the house of the Lord forever."

When *he* finished, lightning lit up the sky and Jazz heard the thunder roll. He felt death was nearby.

The stranger sprang to *his* feet like a panther. Suddenly, panic gripped Jazz like an immovable force around his neck. He knew that more was coming. He struggled to make sense of what had happened. *His* face morphed into something unrecognizable and unreal. The spindly hairs of *his* moustache came to life and reached toward Jazz like hissing serpents poised to strike. *His* face resembled burnt flesh that was scorched by hatred and disgust. *His* eyes changed into bottomless black pits that showed nothing but contempt. What little light the moon provided was sucked into *his* hateful eyes, making the dark night its darkest ever. *His* full mouth stretched into slivers of tightly drawn flesh and Jazz closed his eyes and prepared for his painful demise.

He turned his back to Jazz and recanted the prayer again. Jazz writhed in pain and tried to scoot away from his antagonist, but he was quickly met by another kick to the ribs.

"My son, you have brought my wrath upon you because of your sins and unclean acts. You are an abomination," *he* said in a gritty, throaty whisper that felt like jagged fingernails scraping the skin off Jazz's back; even still, *his* gruff voice carried enough force for Jazz to feel it. Jazz tried not to show panic or fear, even though fear had engulfed him. "But, fear not, my child. I am your redeemer. I have come to save your immortal soul from eternal damnation." *He* snapped *his* head back and looked to the heavens as *he* extended *his* arms as if surrendering to a higher power. A wild and delightful smile covered *his* face as *he* looked up and started to recant another prayer. *His* body swayed from side-to-side and an unsettling smile shone on his face.

"A-ma-zing grace, how sweet the sound, that saved a wretch like me," he bellowed out in an uncanny yet angelic voice. Jazz tried to move along the ground, but could not free himself from that voice. At the same time he was bewildered by pain and bewitched by the spirited song that filled the night air at the same time. He tried to regroup but was startled when he looked up. The stranger's extended arms looked like large black wings that spread the span of *his* reach. When the wings spread out a powerful odor filled Jazz's nostrils and almost made him choke. The stench was so strong and so foul that it lodged in his lungs and made him dry cough.

The sound continued to mesmerize and enchant Jazz—even in this moment—until he forced himself out of the daze. Jazz closed his eyes and shook his head. When he opened them, the stranger peered down on him. The wings were no more. He didn't know if he'd really seen them or if his mind was playing tricks on him.

As Jazz lay on the ground, trying to come to terms with the pain in his head, he could feel *his* greasy hands yanking at his body and then his clothes. Jazz tried to kick him away but to no avail. Jazz's feeble attempt at resistance angered *him*, and *he* pulled Jazz up by his shirt and sent a strong backhand across his face, which sent him reeling back to the ground. Jazz felt as if his jaw had exploded. *He* repeated the prayer, this time in a more coherent voice while *he* continued to disrobe him until Jazz lay naked—his brown flesh exposed to the world.

"W-w-wait, stop—please," Jazz managed to utter, but his broken words landed on uncaring ears. "Why are you doing this to me? Who—who are you?" Jazz asked as he spit blood from his mouth.

He paused. "I am Alpha and Omega; the first and the last; the beginning and the end," *he* said in matter-of-fact tone. "You will lay naked before the throne of God and repent your sins. You will renounce your wicked ways," *he* said in a voice that boomed across the sky. *He* seemed to be in some kind of trance, walking back and forth and back and forth and uttering prayer. *He'd* walk away from Jazz only to return with a kick or a punch. *He* ordered Jazz on his knees and shocked him by punching him in the eye so hard Jazz thought he had been blinded. Jazz had never known pain so profoundly.

When *he* was satisfied that Jazz was weak enough, *he* dragged his limp body across the coarse grass to the tattered fence at the very edge of the property that separated the back of the church from the woods. Jazz felt sharp rocks and shards of broken glass cutting across his skin as he grabbed at mounds of grass in an attempt to anchor his body.

When *he* got to the end of the field, *he* loosened his grip on Jazz and let him go. *He* walked through the hole in the fence and opened the door to a black van that was parked on a dirt trail. Jazz lifted his head to ascertain what was going on, but dizziness forced him back to the ground.

Then, *he* stepped from the van with handcuffs and proceeded to fasten Jazz to the fence before Jazz realized what was going on. Blood oozed from his weakened mouth when he coughed. Then *he* spoke in a hell-inspired voice as a foul stench permeated the air all around them.

"The reason you are alive is because it is the will of God. You have a job to do. You will be my apostle. The world will take little note of what I say here, but it will remember what you tell them. You will tell them all to repent. You will tell them of the coming apocalypse. You will tell them I am watching. I am *always* watching. You will do this in our covenant or I will visit you again. Jazz McKinney, you are my sacrifice to righteousness! Do you understand the task appointed to you?"

Pain sealed Jazz's lips, but his will to survive broke through and he mustered enough strength to mumble the word *yes*. Jazz wanted to see the face of this maniac, but his ragged body would not move.

"Mark this day as a return to righteousness. Walk by my side and you will dwell with me forever. You are to undergo circumcision, and it will be the sign of the covenant between me and you."

Circumcision?

Jazz tried to shake himself free from his bondage, but he barely had strength to dangle the fence. *He* moved closer to Jazz whose wild eyes grew at the sight of the sharp stone held in *his* hand.

"Do not fear, my child. I will protect you in our covenant."

Jazz kicked and wiggled his body to fend off the predator, but a powerful fist to Jazz's face ended his resistance.

He reached down and grabbed the wad of skin atop of Jazz's penis. Jazz closed his eyes. Then, as if studying it, *he* looked curiously at the hull that hid the head of Jazz's organ. Suddenly, *he* took the sharp stone that *he* held and started cutting away the superfluous skin. Jazz screamed as loud as he could as the unbearable sensation rapidly inflamed every cell in his body. A hurt like no other hurt he had ever felt consumed him. Then, he found his voice. The sound that escaped from Jazz's mouth was previously unheard by any human ear; it reached the heavens, circled the distant moon and stars, and came back down landing with a shattering thump.

He stood before Jazz, skin in his hand, and spoke. "Tell them The Messiah has returned. And he is angry."

The weight of his heavy words and the pain Jazz felt sent the night hurling around his head.

"THE LORD is my shepherd; I shall not want," *he* continued. "He maketh me to lie down in green pastures: He leadeth me beside still waters. He restoreth my soul: He leadeth me in paths of righteousness for His name's sake." The Messiah walked slowly through the opening in the fence toward the van, opened the door, and stepped casually into the vehicle.

Still bound to the fence, Jazz heard a rumbling noise from above and the sky grew bright as lightning burned an electric trail.

"For as lightning that comes from the east is visible even in the west, so will be the coming of the Son of Man." His words rung like a church bell in the night.

The Messiah closed the van's door and drove away slowly into the dark. In the final moment before his black van disappeared, the sky opened and rain poured from the heavens in buckets.

It rained for exactly six minutes and sixty-six seconds.

†††

A car winding up the road in front of the church crunched the gravel beneath its tires and pulled Jazz out of his recount of the evening before. Ironically, his hope for rescue would lie in the hands of a stranger, as his demise almost did. He simply closed his eyes and waited, still chained to the fence and unable to move. He knew another judgment would surely come from the "good Samaritan" that was about to find and—hopefully—rescue him. It was a judgment he didn't want to face, yet he knew it would be nothing compared to the one the Messiah had administered on him the night before.